THE BARON'S HEART

HEROES OF RAVENFORD

BOOK 5

F.P. SPIRIT
K.J. FOGLEMAN

BOOKS BY F.P. SPIRIT

The Heroes of Ravenford

Ruins on Stone Hill

Serpent Cult

Dark Monolith

Princess of Lanfor

The Baron's Heart

Rise of the Thrall Lord

City of Tears

Arinthar Collections

Tales From Thac

BOOKS BY K.J. FOGLEMAN

Tales of the Wovlen

The Dragon's Son

The Dragon's Due

Arinthar Collections

Tales From Thac

THE BARON'S HEART

HEROES OF RAVENFORD
BOOK 5

Thanks to Tim for creating the world of Thac, and to Eric, Jeff, John, Mark and Matt for their roles in bringing the Heroes to life. Also, thanks to the rest of my friends and family who gave their time and support into the creation of this book.

TABLE OF CONTENTS

Heartbreak..1
On the Road Again... 12
Magic Circle 18
Sky Knights 29
Dragon Tales... 35
Quit Monkeying Around 50
Something Rotten in Vermoorden 64
Temples of Storms and Magic.. 74
The Wrath of Deepwood.. 79
To Kill a Bard 89
Wizard's Apprentice... 97
Seth and Aksel, Vampire Hunters?................................ 107
Imp in the Fold.. 119
Lost and Found 128
Battle at Haltan's.. 137
Bring Out Your Undead 149
A Matter of Trust 165
What Are Little Girls Made Of?................................... 177
Playing With Fire 189
Letters From a Dead Cleric 207
Fiends in the Dark 223
Invasion of Ravendford.. 237
The Cage 247

Alliances...259

Stop Dragon My Heart Around 270

Unexpected Friends...284

Assassin's Lair 299

An Evil Discovery...313

Welcoming Party 326

Just Desserts 343

Dark Legacy 355

Into the Crypt...369

Resurrection 380

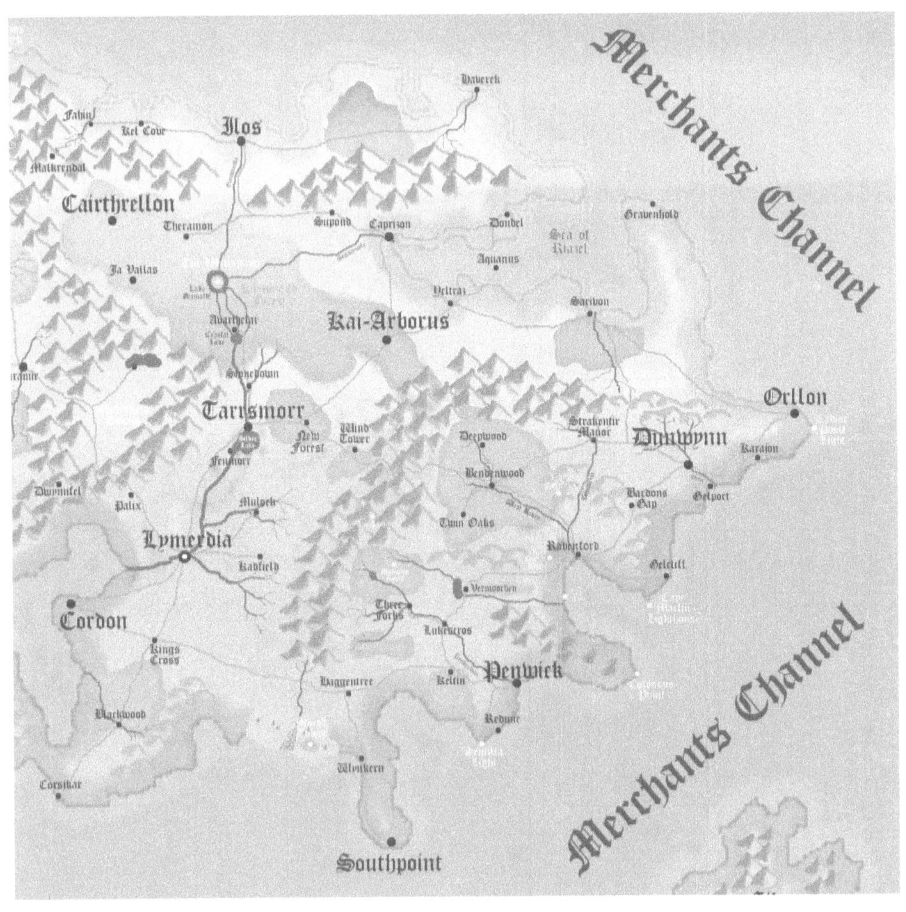

While most of Arinthar worship the Ralnai, or the Material Gods, there are those who revere the darkness. The denizens of the Abyss have always had their eye on this world, its path through the heavens seen as a stepping stone to the higher realms beyond. Those demon lords have their followers in this world, secretive demonic cults that seek to do their master's bidding. Dark rituals, stolen souls, and murder are the agenda these groups seek to promote across the globe. They prey on the weak-willed, exploiting their basest desires, bending them down the path to darkness...

- Lady Lara Stealle, High Wizard of Penwick

1
HEARTBREAK

It looked like some sort of ritual had been performed on him

Night had fallen over Ravenford, house lights struggling to push back the darkness in the dreary weather that had descended upon the town. A blanket of mist had rolled in from Merchant's Bay, the still waters seeming to disappear just a few yards off shore. A thin fog enveloped the entire town, its tendrils grasping at the walls of the keep on the hilltop to the north. Torches lined the parapets, seeming hard pressed to hold back the cold vapors that threatened to overrun the small castle.

The dismal weather matched the mood of the residents of the little town. The Baron of Ravenford, the town's lord and protector these last eighteen years, was dead. Rumors abounded on the details of his demise, but all agreed that it had happened three days ago. The mood was equally somber in the throne room of Ravenford Keep. Glolindir Eodin and the rest of the companions had arrived a short while ago to find the Baroness and the Lady Andrella in mourning.

"We are truly sorry for your loss."Elladan Narmolanya stood a step down from the ornate wooden chair that served as a throne. Even at this late hour, there were a few townsfolk in the rows of benches behind him. Baroness Gracelynn insisted on leaving the chamber open to anyone who wished to mourn their late monarch.

Elladan, as usual, was garbed all in white, except for a green cloak that hung at his shoulders and a pair of brown leather boots. Framed by a smooth mop of jet-black hair, the bard's handsome face was filled with sympathy. His dark eyes glistened with just a hint of moisture as he bowed before the stately woman.

A thin smile spread across Gracelynn's lips as she reached out a hand to the compassionate elf. "Thank you, my friends. We are glad to see you at this dark hour."

Baroness Gracelynn was a strong woman, her demeanor cool and regal despite the tragic circumstances. The only visible trace of strain was the even lighter pallor of her normally porcelain skin against the dark colors she wore this eve. In every other way her appearance was immaculate, from her perfectly coiffed chestnut hair to the dark grey gown that covered the entirety of her lithe frame.

Elladan gently took the lady's hand and kissed it. "Word only reached us late last night, or we would have been here sooner."

"We're just glad… that you are here now," the Lady Andrella managed between sobs.

The young lady had put on a strong appearance when they first entered the throne room. Impeccably dressed in a fine black gown, her stony expression was starkly offset by her striking blue eyes and strawberry blonde hair. Yet the tears began to freely flow when she laid eyes upon the young Lloyd Stealle.

The tall, broad-shouldered youth immediately went to her, his lean but muscular arms wrapping around her slim shoulders. Andrella lay her head upon his scarlet-clad chest, the top of her blonde strands landing just below his chin. Beneath his shock of tousled brown hair, Lloyd's deep blue eyes mirrored her sorrow.

"Please tell us what happened here."

Aksel Alabaster climbed the few steps that led up to the throne and stood next to Elladan. The gnome appeared small in comparison to the elf, the crown of his copper-colored head barely reaching the bard's hip. He too was garbed in white—the clerical robes of his order.

Gracelynn's amber eyes fell upon the little gnome, her expression growing pained as she spoke. "Let us adjourn to a private room"—her voice dropped to a whisper—"the details of my husband's… demise was not made known in general."

Gelpas Ranblade, Captain of the Ravenford Guard, stood silently at Gracelynn's shoulder. As she rose, the grim-faced, red-bearded man stepped down and contritely offered her his arm. He quietly escorted her to a small chamber off the throne room. The others followed, fanning out to take seats around the large table that occupied most of the small room.

Only Kalyn hesitated, the young reddish-brown-haired archer seemingly uncertain where to sit. Kalyn Rhan had joined the companions just a few days ago, assisting in their struggle to defeat the Serpent Cult. Afterwards she opted to join the companions as they rushed back to Ravenford.

"Sit wherever you want," Seth Korzair advised as he brushed by her. The dark-haired, black-clad halfling was not one to be daunted by propriety.

Kalyn fixed her stormy gray eyes on the halfling's diminutive frame, the side of her mouth upturning. "That's easy for you to say, short-stack. You're small enough you *can* sit wherever you want. I ain't never been in such a fancy place. I feel like my backside is gonna leave a stain on these pretty polished chairs."

Seth shrugged, his brown eyes dancing with amusement at her apparent predicament.

Lloyd accompanied Andrella, following just behind Kalyn. The trace of a smile formed on the young lady's lips for the first time since they had arrived. "Oh, I like her. Anyone who can dish it out with Seth is okay in my book."

Kalyn grinned at the young lady, her cheeks reddening with embarrassment.

"Come sit with us," Andrella said, grasping Kalyn's hand.

Moments later, all were seated except for Gelpas, who elected to guard the door. Gracelynn sat at the head of the table, flanked on either side by Elladan and Aksel. Andrella sat at the other end with Lloyd and Kalyn. Glo sat in the middle, opposite Seth and the heretofore quiet Donatello.

The slim, sandy-haired young elf had been unusually silent since they left Bendenwood this morning. They had ridden hard the entire way, reaching Ravenford just a few hours after nightfall. Yet Donnie had said almost nothing the entire time.

Glo assumed his sullenness stemmed from having to part with Alana. The pair had grown close during their adventures these last weeks, but in the end the lady knight had to return to her order.

Once everyone was seated, Gracelynn began her sad tale. "It was three nights ago. Gryswold had retired to his chambers after a long day of town business. I bid him good night and then adjourned to my own room. The guards were all at their regular stations along the hall; no one could have gotten by without them seeing."

"Ahem," Seth cleared his throat.

"Forgive me, Master Seth—no ordinary person." Gracelynn gave the halfling a wan smile before continuing.

"The head butler, Gevies, usually goes in around ten o'clock to turn down my husband's sheets and lay out his nightclothes. He reported the Baron fine when he saw him—tired, but otherwise in good spirits. Yet when Gevies went in to wake him in the morning, he found Gryswold's body on the floor"—Gracelynn's voice fell to a whisper—"with his heart cut out."

Gasps erupted from around the room.

Glo's eyes went wide. Even in a world with magic that could bring back the dead, death was not something to be taken lightly. There were consequences to death. Any attempt to recall the soul might fail. Worse, a malevolent spirit might take its place. Yet in a case like this, where the body was not intact, no spell could restore it enough to even try to recall the spirit.

Across the table, Lloyd grasped Andrella's hand. The young lady's eyes were red, but she valiantly fought back the tears.

Gelpas strode up behind Gracelynn and placed a hand on her shoulder. Elladan, in turn, reached over and gently patted her hand.

Gracelynn gazed up, her lips flattening into a slim smile. "I'm fine. I'm fine. Thank you, gentlemen."

She waved them away, then took a deep breath and went on. "Once we realized what had been done, we called for Abbot Qualtan. He is more experienced a healer than I."

Her blue eyes swept around the room with a fierce intensity. "Qualtan said it looked like some sort of ritual had been performed on him. He could do no more, though. Qualtan placed the body in a magical stasis, but said that if we could not retrieve the heart in a couple of weeks at most, Gryswold would be too far gone to bring back."

Gracelynn sat up staunchly, but her face had gone ashen.

Andrella had gone pale as well. Her grip on Lloyd's hand tightened to the point of turning white.

Kalyn reached out and grabbed her other hand, looking the young lady in the eyes and giving her a reassuring nod. Still fighting back tears, Andrella managed a feeble smile.

Glo found himself speechless. In all his training as a wizard, the tall blonde elf had never heard of such an abominable act. Gryswold was the first friend Glo had lost to death, and he wasn't quite sure just yet how to handle it. He glanced around the table and saw his own shock mirrored in the others' eyes. Even the normally unflappable Seth appeared shaken.

Aksel slowly rose to his feet. "Your ladyship, that is one of the most heinous acts I have ever heard of. I promise you, we will do whatever is in our power to find the Baron's heart and return it so that he may be resurrected."

Gracelynn's eyes misted over as she stared at the little cleric. "Thank you, Cleric Aksel. We knew we could count on you"—her eyes swept around the table—"all of you."

Glo wished he had some words of comfort, but realized the best thing they could do was exactly as Aksel said. The young elf quietly addressed the Baroness. "Lady Gracelynn, would it be possible for us to examine the Baron's chambers?"

Gracelynn took a moment to wipe the moisture from her eyes, then turned to him. "Yes, of course."

She slowly stood up, her shoulders straight and her jaw firmly set. Gracelynn then motioned toward the door. "Captain, please lead the way."

A short while later, the companions gathered outside the Baron's chambers. A solitary guard stood at the door.

Gracelynn addressed the group, her voice subdued. "We kept the room exactly as it was the night he was murdered. No one has been allowed in since Qualtan removed the body three days ago."

Aksel bowed his head. "Thank you, your ladyship."

He shifted his gaze to Donnie and Seth. "I think it best we wait out here while you two check things out."

There was none of the banter between the duo that they all had come to expect. Both merely nodded, Seth leading the way as they entered the Baron's chambers.

Glo peered in after them. It was a large room, with an ornate poster bed against one wall. A round table with some chairs stood in the corner next to the bed. Glo shifted around and spied a mirror, two dressers, and a large wardrobe on the opposite wall.

The wall across from the door held two windows that opened onto a balcony. The gardens were just visible through them, yet those were three stories down. Thus, there was no obvious way in or out of the room other than the doorway.

The bed was turned down and the Baron's night clothes still lay there untouched. On the floor, at the foot of the bed, were stains of dried blood.

Donnie and Seth went straight to that spot, examining it carefully. Meanwhile, Aksel addressed the Baroness. "Could you send for the butler? I'd like to have a word with him."

"Of course," Gracelynn replied. She nodded toward Gelpas.

The Captain bowed. "At once, your ladyship."

He glanced at the guard. "Go fetch Gevies and return with him as quickly as possible."

"Yes, Sir!" The guard responded with a crisp salute, immediately taking off down the hall.

Kalyn stared after the guard, her mouth agape. "Sure are a lot of ladder rungs around here." She abruptly snapped her eyes toward Gracelynn, her cheeks reddening as she moved behind Elladan with an apologetic smile.

In the meantime, Seth and Donnie had fanned out. The former moved to the outskirts of the room, while the latter crawled under the bed.

A minute or so later, Donnie extracted himself and rejoined the others. In his hands he held two items—a gaudy silver button and a strand of golden string. "What do you make of these?"

Elladan took the items and examined them closely. "The button could be from any fine jacket, but this string definitely belongs to a bard."

He paused a moment, his head tilting, his eyes glancing upward. "In fact, if I remember correctly, our friend Balmaroh uses golden strings on his lute."

Gracelynn's tone was incredulous. "Are you suggesting this bard had something to do with my husband's murder?"

Elladan held up his hands in front of him. "It was merely an observation, your ladyship. We just met him while passing through Vermoorden, but the man didn't seem like the murdering type."

Aksel nodded. "I concur, your ladyship. It's really too soon to say anything for certain, but I promise you we will get to the bottom of this."

Any further conversation was interrupted as the guard returned with the butler, Gevies. Aksel had Elladan question the man while the cleric covertly cast a spell. It was expertly done. Glo could barely feel the magic build up and release.

Glo exchanged a glance with the gnome, but Aksel shook his head. *So, the butler didn't do it.*

Meanwhile, Elladan grilled the man. He showed him the two items Donnie had found.

Gevies responded stiffly. "The button is not the Baron's. I know every coat he owned—that doesn't belong to any of them. Furthermore, he didn't play any musical instruments."

Aksel nodded to Elladan and Gracelynn.

The Baroness sighed, then motioned toward Gevies. "Very well. That will be all."

The butler bowed to the Baroness. "Very good, ma'am."

He spun around and headed back down the hall, his boot heels clicking smartly as he went.

Gracelynn swept her eyes around the gathering. "So where does that leave us?"

"How about with a secret passage that leads outside the castle?"

All eyes turned to see Seth, who had just reappeared in the doorway.

"A secret passage?" Gracelynn pulled back, her eyes widening as they fell upon the halfling.

Seth's lips twisted sideways. "Yup. There's a secret door behind the wardrobe, with a dark passage beyond. It leads to a winding flight of stairs, and then a long corridor that comes out right behind the keep."

Glo raised an eyebrow. It was not unheard of for royalty to have a hidden exit out of a castle in case of emergencies. "Lady Gracelynn, did you have any idea that was there?"

Gracelynn's brow furrowed. "No. I had no idea."

"Would Gryswold have known of it?" Donnie added softly.

"Not as far as I know," Gracelynn responded. She gazed at Gelpas. "Captain?"

Gelpas looked as surprised as the Baroness. "I think he would have told at least one of us if he had, your ladyship."

Aksel cleared his throat. "Well either way, now we know how the murderer got in."

"Lady Gracelynn?" Seth spoke up again, his tone tentative.

She shifted her gaze toward him. "Yes, Master Seth?"

"Was the incision in your husband's chest jagged, or a straight line?"

"What kind of a question is that? He's a baron, not a skinned wolf!" Kalyn blurted out, her voice filled with horror.

The halfling fixed her with a dark stare. "It's important."

Gracelynn smiled at the young archer. "No, it's fine if it will help you find the murderer. I believe Qualtan said it was a 'very fine incision.'"

"Those were his exact words," Andrella agreed.

Seth pursed his lips together and took a slow breath. "I thought so. This was no ordinary killing. The removal of the heart was expert, so as to not damage it. That could only be done by a physician—or a highly trained assassin."

A dark shadow seemed to pass over the hall at Seth's pronouncement. Everyone began talking at once.

The mayhem continued until Aksel cried over the din. "Quiet, please!"

All went silent, their eyes shifting to the little gnome.

Aksel, in turn, gazed at Donnie. "You mentioned an assassin's guild on our trip out to Vermoorden."

Donnie looked around and nodded. "Yes, there are rumors of one around the seedier side of town. Though I can't imagine Balmaroh being an assassin. Still, if he isn't, someone is going to an awful lot of trouble to implicate him."

Something had been nagging at the back of Glo's mind ever since they heard about the Baron's death. He finally decided to bring it up. "While I agree that Balmaroh and Vermoorden bear looking into, I can't help wonder the motive behind all this. Could it have something to do with Gryswold's adventuring days?"

Gracelynn cast an appraising eye at the young elven wizard. "We did make our fair share of enemies in those days."

"We?" Elladan asked the bereaved monarch.

Gracelynn slowly ticked off on her fingers as she answered. "Gryswold, myself, the Wizard Maltar, the Abbot Qualtan, the Druid Almax, and our departed friend, Flandril."

Glo arched an eyebrow. It appeared that most of their old companions had settled down in Ravenford with them. "Interesting— though this is the first I've heard mention of this Flandril."

A wistful expression crossed Gracelynn's face. "He was a good friend and quite capable—sort of a cross between yourself, Glolindir, and Master Seth in his talents."

The side of Seth's mouth upturned slightly. "So a pyromaniac thief."

Glo stared daggers at Seth, but Gracelynn let out the smallest of laughs. "Now that you mention it, he did have a penchant for fire spells."

Aksel gingerly stroked his chin. "Anyway, you may be on to something there, Glo. While all the evidence points to Vermoorden, this also bears further scrutiny."

The little cleric shifted his gaze to Seth. "What do you think?"

Seth stood with his arms folded. "I think it's a good idea. I certainly don't want all of you trailing me through the streets of Vermoorden."

Aksel gave the halfling a weak smile. "Point taken."

"Speak for yourself," Kalyn huffed under her breath.

Glo snorted while suppressing a laugh. He shook his head at the exuberant archer, then shifted his gaze back to Aksel. "I agree as well. We should question Qualtan and Almax, but I also think it's time for us to renew our search for Maltar. It's too much of a coincidence that he was also attacked a couple of weeks ago."

"I thought that was the Serpent Cult?" Lloyd said with narrowed eyes.

"Maybe… maybe not," Glo responded slowly. "Either way, I think it's worth a look."

"Agreed," Aksel said. He shifted his gaze back to Seth. "So, who's going with you to Vermoorden?"

Kalyn started bouncing on her toes, holding her hand up, "Oh! Me, me, me! Pick me!" Her voice had turned into an excited squeak.

Seth swept his eyes across the group, halted momentarily on Kalyn, then finally settled on Aksel. "You and Martan."

Kalyn's mouth fell open, her shoulders drooping.

Aksel narrowed his eyes. "That's all?"

Seth shrugged. "That's all I need."

Kalyn huffed and crossed her arms. "Fine. At least I won't have to tolerate Martan if he's with you."

Aksel looked at Glo, ignoring the slighted archer. "And you?"

Gracelynn interrupted before the wizard could respond. "I can invite Qualtan and Almax for dinner tomorrow. You can question them there."

Glo gave the monarch a brief smile. "That would work. As for

Maltar, we've already examined his house. I think I'd like to have a look at his old tower on the keep grounds."

"I have the key," Andrella blurted, her eyes still puffy, but her jaw firmly set. "I can take you there in the morning."

Aksel shifted his gaze from Andrella to Gracelynn. The Baroness dipped her chin in agreement. The little cleric bowed his head and pursed his lips. "Okay then, sounds like we have a plan."

2
ON THE ROAD AGAIN

Nice to see 'a woman among the ranks for a change'

Kalyn Rahn was completely out of her element. When they had arrived in Ravenford yesterday evening, the sun had already set. Between the dark and the fog, she hadn't seen much of the town. Yet now in the bright early morning sun, Kalyn could clearly see streets and buildings stretching out in all directions.

Give me a forest any day! If it weren't for the heroes showing me around, I'd be lost sure as Fran is blind.

Ravenford had to be at least five times the size of Deepwood, if not bigger. Kalyn shaded her eyes with her hand and peered up the hill to the north. The spires of Ravenford Keep glistened a bright white in the morning sunlight.

Kalyn's jaw had drooped open when they first approached the keep. She had never seen anything like it. The walls were taller than Deepwood Fort, and made out of stone to boot. The area inside the walls was so large that most of Deepwood proper could have fit in there.

The keep itself was yet another marvel. The entryway was taller and wider than her parent's tavern. It had evoked many thoughts and feelings as she trudged through there, but two questions in particular stuck in her mind. *How in the world do people live like this? Better yet, who cleans all that?*

There had been other wonders as well that evening. Meeting a real live baroness was one of them. The Lady Gracelynn was the very definition of class. She was poised and elegant, yet tough as nails. She reminded Kalyn of a cross between the High Druid Lysandra of Bendenwood, and her good friend Fran.

The Lady Andrella appeared just as classy as her mother, yet far less aloof. Kalyn had not known what to expect at first, but when the young lady took her hand and insisted she sit with her, it had melted something in Kalyn's heart. The attention Andrella focused on her was almost sisterly. Kalyn hadn't realized till that night just how much she missed having that.

Yet as impressed as she was with Ravenford and its royal family, the young archer could hardly contain her excitement about what was unfolding in front of her at this very moment. She was standing outside the Golden Golem Inn, of all places, watching the Heroes of Ravenford prepare for their next adventure.

"Pinch me," she whispered to Martan.

"What?" the dour-faced archer exclaimed.

Kalyn shifted her gaze toward the man and knit her brow. Martan was tall and lean, his long brown hair outlining a ruggedly handsome face decorated with a close-cropped beard and mustache.

"Do you have any idea where we are?" she explained in a hushed voice.

Martan tilted his head to one side and stared at her. "Um, in the middle of the street?"

Kalyn swiped him across the arm with her hand. "No, orc brain. We're outside the inn where it all began—where the Heroes got their start."

Martan's brow furrowed into deep folds. He paused a moment before responding, "And?"

Kalyn hit him again, this time harder. "Have you no sense of adventure? No love of the stirring tale?"

Martan narrowed an eye at her. "With these folks? I'm just happy to still be alive."

Kalyn's jaw sagged open. "Martan Folke, you... are... no... fun..."

"Hey, you two—less talking and more packing!" Seth called as he exited the doors of the Golden Golem. The halfling had his arms full as he strode across the porch toward a pair of dogs tied to the hitching post.

Both Aksel and Seth were too small in stature to ride horses. Thankfully, the livery here in Ravenford had a couple of canine mounts specifically trained for riding. They were gorgeous animals— tall, strong-looking great danes, one fawn colored, the other a black and white.

A brown and white pinto was hitched to the post beyond the two dogs. Kalyn smacked Martan on the arm and tilted her head toward the waiting animal. "You heard what short-stack said. Get packing already!"

Martan cast a hurt look at Kalyn, then strode off toward his mount, grumbling underneath his breath.

Kalyn wasn't sure exactly why, but she took a great deal of pleasure in needling the gloomy young man. Maybe it was because she had years of teasing to make up for. He and Kalyn had been close 'friends' back in Deepwood—till Martan was accused of murder and took off without even so much as a goodbye.

Kalyn had been harboring resentment toward him ever since, a fact she made quite plain when the two were recently reunited. Yet not long afterwards, Kalyn discovered that her overprotective brothers were behind Martan's sudden disappearance. That assuaged most of her anger, but she still liked needling him nonetheless.

"Don't forget your lunch!" a lovely contralto voice practically sang out the door of the inn.

Shalla Vesperanna stepped through the open doorway, her arms laden with a large wicker basket. Elladan trailed immediately behind her, carrying a duplicate of the basket she held.

Kalyn couldn't stop staring at Shalla as she sauntered across the porch. She was probably the most beautiful woman that Kalyn had ever seen. Shalla was tall and sultry with a heart-shaped face, tiny nose, and high cheekbones. A luxurious mass of wavy brown hair adorned her head, falling well past her slender shoulders.

Kalyn felt just a twinge of jealously as she regarded the lovely woman. *How does she get her hair to fall like that? It's so perfect…*

Yet despite her good looks, Shalla was not conceited in the slightest. Elladan had introduced them last night when the Heroes adjourned for a late dinner. Shalla had welcomed Kalyn with open arms, quipping how it was nice to see 'a woman among the ranks for a change.' Kalyn had taken an immediate liking to her.

After dinner, Shalla and Elladan performed a duet for the patrons of the inn. Kalyn thought she had died and gone to the lands of evergreen. The duo practically glided around each other as they sang on that small stage. The chemistry between them was undeniable. They made quite the pair, the extremely handsome elven bard and the beautiful bardess.

"Sure you got enough packed in there?" Donnie commented. The sandy-haired elf flashed a sparkling smile from his porch chair next to Glolindir.

Shalla responded with a devastating smile of her own. "Don't complain to me, Donatello. You seemed more than content after scarfing down three plates of pot pie for dinner last night."

"Touché!" Elladan grinned at his cheeky companion.

Donnie definitely seemed in better spirits today. Even the normally serious Glolindir cracked a smile at the lively banter.

According to Martan, both elves had recently ended a relationship. Kalyn had met Alana during the fight against the Serpent Cult. When she parted from Donnie afterwards, it was obvious how much she would miss him. Yet Kalyn couldn't fathom how this Elistra had left Glo. The flaxen-haired, blue-eyed elf was not only tall and rather good-looking, but possibly the smartest person Kalyn had ever met.

Kalyn silently shook her head. *That Elistra must be a real shroom-sucker. Some folks just don't realize what they have.*

A black bird abruptly swooped down from overhead, landing on Glo's outstretched arm. It was the wizard's familiar, Raven.

"Nammë avánië, nammë avánië," the dark crow cawed as she hopped around from foot to foot.

The tall elf smiled as he wagged a finger at his small companion. "No, I told you, not this time."

Kalyn's mind wandered to her animal friend, Elfar. He was a big silver lynx she had saved from a trap years ago when he was just a cub. He normally traveled with her everywhere, but he hated town. Kalyn knew he would be unhappy in Ravenford, so far away from his home forest, so she left him with her good friend, Fran. She missed him a great deal and silently cursed him for being such a stick-in-the-mud.

Once the baskets were packed, Aksel pulled Elladan aside. "Can I borrow your portal bag for this trip?"

Kalyn arched an eyebrow at the mention of the bag. Kalyn had never seen one before, but she had heard of them. Portal bags connected to another plane and could store far more inside than it appeared from the outside.

"Sure," Elladan responded as he pulled a plain-looking purple bag from his belt. "Mind if I ask what you want it for?"

Aksel glanced around, his eyes narrowing. "First, has anyone seen Lloyd?"

"He went up to the keep at first light to see Andrella," Glo answered.

"Like that's a surprise," Seth noted with a twist of his lips.

Aksel gave the halfling a hard stare, then continued. "Well, I've been sort of researching how to make armor from dragon scales—and since you still have that little red dragon stuffed in there, I was thinking of making Lloyd a suit of armor from it."

Kalyn's eyes went wide. She hadn't actually seen Lloyd slay the little red dragon. Still, little was a relative term in this case. From what she had heard, the dragon was eight feet long from snout to tail.

Aksel's voice took on a conspiratorial tone. "It's a surprise though, so don't anyone tell him."

Elladan clasped the little gnome on the shoulder. "Well I think it's a great idea, but I have something to ask in return."

Aksel's brow furrowed. "Oh, and what's that?"

"Since you aren't going to be using it, can I have the Boulder's ring?"

Kalyn nearly yelped aloud, her eyes shifting toward the stone creature standing motionless in front of the inn. The Boulder was an impressive sight, standing nine feet tall with broad shoulders nearly half that size. Two eerie glowing eyes were inset into the great stone head that sat above those wide shoulders. Thick arms hung down on either side to the creature's knees, each ending in hands the size of… well, boulders.

Aksel reached into his pocket and pulled out a rather plain-looking gold ring. "Here it is."

A half-smile crept across the bard's lips as he pocketed the ring. "Thanks. You never know when this could come in handy."

With the last of the bags packed, Seth, Aksel, and Martan all swung up into their saddles. Everyone gathered out in the street to send off the trio.

A strange feeling twisted in the pit of Kalyn's stomach as she watched Martan's back slowly recede from her. She cupped her hands together and yelled after him. "Don't go gettin' yerself killed now, Martan Folke!"

Kalyn's face reddened as she felt all eyes turn toward her.

"If anyone's gonna kill ya, it's gonna be me!" she added in an attempt to cover her embarrassment.

Martan glanced over his shoulder at her, both eyebrows raised, but he declined to comment.

Seth, on the other hand, was not so forgiving. "Don't worry, Kalyn! I'm sure he loves you too!"

Kalyn turned red from head to toe.

3
MAGIC CIRCLE

Beyond the door lay another room with three
glowing rings in its center

Andrella Avernos had been raised to believe in "Noblesse Oblige," that with nobility comes responsibility. It meant that her obligations as a noble took precedence over her own needs. It was a Penwick concept, one to which her father and mother firmly subscribed. Yet that belief system had never been so sorely tested as it had these last few days.

Andrella's father was dead, brutally murdered. He had been her rock, her safe haven in a world full of monsters and petty nobles. Whether dealing with a bad dream or some self-centered suitor, Andrella could always turn to Daddy for support. Yet now he was gone.

The young lady wanted nothing more than to curl up into a ball and hide under her bedcovers. If she stayed there, maybe it would turn out to be just another bad dream. She would wake up and Daddy would in his chambers, right as rain.

Yet Andrella could not afford that luxury. Her mother needed her. Mother was strong, but Father had been her heart. Andrella had watched her mother closely these last few days. On the outside she wore a stony mask of nobility, acting as a rock for their people, but Andrella could see the toll it was taking on her. She had stood outside her mother's doorway and heard the sobs in the night. When they took Father's heart, they might as well have taken Mother's, too.

Thus, Andrella couldn't turn her back and hide from the world. She put on her own stony mask and was there for her mother and their people during this trying time.

A pair of strong arms wrapped themselves around her shoulders. "Are you sure you're alright?"

Andrella gazed away from the full-length mirror in front of her, and into a pair of steel-blue eyes filled with concern. The young lady grasped those arms and breathed a deep sigh as she lay her head on the firm chest behind her. "I'll be fine."

Lloyd Stealle was a godsend. He was so much like her father— tall, strong, and handsome. Further, he followed that same moral code that her family held so dear. She felt safe in his arms. He was so unassuming, the exact opposite of the pompous suitors she was used to.

Lloyd spun her around and pulled her closer. "Just making sure. This couldn't have been easy on you."

Andrella lay her head beneath his strong chin, a contented sigh escaping her lips. She could be herself with Lloyd. He understood what it was like to have noble parents and to accept the responsibilities that went with it. He was still a little rough around the edges, but with a bit of polish he would make a fine duke someday.

"It wasn't, but it's much better now that you're here."

A strong hand lifted her chin to stare once again into those deep blue eyes. "Good, because I swear to you, we will find whoever did this, and recover your father's heart."

Andrella's breath caught as wave of emotions threatened to overwhelm her. Lloyd was so much like her father that it magnified her sense of loss. Yet at the same time she felt a deep abiding love for this sweet, tender young man.

She stood up on her toes and pushed her lips against his, kissing him with wild abandon. Lloyd responded in kind, kiss after kiss sending sparks shooting throughout her body. She felt the heat rise to her cheeks, her breath coming in short, ragged bursts. When she could no longer breathe, she pulled away and stared again into that handsome face.

Lloyd smiled at her, his cheeks flushed bright red. "Whoa... if that was meant as incentive, you've done an excellent job."

Andrella's lips curved into an alluring smile. "Well, if you like that, you'll love your reward when you make good on your promise."

Lloyd's eyes widened, his cheeks turning scarlet.

Andrella laughed aloud. Lloyd was so genuine, so easy to embarrass. He was a keeper—she wasn't ever letting him go.

The young lady pushed away, her mood abruptly turning somber. They still had a long way to go if they were to save her father. She opened the jewelry box on top of her dresser and pulled out the key to the tall tower across the courtyard.

"Anyway, the others should be arriving soon. Let's go and see what Maltar has hiding in that tower."

Four figures waited for them at the entrance to the tower—Elladan, Glolindir, Donatello, and Kalyn. Andrella was well acquainted with the first three, but knew nothing about the new girl.

"Do you have the key?" Elladan called out.

Elladan was a strikingly handsome elf. His performances had been the highlight of her birthday party. Yet the bard was surprisingly humble offstage.

"Right here," Andrella replied, holding it up as she strode past them.

"You might want to hand that to Donnie," Glolindir called after her.

Andrella stopped in mid-step and turned to face the tall flaxen-haired elf. Glolindir was quite intelligent—smarter than Maltar, she would daresay. Yet he was also very brave. Andrella would never forget how he took the brunt of a ball of fire to save the guests at her party.

She narrowed an eye at him. "Why's that?"

"From what I heard, Maltar's home had traps on its traps," Donatello quipped.

The slim elf was a bit of an enigma. His boyish good looks and devil-may-care attitude belied the soul of a hero. Yet, he had stood side by side with Lloyd when those giant serpents appeared in the midst of the courtyard.

Andrella held up the key for Donnie to grab. "Be my guest."

"Ladies and gents, there goes the brave elf, to face certain explosion and humiliation. How far will he be blown into the sky this time?" Kalyn said with a half twist of her lips.

Andrella had never met Kalyn before last night. The young woman intrigued her. Lloyd had said she was an expert archer and tracker. She certainly dressed the part in that dirty green outfit.

Elladan snorted. "I think she's got your number, Donnie."

Already at the doorway to the tower, Donnie cast a dark look over his shoulder. "And when have you known me to blow up anything?"

Kalyn clasped her hands behind her back and kicked the dirt with her toe. "Oh, I've heard stories…"

"Don't believe everything Seth tells you," Donnie called back to her as he examined the lock on the door.

Everyone chuckled after that, even Andrella. It was the first time she had laughed in days, and it felt good.

While Donnie continued to fiddle with the lock, Andrella covertly appraised Kalyn. The young woman was certainly feisty, but she also had a marvelously slim figure, a head of long, wavy, reddish-brown hair, storm-gray eyes, and ivory skin. A good bath, the right dress, some makeup to cover those freckles, and a proper styling to that unkempt hair would turn Kalyn into a courtly beauty.

Andrella made up her mind then and there—Kalyn would be her side project. It would be a welcome distraction with everything that was going on right now.

Click.

Donnie grinned as he pushed open the door to the tower. "See, nothing to worry about, folks."

The tower was comprised of circular rooms, with a spiral staircase in the center leading up to the two floors above and a basement below. The group stood on the ground floor, a living area complete with a kitchen and a large open hearth. The second floor was split into four separate bedrooms, while a lab and scant library took up the top floor. Both were mostly empty. Maltar must have brought most of his things with him when he moved across town.

A thorough search turned up nothing of interest until they reached the basement. Another circular area, it was stacked with numerous crates and boxes. Yet off to one side, Donnie found a hidden door. There was some sort of trap on the entryway, but Donnie disarmed it without incident.

Beyond the door lay another room with three glowing rings in its center. The blue rings circled each other in a crisscross fashion, taking up most of the room.

A dazzling portrait of the celestial spheres was meticulously drawn on the ceiling above the circle. It depicted the seven heavens, the area in between, and the many layers of the abyss. A wide oval traversed the portrait, mapping the path of Arinthar through the spheres. An intricate network of piping was suspended from the ceiling, mirroring that path. A single rod hung down from the pipework, with an orb at the top that appeared to be a tiny model of Arinthar.

Once Donnie deemed it safe, Glolindir went to examine the rings, the pipework, and the portrait above. Deep creases lined the wizard's brow. "I'm not completely sure, but I think this is some kind of teleportation magic."

Elladan stood next to him, his arms folded across his chest. "Maybe this is how Maltar left Ravenford unnoticed."

Glo gave his friend a curt nod. "Possibly. The immediate question is how does it work?"

"Magic!" Kalyn crossed her arms, giggling at her own joke.

Glo glanced at the young woman with a single raised eyebrow.

Elladan stood back and gazed up at the ceiling. "I read somewhere that points in the sky can be used to map out locations on the ground."

Glo steepled his hands in front of his lips. "I remember reading that, as well." He walked over to the hanging rod. "This looks like it could be moved along the pipes…"

"…which means it could be used to point out a specific location," Andrella finished for him.

Glo spun around and nodded at the young lady, clearly impressed. "So if that's true, we have the means of setting where we want to teleport. The next question is how the circle is invoked."

"Maybe with this?" Donnie stood off to one side of the room, next to a podium that hadn't been there before.

"Where did that come from?" Lloyd asked as they all strode over for a closer look.

"A hidden panel I found in the floor," Donnie explained. "As soon as it opened, this pedestal popped out of it."

The podium was adorned with a single red lever and a long blue horizontal bar that matched the light of the rings.

Elladan bent down for a closer look. "This lever probably turns on the rings."

Glo gazed back up at the ceiling. "That makes sense. If Maltar used this circle to escape, then the piping should mark the place he teleported to…"

"…which means we could use it to follow him," Lloyd finished his thought.

Glo's expression grew pensive. "Maybe, but I'd still like to know more about how this thing works before we try it."

Andrella cleared her throat. "I think I may know a way."

All eyes turned to the young lady.

Elladan gazed at her with a semi-smile. "I knew you were more than just a pretty face."

Andrella gave the handsome elf an ironic smile. "Thanks… I think. Anyway, when I was younger, I studied with Maltar for a while. I remember seeing a book in the library at his house, with a few drawings that looked just like the map on the ceiling and those rings."

Glo arched an eyebrow at her. "Would you recognize the book if you saw it again?"

Andrella nodded. "I think so. It had a red binding and was written in gnomish, titled something like *Magical Devices from Before the Fall*."

Glo whistled. "A book from before the fall of the Baleful Moon? That's a rare find indeed."

Andrella felt rather pleased at the wizard's praise. She swept her gaze across the small group. They all seemed impressed, except for Lloyd, who looked puzzled.

"Andrella, you can read gnomish?"

The young lady giggled. "Among a few other languages. Uncle Kelvick spared no expense when it came to my studies."

Lloyd picked her up and spun her in a circle. "Andrella, you're amazing!"

His enthusiasm made her giggle once more. "Lloyd, put me down."

The young man immediately complied, a sheepish grin crossing his face. "Sorry."

Glo held his hand out, palm up. "Well then, young scholar, care to lead the way to Maltar's house?"

Andrella executed a perfect curtsy, a grin upon her face. "Why, it would be my pleasure, good Sir."

It had been nearly three years since Andrella had set foot in Maltar's home—the cottage he had moved to when he left the tower at Ravenford keep. Today the once-immaculate place looked like a disaster had hit it. The foyer doors had been ripped clean off the walls, pieces of furniture were strewn all over the hall, and the stairwell was covered with dried blood. Lloyd had told her about the battle they had here with assassins, but the extent of the damage far outstripped her imagination.

A whistle drew Andrella's attention to Kalyn. The young archer stared wide-eyed at all the damage.

"Someone sure had a wild party." Kalyn touched some of the dried blood on the wall before leaning forward and sniffing it.

"Kalyn!" Andrella gasped.

The archer looked at her, perplexed. "What? You can tell a lot about a monster by their blood, and track 'em easier, too."

"Well first, that's probably Glo's blood down here," Lloyd explained with a wan smile. "Second, you won't be tracking those monsters. They didn't exactly leave the house."

Kalyn grinned, crossing her arms. "You guys got 'em?"

Lloyd shook his head. "No. Maltar's trap did that. We were too busy trying to save Glo from a giant whirlwind."

Kalyn's eyes grew wider. She quickly glanced over at the tall elf.

Glo wore a slight smile. "Not one of my finest moments."

Kalyn swept her eyes around the hall again. "Oh! So, *this* is where that story happened! Ha! I'm walking in the remains of a hero battle! This is epic!"

A smile crept across Andrella's lips. Kalyn seemed positively enthralled with the group's past adventures.

The companions wound their way around the wreckage, up to the library on the third floor. Thankfully this room was as pristine as Andrella remembered, filled with row upon row of tall bookshelves that reached all the way to the ceiling. There was a ladder with rollers against each wall, allowing access to the highest shelves.

The six of them split up and scoured the place for any book with red binding. There were a surprising number of them, but none written in gnomish. Nearly three quarters of an hour passed when Lloyd called out, "Is this it?"

The young man floated down from the ceiling, carrying a huge red tome in his hands.

"Couldn't use a ladder like everyone else?" Donnie teased.

Lloyd landed and pointed around the room. "I would've, but they're all occupied."

Kalyn whacked Donnie on the arm. "Hey, I'd be flying too, if I had a cloak like his. Wouldn't you?"

Donnie flashed her a toothy smile. "Probably."

Meanwhile, Lloyd had placed the heavy tome on the table in the center of the room with a loud *thunk*. Everyone gathered around as Andrella gazed at the cover. There was the picture of a fractured moon on the front with a title above written in gnomish.

"You were right, Andrella," Glo said from over her shoulder. "It reads, *Magical Devices from Before the Fall of the Baleful Moon*."

Andrella cast a quick grin at the wizard, then cracked the tome open and paged through it. The book was as long as it was heavy. It took another quarter of an hour before she found the page she was looking for. On that page was an illustration of the crisscrossed rings they had seen in the tower. The next page over had another drawing of the map of the celestial spheres. On the page behind it was a picture of the pedestal with the lever and the blue bar.

Glo and Elladan crowded in on either side of Andrella, and the three of them pored over the text around the illustrations. After a minute or so, the bard cried out exultantly, "I was right! The path of Arinthar through the spheres depicts longitude and latitude…"

"…and the pipes and rod are used to set the destination," Andrella finished for him.

Elladan grinned at her. "Once set, you pull the lever to invoke the teleportation spell."

"And it all works because… magic." Kalyn whispered to Donnie. Donnie winked back at her.

"Yes… that all makes sense…" Glo murmured absently. "But I still want to know… wait, here it is."

The wizard pointed a finger to a passage on the page next to the picture of the device. "The blue bar designates the amount of stored magic available in the circle. The bar must be completely full to invoke teleportation. Once used, the rings must recharge before teleporting again."

Donnie stroked the light-haired stubble on his chin. "Sounds easy enough. The blue bar was full, so we all just need to go through at the same time."

It made sense to Andrella, but Glo still looked uncertain. "Hopefully it's that simple, but that begs the question, where is the circle set to?"

Elladan snapped his fingers. "If I remember right, there were a couple of maps laid out in Maltar's lab."

The elven bard led the way, down the hall to the other end. The door opened to Maltar's private lab.

As she stepped through the entrance, Andrella's eyes went wide with wonder. She had never been allowed in here during her days as an apprentice. The room was lined with multiple tables, their tops covered with vials and beakers of various-colored liquids, many connected by crazy sets of tubing. There were at least a half-dozen experiments sitting there unattended. *Maltar sure must have left in a hurry.*

"Oooh! A fancy whisky distiller!" Kalyn squealed as she hurried up to the table and scanned the vials and beakers appraisingly. "I know a few folk in Deepwood who'd give a basket full of 'shrooms' to get their hands on this."

"By 'a few people,' you mean Fran?" Donnie noted wryly.

Kalyn glanced up at him and grinned. "You said it, not me."

Elladan went to a table with a parchment spread across it. It was a detailed map of the Island of Lanfor, a small island kingdom directly east of Thac. Next to it lay a half-rolled parchment. Elladan picked it up and examined it, his face lighting up.

"Ah ha!" The bard unrolled the thick paper over the other, covering it with a map of the Isle of Thac. Everyone gathered around as he ran his finger across the top, then down. "Based on the location of the rod, the place we are looking for should be… here"—Elladan pointed to a spot near the center of the isle—"right next to the Silver Lakes and the town of Tarsmoor."

"Tarsmoor?" Glo exclaimed. "What would Maltar be doing all the way out there?"

Lloyd appeared equally surprised. "Isn't that where you, Seth, and Aksel were coming from when we first met?"

Glo nodded slowly, but his eyes were unfocused as if his mind were somewhere else entirely. "I think we have company."

A small black bird winged its way into the room and hovered in front of the wizard. It was Raven. Andrella had heard that wizards were linked empathically to their familiars, but this is the first she had seen it in practice.

"*Shalla naa sinome. Shalla naa sinome,*" the black bird cawed.

A moment later, the bardess' voice drifted in from the hall. "Hello!"

Elladan immediately spun around and went to the open doorway.

"Is anybody here?" Shalla cried again.

Elladan strode out into the hall to the top of the stairs.

"We're up here!" he called down the stairwell.

Footsteps drifted up the staircase, and then the lovely bardess appeared on the landing below.

"Ew… this place is a mess," she said, tiptoeing around the dried blood on the stairs. When she finally saw them, she stopped her ascent. "Ah, there you are."

Elladan's comely brow knit together. "What are you doing here?"

Shalla's hands went to her hips. "I thought you'd like to know that a group of Dunwynn Sky Knights just descended upon Ravenford Keep."

Kalyn let out a low hiss, like a cat.

Andrella exchanged a worried glance with Lloyd. Dunwynn Sky Knights?

Shalla's lips twisted into a wry smile. "And you'll never guess who's leading them."

"Who?" Lloyd blurted out.

"Sir Fafnar."

4
SKY KNIGHTS

I see you've been relegated to the status of errand boy

Lloyd Stealle entered the throne room of Ravenford Keep prepared for almost anything. Yet what he observed there caught him completely by surprise. Sir Fafnar Strakentir knelt on one knee at the base of the steps in front of the Lady Gracelynn. It was the last thing Lloyd had expected from the arrogant noble.

When Shalla informed them of Sir Fafnar's arrival, Lloyd had anticipated the worst. The companions rushed across town to find about a dozen hippogriffs and a half-dozen Sky Knights waiting in the courtyard of the keep. The rest of the unexpected guests were already being received in the throne room.

Now Lloyd pulled up short, just beyond the throne room doors. There were a few quiet complaints as his companions nearly crashed into him, but Lloyd maintained his focus on Sir Fafnar.

The noble didn't look much different. Still garbed in a powder-blue Dunwynn uniform, a sword and axe hung from either side of his belt. Light brown hair flowed down his shoulders, and a pencil-thin goatee and mustache adorned his thin face. Yet he no longer wore that haughty sneer Lloyd had become accustomed to. Instead, his expression was rather contrite.

"Dunnies, go home," Kalyn whispered under her breath.

A few chuckles erupted from the companions.

"Shh," Lloyd silenced his friends as Fafnar spoke.

"I understand this is a trying time for you, Lady Gracelynn. If it please your ladyship, I would like to present myself and this small contingent of Dunwynn knights for you to command. Please use our services as you see fit for the benefit of Ravenford."

A hushed silence fell over the room at the Lieutenant's declaration. Considering his attitude the last time they crossed paths, this seemed completely out of character for the Dunwynn noble.

Lloyd felt a slim hand slide into his. He glanced over to see Andrella peering at him, a single brow arched above her eye. Lloyd shrugged. While Fafnar sounded sincere, he found it difficult to believe the noble had changed so drastically in such a short amount of time. Still, there was a way to find out.

As the name implied, there were spiritual elements to the discipline of the spiritblade. It was not something Lloyd excelled at—his brother and sister were far more adept than he. Nonetheless, Lloyd now attempted to use that skill to gauge Sir Fafnar's true intent.

The young man quieted his mind and connected with his inner self. He felt the energy flow from his core through his body. He pushed it out across the room, in the direction of Sir Fafnar. As he did so, the Lady Gracelynn broke the strained silence.

"I must say Sir Fafnar, we are very grateful for your surprisingly generous offer. Still, I do believe we have things well in hand for now."

Fafnar's face momentarily darkened—there was the arrogant noble they all knew. Yet he quickly caught himself, his features softening once again. "I am sure that is not completely true, your ladyship, but I do understand why you may not want my services." The side of his mouth upturned slightly. "I did not exactly make a good impression on my last visit."

Elladan stepped past Lloyd and called across the chamber. "I guess the Duke didn't think so, either. I see you've been relegated to the status of errand boy."

Fafnar stood to face the bard, his expression unreadable. Elladan returned his gaze with a quasi-smile. After a moment or two, a deep sigh escaped the noble's lips. "As you intimate, my poor performance last time I was here did not go unpunished."

"Couldn't have happened to a nicer guy," Donnie murmured under his breath.

Kalyn snorted. "Better put some butter on that burn."

Lloyd's focus wavered momentarily, but he managed to wrestle it back under control. As far as he could sense, there had been brief dark spikes in Fafnar's aura, but they disappeared as quick as they had appeared. There was still a trace of negativity in the man, but that seemed to be directed mostly inward.

Glo strode up next to Elladan, the tall elf trying hard not to choke. "Your ladyship, all good intentions aside, we have more pressing matters to discuss at the moment."

Fafnar cast a curious glance at the elf, but Gracelynn interrupted him as she rose from her seat.

"Sir Fafnar, thank you again for your concern and your generous offer, but you will have to excuse us for now."

Fafnar eyed Glo a moment longer, then turned and executed a deep bow before the Baroness. "As you wish, your ladyship. But please do give our offer some further thought."

Gracelynn regarded the noble for a few moments, then held out her hand to him. "Very well. In the meantime, we are hosting a dinner tonight for a few special guests. Please be kind enough to join us."

"Oh boy. Guess who's coming to dinner," Donnie quipped under his breath.

This time, Lloyd nearly choked as Fafnar took Gracelynn's hand and kissed it. "It would be an honor, your ladyship."

"That hand's gonna need lots o' washin'," Kalyn noted as the companions filed across the room.

"Kalyn!" Andrella admonished the young woman as she tried desperately to suppress a laugh.

Once again they had gathered in the side chamber off the throne room. Elladan had just finished reporting to Lady Gracelynn what they had found in the tower and Maltar's home.

"…to sum things up, your ladyship, we believe Maltar may have gone to Tarsmoor. We would like to follow him there, but all things considered, we are not sure it would be best for us to leave Ravenford right now."

Gracelynn pursed her lips together and dipped her chin. "I understand and appreciate your concern. My people's well-being is paramount, but I am reluctant to give up on my husband's revival so easily."

Lloyd listened quietly to the exchange, at the same time sorting out his feelings about Sir Fafnar. The man had been an arrogant fool, blocking their attempts to protect Ravenford. Yet his defeat in the tournament at Lloyd's hand, and his subsequent demotion by the Duke, appeared to have taken a toll on the noble's ego.

If Lloyd was right about Fafnar, then it gave him an idea. "Lady Gracelynn?"

The Baroness tilted her head and peered at him. "Yes, Lloyd?"

"Maybe you should take Fafnar up on his offer of knights."

Elladan spun around in his chair and narrowed an eye at Lloyd. "Are you crazy? Do you want to hand Ravenford over to Dunwynn?"

A strained smile crept across Lloyd's lips. "I said the knights, not Fafnar. We leave them here, but bring him with us."

Donnie let out an exasperated huff. "Now I know you're crazy. Why would we possibly want Fafnar with us?"

Lloyd took a deep breath and grimaced. "It's hard to explain."

He couldn't exactly blame the elves for their adverse reaction. During their last visit, Fafnar and his ilk had made it plain that they thought non-humans inferior. One Dunwynn guard went so far as to ignore queries from anyone but Lloyd.

Thus, it was unexpected when Glo came to his rescue. The tall elf held up a hand in front of the others. "Hold on a minute. I'd like to hear to him out."

Lloyd smiled at Glo, then took a moment to collect his thoughts. "First of all, I know firsthand that Fafnar is awful handy with that sword and axe of his."

"Granted," Elladan admitted begrudgingly.

"Second, while I'm no expert at this, spiritblades do have the ability to sense auras. From what I was able to tell from Fafnar, he was being sincere."

Donnie grumbled. "Doesn't make him any less a pain in the…"

Elladan cut him off before he could finish. "No, I get it. This is a classic case of keep your friends close, but your enemies closer."

Lloyd threw up his hands and shrugged. That was not what he said, but if that's how they needed to view it, then so be it.

Glo shifted his gaze from Lloyd to Elladan, then nodded. "I believe I agree, Lady Gracelynn. Of course, the final decision is up to you."

Gracelynn pinched her chin between her thumb and forefinger, then turned to Andrella. "What say you, daughter?"

"Don't do it. Dunnies go home," Kalyn murmured under her breath.

The corners of Andrella's lips rose slightly, but she managed to bring them under control. She glanced over at Lloyd, her blue eyes burning into him intently. Lloyd held her stare unwaveringly until she finally smiled at him.

Andrella then shifted her gaze back to her mother. "I agree as well."

"Very well," Gracelynn responded. "I will broach the subject at dinner tonight."

Lloyd was pleased they had listened to him, but another thought abruptly entered his mind. "Begging your pardon, Lady Gracelynn, but would you mind if I talked to him instead?"

Gracelynn glanced at him, her brow furrowing. "Any particular reason?"

"I figure if I make the offer and he agrees, it will show he is willing to work with us."

Gracelynn appeared impressed with his proposal. She tilted her head and nodded. "Hmm. Very well. You may make the offer to him."

Lloyd grinned in response. "Thank you, Lady Gracelynn."

With the meeting adjourned, everyone exited the small room, leaving Lloyd alone with Andrella and Kalyn. The two young women still sat in their chairs, whispering back and forth.

"But I ain't got nothin' to wear to no fancy dinner," Kalyn insisted.

Andrella grinned as she grabbed Kalyn by the arm and pulled her from the chair. "Oh, don't worry. I'm sure we can fix that."

Kalyn peered at Lloyd with pleading eyes as the duo brushed by them. Yet Andrella cut him off before he could say a word. "Don't wait around for us, Lloyd. We'll see you at dinner."

Lloyd watched sympathetically as Andrella dragged the floundering Kalyn out of the throne room. He had the strangest feeling he was looking at how his future was going to be.

5
DRAGON TALES

*It tormented the survivors from the darkness telling them
how many would die that night*

K alyn had only ever worn the dresses her momma made her,
and only when her momma made her wear them. They were
modest, hot, and usually uncomfortable, and thus were only
worn to midsummer parties which were awkward anyway. Though
her momma had poured a lot of love and attention into the making of those dresses, none of them had been as fancy as the ones
Andrella had picked out for her. Kalyn was still in awe of the young
noble, but put her foot down on the bright red, pale yellow, and sky-blue gowns she had chosen.

"What do you think I am? A poppy flower? That one's too red.
That one's too yellow. And that blue one shows not just my collar
bone, but my shoulders to boot!"

They finally settled on a deep green one that reminded Kalyn of
the forest, kept her decently covered, and pleased Andrella.

The dress fit Kalyn quite well, with one exception—the length.

Andrella was about four inches taller than her. Kalyn thought for sure she'd get her leathers back, but the "problem" was quickly remedied. Andrella sent for her friend, Kailay, whose mother was the town seamstress. With the bubbly young woman's help, the dress was ready just before dinner.

Yet that wasn't the end of it. Andrella had insisted on 'painting her up' as well. Kalyn's face felt like it was suffocating, her eyelids heavy, and her lips sticky. She didn't even recognize herself in the mirror. She had flat out refused Andrella's shoes, though—she was certain she would kill herself in those tiny pointed heels. In the end they compromised. The gown she wore was floor length, so Andrella grudgingly agreed to let Kalyn keep her doe-skin boots.

"At least now I only feel kinda neked," Kalyn grumbled.

Now both women stood at the entryway to the main dining hall. Kalyn felt like her stomach was going to drop clear to the floor as Andrella pushed the double doors open.

Kalyn's mouth hung open as she gazed around the hall. It was not as big as the throne room, but there was a large hearth opposite the doors, and two tall windows on each of the remaining walls. Floor-length tapestries hung between the windows with the town's insignia—a black dragon on a red, white, and blue background.

A pair of fancy chandeliers hung over a large table, with seating for easily twenty folks. Several people sat around the table, but Kalyn's eyes focused on the Lady Gracelynn.

The regal woman turned and motioned toward them. "Ah, here is my daughter. Andrella, Kalyn, please come and join us."

Kalyn's feet felt firmly frozen to the floor. Andrella knit her brows, then laced her arm through Kalyn's and practically dragged the stunned young woman into the dining hall.

"Close your mouth," Andrella hissed to her under her breath.

Kalyn had not realized it was still open. She did so, yet her eyes remained wide as she stared around the room.

The Lady Gracelynn sat at one end of that huge table. To her left sat a pudgy, balding, sour-faced man in the white robes of the clergy. To her right was a tall, white-haired gentleman garbed in long brown robes. *I'd know a druid anywhere. That must be Almax, and the feller with the stick up his rear must be Abbot Qualtan.*

Elladan was seated next to Qualtan, with Glo on his other side. Donnie sat next to Almax, followed by Lloyd and Sir Fafnar. There were two more place settings beyond Glo, and one more at the far end of the table, most likely in honor of the fallen Baron.

Kalyn felt extremely uncomfortable as all eyes in the room turned their way.

Donnie's eyes went wide with surprise, as if he didn't recognize her at first. "Well, you clean up nicely."

Elladan stared at her sidelong, his eyes a-twinkle. "Martan would die if he could see this."

The mention of her long time 'friend' stirred Kalyn from her shocked state. "Shut yer pieholes, gents, before ya get maggots in 'em."

"Kalyn!" Andrella hissed at her, the young lady mortified at her reaction.

Yet Kalyn's comment had elicited a round of snorts and chuckles from the table. Almax in particular seemed quite amused. "Oh, I like her." He turned to Lady Gracelynn. "From what I heard, she left quite an impression on High Druid Lysandra. Now I can see why."

That was certainly news to Kalyn. She didn't think the High Druid liked anyone, except for maybe Glolindir.

Andrella seated them both without further incident. Kalyn gazed wide-eyed at the number of forks and spoons spread out before her. She had no idea why there were so many. The young woman folded her hands together and silently prayed to the moon goddess, Synopei, that she would make it through this dinner without further embarrassment.

Elladan Narmolanya was a fairly good judge of character. He'd traveled up and down the eastern half of Thac—everywhere from Kai Arborous to Lukescros. He'd performed in the seediest of taverns to the most extravagant of venues, meeting folks from all walks of life. Over time, Elladan had learned how to read his audience. Yet more importantly, he had learned to read people. It was a talent he put to good use this night at the dinner table.

Elladan took an immediate liking to the druid, Almax. At first the man seemed somewhat reserved, but he quickly exhibited a keen sense of humor. Qualtan, on the other hand, was sour-faced, his speech that fake-friendly you found in diplomats.

Fafnar had been the hardest to read. Initially shocked to see the companions, he nonetheless attempted to be gracious. It was obviously a struggle for the Dunwynn noble, but Elladan gave him credit for trying.

Of all the guests, Kalyn's entrance was the most entertaining. Garbed in a dress fit for a duke's court, she was quite fetching—yet it was obvious that she felt like a fish out of water. Neither he nor Donnie could resist ribbing her. Kalyn's exceedingly harsh comeback proved that she was still herself underneath all that finery.

Once everyone was seated, Gracelynn drew their attention by tapping on her glass with a spoon. "Thank you all for accepting our last-minute invitation. This has been a trying time for us and it is good to be surrounded by friends."

Murmurs of gratitude passed around the table. Gracelynn had the guests introduce themselves, then addressed them all once more.

"I must admit I have an ulterior motive for gathering you here." A faint smile touched her lips. "To that end, I'd like to pass the floor to our good friend, Elladan."

Prior to dinner, the companions had agreed that Elladan should do the talking. Now he rose and smiled, sweeping his eyes around the table. "Thank you all again for coming. At the Baroness' request, my friends and I are investigating the Baron's murder."

Fafnar raised an eyebrow at the statement, but neither Almax nor Qualtan appeared very surprised.

Elladan swept his gaze between the pair. "One of the chief questions is the motive behind Gryswold's demise. That is where you two come in. We were hoping you could share with us some of his exploits prior to becoming the Baron, in hopes of finding some clue."

Almax merely pursed his lips, but Qualtan seemed quite eager to help. "Why, yes. Yes, of course. We'd be more than happy to discuss the adventures of our former little band."

Qualtan did most of the storytelling, though Almax interjected his thoughts from time to time. Most everyone else listened, but occasionally someone would stop them to ask a question or clarify a point.

Gryswold and his friends had started out in Lanfor about twenty-five years ago. They quested there for nearly five years, until the great pirate raid on Penwick. The group followed Gryswold to his home city to help expel the invaders. After the pirates were driven out, they met Gracelynn—a modest Dunwynn cleric on a relief mission to the city. Gryswold and Gracelynn immediately hit it off, and she chose to join the band when they left.

The group traveled around south central Thac for the next two years, until Gryswold finally proposed to Gracelynn. On their way to announce it to her family, the druids of Bendenwood advised them of disturbing reports coming out of Ravenford. Since it was Almax's old home and the druids seemed reluctant to get involved, the group agreed to detour there before heading to Dunwynn.

The closer they drew to the Ravenford, the more dire the news became. They soon discovered that the town had fallen to the same black dragon they had been hearing about for a few months now—one that had previously terrorized two towns in central Thac.

"When we first arrived, Ravenford had been under siege for nearly three weeks. At that point, almost half the population had been decimated, but the dragon kept the rest alive. They were holed up around town, the majority in the basement of the temple."

Qualtan paused to sip his drink. The man seemed to thrive on being the center of attention. He had already talked all the way through the first and second courses of the meal.

"The dragon was enacting a bizarre ritual. It tormented the survivors from the darkness, telling them how many would die that night. Any who tried to escape, it would hunt down, and hang their corpses on the large oak tree in the town square."

Qualtan shuddered, the horror of that visage mirrored in his eyes. As the abbot took a rare breath, Almax interjected a few words.

"Grys wanted to charge right in, but Grace and Maltar thought it best we get the lay of the land first. I sent out a few animals to scout things out, but the story they returned with shocked us all."

Qualtan cleared his throat. "It seems the dragon already knew we were there, but it wanted its story told. It was on a vendetta against the Knights of the Rose."

Almax lifted an eyebrow at the abbot. "Yes, Qualtan, I was getting to that."

Qualtan lifted two pudgy hands in front of him. "Oh, my apologies, Almax. This is your part of the story—I guess it's best if you tell it."

The druid eyed the abbot sharply, then huffed and continued. "As I was saying, this was not the first village Ullarak had destroyed. He and his mate had nearly wiped out the town of Blackwood in southern Thac. Thankfully, Sir Nigel and the Knights of the Rose had arrived in time to save a few survivors. They also managed to kill the dragon's mate..."

"...which is what started its vendetta," Qualtan finished for him.

Almax leveled a hard stare at the abbot.

Qualtan held up his hands once more. "Oops... sorry."

Almax took a deep breath. "Yes, well, the dragon decided to enact its revenge by decimating town after town before Sir Nigel could stop it..."

"...which is how it ended up on the east coast," Qualtan interjected.

Almax glared at the abbot. "You just can't help yourself, can you?"

Qualtan shrugged, a feeble smile crossing his lips.

Almax shook his head in disgust. "Oh, very well. Go ahead and tell the rest of it."

"Are you sure?" Qualtan asked, clearly itching to continue the story.

Almax refused to respond, instead sitting back in his chair and waving a hand at the abbot to go on.

Elladan watched the pair closely. There was a fair amount of friction between the two. He wondered if it was strictly a difference in personality, or if there was a deep-seated reason for the tension between them.

Qualtan cleared his throat again. "Yes, well, the dragon planned on taking its time, slowly killing the populace and decorating that grisly tree with their remains. Once done, it planned to fly off to the next town and continue its macabre practice, leaving behind that horrific sight as a message to Sir Nigel and company."

"So, how'd you slay the ugly brute?" Kalyn sat at the edge of her seat, her eyes wide.

The abbot pressed his lips together, the corners of his mouth upturning slightly. "Why, Gracelynn came up with a plan." He gave the Baroness a deferential nod. "She was the real brains behind the outfit."

Gracelynn's cheeks reddened slightly. "Why Qualtan, you give me too much credit."

"And you, dear lady, are far too modest," Qualtan responded with a thick smile. His eyes lingered on her for a few moments before he caught himself and swept them around the table. "But perhaps Maltar added a point or two."

Almax cleared his throat rather loudly.

Qualtan shifted his gaze back to the druid. "Oh, and Almax, too, of course."

"It was a joint effort," Gracelynn stressed with a nod to both men.

Almax tilted his head toward her. "Thank you, Grace."

Qualtan let out a short breath, then rubbed his hands together. "Well then, it took a bit of preparation on all our parts, but before the sun set that day and another soul was lost, we put our plan into action. It all started with making the dragon think we were rescuing the folks from the temple."

Qualtan swept his gaze around the table as he spoke. All eyes were riveted on the abbot. "Gracelynn used a spell to cut a hole in the back of the temple. Then Gryswold slipped inside and ushered the folks out toward the town wall."

Qualtan's voice rose in pitch.

"As anticipated, Ullarak had been watching. It launched itself out of the river, straight at the escaping folks, only to slam into an invisible wall of force that Maltar had placed in front of the temple."

"Whoa," Kalyn exclaimed, her eyes alight.

Qualtan grinned. "Whoa, indeed. The dragon slid off the wall, right into a puddle of mud our friend Almax here had prepared earlier. The instant it splashed down, the good druid turned that mud to stone, temporarily trapping the creature."

"That probably didn't hold very long," Glo pointed out.

Qualtan waved a finger at the wizard. "It didn't need to. With the trap sprung, the rest of us piled on the creature. Gryswold, suddenly twice his size, waded in with his sword ablaze. Flandril, completely invisible, followed him, firing off red-hot rays."

"It made Grys look like a god of fire," Almax noted with a wry smile.

Qualtan cast a sour look at the druid. "Yes… anyway, that's where Almax and I came in. Our creative friend had been coaxing the oak tree in the town square to life all afternoon. It turns out the tree didn't like being decked out with carrion. The oak charged across the bridge at the dragon, newly decorated with a slew of lantern archons, courtesy of yours truly."

The abbot finished with his hand on his chest.

"It was an impressive sight," Gracelynn agreed with a dip of her chin. "The tree was bathed in an eerie glow that leapt off its branches at the dragon as it closed the gap. It looked like the spirit of the town come to wreak its vengeance."

"All I can say is, don't mess with a druid!" Kalyn gasped.

"You can say that again," Lloyd agreed.

Fafnar, quiet up till now, finally spoke up. "These theatrics are all well and fine, but wouldn't a contingent of knights have been better served in this instance?"

Elladan exchanged a half-smile with Glo and Donnie. *Leave it to Fafnar to totally misread the situation.*

"Perhaps, young man," Almax responded. "However, the Knights of the Rose and a contingent from Bendenwood were still days away at that point."

Fafnar cocked his head to one side. "Ah, I see. So, you had no choice but to resort to parlor tricks." He pursed his thin lips together. "Considering you were fighting a dragon, that's actually quite admirable."

Did Fafnar just compliment someone? Elladan traded glances with Lloyd. Perhaps the young man was right about the Dunwynn fop.

"Please don't let the Dunny stop you there," Kalyn urged them from the edge of her seat.

Fafnar narrowed an eye the young woman, but otherwise chose not to respond.

"Yes, Uncle Qualtan, what happened next?" Andrella fixed the chubby abbot with a winsome smile.

Qualtan blushed at the young lady and went on. "Well, the dragon broke out of its stone prison, but not before the tree reached it. Long branches wrapped around the monster, pinning it in place once more. At the same time, Gryswold and Flandril continued to assault its flanks."

Almax chuckled. "Ullarak was totally flustered at that point. A god of fire on one side, and a spirit of vengeance on the other. He roared in fear and sprayed the oak with its acid breath."

"I'm just glad it chose the tree instead of Gryswold," Gracelynn added somberly.

Qualtan turned to gaze at her. "But isn't that why you were following him around? To heal him in case he needed it? Granted, you were invisible and all, but I assumed you were right there."

Gracelynn wrinkled her nose at him. "Trust me, I was close enough to smell the foul stench of that acid."

Almax narrowed an eye at Qualtan. "I still don't understand why it was Grace following him around when you could have done it just as easily."

Qualtan swung his gaze toward the druid and puffed up like a blowfish. "How many times must I tell you—I was busy summoning the archons!"

Almax's expression hardened. "Yes, you were."

Elladan peered from Qualtan to Almax. *Ah, so that's the source of contention between those two. Gracelynn had been put in the line of fire while Qualtan spent his time 'decorating' the tree with lantern archons.*

"It matters not," Gracelynn interjected firmly. "It was my choice to follow Gryswold, and the tree was effective in distracting the dragon."

"So, I assume the tree was destroyed," Donnie asked.

Almax turned an eye to the sandy-haired elf. "It was."

Qualtan took a quick sip of wine before continuing. "Free of the tree, Ullarak unfolded his wings to take to the skies, yet pulled up short when he saw what waited there for him. The visage of Sir Nigel swooped down out of the clouds, astride a silver dragon with a loud battle cry."

"Maltar's work, I assume," Glo interjected.

"Indeed," Almax replied with a half curl of his lips.

Qualtan rubbed his hands together gleefully. "The vision spooked the dragon so badly that he fled in the direction we wanted—straight back toward the river. He only made it halfway into the water when Maltar sprung the final trap—a sphere of ice that froze the dragon solidly in place."

"Very nice," Glo said with a nod to Almax, Gracelynn and Qualtan.

The abbot practically beamed with delight. "Yes, it was a splendid plan"—his face abruptly fell—"until Gryswold charged in and stuck that huge flaming sword right between the dragon's shoulder blades."

"Whoa…" Kalyn gushed. "That sounds so cool."

"It sure does," Lloyd agreed with a wistful sigh.

"Yes, yes, it was heroic and all." Qualtan waved his hands around in the air. "In fact, somehow that little stunt earned Gryswold all the credit for taking down the dragon." He cast a sidelong glance at Gracelynn. "Guess it pays to have a consummate diplomat as your bride-to-be."

Gracelynn's face flushed. "Why, Qualtan, just what are you accusing me of?"

A sly smile crossed the abbot's lips. "Why, nothing, Gracelynn, my dear." He waved a nonchalant hand. "That's old news now—water under the bridge."

Gracelynn merely smiled at him, but Elladan was again taken aback by the underlying resentment between these folks.

Qualtan let out a deep sigh, then rose from his seat. "Well, thank you for dinner, Gracelynn, but I have quite a lot of things to attend to—not the least of which is keeping after your husband's body."

Gracelynn dipped her chin. "You're quite welcome."

Elladan rose and extended his hand to the Abbot. "Thank you for all those stories. They were quite… enlightening."

Qualtan eyed him for a moment, then took Elladan's hand. "Yes, well I'm glad I could help." The abbot lowered his voice as they shook. "In fact, I think I might be able to help you a bit more if you wouldn't mind seeing me out?"

"Certainly," Elladan responded, curious as to what more the abbot had to tell him. He escorted the clergyman out the doorway, leaving the rest of the guests behind.

Donatello was amazed at the exploits of Gryswold and his band. He himself had not led a quiet life, but some of these stories rivaled his own.

Seated next to Almax, Donnie found himself exchanging side comments with the druid during most of the storytelling. He was pleasantly surprised to find they shared a similarly ironic sense of humor.

Donnie also noted the underlying tension between Almax and Qualtan, though it was surprising to see some of it directed at Gracelynn.

Elladan had just left with Qualtan when Almax pushed his chair back. "I'm afraid I must be going as well."

The druid nodded to Gracelynn. "Thank you, Grace. It was a wonderful meal."

Gracelynn rose and bade him to embrace her. "Come, Almax. We are too old of friends for you to start treating me like royalty now."

The tall druid's face reddened as Gracelynn pulled him into a warm embrace. When she let go, Almax coughed into his hand to hide his obvious embarrassment.

On a hunch, Donnie rose as well and stood next to the druid. "Perhaps I should walk you out, too?"

Almax cocked his head to once side. "That would be most welcome."

The pair left the rest of them behind to finish what was left of the meal.

Lloyd had been riveted by the account of the fight with the black dragon. He had always suspected Gryswold was a formidable warrior, but this story confirmed his suspicions.

With Qualtan and Almax now gone, Lloyd's thoughts turned to tomorrow's plans. The young man swung around to face Sir Fafnar and broached the subject.

"I think you should know, we recommended that Lady Gracelynn take you up on your offer."

Fafnar's eyebrows arched up his scalp as he stared back at him. "Really? Thank you. You are showing remarkable good sense."

Lloyd let out a closemouthed laugh. "Yes, well, there's just one catch."

Fafnar knit his brow and folded his arms in front of him. "I guess I should have known. What is it?"

Lloyd held up his hands in front of him. "Nothing bad—a worthy quest, in fact. We leave tomorrow to seek out the Wizard Maltar, and were wondering of you would join us? As you heard tonight, he and Gryswold spent a lot of time together. Also, Maltar was attacked in his home a couple of weeks ago."

Fafnar's visage softened, a hand going to his chin. "You don't say? While that is suspicious, I would loath to leave the ladies Gracelynn and Andrella alone for any great length of time."

"We won't be gone that long," Glo interjected.

Fafnar stiffened as he shifted his gaze toward the elf, but caught himself once again and visibly relaxed. "And just how can you guarantee that?"

A slight smile formed on Glo's lips. "We found a teleportation circle in the basement of the keep's tower. We believe Maltar used it to travel to Tarsmoor."

Fafnar responded with a slow nod. "Tarsmoor, you say? That would be a journey even by hippogriff. Still, if one could teleport there and back it might be worth it."

"Our thoughts exactly," Lloyd agreed.

Fafnar shifted his gaze toward Lloyd and attempted a smile. "Very well, then. If this is what the Lady Gracelynn wishes."

"It is," Gracelynn confirmed.

Fafnar dipped his chin toward her, then glanced at Lloyd. "Then count me in on this little venture of yours."

"Excellent," Lloyd said, putting out his hand.

Fafnar tilted his head sideways and regarded Lloyd for a moment. The Dunwynn noble then slowly extended his own hand and shook with the young man from Penwick.

The next morning found Lloyd, Glo, Elladan and Donnie headed back up to the keep, with Shalla in tow. On the way, Glo ruminated about last night's dinner party. "It didn't exactly yield much in the way of potential enemies seeking vengeance on the Baron."

"Not unless the black dragon reincarnated into an assassin," Donnie quipped.

Elladan nudged the slight elf in the shoulder. "Only you would think of that."

Donnie smiled and shrugged. "What can I say? I have a creative mind."

"Still, it's interesting how much tension there was between Qualtan and Almax," Glo noted. "I can't believe they accused each other of 'dabbling in the dark arts.'"

On the way out from dinner, Qualtan had told Elladan about Almax's supposed dark designs. Strangely enough, Almax had told Donnie almost the same thing about Qualtan.

Elladan flashed Glo a partial smile. "I believe Qualtan's exact words were, 'Keep an eye on Almax. He may be experimenting with dark magic.'"

Donnie waved a finger at them. "It was Almax who said, 'Qualtan has been acting strange as of late. I hope he is not dabbling in the dark arts.'"

Glo eyed them both critically. "*Potayto, potahto.* Either way it's the same thing."

Lloyd half-listened to the morning banter, his mind in a state of turmoil. He didn't like leaving Andrella and Gracelynn any more than Fafnar did. Still, they had little choice. He had promised he would do all he could to resurrect the Baron. Even if he hadn't, he admired Gryswold and would have helped anyway.

His thoughts were interrupted by Shalla. "Why are you so pensive, Lloyd?"

Lloyd turned his gaze to the bardess, a slight smile creeping across his lips. "I'm fine—mostly worried about Andrella."

Shalla reached up and placed a hand on his shoulder. "I'm sure she's okay. Isn't that why Kalyn stayed with her overnight?"

Lloyd tilted his head and nodded. "True."

Still, he couldn't help worrying. He picked up his pace, hurrying the rest of the way to the keep. When they entered the courtyard, Andrella, Kalyn, and Sir Fafnar were all waiting for them.

Lloyd strode up to Andrella and swept her into his arms. The young lady's face flushed at first, but then she embraced him and kissed him soundly.

After a few moments, she pulled back, though she kept her arms around his neck. "Well, that was a very nice good morning."

"Ahem," Fafnar cleared his throat.

Lloyd glanced toward the Dunwynn noble.

Fafnar wore a mixed expression, partly wistful and partly embarrassed. "Now that we're done with the morning 'greetings,' perhaps we should be going?"

"Only if these two are done playing 'tongue jousting,'" Kalyn snickered.

"Kalyn!" Andrella smacked her in the arm.

"She's not wrong," Shalla noted with a wry smile.

Andrella shook her head. "Not you, too? Whatever happened to camaraderie among women?"

Kalyn and Shalla began to laugh, Andrella quickly joining in.

A short while later, the companions were once again in the tower basement. Nothing had changed since the previous day. The teleportation circle appeared ready to go.

Fafnar held a hand to his chin as he appraised the crisscrossed rings. "A curious use of magic. I suppose it's safe and all?"

"Only one way to find out," Donnie teased, ushering the noble forward.

"No, after you," Fafnar responded, the hint of a smile on his lips as he ushered Donnie in kind.

Lloyd exchanged a curious glance with Andrella. *Is Fafnar actually joking with an elf?*

"We're all going together," Glo said in a matter-of-fact tone.

"Um, about that…" Andrella interrupted.

Lloyd narrowed his eyes at the young woman. "I thought we agreed you needed to stay here and watch over your mother?"

Andrella placed her hands on her hips, her tone betraying her sudden annoyance. "We did, and I am. What I was going to say is that Kalyn has agreed to stay with me as well."

All eyes turned to the young archer. Kalyn's expression was mixed, both excited and disappointed at the same time.

"As long as you don't try to dress me up again," she warned the young lady.

Andrella placed a finger on her chin, a wicked grin spreading across her lips as she appraised Kalyn's figure. "Well, I don't know. I'm not sure I can promise that."

"Save me!" Kalyn squealed in mock terror, grabbing Shalla by the arm and hiding behind her.

Lloyd found the entire thing humorous, but he also felt a keen sense of relief. "Actually, I think it's a good idea if Kalyn stays to watch over you."

"I agree," Glo nodded.

"As do I," Donnie chimed in.

Kalyn folded her arms and glared at them all. "Traitors!"

Donnie pretended to flinch. "Well then, I think it's time we take our leave."

Everyone said their goodbyes, then Glo, Donnie, Elladan, and Sir Fafnar stepped inside the crisscrossed rings. Lloyd waved one last time at Andrella as she pulled the switch on the pedestal, then the world abruptly faded around them.

6
QUIT MONKEYING AROUND

Kill them all! Especially the thin elf!

Glolindir had never actually teleported before. He had no doubt his father knew the spell, but being isolated to the hidden elven city of Cairthrellon, there was no need. Hence, he wasn't ready for the disoriented feeling of disappearing from one place and moments later reappearing nearly three hundred miles away.

"Whoa! Anyone else nearly lose their stomach?" Donnie held a hand over his abdomen.

Elladan rubbed his temples. "Stomach's fine, but my head's a bit woozy."

Glo felt neither, but his vision had blurred. He briefly rubbed his eyes, then glanced around. His eyesight had thankfully cleared, yet the tall elf had to do a double take.

Three crisscrossed blue rings surrounded them, identical to the ones they had just left behind. Beyond the rings stood a podium with a lever, a duplicate of the one back in Ravenford. For a moment, Glo thought they hadn't moved at all, but on a second glance the room had changed.

First, neither Andrella, Kalyn, nor Shalla stood at the podium. Second, a circular stairway descended along the wall behind the pedestal. Four lancet-shaped windows had appeared evenly spaced along the wall that weren't there moments ago. Directly above them, the ceiling still depicted a celestial sphere with sections of piping, but at a greater height than before.

The small group slowly exited the circle and fanned out around the room. Across from the stairs, a long ladder climbed up the wall, leading to what appeared to be a trap door in the ceiling.

Glo halted in front of one of the windows and peered outside. The blue waters of a wide sparkling river filled his view, its breadth split by three islands. The largest one was populated by two tall ornate buildings that were obviously temples. At the farthest end of that isle stood a huge grey keep, surrounded by thick walls and corner towers. Two smaller islands flanked the large one, a third temple inhabiting the most distant of the pair.

Several bridges spanned those isles, leading to a sprawling town with brown and grey tiled rooftops on the leftmost bank. The walls of a second keep were visible in the distance, on the edge of town farthest from the river.

The tall elf immediately recognized the place. "We're definitely in Tarsmoor."

The others crowded around him and peered over his shoulder.

"Indeed, it is," Elladan agreed. "I can see the *Faire Fields* from here." The dark-haired elf pointed to a wide grassy area filled with canvas tents and stands.

"No mistaking it," Donnie chimed in. "Not many towns are large enough to have three temples and two keeps."

"Hmm," Fafnar murmured. "Adequate for a town, I suppose, but not quite as grand as Dunwynn."

Lloyd let out an exasperated sigh. "Why must you do that?"

Fafnar arched an eyebrow at the young man. "Do what?"

Lloyd eyed the knight incredulously. "Compare everything to the 'grandeur' of Dunwynn?"

Fafnar's brow knit. "I do?"

"Yes," everyone replied in unison.

Recognition dawned in the Dunwynn lieutenant's eyes as he swept his gaze around the group. "Oh…"

Lloyd placed a hand on the noble's shoulder. "It's alright. I did the same thing when I first met the others. I couldn't help comparing everything to Penwick."

Fafnar gazed uneasily at the hand on his shoulder, but his expression lightened when he met Lloyd's eyes. A thin smile spread between Fafnar's mustache and goatee. "Well… if you were able to curb your city 'pride,' then I will endeavor to do the same."

Lloyd grinned back at the thin noble.

Glo exchanged an impressed glance with Elladan and Donnie. Lloyd's genuine nature was slowly melting even Fafnar's icy demeanor.

A noise on the steps behind them made everyone turn around. A large figure shambled slowly into view as it ascended the circular stairwell. Glo nearly retched at the sight.

The creature appeared humanoid, but stood at least two heads higher than any of them. It was garbed in a tight-fitted coat and pants that seemed two sizes too small for it, exposing a good portion of flesh. The creature's skin varied in color, separated by lines of thick stitching along the arms, legs, and neck.

"Is that what I think it is?" Elladan asked in a hushed voice.

Glo nearly gagged as he tried to respond. "Fl… flesh golem."

"Well that's *definitely* not the first thing I wanted to see on this trip," Donnie remarked with a faint smile.

Lloyd positioned himself in front of the others and drew his blades. Fafnar followed suit.

The golem shuffled to the top of the stairs and halted, then stood there staring at them mutely.

"Any idea what this *thing* wants?" Fafnar asked with a hint of anxiousness.

"No idea," Glo answered while mentally sifting through the spells he might use against the creature. He abruptly noticed two things he had not seen before—the golem had a bowtie around its neck and carried something large rolled up under its arm.

Without warning, the golem grasped the object and slowly stooped down, unfurling it on the ground between them. It unraveled across the short distance, stopping about two feet in front of Lloyd.

Glo's eyes went wide as he realized what it was.

Elladan let out a nervous laugh. "Don't look now, but I think that thing just rolled out the red carpet for us."

Donnie jabbed him in the side with an elbow. "Maybe it recognizes a celebrity when it sees it?"

Elladan responded with a withering stare.

The golem slowly stood back up, then motioned for them to follow as it began to descend the stairs.

The five of them exchanged glances.

Fafnar shrugged. "It seems to be showing remarkable good sense."

Lloyd responded with a slow nod. "Maybe, but let's be on our guard anyway."

"Agreed," Fafnar said as the two of them sheathed their swords.

The duo led the way down the stairs after their strange host.

The golem led them down a level to an open doorway. Through it, Glo spied rows upon rows of shelves lined with books of all sizes and colors. Their large host led the way in, the rest of them keeping a respectable distance.

Glo spun around, his mouth agape as his gaze fell on bookshelves in all directions. Based on the number of shelves and their size, he estimated the room to contain somewhere between twenty to twenty-five thousand books. *This is easily as large as my father's library back home.*

A jab in his side caused him to return his gaze to their strange host. The golem had stopped in the middle of the room, next to a perch with a monkey on it. The little simian wore a small deep blue fitted robe.

As they stopped and stared, the monkey spoke. "I am the great Gaither. What brings you unbidden to my humble abode?"

Glo arched a single eyebrow. Gaither was a powerful wizard

during the time of the mad Emperor Naradon. The tall elf pushed his way in front of the others. "Gaither? The wizard Gaither?"

The monkey looked over either shoulder, then twisted his lips to one side. "Do you see another one?"

Glo exchanged a glance with Elladan and Donnie. Both appeared as perplexed as he. He returned his gaze to the small primate. "How is that possible? Gaither vanished over seven hundred years ago, along with the Emperor Naradon."

The monkey turned to the golem and cackled. "You hear that, Mog? The elf dresses like a wizard, but can't figure out something as simple as reincarnation."

The golem remained silent.

Raven fluttered her wings on Glo's shoulder. *"Monkeui edan. Monkeui edan." Monkey man, monkey man.*

The monkey screeched with laughter. "Ha! The bird's smarter than the elf!"

The wizard glared at the little simian.

Elladan sidled up next to Glo. "Wait a minute. If I recall correctly, there's a tower on the northmost island of Tarsmoor that belonged to Gaither."

The monkey grinned at him. "Look at that, Mog. This elf actually has a brain."

As Elladan eyed the simian sharply, Donnie inched up on Glo's other side. "I thought that tower was sealed—that no one's been in or out since Gaither disappeared?"

The monkey threw up his hands and shrugged. "Okay, you got me. I'm not Gaither. I'm his familiar—but he left this tower to me!"

The three elves exchanged another glance.

Glo narrowed an eye at the little simian. "So, this whole time you've been holed up in here?"

The monkey swept his hand around him and bent his lips sideways. "What can I say? I've had a lot to read."

Fafnar huffed behind them. "Are we done talking to this idiotic *thing?* Don't we have more important matters to attend to?"

The monkey jeered at the noble. "Who are you calling an idiot? With all the knowledge I've amassed over the years, my brain is probably twice the size of yours."

Fafnar leveled a haughty stare at the small primate. "I highly doubt that."

The monkey folded his arms and glared at Fafnar.

Lloyd stepped between the pair and held up his hands in front of him. "Sorry if we offended you, Gaither. We just came here looking for someone. Maybe you know him? The wizard Maltar?"

The monkey turned his nose up in the air. "Maltar. That hack? Yes, he was here. Come and gone."

Glo eyed the monkey curiously. "What do you mean come and gone?"

The small simian glared at Fafnar, then turned its head away. "I'm obviously too stupid to answer you."

"Dunwynn diplomacy strikes again," Donnie muttered under his breath.

Fafnar fixed the elf with an unkind stare.

Meanwhile, Lloyd tried to mollify the monkey once more. "Please don't be like that. Would it help if Fafnar apologized to you?"

Fafnar folded his arms across his chest. "You're crazy if you think I'm going to apologize to that little hairy creature."

The nobleman turned his head away. Man and monkey stood there silently mirroring each other's pose. It would have been comical if the need to find Maltar wasn't so pressing.

"Do you want to help revive the Baron or not?" Lloyd urged the noble.

Fafnar glared at him, then let out an exasperated sigh. "Oh, very well." He shifted his gaze to the little simian. "I am quite sorry if I have leveled any offense in your direction. Now, can you please tell us where Maltar went?"

It appeared for a moment as if the monkey was going to capitulate, but then he drew itself up and said, "It's too late for that. You've worn out your welcome." He glanced at the large golem. "Mog, please escort this 'riffraff' out of our home."

The large creature nodded then lumbered forward toward the companions.

Lloyd stepped back and drew his blades. "Can't we talk about this?"

"The time for talk is over," the monkey insisted.

As the large golem reached for them, Lloyd's blades came alight with red flame. The tall warrior waded in under the golem's slow-moving arms and slashed it twice across the torso. They were shallow cuts causing minor damage, but the creature paused in its tracks and uttered a single word.

"Ow."

The monkey shrieked at the top of its lungs. "You hurt Mog! Tog, get in here!"

A door on the other side of the room swung open and a second flesh golem lumbered through it. This one was as big as Mog, but was wearing an ill-fitted cook's outfit.

"Kill them!" the monkey shrieked. "Kill them all!"

As Mog and Tog lumbered forward, the monkey leaped off his perch to the top of a nearby bookshelf. From there he leapt all the way up to a chandelier hanging above them.

Down below, Fafnar drew his weapons as he and Lloyd prepared to face the golems.

"Catch the monkey!" Elladan cried. "Then we can force him to call off his servants."

Easier said than done, Donnie thought to himself. He'd been in some strange predicaments before, but this might just be one of the weirdest.

Donnie swept his eyes across the ceiling and around the room. The chandelier was too high to reach from the ground, but it wasn't that far from the ceiling. It gave him an idea.

Donnie leaned close to Glo and whispered, "Keep the monkey distracted. I'm going to try something."

The wizard responded with a subtle nod.

Music filled the room as Lloyd and Fafnar engaged the golems in earnest. Elladan had conjured his lute and played an inspiring tune for his comrades.

Meanwhile, Glo had sent Raven to fly around the chandelier. The wizard then cast a spell and floated up to join them. As he approached, the little simian screamed.

"Get away from me! I'm warning you, I'll hit you with a fire ray." The monkey lifted his small hand and pointed a finger at the wizard.

Glo momentarily flinched, but nothing happened.

"Seriously, can't we just talk this over?" the wizard implored.

While Glo kept the monkey busy, Donnie rushed over to the opposite wall. He spoke the words that invoked his *Boots of the Spider*— "*Aranea Ascenditur*"—then began to climb upward.

As Donnie reached the ceiling and clambered across, he caught a glimpse of the battle below. Lloyd and Fafnar were locked in a fierce struggle with the two golems. Magic had little effect on those creatures, so neither the fire nor the ice the two warriors generated did any good. Yet Lloyd's black blade appeared to be doing damage.

Of course. It's made of star metal.

The material was so strong that it could cut through almost anything. Donnie hoped it would be enough to hold off the golems, at least until they could catch the monkey.

The thin elf was close to the chandelier now. Glo had the little simian completely turned in the opposite direction.

"I'm telling you, I'll fry you!" the monkey threatened again. The creature abruptly shifted its aim toward Raven. "Forget that. I'll fry your bird!"

Glo face darkened with anger. He leveled a finger back at the small primate. "If you're not careful, you're the one who's going to get fried."

The monkey responded by skittering around the chandelier. "Go ahead, take your best shot."

Donnie sighed inwardly. This was not going to be easy. A sudden idea came to him from his days on the pirate coast. The slim elf reached back and pulled off his cloak. He wound it around his arm, then waited until the monkey was nearest to him.

Snap!

The end of the cloak shot out and wrapped around the small simian's waist. Donnie gave it a swift yank, and the monkey flew backwards, right into his waiting arms.

Donnie spun the little primate around to face him. Its tiny body trembled with fear. Donnie felt a moment of remorse, then realized his friends' lives were at stake.

"Call off your servants!" he barked at the small creature.

"Stop!" the monkey wailed at the top of its lungs.

Directly below them, the two golems halted their attack. Lloyd appeared relatively fine, but Fafnar already had a couple of bruises.

Unfortunately, Donnie had taken his eye off his small captive. The monkey savagely twisted his body out of Donnie's grasp and fell to the floor below. The creature landed on all fours, then scampered toward the stairs with a loud cry, "Kill them all! Especially the thin elf!"

Donnie cursed himself as he leapt from the ceiling to the floor below. A puddle of grease suddenly appeared in front of the monkey, yet the agile creature slid through it, shooting out into the stairwell.

Elladan snapped his fingers. "Dragon dung! I thought I had him!"

As Donnie skirted around the puddle, Glo and Raven shot through the air past him. Donnie was right behind them as they hastened after their quarry.

The monkey careened down the stairs, screaming for help the entire time.

"I hope there aren't more of those golems," Donnie yelled to Glo.

"There are more," the little simian taunted over its shoulder. "A lot more!"

Donnie cast a quick glance at Glo. "If we don't stop him soon, we're all as good as dead."

The monkey reached the next landing and skittered through the doorway. The two elves passed through the threshold a few moments later. This was another circular room similar to the two above them, but this one was decorated like a dining area.

The monkey leapt onto the dinner table and skittered along its length, still screaming for help. Glo went around the one side, avoiding the chandeliers, while Donnie hurried down the other.

The nimble elf reached the end of the table just before the monkey, but the agile simian leapt right over his head. Donnie grasped for the creature nonetheless, but it was too late.

Yet before the monkey could reach the doorway, a black blur swept in front of him. Raven hovered before the little simian, blocking his path.

"I warned you not to get in my way!" the monkey jeered. He swiped a long limb at the black bird knocking it out of the air.

A scream erupted from behind Donnie, the slender elf flinching as a red-hot beam shot past him. It connected with the monkey, the small creature immediately erupting into flames. Hot fur flew in all directions. By the time he hit the ground, all that was left of the little monkey was a single paw.

Lloyd Stealle fought with everything he had against the large golem. The creature was slow and not very bright, but those big arms were extremely dangerous. A grazing blow from one of them had felt like being hit with a battering ram.

After that one shot, the young warrior employed a strategy that worked like a charm. He would feint to one side, and when the golem swung at him, would attack the other flank with his black blade. The weapon had now bitten numerous times into the creature's hide, and huge pieces were now missing from its patchwork body.

Unfortunately, Fafnar was not having as much luck. The knight had mimicked Lloyd's strategy, but his weapons could not hurt his opponent like Lloyd's black sword. His frustration made Fafnar careless, and the knight had paid severely for it. He was now battered and bruised, but to his credit, he fought on nonetheless.

It seemed like these things were taking forever to fall, when Lloyd's blade sliced clean through his opponent's torso. Split in two, the golem fell to the ground and went still.

Lloyd felt elated, but a chill went up his spine as he heard a loud *crack!* He spun around to see Fafnar laid out on the ground, his eyes unfocused and his weapons scattered.

A puddle of grease abruptly appeared between the golem and Fafnar, but the creature shambled through it as if it weren't there.

"Do something, Lloyd, or he's a goner!" Elladan cried.

As the hulking golem lumbered over the downed knight, Lloyd reached down deep inside. The world suddenly slowed around him, and in the blink of an eye the young warrior reappeared in front of Fafnar.

The golem unloaded a huge fist down at Lloyd. The young warrior held up his sword and silently prayed it could take the blow. The golem connected with the blade, sending Lloyd flying across the room.

Lloyd hit the ground with a solid *thud*, yet forced himself immediately back up. A grim smile crossed his face when he saw the black blade in his hand was still in one piece.

With a loud cry of "Penwick!" the young warrior charged the golem and ducked under its massive arms. He sliced through its torso, but kept going past the creature.

Lloyd halted a few yards away, then spun around and charged again. He kept up the crazed barrage, though his arms and legs were growing weary.

The sound of music suddenly flooded the air, renewed vigor pumping through his limbs. Lloyd gave a brief nod to Elladan.

"Thanks!"

Abruptly, Fafnar rose from the ground and retrieved his weapons. Wincing with pain, he called out to Lloyd, "Let's do this together."

With a nod, the two of them rushed the golem in tandem.

Fafnar drew off the golem's attacks, somehow managing to avoid them, while Lloyd drew in close and gutted the creature. In less than a minute, it was all over. Like its brethren, the golem lay twain in two on the ground in front of them.

Huffing with exhaustion, Fafnar limped his way over to Lloyd. The battered Dunwynn knight stood up as straight as he could and held out a hand to the Penwick warrior. "I owe you my life. I only hope that someday I can repay the favor."

Lloyd was stunned by the declaration. He paused a moment, then sheathed his sword and took Fafnar's hand. "It's what comrades do for each other."

Fafnar raised an eyebrow. "Comrades? A Dunwynn knight and a man of Penwick? Who would have thought?"

Elladan couldn't believe his eyes or his ears. Lloyd had saved the once haughty Sir Fafnar, and the Dunwynn noble had actually been appreciative. He'd even gone as far as to shake Lloyd's hand.

Elladan still wasn't ready to buy Fafnar's apparent change. He had seen too much in his life to so readily accept this about-face in character. Yet the man was handy with a weapon, as Lloyd had attested.

The bard shrugged and joined the pair. "If the two of you can sit down, I can perform some minor healing on you both."

Lloyd gazed at him curiously.

Elladan held up his hands. "Don't get me wrong, I'm no Aksel. I can patch you up a bit, but you both took some serious shots there. Fafnar in particular could use a real healer."

"I won't argue that point." The Dunwynn knight sat on the ground with a deep sigh.

Lloyd seated himself next to him.

Elladan peered closely at the Dunwynn noble. Maybe he has changed a bit, but I'm still not turning my back on him.

The elven bard called down some minor healing light on the duo. He had just finished when a familiar voice rang out behind them.

"Looks like you have things well in hand!"

Elladan spun around to see Donnie and Glo stride through the open doorway. "What about the monkey?"

Donnie held up a fur-covered claw and grinned. "Thanks to Glo, this is all that's left."

Elladan narrowed an eye at the wizard. "Isn't that a bit of overkill?"

Glo reached up and petted the black bird perched on his shoulder. "That's what it gets for attacking Raven."

"Plus, it was calling out for more golems," Donnie added.

A cold shiver went up Elladan's spine. "There are more of those things in here?"

Glo shook his head. "I really don't want to find out."

"Anyway, I think I'll keep this thing for good luck." Donnie unstrung a pouch at this hip.

"That's a rabbit's foot, not a monkey's claw," Elladan chided him.

"Potato-potahto," Donnie responded as he placed the paw in his pouch and drew the strings closed.

Elladan shrugged, then shifted his gaze to Glo. "If there are more of those golems skulking around, maybe we should just head back the way we came."

A faint smile crept across Glo's lips. "I don't think that's going to be possible. We probably won't be able to use the teleportation circle for a while."

Elladan knew that as well, but he really didn't want to face more golems, especially with Lloyd and Fafnar still in need of healing. "It wouldn't hurt to check."

"You all go ahead," Donnie agreed. "I'll take a quiet look down below and see how many more of those things there are."

Elladan placed a hand on the slender elf's shoulder. "Sure you want to do that with that monkey's claw on you?"

Donnie flashed him a sparkling smile. "I'll take my chances."

Elladan half-smiled back at his friend. "Your funeral."

As usual, Glo ended up being correct. They had only been in Tarsmoor less than an hour, and the mana level on the bar had barely risen. "We probably can't use the circle again until the day after tomorrow."

Lloyd appeared apprehensive. "So we're stuck in Tarsmoor?"

Elladan placed a sympathetic hand on the young man's shoulder. It was obvious he hated the thought of being separated from Andrella. "It's our best bet unless you want to rent horses…

"…which would be almost a week's journey over the mountains this time of year," Glo finished.

Lloyd let out a huge sigh. "Okay, I guess we'll wait."

"Cheer up. My men will watch over the ladies." Fafnar attempted to reassure him with a faint smile.

Elladan exchanged a glance with Glo. The tall elf's skeptical expression spoke volumes—even the normally optimistic Glo was wary of the Dunwynn noble.

Elladan let go of Lloyd and strode over to the window. The sky shone a brilliant blue, the town of Tarsmoor bustling under the near midday sun. "Right now, I'd settle for just getting out of this tower."

"Well, we aren't going out through the front door."

Elladan shifted his gaze toward the stairwell where Donnie had just reappeared.

"What did you find?" Glo asked pensively.

The slim elf shrugged. "The place is practically crawling with flesh golems." A wry smile formed on Donnie's lips. "There was even one in a maid's outfit."

Elladan shuddered at the thought.

"Well, we need to do something. These two need healing." The bard pointed a thumb at Lloyd and Fafnar.

Donnie swept his gaze over the pair, his eyes filled with concern. "Then let's see where that ladder goes."

The wiry elf briskly strode across the room and climbed up the ladder to the trap door above. There was a single bolt holding the door shut, which easily slid out of place. Donnie pushed the door upward and sunlight flooded through it. "Looks like it opens to the roof! I'll check it out."

The agile elf climbed through the hatchway and disappeared from sight. A minute or so passed when his head popped back through the hatch. "It's all clear. A short flight and we should be in Tarsmoor."

Feeling suddenly liberated, Elladan clasped his comrades on the shoulders and grinned. "Well then, all aboard for the Lloyd and Glo-lindir express."

7
SOMETHING ROTTEN IN VERMOORDEN

I told you not to go around bad mouthing them.
Now they're out to get us

Aksel Alabaster stood in front of a rather large wooden structure seated on a grey stone foundation. A decorative sign stretched across the front, covered with scripted multicolored lettering that read *The Theater of the Festive Spirits*.

It was midafternoon in Vermoorden, and the streets were filled with folks hurrying about their business. Down the road to the west, the golden rays of the sun sparkled across the calm shores of Lake Strikken. Fishing boats dotted the waters, their nets drawn in as they headed back to port for the day.

Aksel, Seth, and Martan had arrived in town a short while ago. The trio set up camp in a vacant farmhouse north of town that Aksel had spied on his last trip here. All three then went their separate ways to gather information.

It was Aksel's task to question Balmaroh. He assumed he would find him at the town theater rehearsing for his next performance.

The little cleric glanced around before entering the theater. Aksel thought himself a fairly good judge of character. Despite the evidence, he couldn't imagine Balmaroh being involved in the Baron's murder. Still, if he wasn't, someone had gone to a lot of trouble to implicate him.

If the Assassin's Guild were trying to frame him, Aksel assumed they would be watching the bard. Yet no one around here seemed the least bit interested in the theater. Still, there were other ways to keep an eye on someone—magical ways.

Aksel shrugged and pushed his way into the building. Inside, a thin, light-haired man stood in the middle of the stage. He was dressed in fine attire—a puffy white silk shirt under a fancy gold vest, light brown pants, and knee-high brown leather boots.

As expected, Aksel had found Balmaroh. The bard was flanked on either side by his helpers, the illusionist Rhith and the wizard Newin. The companions had met all three when they stopped here on their journey to the Darkwoods Monolith.

Up on stage, Balmaroh strummed a loud chord on his lute, then nodded to his crew. "Now, Newin!"

The tall, thin, hawk-nosed woman brushed back a lock of her long brown hair, then cast a quick incantation. Green clouds of smoke billowed up from the bard's feet, swiftly engulfing him till he completely disappeared.

Violent coughs erupted from the area where Balmaroh had just vanished.

"Whoa!" The mousy-looking, grey-robed Rhith jumped backward, nearly losing his spectacles in the process. Newin, on the other hand, in an iridescent blue robe, scrambled her way onto the stage.

"Sorry, sorry," the wizard exclaimed as she tried to fan the greenish cloud out of the way.

Aksel leapt out of his seat and hurried down toward the stage. He had just reached the edge of the seats when Balmaroh staggered out of the smoke, still coughing.

"It's… it's okay… Newin. We'll get it… next time," he managed in between spasms.

Aksel hurried over till he stood just below the bard. "Are you alright?"

Balmaroh wiped his eyes, then shifted his gaze downward.

"Why, if it isn't Cleric Aksel!" His exclamation drew another round of coughing fits.

Aksel waved him to climb down. "Here, let me help you."

Newin grabbed the bard by the arm and helped him down off the stage. She and Aksel then ushered him to a seat.

Once there, Aksel ran his hands a few inches from the bard's body. His inner senses immediately detected irritation in the man's throat and chest. Aksel stilled his hands over those areas, and with a quick prayer, called forth the healing light of his goddess.

White light emanated from his palms, swiftly engulfing the bard. Balmaroh's breath eased almost immediately, a wry smile creeping across his lips. "Good thing... you were here."

"Don't talk 'til I'm finished," Aksel admonished him.

Balmaroh arched his eyebrows, then pressed his lips together and reached up, drawing his fingers across them as if closing a zipper.

A faint smile touched Aksel's lips as he continued pouring healing light into his patient. The man had an irrepressible sense of humor. He reminded Aksel of a cross between Elladan and Donnie.

Aksel poured white light into Balmaroh until he could no longer detect any sign of irritation. The little cleric then drew back the light, finishing with a prayer of thanks to his goddess. He nodded to the bard. "Now you can talk."

Balmaroh cleared his throat, then smiled brightly at Aksel. "Whew, that's much better. As I said before, good thing you were here—why are you here, by the way?"

Aksel turned to see that Rhith had joined them. The illusionist stared at him suspiciously over the top of his spectacles.

As Aksel debated what to reply, Newin strode over and pushed Rhith hard in the shoulder. "Is that any way to treat someone who just healed our boss?" She folded her arms across her chest and eyed the mousy man darkly. "And just what were you doing this entire time?"

Rhith's face took on a look of terror. "I... I..." he stammered.

Newin pointed a finger at him, her voice harsh. "You ran from that cloud like a frightened school girl."

Balmaroh stood up and inserted himself between the pair. "Now, now, you two. It was an unexpected turn of events. I might have done the same as Rhith if our places had been switched."

Newin smiled briefly at the bard, then folder her arms and fixed her grey-robed partner with a hard stare. "Somehow I doubt that."

Balmaroh let out a deep sigh. "Well then, that is probably enough for the day. Let's adjourn to the house for some tea." He turned to Aksel. "Would you care to join us, my friend?"

Aksel tilted his head to the thoughtful man. "I would be delighted."

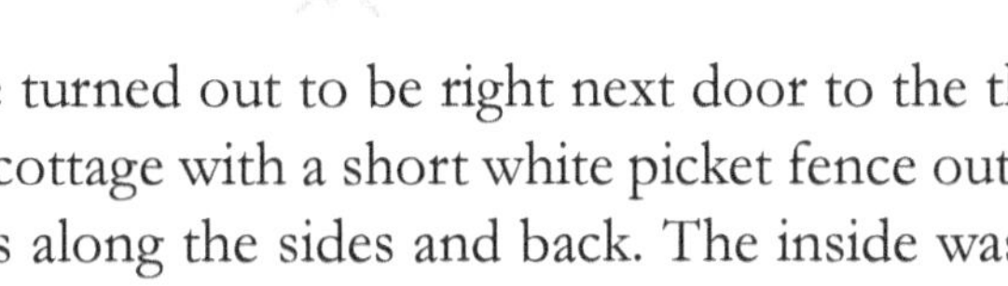

Balmaroh's place turned out to be right next door to the theater. It was a small stone cottage with a short white picket fence out front, and a row of hedges along the sides and back. The inside was quite comfy. Beyond the entrance was a narrow hallway, paralleling a set of stairs that led to the second floor. An archway opened to a good-sized living area decorated with a couch, a few chairs, a harpsicord, and an open hearth at the other end.

At the end of the hall was a good-sized kitchen, complete with a long counter, a table big enough for four, and a warm cooking hearth. A large black dog lay in front of the cooking fire. As Aksel entered, it raised its head and stared at him.

On closer inspection, Aksel noted splotches of yellow-brown around the big fellow's snout and underside. The little cleric immediately went over and held out his hand. The dog looked up and sniffed him a few times before a long tongue slipped out and licked his digits thoroughly.

Balmaroh knelt next to them and scratched the dog behind the ears. "It appears Wraith likes you."

"He's a fine-looking animal," Aksel responded, gently scratching Wraith under the chin.

"And you are a fine-looking gnome," the dog responded.

Aksel raised an eyebrow. He had heard of talking dogs before, but had never met one. He executed a low bow. "Thank you. You are very kind."

"Wraith is a special dog," Newin advised them from the kitchen table, a touch of pride in her voice. "Not only can he talk, but he can 'blink' as well."

A blink dog? Now that is special.

Blink dogs could teleport short distances quickly and at will. They were also highly intelligent and quite rare.

Balmaroh had gotten up and was pouring cups from a steaming teapot. "We found him on a trip to Lymerdia a few years ago. He wasn't being treated very kindly by his master, and we sort of 'liberated' him. I couldn't very well stand by and do nothing, but I still feel a twinge of guilt about it to this day."

"You shouldn't," Wraith responded. "The man was a brute."

Aksel shifted his gaze from the dog to the bard. Either Balmaroh was a consummate actor, or he was genuinely a good soul. Aksel felt he was the latter, but he had to be sure.

The bard presented him with a hot steaming cup, then went to fetch some cookies. Newin was busy feeding Wraith. Rhith, however, sat across from Aksel, watching him closely.

Yet Aksel had become an expert at covert casting these last few months. While sipping his tea with one hand, he motioned under the table with the other. As he finished, he mumbled two words into his cup. "*Deprehendere Malum.*"

The magic released so slowly that it was virtually undetectable. It gently flowed across the room touching upon the occupants of the house. A white fire suddenly appeared over each of their hearts. Balmaroh's shone the tallest and brightest, with Newin's a close second. Rhith's flame, though markedly duller than the others, still burned an off-white.

Aksel breathed a sigh of relief. None showed any signs of evil, yet his clandestine inspection had not gone completely unnoticed.

Wraith raised his head from his bowl and eyed Aksel curiously.

Aksel noted a white flame emanating from the dog's heart as well. He smiled at the dog and said, "Good boy."

Wraith tilted his head sideways, then responded, "Good gnome." The dog then went back to eating.

Balmaroh returned with a plate of cookies, then he and Newin sat down and joined them for tea. "So, to what do we owe the pleasure of this visit?"

Aksel let out a deep breath. There was no point in mincing words. He reached into his pouch and pulled out the silver button and gold lute string they had found in the Baron's room. "Have you ever seen these before?"

Balmaroh's eyes went wide. "Why that's the missing button from my dress vest… and that looks like a string from my lute. Where ever did you find them?"

Aksel launched into a brief explanation of the Baron's murder and their subsequent search of the room. Balmaroh and Newin listened with growing horror, yet Rhith folded his arms and stared darkly at the little gnome.

When Aksel finished, Newin was the first to speak. "That's absolutely dreadful. I can't imagine what the Baroness and the Lady Andrella are going through."

Balmaroh gazed at Aksel, his expression haggard. "I hope you don't think I had anything to do with this."

"That's exactly what he thinks," Rhith said in an accusing tone. "Why else would he be showing these to us?"

Aksel let out a deep sigh and folded his hands before him. "We didn't think you were involved, but we had to be sure."

Balmaroh stared at him with haunted eyes. "And now?"

"Now I know you all have good hearts," Aksel admitted.

Wraith came padding over to the table and looked up at Aksel. "So that's what that spell was. It was so expertly done, I almost didn't notice it."

Rhith eyed him sharply. "You cast a spell on us?"

Aksel bowed his head and nodded. "Just to see if any of you had any trace of evil."

Rhith made a disapproving sound. "Hmph. I say we kick him out now."

Newin eyed Aksel uncertainly, but Balmaroh held up his hand. "Wait. Let's not jump to any hasty conclusions." He peered intently at Aksel. "Now that you know we are not evil, what is it you want?"

Aksel kept his eyes locked on Balmaroh's. "Since you couldn't have been involved, the next most likely suspect is the Assassin's Guild."

"I knew it!" Rhith practically squealed. He shifted his eyes to Balmaroh, his tone suddenly filled of fear. "I told you not to go around bad-mouthing them. Now they're out to get us."

Newin placed a hand on the mousy man's arm. "Calm down, Rhith."

"Yes, calm down," Balmaroh agreed. He turned his attention back to Aksel. "What Rhith is referring to is my attempt to straighten things out in this town. There've been too many robberies and stabbings as of late, but no one ever seems to get caught. I tried to bring it up with the Mayor, but she is too 'busy' to see anyone right now."

"We were starting to wonder if she and the magistrate were being paid off by the guild," Newin added.

Aksel let out a deep breath. "That is very disconcerting news. If the mayor and the magistrate are somehow involved in this, then the guild has a farther reach than any of us suspected."

Balmaroh banged his hand on the table. "I am sick of all this. It's getting so a man can't make an honest living in this town."

He swept his gaze around the table. Newin responded with a nod. Rhith still appeared frightened, but finally nodded as well.

Balmaroh glanced back at Aksel. "You lot made short work of those lake monsters last time you were here. If you plan on taking on the Assassin's guild, you can count us in."

Aksel tilted his head in response. "That's good to know, but for now I think it best to keep it quiet. We'll let you know if and when we need your assistance."

Balmaroh let out a long breath, then flashed a smile around the table. "Very good. Now let's finish our tea before it gets cold."

Martan Folke sat quietly in a corner booth in the back of the common room at the House of Barmann. The dour archer had been saddled with the task of watching the seedy potion vendor, Philmar. The vendor had attempted to cheat Aksel and Ruka on their last visit to town. Thus, Aksel felt the man might have some connection to the underside of Vermoorden.

Martan had not been comfortable with the idea of playing spy amidst a room full of people. He was far more at home in the woods amongst the animals and the trees, yet he had been pushed way out of his comfort zone since meeting the Heroes.

Martan let out a deep sigh as he placed his ale upon the table. He was just a simple man. His sword did not burst into flames, he could not dodge arrows, turn invisible, cast lightning bolts, or even heal his comrades. Thus, it was beyond him why the Heroes kept him around.

Worse, they continually dragged him into dangerous situations. They were a talented lot, but they were also quite reckless. Martan firmly believed that one day they would get him killed. In fact, they nearly had less than a week ago.

Martan shook his head. *Why again am I still here?* The answer immediately came to mind. *Kalyn.*

He had been reunited with the fiery young woman less than a week ago. As soon as he had seen her, old feelings began to stir.

Kalyn had been his only friend back in Deepwood. They might have been more, had fate not gotten in the way. Martan had been accused of murder, and ran for his life. True, Kalyn's brothers had coerced him into running, but either way, he had abandoned the young woman.

Martan had not realized just how much he hurt her until they recently reunited. He firmly resolved to make it up to her, refusing to run away again even if it killed him—and it nearly did.

The glum archer shrugged as he cast a covert eye across the room. The common area was long, with a bar at one end, a hearth along the side, a couple of booths back where Martan sat, and tables scattered in between.

Philmar sat alone at a table near the hearth, his hands holding the single tankard in front of him. He certainly was an unsavory-looking character. Long, straggly black hair hung limply around a hawk-like face covered with dark stubble. A patched and stained what-used-to-be-tan longcoat hung loosely off his thin shoulders.

The vendor appeared to be talking to his tankard, but every once in a while would glance up and peer around the room. Martan made certain to be looking the other way when that happened.

Philmar remained alone until another figure entered the tavern— a long-haired man with a thick black beard, garbed in a tricorne hat and a blue longcoat. Martan immediately recognized the figure as Captain Morled, the skipper of the *Rusty Nail*. Morled had sailed the Heroes up into the Darkwoods a little over a week ago. The voyage had taken a couple of days, thus Martan was certain Morled would recognize him.

Martan pulled his hood down further and slumped in his seat as Morled strode directly over to Philmar. He strained his ears as the seaman sat down and conversed softly with the vendor, but he could not catch what they were saying.

After a brief talk, the pair stood up. Philmar dropped a few coppers on the table and the duo exited together.

Martan waited till they were gone, then left as well. He caught sight of the duo headed up the road to Vermoorden Keep. Martan kept to the trees along the path as he followed them up the hill, but stopped at the last tree, a few dozen yards from the gate.

The pair were halted by the keep guards; a brief conversation ensued. Martan could not hear what they were saying, but his keen eyes were able to read the guard's lips.

Come with me—I'll let the Mayor know you're here.

The duo were then escorted into the keep.

Martan raised an eyebrow. He had met the Mayor the last time they were in town, and she had not struck him as the accommodating type. Thus, it was rather surprising that she would see the unseemly pair, especially on such short notice.

Unable to follow further, the archer slipped quietly back into the trees, curious as to what the others would make of this interesting development.

Seth swept his eyes around carefully as he entered the common room at Barmann's. An hour earlier, he had been poking around town when he ran into Captain Morled. The halfling let it be known he had a falling out with the Heroes and was looking for work. He also inferred that he didn't care what kind of work, as long as the pay was decent.

Morled had seen Seth in action and seemed impressed. He told him he knew a guy, and instructed Seth to wait an hour, then head over to Barmann's.

Seth's eyes now fell upon his contact—a small man with an eye patch sitting in a corner booth. He slowly made his way across the room and slid into the seat across from him.

Neither said anything for a few moments. Seth finally broke the silence with a hushed question. "You got any work for decent pay?"

The one-eyed man regarded him intently before replying, "The pay is very good—if the job gets done right."

Seth leaned forward, lowering his voice even further. "What's the job?"

The man briefly gazed around, then fixed Seth with his one good eye. "There's a certain bard in town with a big mouth. Says a bit too much for the liking of my associates. The job is to silence him."

So, the frame-up failed, and now they are going directly after Balmaroh. Seth was not surprised in the least. Coming from a background of thieves and cutthroats had a tendency to harden you.

"How much?" Seth responded without batting an eye.

"Ten thousand gold. Half now and half when the job gets done." The one-eyed man snickered. "Of course, if it gets botched, we'll want our five-thousand back."

The side of Seth's mouth upturned slightly. "I always do the job right."

"Let's hope your good fortune continues," the one-eyed man said as he pushed a pouch across the table.

Seth took the pouch and opened it, carefully eyeing the contents inside.

"Don't trust no one, do you?" the one-eyed man noted.

"Well, not you," Seth answered as he pulled the drawstrings closed.

"Good," the one-eyed man chuckled.

Seth slid out of the booth without responding and walked away.

8
TEMPLES OF STORM AND MAGIC

Arm all bandaged and twisted at a weird angle—holding onto it as if he expected it to fall off

Glolindir stood just outside the Temple of Magic in Tarsmoor. Though it did not have the natural flowing lines of elven architecture, it had a charm of its own. A row of white arched columns decorated the front of the flat white stone building, with a tall pinnacle rising in its center. Glass panes ran up the pinnacle, capped with a circular glass window containing two pairs of curved lines that crossed each other slightly off center.

The symbol of Enuii, the Ralnain God of Magic, Glo noted as he climbed up the beautifully carved stone steps toward the entrance of the building. The tall elf had come to this temple on the main isle in search of information regarding Maltar.

Elladan, in the meantime, had taken Lloyd and Fafnar to the Temple of Storms on the southernmost island. Though a God of Storms, Alaric also promoted healing, something the duo sorely needed. At the same time, Donnie had gone off on his own to find them lodging in the town proper.

The entryway to the Temple of Magic opened to a two-story foyer with a marble floor. A set of tall white columns ran along the room on the left and right, with doors leading off to either side. At the end of the line of columns were a set of ornate double doors leading into the main temple. These were blocked off by a marble desk occupied by an aged man in grey robes.

As Glo approached, the old man peered up and laid down his quill. "How may I be of service to you today?"

Glo smiled at the aged gentleman. "I am looking for my master, the Wizard Maltar. He traveled here to Tarsmoor a couple of weeks ago. It is imperative that I find him."

The old man cocked his head to one side. "Maltar, you say? As a matter of fact, he was here in this temple about a fortnight ago." The grey-robed man gently stroked his chin. "He was in pretty bad shape, if I remember correctly. Arm all bandaged and twisted at a weird angle—holding onto it as if he expected it to fall off."

Glo's eyes widened in horror. That did sound pretty bad. Yet it didn't seem like the approach an assassin would use. "Did he say what happened to him?"

The aged gentleman shook his head. "A closemouthed one, that Maltar. Though I did get the impression it was from some kind of magic encounter."

Glo snorted softly. *Dark magic, most likely.*

The old man leaned in close, his voice taking on a conspiratorial tone. "He was so badly hurt we took him straight to the headmistress."

Glo bent down and whispered back. "What did she think of all this?"

A toothy grin spread across the old man's mouth. "That's the funny thing, she never did say. She went into seclusion with him, and when he left a few days later, she went with him!"

Glo eyed the aged man skeptically. "And she never came back?"

The old man shook his head. "Nope."

Deep creases folded along Glo's brow. *Well things just keep getting stranger and stranger.*

"Do you have any idea where they went?"

"Again, nope," the old man responded. "The last they were seen was headed down the south road out of town."

Glo smiled at the aged gentleman. "Thank you for your time."

"No problem," the old man replied with a grin.

Glo's mind raced as he strode out of the temple. *The south road? Perhaps they were headed to Lymerdia?*

It was a huge city—a good place to hide if someone, or something, were looking for you. Still, that didn't mean they hadn't doubled back and used the teleportation circle in Gaither's tower. It would be a classic ploy of misdirection.

Glo had memorized the settings on the diagram above the circle before they left the tower. He'd have to check a map and see where it was set to, but somehow he doubted it was Lymerdia.

When Elladan dropped off Lloyd and Fafnar at the Temple of Storms, the clerics there insisted they would have them healed in no time. Yet Fafnar had seemed a bit dubious at first. Alaric was a god of nature, his doctrine aligned with the randomness of life, in direct contrast to the Dunwynn Lady of Law, Iustatia.

Lloyd once again came to the rescue. "In Penwick, we worship Arenor, the Hand of Light."

Fafnar responded with a curt nod. "A respectable god."

A smile touched Lloyd's lips. "We think so. Anyway, Arenor would never turn away a follower of Alaric that needed healing. I can't imagine that Iustatia would, either."

Fafnar's brow knit for a moment. "Probably not."

Lloyd placed a hand on Fafnar's shoulder. "Well then, why would she have a problem with Alaric healing you?"

Fafnar's eyebrows knit together, deep creases lining his forehead. After a few moments he shook his head. "I guess she wouldn't." He waved a hand at the surrounding clerics. "Very well, let's get on with it."

Elladan was quite impressed with the young man's handling of the situation. Lloyd had come a long way, due in no small part to Elladan's coaching.

Afterwards, the elven bard headed off to town for a whirlwind shopping spree. The dangers they had faced this day convinced him they needed better gear, and Tarsmoor was full of shops of all kinds.

A visit to Stonehead's Armory had netted him a full set of mithral chainmail for Lloyd. He had momentarily considered getting one for Fafnar, but was certain the Dunwynn noble would break out into a rash, given the elven-wrought mail. Elladan also procured a holy sword for Lloyd at the Weapon's Shop. A trip to the Curio Shop had resulted in the bargain purchase of a magical vest for Donnie that would make the wiry elf even harder to pin down. He had also talked the shop owner into throwing in a brand-new set of cookware.

All in all, Elladan was feeling better about things as he returned to the Temple of Storms a few hours later. The temple itself was beautiful, with ornate columns on the outside, handsomely carved stone steps that led up to two large highly wrought iron doors, and a wide foyer with a marble floor. The foyer was filled with statues dedicated to Alaric and his staunchest followers. In one corner, there was a statue of the great warrior cleric "Ceri Al Drakkar."

A cleric with a serene smile led Elladan to a waiting room. Donnie and Glo were already there lounging comfortably on a set of deep cushioned seats. A platter of fruit and decanter of wine was laid out on a nearby table.

Elladan gave the pair a bent smile. "Well, this certainly looks comfy."

The bard sat down to eat and drink as the trio exchanged notes. Glo explained what he had found out about Maltar. Donnie then relayed that he had procured them rooms at the best inn in town, the Slumbering Dragon. The sharp-eyed elf had then scoped out the taverns, but found not a hint of Maltar's presence. He did note that the news of the Baron's demise had reached Tarsmoor.

They were able to obtain a map of Thac from one of the attendants. Elladan swiftly traced down the settings on Gaither's teleportation circle to Lukescros.

"I knew it!" Glo declared. "Lymerdia was just a false trail."

"What about Lymerdia?" A familiar voice spoke behind them.

Elladan turned to see Lloyd and Fafnar enter the waiting room. The pair looked completely healed and refreshed.

Glo swiftly re-explained what he had heard at the Temple of Magic.

After listening to him, Lloyd nodded. "Lukescros has a lot of different sections. If Maltar wanted to hide there, it wouldn't be that difficult."

Fafnar dipped his chin as well. "I've been to Lukescros a few times myself, and I must concur."

Elladan swept his eyes around the seated group. "So that begs the question, where do we head next?"

Lloyd's face took on a wistful expression. "Much as I want to track down Maltar, I really don't like the idea of being away from Ravenford too long."

Elladan raised an eyebrow when Fafnar placed a hand on Lloyd's shoulder. "I must agree yet again. If I can get a message to my sky knights, one of them could head to Lukescros. It would be no more than a two-day trip by air. There is a Dunwynn embassy in Lukescros, where he could recruit help in finding this wayward wizard."

Lloyd's face brightened. "That sounds like an excellent plan!"

Fafnar smiled, then stood. "Very good. I shall find a cleric, then, to send a message."

Once the noble was gone, Donnie grabbed Lloyd by the arm. "What in the world have you been feeding him?"

Elladan chuckled. "He has been rather helpful of late." The bard furrowed his brow. "Maybe too much so."

"What did you say before—keep your friends close and your enemies closer?" Glo reminded him.

Elladan smiled at his fellow elf. "Now you're learning."

9
THE WRATH OF DEEPWOOD

Which pansy blue hippogriff manure shoveler is next?

Kalyn Rhan tromped through a mud puddle as she and Kailay Finespun walked from Ravenford keep toward the Golden Golem. The bubbly strawberry blonde squeaked when some of the mud splashed at her skirts. She shoved Kalyn in the shoulder playfully.

"You're such a tomboy!"

Kalyn giggled, then frowned. "What's a tomboy? Is it a good thing?"

Kailay looked at Kalyn, her brown eyes wide, then she threw her head back and laughed. A sweet smile graced her lips as she wrapped her arm through Kalyn's and pulled her close. "Kalyn, you're a hoot!"

"What's so funny?"

Kalyn turned to find Xelda Sheenarn approaching them. She had met Xelda earlier that day when Andrella took her on a tour of the town. It had been the first time she'd ever seen a half-elf.

Xelda's dark eyes gleamed with curiosity, a small smile cracking her diamond-shaped face. Kailay hooked her free arm into Xelda's, linking the three of them together.

"Kalyn doesn't know what a tomboy is," she whispered conspiratorially to Xelda.

Xelda pushed a long strand of black hair from her face, her eyebrow rising. "Are you serious?"

Kalyn shrugged. "I'm assumin' it has something to do with mud puddles and it being something that boys like. To me, boy or girl, everybody enjoys jumpin' in a mud puddle once in a while."

A bright smile lit up Xelda's face. "You aren't wrong." She glanced around. "Where's Andrella? I thought she was joining us tonight?"

"She had to change her dress and slather her face with paint." Kalyn rolled her eyes. "I don't know what was wrong with the dress she had on."

Xelda laughed while Kailay patted Kalyn's arm. "We'll explain the fancy dress rules to you later."

The trio walked arm-in-arm up to the inn. Rather than unlinking their arms, they walked through the door sideways. As soon as Kalyn stepped through, she felt a change in mood and atmosphere. The Dunwynn Sky Knights were all drinking together, clustered at a table in the center of the room. The regular patrons were silent as the knights laughed loudly, chugging their drinks down as if they hadn't a care in the world.

Kalyn spied Shalla standing behind the bar, her brows knit and a frown engraved on her face. The young archer's eyes flickered back to the knights as she picked up some of their conversation.

"...and he ordered that we shouldn't insult the elves serving Lady Gracelynn, and I was like 'Well, if calling them leaf-ears is out of the question, what about calling them senior citizens, since they live so long?'"

Kalyn snorted as the men all laughed, but she quickly regained her composure and looked at Kailay.

"Let's sit near the bar." Kailay suggested, her normally cheerful smile bare and thin.

The three girls quietly moved in Shalla's direction, doing their best to ignore the ruckus going on.

"…I don't know. I couldn't ever bear to touch one myself, much less think about kissing one. Like that one walking by there—I could stand for a little of that blondie, but that elf spawn makes my skin crawl. Don't see how anyone could make them, much less love them."

Kalyn clenched her fists as she watched Xelda's jaw tighten.

"Well, why don't ya ask that bard wench what it's like!" One of the men turned and staggered a few steps forward, catching himself on a chair, sloshing his drink across a patron. He mumbled a weak apology, then glanced at Shalla. "Hey! Bartender woman! What's it like to dance and sing with an elf all night long? Does he have any chest hair?"

His comrades laughed at the question. Shalla narrowed her eyes, her frown sharpening into a glare. "I don't know. Do you have any chest hair, boy?"

"Judging by that rabbit's foot hanging under his nose, I'd guess he don't have much." Kalyn turned and leaned against the bar, crossing her arms and eyeing the knights darkly. Kailay joined her on one side, propping her elbows on the bar, while Xelda stood on the other side, a drink in hand.

The man glared back at his comrades when they chuckled at Shalla and Kalyn's comebacks. "I wouldn't expect a bunch of backwater harlots like you to know the difference between a twig man and a real man. You'd all marry dogs if you could, and leave your spawn behind for the rest of us to feed, just like *that*." He pointed his drink at Xelda, sloshing the liquid across the floor. "If you ask me, the baron got what he bloody well deserved for treating the likes of you as equals."

Kalyn pushed up to her feet, dropping her hands to her sides. Several of the patrons stood to their feet as well, pushing their chairs out of the way. The other knights quickly followed their example.

Shalla walked around the bar and stood in front of the girls, feet spread and fists on her hips.

"You need to leave now."

Kalyn moved to Shalla's side, resting her hands on the back of the nearest chair while glaring at the man. "Dunnie go home—while you can still walk."

He cast his gaze around the room, peering at the stern-faced patrons. "Ya hear that, boys?" He turned to his men. "Looks like fine human company ain't appreciated around here. Maybe we ought to show these bloody elf-huggers a lesson."

"Oh, shut up, ya slobbering goblin licker." Kalyn picked up the chair and crossed the space between them quickly. As he turned and locked eyes with her, she brought it down on his head. There was a satisfying *crack*, and the chair splintered. The man weaved on his feet and went cross-eyed, then fell flat on his back.

The other knights stared at him for a moment before looking up in unison. They gaped in disbelief at Kalyn, who still held the back of the chair in her hands.

"Okay, which pansy-blue hippogriff manure shoveler is next?" she shouted.

All at once, the inn erupted into a flurry of action. The knights and Kalyn charged each other with angry shouts. The patrons charged the knights with curses.

"Fighting is stupid… you… idiots!" Xelda screamed just before she and Kailay started throwing whatever they could get their hands around. Mugs and bottles were sent sailing through the air. Shalla grabbed a leg of Kalyn's shattered chair and used it to thump anyone wearing powder-blue Dunwynn uniforms.

Kalyn tossed a man over her shoulder, flopping him onto a table that gave way under his bulk. She jammed the back of her chair into the throats of two oncoming Dunnies, then punched one beside her.

Someone grabbed her braid and pulled on it. Kalyn twisted sideways and wrapped herself around a tall soldier, grappling him and sinking her teeth into his elbow. He howled and tried to pry her off, but slipped and fell to the floor, where Kalyn landed a solid punch to his jaw.

Someone's foot haphazardly connected with the middle of Kalyn's face, sending her sprawling. Blood poured from her nose almost instantly. She rolled over to her hands and knees, struggling to her feet. A pair of strong arms wrapped around her middle and hoisted her into the air.

"You'll pay for that chair move, you little Deepwood rat!" She heard the rabble-rouser growl in her ear.

She twisted in his arms, her elbow connecting solidly with the side of his head. The knight dropped her and clutched at his ear with a howl. Kalyn jammed her fist into his middle as hard as she could, making him buckle over. She jerked her knee up, smashing it into his forehead, sending him straight onto his back again.

"Ha! You'll feel that Deepwood wrath poundin' in yer head tomorrow mornin', ya Dunnie dog!"

Another pair of arms wrapped themselves around Kalyn, trapping her arms to her sides. She kicked her feet up, punching her boots into the chest of an oncoming soldier, at the same time sending the one holding her stumbling into a table. He couldn't regain his balance as Kalyn squirmed and kicked, and eventually fell to the floor. She jammed her elbow into his ribs, wiggling away from him, then grabbed a chair leg and hoisted it over her head, aiming for the middle of his back as he tried to crawl away.

"I said *enough*!" The piercing cry was followed by a couple of red-hot rays lancing over their heads, hitting the ceiling with a *hiss*.

Everyone froze and ducked in unison. They turned to the door to find the Lady Andrella, fuming, hands in motion as she prepared another spell.

"Sky Knights, return to your rooms *now*!" She waited until the soldiers had picked their drooling comrades up off the floor before addressing the patrons. "The rest of you, go home! Xelda, Kailay and Kalyn, stay! I want to have a little talk with you."

Kalyn looked at the chair leg in her hands and quickly lowered it, slipping it behind her back.

Once the inn was clear, Andrella sighed and lowered her hands. "Whew. What a mess." She stepped over a broken chair and looked at the other girls. Her eyes widened when they came to Kalyn. "And *you're* a mess!"

Kalyn wiped her bloody nose on her sleeve, glanced around the room, then shrugged. "Sorry." She peered at Shalla. "Really sorry. I'll clean it all up."

Shalla smiled, pushing back her messy hair and revealing a black eye. "No apology necessary. We'll clean it up later. Right now, drinks are on the house!"

"And when it's time to clean up, we'll all do it together," Kailay said, hurrying around behind the bar to set out clean mugs.

Kalyn stared at each girl in turn as they took seats at the bar. "Wait. Aren't we in trouble? I would be if I were at home." She gazed at Andrella. "I thought you said you wanted to talk to us?"

Andrella shrugged with a grin. "Yeah. Sure. What do we want to talk about tonight? Boys?"

Everyone giggled.

Andrella stepped up to Kalyn and set her hands on her shoulders, looking her over. She shook her head, a wry smile turning up the corners of her mouth. "I seriously have my work cut out for me, don't I?"

Kailay laughed as she filled a mug. "More work than Titan was, that's for sure!"

Xelda chuckled. "… And that's saying something!"

Andrella sighed and pulled a handkerchief from her dress pocket, passing it to Kalyn. "Why is it I always get the tomboys?"

Shalla chuckled. "Because you can't help yourself?"

All the girls laughed, except Kalyn. She stared at the white lacy handkerchief with a repulsed expression, then looked at herself in the mirror behind the bar.

"What's wrong with me?"

The corner of Shalla's lips upturned slightly. "Oh, honey. Where do we start?"

Kalyn stared at Shalla for a moment, but looked back as Andrella snapped her fingers. Instantly all the bloodstains on Kalyn's clothes disappeared.

Kalyn jumped, staring at her clothes in surprise. "Whoa. That's slicker n' snot!"

Andrella giggled. "Xelda and I used that spell a lot when we were fresh apprentices and ran with our old friend, Titan. Oh! Some of the messes we'd get into!"

Xelda laughed behind them. "Literally! Like the time all three of us fell from that barn roof and landed in that giant manure pile. I was thankful for the soft landing, but if it hadn't have been for that spell, there's no telling what kind of trouble we would've gotten into.

Especially had Titan's father seen what a mess we were."

"Oh! I remember that!" Kailay piped up, setting a full mug down in front of Kalyn, "You got rid of the nasty stains, but still smelled awful! We went swimming to cover it up."

"Oooh! Stories!" Kalyn limped up to the bar and sat down, grinning from ear-to-ear. "I'm always in the mood for a good story! Do tell!"

Kailay and Shalla poured everyone drinks as Andrella and Xelda launched into a narrative of the crazy antics they would get into as young apprentices to Maltar.

The five women talked late into the evening.

Kalyn had to re-evaluate her first opinions of the women surrounding her. Andrella was not nearly as much of a sissy as she first thought. Even Kailay seemed to have her "tomboy" moments growing up. As for Xelda, much like Glo, her book smarts tended to overshadow her dry sense of humor, which Kalyn found to be a hoot. The longer the girls talked about their younger days, the more Kalyn wished she had met Titan. She sounded more fun than an air elemental at a fairy tea party, and tough as Lloyd to boot!

At some point, the conversation turned to boys. It all started when Andrella mentioned how much she missed Lloyd.

Shalla looked her in the eyes with a wry smile. "Would you just marry him already?"

Andrella grinned mischievously. "Oh, I intend to. Trust me. He just needs a little more polishing."

Kalyn shook her head. "What is it with you and wantin' to fix folk who ain't broke?"

Xelda leaned forward, propping her arms on the bar. "You should have seen Lloyd before, though! Like a bull in a china closet, that one, always acting first and thinking later."

Kailay raised a finger. "There was nothing wrong with that per se, but he has grown a lot just in the few weeks I've known him. Andrella has done a smashing job, if you ask me." She nodded and took a sip of her drink.

Kalyn shrugged and turned to Shalla. "So, any polishin' you need to do to Elladan before the both of you get hitched?"

Shalla paused mid-drink, her cheeks brightening. She lowered her drink, a demure smile crossing her lips. "Oh, we're just friends. I'm not the settling-down type."

"Oh yes. We could tell. *Really* good friends, I'd say." Kailay giggled.

"You're a fine one to talk!" Xelda snorted, "Throwing yourself at Lloyd when he first showed up."

Kailay blushed, her wide eyes turning to Andrella.

Andrella giggled and waved her off. "I know you well enough to know it was harmless."

Kailay shrugged and took a drink. "Well, I switched over to Glo anyway, but couldn't get a rise out of him."

"I heard he fancied a gypsy woman, or something like that." Xelda looked down at the liquid in her mug, swirling it around. Kalyn raised an eyebrow as she noticed color rise to Xelda's cheeks.

Kalyn shrugged. "He did, but the floozy ran off and broke his heart. Didn't know what a treasure she had, if you ask me."

Xelda's face reddened a little more as she peered intently at Kalyn. "You don't say?"

Shalla licked her lips, leaning forward. "Ya interested, Xelda?"

Xelda sat up straight. "Oh! No, not at all. I was just… curious."

Kalyn snorted, a grin splitting her face. "Sure ya are."

Xelda rolled her eyes, lifting her mug to her lip. "How about that Donatello, though? I'm surprised someone hasn't snatched him up yet."

Kalyn laughed. "They'd have to nail him down first!"

Andrella blinked, her eyebrows knitting. "But I thought the lady knight Alana had him enthralled?"

Kalyn nodded with a sigh. "Yeah, and she was pretty smitten by him too, but she had her knightly duties to attend to, and he didn't. So they said goodbye and went their separate ways in Bendenwood. I have to admit, it did seem to depress the lil' feller for a while."

Shalla waggled her finger. "That explains why he's been so placid lately."

Kalyn nodded, tilting her mug back and taking another drink.

Kailay's eyes swiveled to Kalyn, a mischievous smile touching her lips. "So, Kalyn… how about that Martan?"

Kalyn swallowed wrong and spewed the liquid back into her mug. "Troll-haunches! That burns!" She wiped the amber liquid dripping from her nose while the other girls laughed.

"I told you she would be that way!" Kailay said between giggling fits.

Kalyn shook her head, setting her mug down. "You guys are more trouble than you look, ya know that?"

Xelda leaned into Kalyn's shoulder. "It makes us more fun."

Shalla smiled, "Seriously, Kalyn. I know you and Martan have some sort of rough history, but when are you going to kiss and make up?"

Kalyn crossed her arms, "When pigs fly!"

The other girls all groaned. Andrella put a hand on Kalyn's shoulder. "It was cute before, sweetie, but now it's just old. We all know you like him."

Kailay giggled. "If not him, then who else?"

Kalyn narrowed her eyes and stared at each of the other women in turn. Finally, she shrugged and propped her elbows on the bar, picking up her mug again, a smile touching her lips.

"I'm don't know, I'm more of a Seth kind of girl, myself."

All the women burst into fits of laughter that lasted a good while.

"You and Seth? What an image!" Xelda coughed, gasping for a breath of air as she wiped tears from her eyes.

"I wouldn't know who to pity most. You'd both drive each other insane!" Shalla chuckled.

Kalyn shrugged and took another drink. "You're probably right. He deserves Aksel more."

The room filled with boos and hisses as the other girls voiced their disapproval.

"Poor Aksel! He's such a sweetie. What'd he do to deserve such a fate?" Kailay narrowed an accusing stare at Kalyn, even as a grin touched the corner of her lips.

Kalyn shrugged. "He didn't! But with everyone else all paired up, who are Seth and Aksel left with?"

Xelda waved her hand dismissively. "Seth has himself. He's happy that way."

"…but Aksel…" Shalla trailed off.

All the girls exchanged glances, eyes widening, then they gasped in unison, leaning in close to one another.

"I know a cute little gnome girl in Lymerdia!" Shalla whispered.

Kailay squealed, shaking her hands excitedly.

"Tell us about her!" Andrella slapped her hand on the bar.

"Hold it! Before we go any further, don't Aksel get a say in this?" Kalyn asked.

All the women turned her way, eyes narrowed, or eyebrows raised.

Xelda set her hand on Kalyn's shoulder. "Sometimes, Kalyn, a man needs expert intervention."

"So don't you *dare* tell Aksel about this!" Kailay warned.

"Okay! Sheesh." Kalyn leaned in closer, eyes wide and smile growing "I haven't ever been to a matchmaker's meeting before. This is fun!"

Everyone laughed, then fell into conspiratorial whispers.

10
TO KILL A BARD

The light from inside fell on a tall figure garbed in dark red

The dusky blanket of night stretched over the darkening skies of Vermoorden as Seth silently stalked his target. The invisible halfling had seen Balmaroh leave the small house next to the theater about an hour ago. He tailed the thin man through the worn down, pot-holed streets of the town, watching from a careful distance as he stopped at the tailor shop and the winery. Balmaroh then reversed directions and headed across town to the general store before finally heading back home.

The sun had dropped below the horizon, and darkness enveloped the street as the blond-haired man approached the white picket fence in front of his house. On silent feet, Seth stole around the bard, ducking through the hedges off to the side. There he crouched down and waited patiently for his target.

The thin man stopped at the three-foot-high gate, juggling packages as he unlatched it. The white gate creaked a bit as he pushed it open, and again when he closed it behind him.

"I really should fix that one of these days," Balmaroh murmured as he readjusted his load and strode up the walkway.

As the thin man passed by his hiding spot, Seth stole from the bushes and silently closed the gap between them. His target was only halfway up the walk when Seth finally caught up with him.

The bard never saw the knife that slid upward into his back. A loud cry left his lips as the packages dropped to the ground below. The thin man then fell to his knees, grasping vainly at the spot where he had just been stabbed, but the knife was no longer there. His eyes fixed on the short dark figure that crouched just a few feet away.

"Why?" The single word left Balmaroh's mouth before he fell forward and hit the ground, the life draining from his body.

Still in a crouch, Seth began to back away when a sudden bark made him nearly jump out of his skin. He whirled around and came face to face with a big black dog that hadn't been there a moment ago.

The dog bared its teeth and growled at him. Seth prepared for the worst when surprisingly, the dog spoke. "You scoundrel, you've killed my master!"

The halfling tensed for the inevitable charge when a cry caught both their attention.

"Wraith, what's going on out there?" Two figures exited the house, their dark silhouettes outlined by the light from inside.

Seth took advantage of the momentary interruption, reaching to his belt and throwing a round object on the ground in front of him. There was a loud pop as grey smoke abruptly hissed out in all directions.

The whimpering and cries died down by the time Seth reached the other side of the theater. Yet it was soon replaced by the mournful howl of a dog, wailing over the death of its master.

Aksel was worried. Night had fallen and there was still no sign of Seth.

The little cleric had returned to the deserted farmhouse a couple of hours ago. Martan had shown up shortly thereafter. The pair had compared notes, their findings confirming Aksel's suspicions about the mayor.

Aksel now sat alone, Martan having gone to gather some firewood. A few red dragon scales laid spread out on the table before him. The little cleric tried to keep occupied by working on Lloyd's new armor, but thoughts of all that had happened kept creeping into his mind.

Aksel had not shared with anyone his suspicions about the ghoulish ritual that had been performed on the Baron. If he were right, Gryswold's spirit had been bound to the missing heart by magics dark and foul. If so, they had to recover the heart, or the Baron's very soul might be lost forever.

Finally giving up on the armor, Aksel sat back, his eyes wandering around the vacant home. The place was small but comfortable, consisting of one large room that made up both the kitchen and the living area. Most of the furniture was gone, except for the table Aksel sat at, and an old beaten-up couch with a rickety endtable beside it. A hallway led off to one side, adjoining three small bedrooms to the main house.

Aksel's lamp sat on the table in front of him, and Martan's over on the endtable, together illuminating the large room. The hearth behind him lay dark, waiting for the wood Martan had gone to fetch.

Aksel nearly jumped out of his seat when the front door flew open. He swung around to see Seth standing there, the halfling huffing as if he had run clear across town.

"Well, it's about time you showed up," Aksel admonished him.

Instead of the typical snarky comeback, Seth merely slammed the door shut.

Aksel's brow creased as he stood up. "What happened?"

"Stuff… with the… Assassins Guild…" Seth panted, taking a quick peek out the window.

Aksel strode across the room, narrowing an eye at his edgy friend. "That bad?"

"That bad," Seth nodded without looking at him.

Seth's strange behavior magnified Aksel's own anxiety. He had never seen the halfling in such a rattled state. Aksel placed a hand on Seth's shoulder. It felt tense beneath his touch. "Come have a drink and you can tell me about it."

Seth took one last look through the window, then followed Aksel back to the kitchen table. The pair sat down and Aksel handed him a canteen. The halfling took a long swig, then set it down and let out a deep breath.

"So?" Aksel said impatiently.

There was a strange look in the halfling's eyes. "Balmaroh's been assassinated."

Aksel felt a sudden sinking in the pit of his stomach. "But… I was just… with him…"

Seth's eyes glowed with an odd intensity. "It only happened a short while ago."

Aksel narrowed an eye at the halfling. Something was not right. "What aren't you telling me? Did you see it happen?"

Seth's expression grew pained. "Sort of…"

The look in his friend's eyes sent a shiver down Aksel's spine. "Seth… you didn't…"

"Well…" Seth began, his eyes drifting away from Aksel's.

A sudden knock on the door made both of them jump out of their seats. The pair exchanged a nervous glance.

"You expecting company?" Aksel asked.

"No," Seth responded, sweeping his eyes around the room. "Where's Martan?"

"Out gathering firewood," Aksel told him.

There was another knock at the door, this one sounding more urgent. Aksel shrugged. "Guess we should see who it is."

Seth ushered him forward. "You first."

Aksel raised an eyebrow, then strode over to the front door. Seth followed, positioning himself so he couldn't be seen through the doorway.

Aksel gave him a curious look, then opened the door. The light from inside fell on a tall figure garbed in dark red. Aksel's eyes drifted upward to the face of a striking woman with flaming red hair.

The woman's eyes drifted downward, regarding him with a cool stare. There was something vaguely familiar about her. When she spoke, there was an icy edge to her voice. "I'm looking for my son. Have you seen him?"

The hairs on the back of Aksel's neck stood up. "I'm… not sure. Who is your son?"

"Oh, you'd know him if you saw him," the woman said with confidence as she took a step forward through the open doorway.

Aksel unconsciously stepped backward. "Th—there's no one else here but me and my friend."

"I wouldn't be too sure about that," the woman replied, her tone assured as she continued to walk forward.

Aksel moved out of the way as she strode past him to the center of the room. Seth came out from behind the door and stood beside him, knife in hand.

Yet the woman paid them no heed as her eyes settled on the kitchen table. She strode purposely over to it and picked up one of the red scales lying there. The woman stood there a moment as if transfixed, then spun around, her face contorted with rage.

"Where's the rest of him? Where is my son?" she screamed.

Aksel's body began to shake with fear. *The scales? Her son?*

The blood drained from Aksel's face as the realization set in. Yet before he could say a word, a knife flew across the room, straight at the raging woman. At the same moment Aksel felt a hand on his arm, dragging him backward.

"Run!" Seth cried as the woman abruptly began to glow.

Aksel felt numb as he watched the knife bounce harmlessly off the brightening form. Seth continued to pull on him, but Aksel's feet were firmly rooted in place.

The glowing figure swelled in size, the neck elongating as two huge bat-like wings sprouted from its back, and a serpent-like tail extended out behind it. It grew so large that it burst through the roof, the entire house collapsing around them.

Everything went black till a roaring voice brought Aksel to his senses. "Give me the rest of my son!"

Aksel's eyes snapped open. Darkness surrounded him, a heavy weight pinning him to the ground. The little cleric twisted his body around—there was an opening in the rubble ahead of him.

Seth's voice reached his ears. "I don't have him."

Aksel swiftly crawled out on his belly, then stood. His eyes nearly popped out of his head as they fixed on a frightening sight.

A huge dragon stood in the midst of what once was the small farmhouse. Easily fifty feet long, the creature was covered from the top of its serpentine neck to the tip of its long, sinuous tail in thick leathery scales that shone vaguely crimson in the pale moonlight. Long, tapered, bat-like wings extended from the dragon's back, also pale crimson in color, though darker along the bottom edge.

Two massive horns swept back atop the skull, flanked by a pair of crimson-fringed ears. The head was capped by a backswept crest that ran down the neck and along the spine, all the way to the tip of its long, twitching tail.

Small flames danced across the beast's nostrils and eyes, a forked tongue flickering in and out of its beaked snout between wicked dagger-like teeth.

The huge dragon held a tiny figure clutched in its giant claw.

The dragon lowered its head, its deadly teeth drawing within a few feet of the halfling. "Then who does?"

Aksel gulped at the horrifying sight, fear nearly overwhelming him once more. Yet Seth would be a goner if he didn't do something quick.

Swallowing his fear, the young gnome pulled a bag from his belt and stepped out from behind the rubble. "He's in here!"

The dragon swiveled its great head around, a pair of molten-colored glowing eyes fixing on the little cleric. Aksel felt his knees nearly buckle.

"Show me," the dragon rumbled in a menacing voice that shook his very bones.

Aksel steadied his arm a few times before opening the drawstrings of the portal bag. Beads of sweat broke out across his brow as he rummaged around inside. He glanced up at the dragon and was sorry he did. The creature stared at him with such malevolence that Aksel nearly dropped the bag.

"Any day now!" Seth cried, still pinned in the dragon's huge claw.

Abruptly, his hand brushed against something scaly. Aksel grabbed onto it and pulled with all his might. Whatever it was, the thing was heavy.

Aksel laid the bag down and stuck his other hand into it. With a mighty heave, he managed to pull out the tip of what he had found before losing his footing and falling to the ground. Before him lay the tip of a pale crimson tail.

The huge dragon roared. "Scortch! What have they done to you?"

The earth shook repeatedly as the huge dragon lumbered forward. Aksel swiftly scurried back as two giant claws reached down to claim the bag.

Seth tumbled to the ground a few feet from where Aksel lay. The halfling motioned for Aksel to move, then disappeared from sight.

Above him the huge dragon pulled the rest of her son's body from the bag. She took the inert form and cradled it in her arms, crooning to it, "Scortch… Oh, Scortch…"

Ripping his eyes away, Aksel cast a quick spell to make himself invisible, then took off toward the nearby woods. He had barely reached the trees when a terrible roar erupted behind him.

Aksel turned to see a torrent of flame engulf what was left of the fallen farmhouse. It was so hot, he could feel the heat even from where he stood. Aksel fled further into the woods as sparks of flame flew in all directions. Behind him, the trees began to catch on fire.

There was another loud roar, and then a scarlet streak shot overhead, flames trailing behind it as it went.

Aksel ran head long into the forest, dodging and weaving through the trees. He finally stopped when he could no longer smell the burning woods behind him.

The little cleric laid his back against a tree and huffed as he tried to catch his breath. Abruptly something touched his shoulder. Aksel nearly jumped out of his skin.

"You alright?"

A familiar figure stood next to the little cleric—it was Seth. Aksel breathed a sigh of relief. "I'm fine. What about you?"

The halfling grinned, then winced and grabbed his side. "A broken rib or two, but otherwise fine."

Seth suddenly spun around and crouched low, a knife appearing in his hand. Aksel froze in place as a dark figure emerged from the nearby brush.

"Easy, it's me."

It was Martan. Aksel let out another sigh as the tracker rejoined them.

Martan nodded toward the still-burning forest half a mile or so behind them. "What in Thac happened back there?"

"A dragon happened," Seth responded blithely.

"A dragon?" Martan parroted with more than a tinge of fear in his voice.

"It's gone now," Aksel reassured him. "Still, it wasn't exactly happy with us. Probably best we put as much distance between us and Vermoorden as possible."

"I couldn't agree more," Seth said, still wincing a bit.

Aksel gazed at the halfling with concern. "Want me to fix that?"

Seth shook his head. "Later. Right now, less talking and more walking."

As luck would have it, their mounts had bolted into the woods, escaping the dragon's wrath. The dogs soon sniffed them out and led them to Martan's horse.

Mounted again, the trio took off across the fields away from Vermoorden, their eyes constantly scanning the skies above.

11
WIZARD'S APPRENTICE

Maltar? Hard to believe he has any friends

The next morning found Glo, Elladan, and Donnie walking across the many bridges of Tarsmoor. The three elves' destination was the small island just south of Gaither's tower.

"I've been to Tarsmoor a few times," Elladan was saying, "but I've never been to this shop before."

"I never even knew it existed," Donnie added with a wry smile.

Glo let out a closemouthed laugh. "Not many folks do. It's a well-guarded secret, it seems. I only learned about it thanks to a wizard we met in town the last time we were here."

Elladan shaded his eyes from the late-morning sun and gazed at the isle just ahead of them. Nothing was visible from this vantage point, but he knew the building was there—they had seen it quite clearly from Gaither's tower.

"So, you're thinking Maltar knew about it as well?" Donnie speculated.

Glo nodded. "More than likely. If he was in town, he would have come here to stock up on magical supplies."

The trio crossed over the last bridge and onto the small isle. The road turned south meeting another bridge about a hundred yards in the distance. The river ran along the east side of the path, while a dark green hedge bordered it to the west.

There were no visible breaks in the tall hedge, but about fifty feet down, Glo called them to a halt. The wizard raised his hands and spun them in a pattern.

Elladan felt the release of magic, and a moment later an opening appeared in the dark green leaves of the thick hedge. Glo stooped his head and entered, Donnie, and Elladan following right behind him.

Beyond the hedge lay the grey building they had seen from the tower. A single sign hung from its brown tile roof, reading simply, *Wizard's Shop*. A maze of thick vines and brambles stood between them and their destination.

Glo took the lead, winding through the natural labyrinth.

"The owner sure seems to love his privacy," Donnie commented as they circumvented a particularly nasty-looking set of vines.

Glo laughed again. "He is a bit of a strange one."

"What did you say his name was again?" Elladan asked.

"Horcrum."

Elladan tilted his head sideways. "Never heard of him, but the name is kind of catchy."

A short while later, the trio stood before the only door visible in the big building.

Donnie swatted a mosquito off his neck. "I feel like I just trekked through a jungle."

Elladan scratched at a bite on his arm. "You and me both."

"Lloyd was the smart one, staying back at the inn," Donnie commented as he swatted after a second bug.

Elladan snorted at his friend. "You could've stayed as well."

Donnie fixed him with an incredulous stare. "And spar with Sir Fafnar? I think I'll pass."

Glo stared at them with narrowed eyes. "Are you two done?"

Elladan and Donnie exchanged a grin. "For now."

The elven wizard arched an eyebrow, then knocked on the door in front of them. There was no response at first, but after a while it opened a crack, a chain visibly holding it in place.

A halfling woman peered through the thin opening, her eyes gazing up at the tall wizard. It was hard to see her from this angle, but she was garbed in brown robes, gray streaks running through her coffee-colored hair.

"May I help you?" she asked in a polite but reserved tone.

"Yes," Glo replied. "Is Horcrum here?"

The halfling woman shook her head. "No, I'm sorry, the master is away at the moment. You'll have to come back another time."

The woman started to close the door, but Glo placed a hand on it and held it open. "Wait…"

The halfling's eyes narrowed, glaring at the tall elf.

A wan smile graced the wizard's lips as he pulled his hand away from the door. "I'm sorry. It's just we're only in town for a couple of days, and we are in dire need of some information."

The halfling folded her arms across her chest and leveled a hard stare at the elf. "And what information is that?"

"The Baron of Ravenford is dead…" Glo began.

"Old news," the halfling replied, starting to close the door once more.

"…and his heart was cut out," Glo blurted as the door slammed shut.

The elven wizard turned toward the others, his frustration quite evident, when the sound of a latch being pulled came from the other side of the door. Glo spun around in surprise as the door swung all the way open.

"Well, don't just stand there with your mouths hanging open," the halfling woman barked at them.

The trio exchanged a quick glance, then entered the shop. Elladan swept his eyes around the place. At first glance, it wasn't much different from any other magic shop he had seen. There were long aisles filled with shelves of everything from potions to wands to spell ingredients.

The halfling closed the door behind them, then turned around and folded her arms once more. "I take it you are from Ravenford?"

"Yes, ma'am," Donnie drawled, flashing her one of his toothiest smiles.

She cocked her head to one side and narrowed an eye at him. "What's the matter with your face?"

"N-nothing," Donnie stammered, taking a step back from the woman.

Elladan nearly laughed out loud, but somehow managed to stifle it. It seemed Donnie had finally met a woman immune to his smoldering stare.

The halfling shifted her gaze to Glo, her eyes focusing on his shoulder. "Oh, what a pretty bird. Come here, sweetie."

As the halfling held out her hand, Raven flew from the tall elf's shoulder and perched on her arm.

Elladan watched curiously as she stroked the bird's feathers and cooed to it in elvish. *"Bein dulin. Bein dulin." Pretty bird. Pretty bird.*

Glo arched an eyebrow as he exchanged a glance with Elladan. "She appears to like you."

The halfling responded with a curt nod. "She's got good taste. Now, you said the heart was cut out?"

The wizard glanced at Elladan once more. The bard wasn't exactly happy that Glo had mentioned that, but he had to admit it got them in the door. Since the cat was out of the bag anyway, they might as well continue on. Elladan shrugged at the tall elf.

Glo shifted his gaze back to the halfling. "A clean cut, as if done by someone expert with a knife."

The halfling brooded on that information for a few moments. "Probably will be used in some dark ritual."

"That's what our cleric friend surmised," Glo concurred.

The woman regarded them a moment further, then strode down the aisle past them, motioning for them to follow. "Might as well get comfortable. I have a feeling this is going to be a long discussion."

Elladan fell in behind Glo, Donnie trailing behind him. The halfling led them to the back of the store and through a doorway. On the other side was a living area decorated in a quaint but stylish fashion.

The halfling waved at a comfy-looking couch and a pair of chairs in the center of the room. "Grab a seat. I'll get us some refreshments."

Elladan and Donnie sat on the couch while Glo took one of the two chairs. The elven bard then swept his eyes around the room. There was really nothing out of the ordinary here, nothing to indicate it was a wizard's home. There were a few portraits on the wall, yet they all depicted humans.

Elladan leaned forward and whispered to Glo. "I trust this Horcrum was not a halfling."

"No, he's definitely human," Glo whispered back.

A moment later, the halfling re-entered the room carrying a tray with a teapot, tea cups, and a plate full of cookies. She set them down on the small table in front of the couch, then sat in the remaining chair and poured herself a cup of tea.

Steam rose from the cup as the halfling woman sat back and took a sip. "Ah, that's better." She glanced around at her guests. "Go ahead, help yourselves."

Elladan poured himself a cup of tea, but would not touch the cookies. The halfling woman narrowed an eye at him, then grabbed a cookie off the plate and shoved it in her mouth. She munched it down and swallowed hard, then glared at him through dark eyes. "Satisfied?"

Elladan gave her a quasi-smile. "Yes, ma'am." The bard then grabbed a cookie and ate it while she watched. It was rather good—very good, in fact. He would have to see if he could get the recipe.

The halfling settled back in her seat, the chair a bit large for her, then gazed at Glo. "So, where's the body now?"

Once again, Glo cast a quick look at Elladan. The bard responded with the barest of nods. He still didn't quite trust this halfling, but he was curious to see where this would go.

"It's safely tucked away at the temple in Ravenford, under a preservation spell," Glo answered.

The woman tapped the side of her mouth. "Hmm, that would only last for a couple of weeks at best." Her eyes narrowed at the wizard. "So, you came here searching for the heart?"

A strained smile crossed Glo's lips. "Sort of. We came here looking for the Baron's old friend, Maltar. We thought he might have information regarding any old enemies of the Baron."

"Maltar? Hard to believe he has any friends," the halfling scoffed.

The three of them chuckled softly.

"Can't argue with that," Glo admitted. "Still, he was a traveling companion of the Baron's in their adventuring days."

The halfling's expression turned thoughtful. "Maltar was indeed in town a couple of weeks ago. He stopped here for some supplies. Looked pretty banged up."

"So we heard," Donnie responded, a toothy smile crossing his lips once more.

"You know, you really should get that checked," the woman noted critically.

Donnie sat back on the couch, a hurt expression on his face as he pulled a pillow into his lap. The lean elf murmured softly, "Some women find me charming."

"And some women have no brains in their head," the halfling answered him.

This time Elladan couldn't help laughing.

The halfling turned her attention to him. "And I suppose most women find you charming as well?"

Elladan regarded her silently for a few moments. This one was a tough nut to crack. A partial smile spread across his lips. "Some, perhaps, but not all."

She eyed him for a moment, then nodded. "Well, at least you're not all puffed up with your good looks."

Elladan continued to smile at her. "Thanks, I think."

"Anyway," Glo interjected, "do you have any idea what happened to Maltar?"

The halfling returned her attention to the tall elf. "Not sure, really. He's pretty closemouthed, that one."

Elladan still didn't trust this woman, but was curious to see how she would react to Maltar's darker practices. "Tell her what we found in his home, Glo."

The elven wizard arched an eyebrow, then launched into a description of the summoning circle they found in Maltar's house. That type of magic was only used for one purpose—to summon demons or other interdimensional monsters. It was dark magic, something no self-respecting wizard would delve into.

When Glo was done, the halfling sat back in her chair and let out a deep sigh. "Ah, we were afraid of that."

Elladan peered at her intently. "We?"

The halfling glared at him for what seemed like forever. It felt as if her dark eyes were digging all the way down to his very soul. It was extremely uncomfortable, but not painful, and only lasted a few seconds.

The halfling then shifted her gaze to Donnie and finally Glo. When she was done, she sat back and sighed. "Very well. I detect no malevolence in you. My name is Franzire, and I am a member of the Wizard's Council."

The revelation caught the three of them by surprise. Elladan could sense the woman was hiding something, but a member of the Wizard's Council—that was rare indeed.

The Wizard's Council was a ruling body of high powered mages based in Lymerdia, the capital of Thac. Together they held sway over all uses of magic across the isle. If this Franzire were indeed a member of the council, then she was more powerful than all of them in this room put together.

Franzire regarded them intently from her chair. "Maltar has been vying for a seat on the council for a number of years. Some members already approved his application, but the vote needs to be unanimous. There are a few of us who never quite trusted him. Now I'm glad we didn't."

That admission made Elladan more comfortable with the halfling wizard. Her distrust of Maltar went a long way in his book. Furthermore, a charlatan would pretend to be your friend, and this Franzire was anything but friendly. He was starting to like her.

Glo continued to question Franzire. "If you don't mind my asking, what are you doing in Tarsmoor? Does it have anything to do with your disappearing members?"

Franzire whirled upon Glo, her demeanor deceptively calm, but Elladan could detect a dark edge to her voice. "How do you know about that?"

Glo opened his mouth to answer, but Elladan cut him off. This was quite obviously a touchy subject and needed to be handled delicately. "We are friends of the Greymantles."

Franzire shifted her gaze to Elladan, her dark eyes practically boring into him. "Is that right?"

Elladan stared back at her evenly, carefully gauging his words. "The sisters overheard their father's conversation with the council members. Now Rodric has gone missing. They are rather worried."

Franzire gave him a slow nod, still holding his stare. "We haven't heard from him either in months now. That's why we disbanded."

Elladan pursed his lips together. "That's probably wise. We promised the girls we would look for their father, but now we've gotten caught up in this search for the Baron's heart."

Franzire visibly relaxed, a short sigh escaping her lips. "Well, if you find out anything more, please let me know." She swept her gaze around the room. "Now, was there anything else I can do for you?"

Glo sat forward in his seat. "Do you have any idea where Maltar was headed next? The clerk at the Temple of Enuii said he was last seen headed down the south road."

Franzire tapped the side of her mouth once more. "Not specifically, though now that you mention it, Illiana did caution him about the goings-on at the capital."

Glo cocked his head to one side. "Illiana? Is that the headmistress of at the Temple of Enuii?"

Franzire gave him a curt nod. "Indeed, though why she was hanging around with Maltar escapes me."

Elladan narrowed an eye at the halfling wizard. "How did this Illiana know about what's going on with the council?"

Franzire's face fell. "That's my fault. She's an old friend, and I entrusted her with the information. I'll not make that mistake again."

Keen sympathy welled up inside Elladan for the halfling wizard. He had made a similar mistake when he was younger. It was a hard lesson, but he had learned it well. "It happens to the best of us."

Franzire's eyes softened as she peered at him. "Is there anything else I can do for you?"

Elladan couldn't think of anything at first, but then an interesting idea struck him. "Would you happen to have a scroll of *Malefic Mutation*?"

Glo and Donnie both choked at his request. Malefic Mutation

was the spell Princess Anya had used on Elladan to turn him into a little grey bunny.

Franzire gazed at the pair curiously, then back at Elladan. "I do, but am I missing something?"

Elladan smiled at the halfling. "Let's just say it's a 'surprise' for a special friend."

The side of the halfling's mouth upturned slightly as she produced the scroll out of thin air. She held it out for Elladan to take. "I hope your 'friend' enjoys their surprise."

Elladan's smile widened into a grin. "Oh, I'm sure she will."

Franzire stared at him with clear amusement, then turned to the others. "Anything else? Anything that might help you with the quest for the Baron's heart or finding Rodric?"

In the end, the halfling wizard provided Glo with a few more scrolls of higher order spells. That alone would save the elf months of research.

Franzire then ushered them out, slamming the door to the Wizard's Shop behind them.

Donnie glanced at the now-closed door. "Well, that was rather rude."

Elladan chuckled. "You're just saying that because she didn't fall for your charming smile."

Donnie glanced at Elladan and shrugged. "She wasn't exactly fawning over you, either."

"Gentlemen," Glo interjected. "She was obviously beyond those types of concerns. If Arenor himself appeared on her doorstep, I doubt she would be impressed."

Donnie gave the tall elf a sly look. "I don't know, Glo. I think she kind of liked you."

Glo gave his droll friend a withering stare. "She's not exactly my type."

Elladan peered at Donnie and winked. "Still, she might take you on as her apprentice, in exchange for certain 'favors.'"

Glo swept his gaze between the pair, his cheeks turning a pale shade of red. "You two are absolutely incorrigible!"

Elladan grinned at Donnie. "Yes, we are, aren't we?"

The duo each placed an arm on Glo's shoulder, laughing raucously as they left the Wizard's Shop behind.

SETH AND AKSEL, VAMPIRE HUNTERS?

Nearly half the town had already been turned

It was late afternoon when Seth, Aksel, and Martan arrived back in Ravenford. The trio had ridden hard the night before, not stopping until well past midnight. After only a few hours' sleep, they mounted up again and rode at a steady pace the rest of the way.

As soon as they reached town, Seth and Aksel went straight to see Lady Gracelynn. Martan, in the meantime, took care of the mounts.

Captain Gelpas met the duo at the front gate. "Cleric Aksel, Master Seth. Well met. How went things in Vermoorden?"

Aksel glanced at Seth before replying. Seth stared back at him, his arms folded.

"Let's just say it was an interesting trip," Aksel responded in a soft voice.

Gelpas arched an eyebrow at the pair, but asked no more about it.

"The Baroness is already in conference, but I am sure she will want to see you immediately. Follow me." The Captain motioned for them to fall in behind as he led them through the keep.

As they went, Seth's thoughts drifted back to Vermoorden. He wasn't completely happy with the way they had left things. Still, it couldn't be helped. Earning his way into the Assassin's Guild was key if they were going to find the Baron's heart in time. Unfortunately, Balmaroh's 'demise' had been the only way to ensure that.

Seth's musings were interrupted as Gelpas ushered them into the chamber off the throne room. Four familiar figures sat huddled around the table there.

Lady Andrella was the first to stand and greet them. "Aksel! Seth!"

Lady Gracelynn rose as well. "Welcome back, gentlemen."

"Ho there, short-stuff!" Kalyn waved as she also stood.

"Well if it isn't my favorite cake-loving halfling!"

The fourth person at the table was someone Seth hadn't expected to see again so soon, if ever. The halfling narrowed an eye at the newcomer. "Raina? What are you doing here?"

Raina was a young druid they had met in the Bendenwoods. A friend of Kalyn, she had aided them in their quest to dismantle the Serpent Cult.

"Well that's a fine greeting." A cheery smile crept across the short human's freckled face. Her bright green eyes twinkled and her vibrant red dreadlocks bounced up and down as she came around the table to greet them.

Seth noted that she still wore the same patchwork clothes as the last time he saw her—a strange mish-mash of different fibers and colors, all styled to look like bark and leaves. Feathers adorned both her hair and outfit in numerous places, and she was still shoeless.

Aksel attempted to cover for his friend's lack of social skills. "I think what Seth meant to say was, didn't we just leave you in the Bendenwoods?"

Raina shifted her gaze to the gnome cleric, her cheeks reddening slightly. "Yes, well… it's a bit of a long story…"

"…which we will get to in a moment," Gracelynn interrupted her. "First, any news from Vermoorden?"

Seth sat next to Aksel as his friend briefly explained what they had found. He noted with interest that Aksel left out the part about Balmaroh's assassination.

Gracelynn's brow knit into deep creases as he finished. "I never did warm up to Mayor DeWyness, but to find that she might be in league with the Assassin's Guild? That's unconscionable."

Aksel responded with a curt nod. "Our thoughts exactly, your ladyship."

Gelpas, standing behind Gracelynn, scoffed. "I never did trust that election system of theirs. Too easy to rig something like that."

Seth had to suppress a laugh. Gelpas had practically read his mind.

Andrella eyed Seth and Aksel curiously. "So, you don't think this red dragon had anything to do with the assassins?"

Seth's mouth twisted sideways. "Nah. She's Princess Anya's pet, if anything."

Kalyn snorted. "Ha. She was prob'ly after that lil' red dragon Lloyd chopped up back n' the woods."

Aksel responded with a curt nod. "It was her son."

Gracelynn sat back in her chair, her hands steepled in front of her. "Well then, you ruled out this Balmaroh as a suspect, and even enlisted his potential aid. Also, you made contact with the guild. So how soon do you plan on going back?"

Aksel glanced at Seth.

Seth didn't relish the thought of running into that red dragon again, but he also didn't think it would return to Vermoorden anytime soon. He was far more concerned with facing an entire guild of assassins. "That depends on the others."

Aksel swept his gaze around the room. "Where exactly did they go?"

Andrella briefly explained the discovery of the teleportation circle in the tower basement. She further described how it was set to Tarsmoor, and how the others left the same morning Aksel and Seth had.

Once she was finished, Aksel sat quietly stroking his chin. "Probably best that we wait for them to return." He shifted his gaze to the Lady Gracelynn. "May we stay in the tower while we wait?"

Gracelynn dipped her chin. "Why, of course. In the meantime, we have another matter that we could use your help with." She waved a hand toward Raina. "I'll let our young druid friend elaborate."

All eyes turned toward Raina as she cleared her throat. "I already explained some of this to the others, but I'll backtrack a bit for you two." She sat forward in her seat and peered intently at the duo. "Just after you left Bendenwood, some alarming reports came in from Twin Oaks. They'd been dealing with an uprising of undead."

Seth narrowed an eye at the young woman. "What kind of undead?"

"Vampires."

Seth sat back in his chair and glanced at Aksel. Aksel stared back at him, his expression grim.

Vampires were a far greater threat than the skeletons and zombies they had faced up at Stone Hill. Abnormally strong, vampires regenerated like trolls, controlled minds with a gaze, and drained their victims of both blood and life essence. On top of that, they could shapeshift into rats, bats, or wolves, or disappear in a puff of smoke only to reappear behind you moments later. They could even turn normal folks into vampires if they didn't completely drain them first. Overall, vampires were intelligent, deadly foes.

After a few moments' pause, Raina continued her story. "Members of our order were already on hand, but they could barely hold off the growing numbers of undead. High Druid Lysandra immediately dispatched those of us who could still fight after the battle with the Serpent Cult."

Raina's face grew ashen. "When we got there, nearly half the town had already been turned. We immediately set to work tracking down the undead and driving them from their lairs. In the end we cleansed the town, but the cost was… high."

The young druid's voice cracked at that last word.

Kalyn reached over and grabbed Raina's hand. "I'm sure you did all that you could."

Raina gazed at Kalyn, a haunted look in her eyes. "That might be, but it still wasn't enough. One of the devils escaped. A few of us set out tracking it. I finally found the trail, but lost it once it left the woods. Still, it looked like it was headed straight for Ravenford."

Lady Gracelynn cleared her throat. "This may or may not be related, but there have been reports of townsfolk gone missing this last week. We thought at first they might be picking up and leaving town. Folks have been nervous, with the Baron gone and the Dunwynn knights showing up."

Gracelynn stopped and took a deep breath.

Seth peered closely at the monarch. She looked positively haggard. A deep sympathy welled up inside him for the stately woman. Not only had she lost her husband, but now she had to deal with this, too.

After a moment's pause, Gracelynn resumed speaking. "With folks on edge, I don't want to create any more of a stir."

Aksel sat forward in his seat. "What does Abbot Qualtan have to say about this?"

Raina responded in a subdued voice. "I stopped at the abbey before coming here. They told me that the Abbot was sequestered and not to be disturbed."

"He picked a fine time for it," Gelpas muttered angrily.

Seth had to agree. It was just too much of a coincidence. He thought back to what Almax had said about the Abbot. *Could he somehow be involved in all this?*

Andrella's face had reddened with anger. "I was just about to march down there and demand to see him when you two showed up. Now that you're here, I say to the abyss with him!"

"Andrella!" Gracelynn cried. "Whatever has come over you?"

Seth noted Kalyn sliding down in her seat, trying to make herself less noticeable. The halfling's mouth bent to one side. Here Andrella was trying to make a lady out of the Deepwooder, but it seemed that instead Kalyn was bringing out Andrella's rougher side.

Andrella stared her mother in the eye. "Between the five of us, we don't need him. Aksel, Seth, Raina, Kalyn, and I can split up and search the town easier than that old fuddy-duddy."

Gracelynn's expression hardened as she regarded her daughter. "Andrella, the last thing I need right now is you putting yourself in danger."

Andrella's demeanor grew just as hard. "Mother, I am not a child!"

Gracelynn's expression did not change, but Seth could see the hurt in her eyes. Andrella must have observed it as well, because she immediately flew out of her seat and threw her arms around Gracelynn.

"Oh Mother, I'm so sorry."

Lady Gracelynn patted her daughter gently on the back. "It's alright, dear. I'm only worried about your safety, after all."

Andrella stood up and wiped the moisture from her eyes. "I know, but I also can't just stand around while our people are in trouble."

Gracelynn's expression abruptly changed from one of concern to one of pride. At the same moment, Kalyn stood and grabbed Andrella by the arm.

"Don't worry, ma'am. I'll keep a real good eye on her."

The Lady Gracelynn smiled in earnest at the young archer. "That you will… as will Captain Gelpas." She turned to the Captain of the Guard. "You will escort the ladies around the town as they search for signs of undead."

Gelpas gave her a crisp nod. "I will guard them with my life."

"I know you will." Gracelynn smiled back at the stalwart soldier.

Aksel cleared his throat. "Your ladyship, may we take a castle guard with us as well?"

"Of course." Gracelynn once again addressed Gelpas. "Send Lieutenant Relkin with them."

"What about Almax?" Seth interjected.

Gracelynn sighed. "This is incredibly poor timing, but he was called to Bendenwood shortly after the others departed for Tarsmoor."

"Probably had something to do with what happened in Twin Oaks," Aksel guessed.

"Well in that case, can we also take Francis?" Seth asked. The guard had been quite kind to them when they first arrived at the keep. Seth had taken an uncharacteristic liking to the genuine young man.

Gracelynn gazed at him curiously. "I don't see why not. In fact, that's an excellent idea." She looked at Gelpas once more. "Just to be on the safe side, take a second guard with you."

Captain Gelpas bowed to the beleaguered monarch. "As you wish."

Andrella and Kalyn walked silently side-by-side down the street, Gelpas and two guards keeping pace behind them while Raina took the lead.

Since Aksel and Raina each knew a similar spell that allowed them to track undead, they decided to split into two groups to cover more territory. Aksel, Seth, and company took the north side of the river, while Andrella, Raina, and Kalyn crossed the west bridge and took the south side of town.

Raina suddenly paused and lifted her hands, rolling her wrists in circles. White light filled her palms, encircling her weaving fingers. She closed her eyes in concentration, tilting her head as if she were listening to something.

Andrella took the opportunity to assess Raina's attire. At first glance she thought it was worse than Kalyn's. Yet, as she studied it, she noticed how well thought out each piece was. Every bead and leaf was strategically placed on the strange forest-like dress.

It was certainly not to Andrella's tastes, but it was cute, and it fit Raina's petite figure perfectly. Those red dreadlocks, though, would have to go.

"This way," Raina pointed toward the river, looking back at them with a feeble smile. She paused when she met Andrella's eye. She glanced down at her dress, then back up at Andrella, a puzzled expression in her green eyes.

"Is something the matter?" Raina asked.

Andrella quickly shook her head. "Oh, no. Please, lead the way."

Kalyn snorted as they started walking again. "Somebody is thinking about fixin' something that ain't broke."

"I am not as predictable as you and Shalla think I am." Andrella huffed.

Kalyn crossed her arms. "Sure yer not."

Andrella crossed her arms as well and looked away.

The three of them walked down to the river, finally stopping in front of a riverside tavern.

"The presence leads inside here." Raina pointed at the building, looking back at Andrella.

"This is Falcon Breem's place," Andrella frowned, "What would undead be doing here?" Falcon Breem and his wife were good folk, both dwarves, two of a few living in Ravenford.

Kalyn giggled. "I reckon even vampires need a good drink once in a while."

Andrella smirked, then led the way up the steps and into the building. They were immediately met by a young dwarf wiping down tables. He paused and looked toward them.

"Hi there," the words rolled from his tongue in a thick brogue, "What can I do fer ya?"

"Are you the manager of this fine establishment?" Raina asked.

The dwarf smiled at her and crossed his arms, puffing his chest out. "Aye! That I am, lassie. I must say, it ain't often I see another reasonable-sized person around these parts. All these humans are too tall! Are ya lookin' for a job? I'll set ya up with one in a heartbeat!"

Raina's cheeks brightened. "No. I have a job already. I'm working for the baroness and Lady Andrella today." At that, she motioned to the young lady behind her.

Andrella crossed her arms as the dwarf lowered his, her face forming a frown. "Alright, Keegan. The fun is over. We need to see the *real* manager, if you don't mind."

The dwarf sighed, "I try to make a good impression on a pretty girl, and it gets ruined every time." He turned to leave, then paused, looking back at Raina. "Eh, ya wouldn't happen to be single, would ya, missy?"

Raina's cheeks flushed brighter.

Andrella huffed, "Enough, Keegan! Bring Falcon to us right away!"

Keegan walked away, grumbling under his breath. "Can't find a decent girl around this wee town to save my life. If they ain't too tall, they're working for someone who is…"

Kalyn chuckled. "I need to spend more time with short people like you, Raina! They're funny!"

"I'm not that short." Raina waved her hand dismissively.

"Not as short as Seth, you mean?" Kalyn's lips curved to one side.

Andrella looked at the young druid, a thought occurring to her, "Raina, forgive my asking, but *are* you single?"

Raina looked sidelong at Andrella, a half smile on her lips. "Yes. But not for a dwarf like him!"

They all giggled.

"So, dwarves like Keegan are out of the question. What kind of man are you looking for?"

Raina shrugged, pulling at one of her dreadlocks. "Well, I guess I want what every other girl wants: someone kind, thoughtful, and hardworking. Being handsome is a bonus."

Andrella's smile grew. "Do you have a height limit?"

Raina giggled. "No, not really. Just an intelligence limit."

"Doesn't that disqualify *all* men, then?" Kalyn scoffed.

Raina laughed, but Andrella nudged Kalyn in the arm, her eyes widening. "Not all men! *Aksel* is very intelligent."

Kalyn shrugged. "You're right. I guess Glo is pretty bright, too."

Andrella grit her teeth with a roll of her eyes, nudging Kalyn again, "But Aksel is *very* intelligent, and kind, and thoughtful, and hardworking."

Kalyn stared at Andrella, clearly confused. After a moment, her face lit up and her eyes grew wide.

"Oh! Well… yes. Of course Aksel is super smart and… and… you can't get much nicer than Aksel. He's a real sweety, that one. I can't figure why he's still single."

Andrella closed her eyes and rubbed her temples.

What am I going to do with her?

Raina tilted her head just the slightest bit and raised an eyebrow at Kalyn. "I see."

Presently, an older, balding dwarf came from the back room. He greeted Andrella with a wide, warm smile. "Lady Andrella! Glad ta see ya! What can I do fer ya? Anything at all, just name it."

Andrella curtsied. "We are here on important business, Falcon. I don't mean to cause any alarm, but this good druid has been sent by the Bendenwood council to investigate a delicate matter."

The dwarf lost his smile and raised an eyebrow, but it was Kalyn who spoke up next. "Delicate? How is undead delicate?"

Andrella whirled around, clamping her hand over Kalyn's big mouth. Thankfully, it was dinner time, and most people were home. Only a few patrons were in the tavern at this time, and most seemed content to mind their own business.

Kalyn's eyes went wide as she mumbled into Andrella's hand. "Wub I shay?"

Falcon looked between Andrella and Kalyn, his eyes widening. "Undead?"

Andrella sighed, then responded in a hushed tone. "We don't want to cause a panic, but there is a possibility that an undead creature has infiltrated our town. We intend to rout it out before it can cause any trouble."

Falcon stroked his long graying beard. He answered in a soft voice. "Might explain a few of the disappearances 'round here, eh? Of course I'll help you in whatever way I can. What do you need?"

Raina shifted on her feet, dropping her voice as well. "I've followed a faint undead presence here and can sense traces of it beneath us. Do you have a cellar?"

Falcon nodded, his face darkening. "Aye, that I do. I store the wine down there. KEEGAN!"

All the girls jumped when the dwarf bellowed the name.

There was a crash from the back room, followed by the younger dwarf stumbling out the door and rushing up to Falcon.

Falcon faced Keegan, placing his fists on his sides. "Just what have ya been storing in my cellar?"

Keegan shrank a couple of inches, his eyes widening. "Just the elf wine, Falcon. I swear I haven't let the pig down there again. I learned my lesson the last time!"

Andrella bit the inside of her cheek, trying not to laugh.

Falcon's shoulders tensed. "I'm not talking about that blasted pig! Have you completed the manifest of what's down there, or did ya just store it and leave it, like always?"

Keegan's cheeks brightened. "I-I... no sir, I haven't finished the manifest yet."

Falcon audibly growled, then stormed behind the bar. "Here! Take this!" He lifted a crowbar and tossed it at Keegan, who barely caught it. "We're taking these young ladies down to the cellar to check it out. I want you to crack those crates open yourself, and if something jumps out all angry-like, I'm feeding you to it! Get goin' lad!"

Keegan stumbled over his feet as he turned and hurried to the cellar door. He threw it open and hastily lit a lantern. Falcon followed him up to the door, a club in hand. He took the lantern from Keegan and turned to the girls.

"Follow us, if ya will. But keep a safe distance. Dwarves swing wide." He wagged his club from side to side, then turned and marched down the stairs after the younger dwarf.

Raina hurried after him. Andrella followed her while Kalyn took the rear, drawing her bow.

The cellar was small compared to the rest of the tavern, only being half the size of the common room, if that. The walls were lined with shelves for wine and cheese, and two long crates sat near the door, stacked atop one another.

"I thought there were three crates?" Falcon's tone was low and gruff.

Keegan nodded, raising his crowbar. "The third one is sitting behind those two."

Falcon motioned for the girls to stay near the stairs, then the two dwarves crept forward. They split off and crept around the crates on opposite sides, disappearing behind them.

Raina raised her hands, her fingers glowing with a prepared spell. Andrella followed her example, reaching into a pouch next to her side and touching a powder, the incantation ready to fall from her lips at a moment's notice. Kalyn moved past Andrella and raised her bow, arrow nocked. Andrella's eye was momentarily drawn to a faint purple glow wrapping itself around Kalyn's arrow like a snake. She briefly wondered what kind of magic Kalyn had hidden in her quiver, but she quickly refocused herself on the task at hand.

After a few breathless moments, Falcon's booming voice startled all the girls again. "It's empty! Too bad. I was lookin' forward ta feeding ya to something vicious." He reappeared from around the crates and waved the girls over, "Ain't nothin' dangerous here, but ya might not like what ya see."

Andrella followed Raina around the crates, stopping short when her eyes fell on a broken one, a giant hole in the lid, the splinters jutting outward and lying around it on the floor.

Keegan tapped it with his crowbar, "Burst from the inside, I'd say."

Falcon grunted. "Aye. Weren't no wine in there, that's fer sure."

Raina knelt next to the crate and carefully inspected the edges of the opening. She reached inside the box and pulled out a handful of dirt. She frowned and waved her hand over the dirt, her fingers glowing. "Yes, the presence is strongest here." Her brows formed into a line of concern as she looked at Falcon. "When did this shipment arrive?"

"Much to me chagrin, my wife has insisted I leave the inventorying to her nephew." The older dwarf turned a stern frown in Keegan's direction.

Keegan shrank back a few inches. "It, um, arrived two weeks ago… I was going to take care of it today, though!"

Andrella watched as Raina caught her breath, stiffening.

"Two weeks ago?" Falcon bellowed, "If ya weren't me wife's nephew, I'd call ya a lazy piece of slag for lettin' this sit here that long!"

"What is the matter, Raina?" Andrella asked, drawing everyone's attention to the druid.

Raina cast a worried glance at Andrella. "The undead I was following was only a few days old. If this arrived two weeks ago, then I'm afraid we have a much worse problem on our hands."

13
IMP IN THE FOLD

It had red scales, tiny horns, small wings, and a long barb-ended tail

Seth watched Aksel with growing impatience as the little cleric swept the town for any signs of undead. It was a slow, painstaking process. The spell Aksel used had a limited range at best—no more than fifty to sixty feet in all directions. This meant they had to crisscross their way across town to cover every dwelling.

Seth, Francis, and Relkin followed a short way behind Aksel so as not to disturb his concentration. Thankfully it was near dinner time. Few folks were out and about, so no one interfered with their progress. Still, in fifteen minutes they had only made it from the northwest guard post to the road leading to the keep.

At that point, Francis bent down and whispered to Seth. "You sure there's not a faster way to do this?"

Seth snorted. "I wish. This is about as much fun as watching grass grow."

"Just be glad we don't have to cover the south side of the river, too," Aksel called back to them.

Seth snickered at the mortified expression on Francis' face. The young human was obviously not aware of gnomes' extraordinary hearing. "Sorry, Cleric Aksel. I didn't mean to question your ability."

Aksel barely nodded as he kept moving. "No offense taken. I would appreciate some quiet, though."

Lieutenant Relkin seemed as amused as Seth as he smacked Francis on the arm. "You heard him, zip your lip."

Francis gave the Lieutenant a mock salute, then pulled his fingers across his lips as if zipping them shut.

Luckily, there were not as many dwellings in the eastern part of town. Fifteen minutes later, they passed Maltar's and drew up in front of Haltan's shop. Haltan was a merchant who dealt in rare commodities. Seth and the others had run into him before; he was not exactly the friendliest person in the world.

Seth stole up behind Aksel. "You sense something?"

Deep creases stretched across Aksel's brow. "Yes. It's faint, but there's definitely something here."

Seth's shoulders tensed as he swept his eyes around them. It was late in the day and long shadows had spread behind Haltan's and across the large warehouses behind it down to the river. All the buildings were dark, and there was no one else in sight—it was as if this end of town had been completely deserted.

Francis and Relkin huddled around them, the guard's voice wavering ever so slightly. "You mean there's something here right now?"

Aksel gazed sympathetically at the nervous guard. "There are lingering traces of negative energy—more like something evil passed this way quite recently."

Francis let out a deep sigh. "Well, that's a relief—I think."

Seth's lips twisted sideways. He couldn't exactly blame the guard. A sudden movement caught his eye. A shadow had appeared in Haltan's window that hadn't been there a moment ago.

Seth whispered to the others without turning. "Don't look now, but someone, or something, is watching us from inside the shop."

Francis froze in place, practically squealing his reply. "Any idea what it is?"

"Well there's only one way to find out," Aksel said. The little cleric deliberately strode up to the shop door and knocked on it.

About half a minute went by before the door opened. A burly man stood in the doorway, garbed in a loose shirt and baggy pants held in place by a rope belt. The unshaven man peered down at Aksel, his tone gruff. "What do ya want?"

Aksel exchanged a curious glance with Seth. "We were wondering if the shop was open?"

The man looked them over, his eyes widening as they fell on Francis and Relkin. His tone abruptly turned more formal. "I'm sorry, good sirs, but the place is closed fer inventoryin'. My boss would have my head if I let ya's in."

Lieutenant Relkin stepped forward. "The merchant Haltan is good friends with the Baroness. I'm sure he could see fit to let us into his establishment in her name."

The burly man shook his head. "Nah, didn't ya hear? Haltan sold the shop—left when he heard Dunwynn was comin'. Phulbit owns the place now. I could ask 'em, but I doubt he'd let ya in if ya was the Duke himself."

Relkin was about to reply when Aksel held up a hand. "That's alright. We got what we came for anyway. Thanks for the information."

The big man eyed Aksel darkly for a moment, then slammed the door shut. A bolt could be heard sliding in place from the other side of the door.

The side of Seth's mouth curled upward as they stepped away from the shop. "Well, he's friendly."

Relkin glanced at Aksel. "Are you sure we don't need to go in there?"

Aksel gently stroked his chin as he swept his eyes around the area. "No, whatever I picked up wasn't in Haltan's"—he took a few steps in the direction of the warehouses—"but there seems to be a trail headed this way."

Seth exchanged a brief glance with Francis and Relkin, then fell in behind the little cleric as he led them down toward the riverside.

Aksel led them down to the Raven River, then west along the bank. They soon reached the east bridge. The little cleric continued to follow whatever trail he sensed up and over the bridge, then into the fields and up the hill on the other side.

Seth's eyes narrowed as Aksel headed straight for the abbey at the top of the hill. "Knew it."

"Knew what?" Relkin whispered.

Seth swiftly explained his suspicions about the Abbot. He repeated what Almax had told Donnie about Qualtan messing with the dark arts. He added how the Abbot was sequestered when Raina came looking for him.

Relkin's expression hardened. "Well then, we will demand to see him on Lady Gracelynn's authority."

Yet Aksel held up a hand before they could enter the building. "Better safe than sorry."

The little cleric weaved his hands in a familiar pattern, ending his spell with four words. "*Magicae Circuli Contra Malum.*"

The moment the magic released, a white circle engulfed all of them. Though the circle swiftly faded, Seth could still feel the magic radiating outward from where Aksel stood.

Aksel motioned them forward. "All right, that should keep us safe from any negative influences for a while."

Relkin took the lead as they entered the abbey. A wizened old gentleman in white robes came through a side door to greet them. "May I be of assistance?"

Lieutenant Relkin halted in front of the old cleric. "Huorgan, we're here to see the Abbot Qualtan. Can you please notify him the Baroness wishes to speak with him?"

Huorgan's expression grew anxious. He wrung his hands together as he replied. "Oh, I'm afraid that is out of the question. The Abbot is in a state of deep prayer. He cannot be disturbed at this time."

Seth's mouth twisted sideways. "Sure he is—just when the town is going to hell around him."

The old cleric cast an eye at the halfling. "And just what do you mean by that, young man?"

Relkin grasped the cleric firmly by the shoulders. "What he means is that the town is facing a dire emergency—one that only the most experienced of the clergy can help us with."

The old man winced under Relkin's firm grasp. The Lieutenant's expression abruptly softened, and he let him go. "Forgive me, father, but it really is urgent."

Huorgan brushed himself off, then nodded, his expression serene once more. "I understand, my son. Yet I cannot disturb the Abbot. You will need to do that yourself."

The wizened gentleman led them through an archway at the back of the foyer and into a long hall. Numerous doors lined the hallway. The old cleric pointed to the one at the very end. "That is the Abbot's room. I suggest you knock before entering."

With that, the old man left them alone. Relkin led the way down the hall.

Seth noted that Aksel remained firmly in the middle of the group. Seth could still feel the magic radiating off his friend. He silently hoped it would be enough if they came across any vampires.

Relkin stopped in front of Qualtan's door and knocked. There was no answer. After a few moments, he called inside. "Abbot Qualtan?" There was still no answer. "Abbot Qualtan? The Baroness wishes to see you."

The silence continued beyond the door. Relkin tried the handle, but it was locked.

"Maybe he's not in there?" Francis offered.

"One way to find out." Seth stepped forward, lock pick already in hand. A simple pin and tumbler mechanism, he had it unlocked in under ten seconds.

"Child's play," he murmured to himself.

A sudden crash came from beyond the door. It was followed by a guttural curse.

"Well, that doesn't sound very holy," Seth noted wryly.

Relkin and Francis drew their swords, as Seth pushed the door open. The room beyond was dim, the last vestiges of the fading sunlight barely illuminating it. There was a single bed against one wall, a table with a single chair, and a desk opposite it. A tall bookshelf lay empty, its contents scattered across the floor.

Something stirred under the pile of books. Seth's eyes went wide as a small creature emerged from beneath the mound. It had red scales, tiny horns, small wings, and a long barb-ended tail. The creature turned toward them with a wicked grin.

"What is that thing?" Francis asked, his voice filled with trepidation.

Aksel's tone was one of disgust. "It's an imp."

Imps were small devils. They were not physically strong, but they were extremely clever. Imps typically preyed on weak-minded mortals, leading them down the path to darkness through trickery and deceit.

Seth eyed the creature warily. Qualtan's straying from the light suddenly made a whole lot more sense.

The little devil snarled at them, baring a row of deadly-looking teeth. Abruptly it rushed them.

Seth automatically fell into a crouch, a knife appearing in his hand. Yet when the creature got within ten feet of them, it suddenly bounced back as if hitting an invisible wall.

Aksel's circle of protection worked!

With the realization that the imp could not touch them, Francis and Relkin stepped forward with readied swords.

"Sick 'im, Francis!" Seth cried, cheering on the emboldened guard.

Francis swung at the imp, but his sword merely bounced off its tough scales. Relkin followed suit, but with the same result.

They had reached an impasse. Apparently neither side could hurt the other. The imp stood back and hissed something at them in its hellish tongue. It then picked up the lone chair and flung it at one of the windows.

The chair smashed through the glass, shattering it into a thousand pieces. With a few flaps of its tiny wings, the imp lifted into the air and shot toward the now open window.

"It's getting away!" Francis cried. In a sudden fit of bravado, the guard rushed across the room after the creature.

Everyone else followed, but before they could reach the imp, it flew through the window and into the open air beyond. Yet just when all appeared lost, a bright white beam lanced past them and struck the creature with deadly accuracy.

The imp let out a horrific cry that sent chills up Seth's spine, before falling out of the air. The creature slammed into the ground below and lay there unmoving.

Seth cast a quick glance back over his shoulder. Aksel stood there, hand still raised, a look of triumph on his face.

Seth gave his friend a quick nod. "Nice shot."

The halfling then vaulted out the window. Aksel and the others swiftly followed, then the four of them closed on the downed creature. As they drew within a few yards, they all slowed down, weapons at the ready.

The imp had not moved. It lay sprawled in an awkward position on the ground, its red eyes lifeless as it stared up at the heavens.

Seth watched warily as Aksel ran his hands a few feet over the body. After a few moments, the gnome cleric let out a sigh. "It's dead."

"What's dead?" A familiar voice called out from down the hill.

Seth turned to see Kalyn, Andrella, Raina, Gelpas, and a guard he didn't know hurrying toward them.

"An imp," Aksel responded, pointing to the body upon the ground.

The others all gathered around. Raina stared at the creature with obvious revulsion. "Where in Thac did you find that thing?"

Aksel quickly recounted the trail that led them to the abbey, and the surprise 'guest' they found in Qualtan's quarters.

Kalyn lips curved into a lopsided smile. "That itty bitty thing gave ya that much trouble?"

Seth fixed her with a dark stare. "Go ahead. See how far shooting those little sticks of yours gets you against devils and vampires."

Kalyn glared back at him, but Andrella stepped in before anything else could be said. "Was there any sign of Abbot Qualtan?"

Seth turned his gaze to the young lady. Mixed emotions played across her face. He hadn't realized till that moment that Andrella cared for the older cleric. Seth guessed it sort of made sense. Qualtan was probably like an uncle to her.

"We didn't get a chance to search the room thoroughly, your ladyship, but Qualtan was definitely not there," Relkin reported.

Andrella tapped the side of her mouth with a finger. "Well then let's go back and search it. Perhaps we'll find some clue to Qualtan's whereabouts."

Aksel stared down at the tiny corpse on the ground between them. "If you don't mind, I'd like to take care of the body first."

Andrella glanced at him. "What do you suggest?"

Aksel pursed his lips together. "Burning it should work."

A slight smile formed across Andrella's lips. "Then that is what we shall do."

Seth watched with fascination as the young monarch pointed a finger at the imp's body and spoke two words that he had, to date, only heard from Glo. "*Radius Ardens.*"

A red-hot beam lanced from her fingertips and connected with the small body a few feet in front of her. They all stepped back as sparks flew everywhere. Abruptly the body burst into flames.

Andrella gazed around with an expression of satisfaction. "Will that do?"

Aksel gave her an appreciative nod. "Yes, that will do quite nicely."

"Well then, shall we?"

Seth fell in next to Aksel as Andrella led them all back to the abbey. His voice dropped to a whisper. "Don't look now, but I think we have *two* pyromaniacs on our hands."

Aksel nearly choked. "I'm not sure the world is quite ready for that."

On the way back to Qualtan's room, Raina explained what they had found at Falcon's. The group of them had just left the tavern when they heard the imp's death cry and came rushing up the hill.

Seth exchanged a glance with Aksel after hearing Raina's story. It did not bode well. If a second vampire had been in town for a few days, unchecked, it probably had already turned a number of people. At this point, they were most likely dealing with a full-fledged vampire epidemic.

When they reentered the abbey, the rest of its occupants stood there waiting for them. Aksel, Andrella, and Relkin stopped to explain what had happened, while Seth and the others returned to Qualtan's room.

Seth led a careful search, eventually finding a secret compartment hidden under one of the desk drawers. In it was a parchment with a short message written on it.

Good job. You did well. Meet me tonight at the usual meeting place.

The letter was dated two days ago. According to Kalyn, it was the same evening Qualtan had dinner with them all up at the keep.

"Come ta think of it, he did run off rather quick-like," Kalyn noted in retrospect.

Seth shrugged. "Most likely to meet whoever wrote this letter."

Raina took the letter from Seth and quickly read it over. "We should probably show this to the Baroness…"

"…and warn her about the undead infestation," Seth added drolly.

A lopsided grin crossed Kalyn's face. "Too bad they don't make bug spray for that."

Seth gazed at her with a wicked grin. "At least it's not snakes."

During their time hunting the Serpent Cult, Seth had found that snakes were Kalyn's worst nightmare. The young archer visibly shuddered at the thought.

"Ya had to bring that up, didn't ya?"

"Yup," Seth nodded. He strode away with the satisfaction of finally getting the last word.

14
LOST AND FOUND

I tried to warn him about that monkey claw

It was late at night, the inside of the keep's tower silent as death. A single lamp struggled to illuminate the wide first floor, its dim light fading into eerie shadows in the farthest corners.

Martan sat alone in the center of the room, adjusting the fletchings on his arrows to while away the time. Aksel and Seth had long since gone to bed, both exhausted from too little sleep the night before, and the day's adventures in vampire hunting.

Martan was thankful they hadn't included him this time. The thought of facing undead set his nerves on edge. That feeling was compounded by the fact that they failed to find any vampires. It had gotten too late, and even Martan knew better than to face such creatures after nightfall.

The gloomy archer swept his eyes around the room, his gaze halting at every shadow. He half wished he had been left in the dark like the rest of the town. The Baroness had elected to keep the matter quiet without absolute proof of an undead presence.

Both Aksel and Raina had protested her decision, the latter citing what had happened in Twin Oaks. In the end, the Baroness compromised. She had Gelpas set up a town watch, consisting of Dunwynn Sky Knights and castle guards patrolling the streets in pairs of twos and threes.

Unfortunately, that left a barebones crew at the keep itself. Thus, Kalyn and Raina had elected to stay with the Baroness and Andrella for added protection.

At the same time, Martan watched over the tower while his companions slept. Though he was also tired, his experience in the wild had taught him to remain awake with minimal sleep. Yet there was something heavy in the air this night, something that caused his eyes to droop until they were completely closed.

Bang!

Martan lurched to his feet, his heart in his throat as the sudden noise brought him wide awake. Bow in hand and arrow drawn, he swung around violently in all directions. Yet there was nothing in sight.

Bang!

There it was again. Martan spun around till he faced the stairwell to the basement. The noise had come from down there.

The hair stood on the back of his neck as Martan padded on silent feet to the basement stairs. A dim light drifted up the circular stairwell from below. It was accompanied by the sound of soft voices.

Martan gulped. *What if the vampires had dug their way underground into the keep? The Serpent Cult had done the same thing a couple of weeks ago.*

Martan's eyes narrowed as common sense took hold. *But would vampires need light?*

He struggled with his fears a few moments longer until reason won out. Either way, it didn't matter. He had promised to watch out for the others, and that was what he was going to do.

It'll more than likely get me killed in the end, Martan thought wryly.

With bow still in hand, the gaunt archer steeled his nerves and silently made his way down the stairs to whatever was waiting below.

Bang!

The world had just come into focus around Glolindir. His eyes went wide as a puff of dark smoke mushroomed up directly in front of him.

"Where's Donnie?" Elladan rushed to Glo's side, his eyes glued to the spot where their friend should have been.

Glo's mind raced through everything he had ever heard or read about teleportation, yet he couldn't recall anything like this.

Bang!

Glo started at the second explosion, another puff of dark smoke rising up before them in place of the absent Donatello.

Lloyd carefully approached the second cloud, a hand on each blade hilt. "Isn't that where he was standing right before we teleported?"

"In that very spot," Elladan agreed.

Fafnar edged up next to Lloyd, his eyes fixed on the rising smoke. "Forgive my ignorance, but is it supposed to do that?"

Glo slowly shook his head. "In a word, no. Teleportation is supposed to be clean and simple"—he waved his hands at the smoky cloud—"not explosive."

Elladan inched up to the spot where Donnie should have been standing. "It was that monkey's claw, I tell you. I told him it would bring him bad luck."

Lloyd let go of his sword hilts and narrowed an eye at the bard. "You're kidding, right?"

Elladan shifted his gaze to the young warrior and gave him a half-smile. "You never know. I've seen some pretty strange things in my time."

Glo had nowhere near the worldly experience of Elladan. He had been hidden away behind a wall of magic from the rest of the world up until a few months ago. Still, there was a difference between strange and impossible. What they were seeing now was closer to the latter, unless—unless there was dark magic involved.

The alarming idea spurred Glo into action. He stepped out of the circle and doffed his backpack. "Either way, I'm going to scry for him."

The others gathered around as the tall elf pulled a melon-sized crystal ball out of his pack. He placed it on the ground and waved his hands over it, his focus on Donnie as two magic words spilled from his lips. *"Usque Vigilantes."*

The clear crystal began to glow, illuminated by the gray clouds that formed and swirled around its inside. Yet no picture of their missing friend came to light.

Glo's brow furrowed with concentration as he waved his hands over the crystal one more. Still, the outcome was no different. Swirling clouds filled the ball, refusing to coalesce into a vision of the lost elf.

Glo tried one more time, but his concentration waned. He finally sat back and gingerly rubbed his temples. "I can't seem to locate him. There appears to be some kind of magical interference."

Elladan eyed him sharply. "You mean dark magic."

Glo responded with a curt nod. "More than likely."

A deep sigh came from the doorway behind them. Glo spun his head to see Martan standing there. The archer held his bow aloft with a nocked arrow, his face as white as a sheet. "Thank the gods it's only you."

"That's a fine hello—and mind pointing that thing somewhere else?" Elladan waved a hand at the archer.

Martan lowered his bow and un-nocked the arrow. A sheepish grin spread across his lips as the color slowly returned to his cheeks.

Lloyd stood up and grinned back at the archer. "You look like you were expecting a ghost."

Martan's expression turned abruptly grim. "More like a vampire."

Lloyd, Glo, Elladan, and Fafnar all exchanged a glance.

Fafnar threw his hands up in the air. "Correct me if I'm wrong, but weren't we only gone for a couple of days?"

Elladan shrugged at the noble, then strode over and put his arm around the archer. "Maybe you should explain to us what's going on, from the very beginning."

Aksel sat straight up in bed, a wave of dizziness momentarily washing over him. His eyes darted around the dark room. *Where am I? Did someone just call my name?*

A dim light seeped through the open doorway. A tall silhouette stood there, holding a lantern in its hand. "Aksel! Seth! Wake up. The others are back."

Aksel breathed a sigh of relief. *It's only Martan.*

Seth's voice floated in from across the hall. "People are trying to sleep here! Tell them to come back tomorrow!"

Aksel's eyes went wide as the cobwebs suddenly cleared from his brain. "Ignore Seth! Tell them we'll be right down."

The little cleric leapt out of bed, hope rising in him for the first time in days. He hadn't relished the thought of facing vampires, but with the others back, they might actually survive the encounter.

Aksel rushed toward the stairwell, nearly colliding with a half-dressed Seth. "I thought you were going back to sleep?"

The corner of Seth's mouth lifted as he finished buttoning his shirt. "Right. Like that was going to happen."

At this point, Aksel was used to Seth's brand of sarcasm. A slim smile crossed his lips. "You know, you're welcome to hunt vampires on your own if you want."

Seth didn't bat an eye as he pulled on his boots. "Nah. You'd all die without me."

Aksel narrowed an eye at his friend. "You're not wrong…"

When Seth and Aksel reached the first floor, all their friends were there to greet them—all except one.

Aksel cast a confused gaze around the room. "Where's Donnie?"

Elladan gave them a quick summary of their trip to Tarsmoor, finishing with the teleportation incident. "I tried to warn him about that monkey claw, but he wouldn't listen to me."

Seth snickered softly beside Aksel. "Monkey claw…"

Aksel cast a sidelong glance at the halfling, but otherwise chose to ignore his amusement. "Well, Donnie's whereabouts will have to wait for now—we have bigger problems to deal with at the moment."

Lloyd stood with his arms folded, his expression grim. "Martan already told us about the vampires."

Sir Fafnar stood next to Lloyd, his countenance equally grave. "Indeed. I shall gather my sky knights and we shall rout these filthy creatures out of town."

Seth regarded the Dunwynn knight dubiously. "That'll be fun when they all get turned. Don't think I've ever seen a vampire riding a hippogriff."

Fafnar stared at the halfling with obvious irritation until Lloyd placed a hand on his shoulder. "Seth's right. Creatures of the dark thrive on deceit and trickery. We cannot expect a fair fight from them."

Fafnar regarded Lloyd for a moment, then his demeanor visibly softened. "Very well, then how should we proceed?"

Aksel hesitated before answering—Fafnar's sudden change in temperament had taken him by surprise. "The Baroness wants us to be discreet. She feels the townsfolk have enough to worry about— but I'm afraid the longer we wait, the more vampires we'll have on our hands."

Seth let out a derisive snort. "Don't forget Qualtan. He's already flipped to the dark side."

Glo arched an eyebrow. "So Almax was right about him." The elf turned and reached for his pack. "I could scry for him right now if you want."

Lloyd cleared his throat. "Maybe we should report to the Baroness first?"

"Miss Andrella that much?" Seth snickered.

Lloyd cast an acid glare at the halfling. "Funny, Seth—but I still think the Baroness should be made aware of our return first."

Aksel grasped his chin and nodded. It was interesting to see this change in Lloyd. A month ago, he would have been charging head long into danger just like Fafnar. "Lloyd's right. First things first. We'll report to Lady Gracelynn and then scry for Qualtan."

Everyone agreed.

As they strode across the courtyard toward the keep, Elladan nudged Martan in the arm. "So, where's that girlfriend of yours?"

Elladan grinned as Martan's face flushed. "She's… not… my girlfriend."

Seth's lips twisted sideways. "He's right. They bicker like they're already married."

Martan's face went from flushed to bright scarlet. He began to cough violently.

Elladan patted him firmly on the back. "Easy, man. Don't die just yet—at least not until after you've said your vows."

Martan's face changed from red to white at the mention of matrimony.

Lloyd pushed his way between the two and grabbed the archer by the arm. "Don't let them bother you. Kalyn seems like a sensible girl. I'm sure marriage is the farthest thing from her mind."

A wicked grin crossed Seth's face. "Don't be too sure about that. She and Andrella have become thick as thieves. They're probably planning a double wedding."

This time, Lloyd and Martan both turned red.

Aksel had let the teasing go till now, thinking it might lighten things up. Yet as usual, Seth had taken it one step too far. "Can it, Seth. I need them focused on the battle to come, not some imagined nuptials."

The side of Seth's mouth lifted ever so slightly. "Killjoy."

Andrella had been wrestling a brush through the thick mass that Kalyn called hair when the knock came on her door. "Lady Andrella! Pardon the interruption, but the young Lord Stealle has returned with his company."

Andrella nearly dropped the brush in her hand. "Lloyd is here now?" The young lady glanced at herself in the mirror, her jaw dropping open at what she saw. "But he can't be. I'm a mess!"

Kalyn spun around in her seat and gazed up at Andrella, a mixture of relief and confusion on her face. "What do you mean a mess? You look just fine."

Andrella shifted her eyes down toward Kalyn and slowly shook her head. "Whatever I am going to do with you?"

"We'll be there presently!" Andrella yelled at the door, then grabbed Kalyn by the hand and dragged her toward the wardrobe.

A half hour passed before Kalyn and Andrella entered the side chamber off the throne room. Elladan halted his narration as all eyes fell on the two young women.

Andrella noted the appreciative stares with pleasure. Yet she was particularly pleased with the awed expressions of both Lloyd and Martan. *And Kalyn thought the 'primping' wasn't worth it.*

"Ah, Andrella, Kalyn, there you are. Come take a seat." Her mother waved to two empty chairs between Lloyd and Martan.

Andrella smiled demurely at Lloyd as he held out her chair for her. Martan took a cue from the young noble and attempted to do the same for Kalyn. Unfortunately, the young woman still had a lot to learn.

Kalyn smacked Martan's hands away. "Do I look like I can't seat myself?"

Andrella sat and shook her head silently as a round of light laughter traveled across the table. Thankfully, her mother put a quick stop to it.

"Ahem. Elladan, would you mind reiterating the highlights of your journey for the ladies?"

Elladan bowed to the Baroness. "It would be my pleasure, your grace."

The elven bard swiftly summarized what they had encountered on their trip to Tarsmoor.

Andrella was hard pressed not to smile when he described the monkey 'Gaither.' Yet her amusement swiftly died when things turned into a deadly battle. She looked at Lloyd, first with concern, and then with pride as he saved Sir Fafnar's life.

A laugh finally escaped her lips when Donnie returned with the monkey's claw.

"The critter got what he deserved, if you ask me—cute or not," Kalyn muttered under her breath.

Once Elladan finished his story, Andrella sat forward and pursed her lips. "So you think Maltar went to Lukescros?"

Across the table from her, Glo nodded. "That's where all the evidence points."

"Is that where you're headed next?"

"Once we tend to things here." The tall elf shifted his gaze to her mother. "With your permission, we'd like to try scrying for Qualtan."

The Lady Gracelynn waved a hand at him. "By all means."

Glo pulled his melon-sized crystal ball out of his pack, and placed it in the center of the large table. Andrella watched on with fascination as the tall elf waved his hands over the crystal and spoke a two-word incantation. *"Usque Vigilantes."*

The clear crystal began to glow, lighting the gray clouds that had formed inside. The mists then swirled and parted to reveal a familiar visage.

Andrella gasped. "It's Uncle Qualtan."

The old abbot's face appeared there as clear as day. Yet as Andrella looked closer, she noticed he looked different. The abbot's face appeared gaunt, and there was a haunted look in his eyes.

Everyone watched as the image panned back to reveal a dark room lit by a single candle. A shadowy figure stood next to her uncle, a knight in black armor. There was a symbol emblazoned on the knight's chest, a green tree on a yellow background.

Andrella thought it looked familiar, but couldn't quite place it. "Does anyone…"

"Shh!" Glo cut her off as a voice emanated from the crystal.

"…loading the wagons. Once they're done, we can set some spells and leave."

That was definitely her uncle, but he sounded rather shaky, as if he were frightened beyond his wits. The black-armored knight responded to him in an unearthly voice. "Very good. Now go check outside and make sure you weren't followed."

"Out—outside?" Qualtan stammered.

The black knight towered over him. "Do you have a problem with that?"

Qualtan took a step backward and held up his hands. "N-no. Not at all."

The frightened abbot spun on his heel and almost ran from the room. The crystal followed his progress as he swiftly ascended a flight of stairs and stepped through a curtained doorway. He scurried across another dark room, then opened a door and stuck his head outside. The crystal image slowly panned back to reveal a familiar storefront.

"That's Haltan's!" Elladan exclaimed.

A stunned silence felt over the room. It was broken a few moments later by her mother's harsh cry. "Gelpas, summon the castle guards! This ends now."

15

BATTLE AT HALTAN'S

There's nothing subtle about a stone golem

Lloyd led the companions straight to Haltan's, while Gelpas and Fafnar gathered their men. Elladan split off from them on the way to pick up the Boulder.

When the companions drew in sight of Haltan's, the shop appeared dark and empty, yet there was a dim light coming from one of the nearby warehouses. Glo cast a spell so they could keep in contact, then the companions surrounded the place.

Lloyd and Glo watched the front of the shop, while Seth stole around the back. Aksel turned invisible and went around the other side. Kalyn and Martan stole through the trees, down to the warehouse.

When Lloyd and Glo got there, they found a small group still loading the wagons. Yet none of them appeared to be Qualtan or the black knight. At the same time, Seth heard voices from inside the house. Thus, the heroes assumed that their quarry was still in there.

Still, Lloyd was worried that Gracelynn and her men might not arrive in time, so the companions prepared to rush the shop and warehouse if necessary.

A minute or so later, the ground around Lloyd and Glo began to tremble. Lloyd glanced back down the road and saw a huge figure lumbering their way. Two smaller figures marched beside it, one all in white.

Lloyd rushed to meet them, holding up his hands. "Whoa! Why don't you just sound a horn that we're out here?"

Elladan, Shalla, and the Boulder all drew to a halt. The white-clad bard fixed him with a semi-smile. "Well if that's what you want, I'm sure I have one in my pack somewhere."

Shalla placed a gentle hand on each of them as she stared up at the huge golem. "He does make a fair point, though. Our large friend here is not exactly subtle on his feet."

Elladan chuckled softly. "True. There's nothing subtle about a stone golem."

Lloyd gulped, his cheeks burning and his tongue tied. Though smitten with Andrella, Shalla was perhaps the most beautiful woman he had ever seen.

A sudden movement down the road was a welcome distraction. A small army of figures were headed their way with a couple of riders. The Lady Gracelynn soon drew up with Andrella, Fafnar, Gelpas, and a host of town guards.

"What's the status?" Gracelynn asked as she swung down out of her saddle.

"We've got the place surrounded," Lloyd reported. "No one's gone in or out, but according to Kalyn, they're almost done loading the wagons."

A determined smile pressed across Gracelynn's lips. "So we've got them."

Lloyd responded with a curt nod. "It appears that way. Unless anyone slipped away before we got here."

"Even if they did, they'll never get past my sky knights," Fafnar declared with firm conviction. "I sent them to watch the roads out of town."

"Excellent." Lloyd grinned at the knight for a moment, then returned his attention to the Baroness. "Lady Gracelynn, since we are already in position, would you mind if we spearhead the attack?"

Gracelynn pursed her lips together as she mulled over his request. Finally she dipped her chin. "You may. I'll have my men set up a perimeter." She motioned to Gelpas. "Captain?"

Gelpas responded with a crisp nod. "I'll have the men spread out, your ladyship."

As Gelpas strode off, Lloyd felt a light tap on his arm. He looked down at a young woman garbed in an odd outfit of bark and leaves. Lloyd guessed she was the small druid that Gracelynn had told them about. "Raina?"

A bright smile momentarily crossed her freckled face. "Yes." The smile quickly disappeared. "Do you know where Kalyn is?"

Lloyd pointed through the grove of trees toward the river. "She's watching the warehouses with Martan."

Raina smiled cheerfully once more. "Thank you. I'll go give them a hand."

The young woman stepped back, and her body twisted before his eyes. Moments later, a red wolf sped off into the woods in the direction of the river.

Lloyd watched with fascination as she disappeared into the trees until he felt another tug on his arm. He turned to see Andrella peering up at him.

"Lloyd?" she said his name softly.

Lloyd involuntarily grimaced. He knew what was coming next. Andrella had taken a more active role in their absence, and she would want to join them now. Yet there was a difference between searching the town and going into battle. He placed his arms around her slim waist, his eyes meeting hers.

"Andrella…" Lloyd paused, unsure how to phrase his concerns without starting a fight.

Yet before he could continue, she hushed him with two fingers to his lips, and spoke instead. "Promise me you won't do anything stupid."

Lloyd's brow knit in confusion. That was not at all what he had expected her to say. The young man stammered helplessly as she wrapped her arms around his neck and kissed him on the lips.

"Ah, young love," Elladan said in a mock wistful tone.

Shalla's response was equally melodramatic. "Ah yes. It brings back such fond memories."

Lloyd's cheeks began to burn once more.

Even Sir Fafnar joined in the fun at his expense. "Don't worry, fair lady, I will keep an eye on him."

Lloyd was now thoroughly baffled. Andrella hadn't said one word about coming with them. Instead she now giggled at his apparent embarrassment. Elladan and Shalla added to the mix with soft laughter of their own. Even Fafnar let out a wheezing half-snort.

Lloyd sighed, thankful for not having to fight with Andrella. A sheepish grin crossed his lips as he regarded the uncharacteristically flippant Fafnar. "You might as well join us, since you promised to 'keep an eye' on me."

"It would be my honor." Fafnar bowed while still half-wheezing in laughter.

Lloyd cast an eye on Elladan. "Okay then, my easily-amused friend. Care to lead the way?"

The bard's mouth split into a grin. "I thought you'd never ask."

Elladan strode over to the huge stone golem and held up a hand adorned with the creature's ring. "Boulder, go and 'knock' on the front door."

Seth didn't need Glo's warning to know that the Boulder was coming. The ground shaking around him was more than enough.

Already invisible, the halfling waited at the back door. He didn't have to wait long. Less than a minute later, there was a loud boom and the entire house shook.

He heard a voice cry out from the other side of the door. "What's that?"

A second calmer voice answered. "Whatever it was, I'm sure the others can handle it."

A few seconds later there was another loud boom. The house shook again.

"You sure about that?"

"Just hold your position."

A couple of seconds later there was one final boom. The shaking this time was accompanied by a loud crash.

"Sounds like the whole place is coming down!"

"You might be right about that."

I don't doubt it, Seth chuckled to himself. He'd seen firsthand what the Boulder could do back up at Stone Hill.

Figuring this was his best chance to slip in undetected, Seth carefully opened the back door. A dim light filtered out into the night as he slipped inside. Unfortunately, there were two armed men standing directly in front of the door. Both had their backs turned to him, but one glanced over his shoulder before Seth could completely close the door.

"Hey! The door just moved by itself!"

"You idiot! There's someone else in here!"

Seth hit the ground as both men spun around and swung their swords in the space above his head. Seth launched himself forward, tumbling between the two. He came up behind them, chuckling silently to himself. *Two idiots, with half a brain between them.*

Do you need help? Came the thought from Glo.

Nah, I got this.

"There's nothing here!" the one man cried.

"Well, doors don't just move by themselves."

At that moment, shouts erupted from the front room.

Seth already had an idea on how to handle these two, but he needed to keep them distracted for just a bit longer. Casting a quick spell, he cried out as he leapt for the ceiling. "Behind you, morons!"

The duo spun around back to back, both swinging at the air around them.

Clinging to the ceiling above the pair, and still invisible, Seth cast another spell, creating five duplicate images of himself. He then spun his belt around. There were six flasks of oil attached to it.

"Maybe this place is haunted," one of the men whispered.

Seth snickered as he lit all the flasks on fire and cut his belt with a swift flick of his knife. His flasks and the duplicate images all became visible at once, making it appear as if fire bombs were raining from the ceiling.

The men screamed as the bombs hit the ground, smoke and flames leaping out in all directions. Some sparks even caught their clothes, setting them partially on fire.

The two men were so busy trying to put out the flames that they didn't notice the six halflings laughing silently on the ceiling above them.

The Boulder had "knocked' so hard on the front door that it caved in half the wall. Elladan then sent the golem into the building. Lloyd and Fafnar exchanged nods, then split up, flanking the Boulder on either side.

Lloyd stepped over the debris and into the front room of the shop. The shop was dimly lit, but well enough to see the mess. Shelves were crushed, others toppled over. Dozens of items lay strewn upon the floor.

A sudden movement caught Lloyd's eye. A figure leapt from behind the wreckage and swung a sword at him.

Lloyd deftly caught it with his blade and countered the strike, throwing the man off balance. He quickly came around with his other sword, catching the attacker in his midsection. The man went down, not to rise again.

Out of the corner of his eye, Lloyd saw four more figures rush forward. One launched itself at Sir Fafnar, only to be cleaved by his axe. A second fell as four purple missiles of light wove around Lloyd, slamming into the man.

Glo's magic projectile spell. The wizard had confided to Lloyd that the spell never missed. Even if there were things in the way, it would zigzag around them.

The other two men made the mistake of attacking the Boulder. The pair went flying across the room in opposite directions, hitting the wall and falling limply to the ground.

A grim smile crossed Lloyd's lips as he moved forward. He knew what it was like to be hit by a golem. Very few could survive even one punch.

Lloyd's skin suddenly began to tingle. He stopped in his tracks as two blue rings of light surrounded his body. Lloyd tried to take a step, but couldn't even budge an inch.

At the same moment, two more figures came rushing toward him. The first fell to another rain of purple projectiles, but the second continued to close the gap between them.

Lloyd watched in horror as the dim light glinted off a sword aimed straight for his skull. The young warrior strained against his bonds, but his efforts proved in vain. Tears welled in his eyes. *It can't end like this. I never even told Andrella…*

At that moment, an icy axe interposed itself between Lloyd and his attacker. The killing strike was pushed aside, and an icy sword finished the man off.

Fafnar stepped in front of him and winked. "Guess that makes us even."

Lloyd silently thanked the gods. He tried to thank Sir Fafnar as well, but the magic prevented even his jaw muscles from moving.

At that moment, Elladan's voice rang out across the room. "Qualtan's got Lloyd pinned. Boulder, get him!"

The huge golem lumbered forward, smashing through the remaining shelves.

"Stop that thing!" A familiar voice squealed from the back of the room. Out of the corner of his eye, Lloyd could see the white-robed Qualtan. The abbot stood by the curtain to the back room.

Another figure heeded his cry, running to block the golem's advance. Yet one swipe sent that man flying into the wall, where he crumbled to a heap.

Qualtan squealed in terror, then turned and bolted through the curtained doorway. The golem lumbered after him, smashing through the wall, leaving a giant-sized hole behind. At the same moment, Lloyd's bonds fell away. The young man let out a sigh of relief. That had been far too close.

Glo and Elladan suddenly appeared at his side.

"Are you alright?" the tall wizard asked.

Lloyd gave a nod towards Fafnar. "Thanks to our friend here."

Elladan clasped Lloyd on the shoulder. "Glad to see you're okay, but Qualtan's getting away."

The elven bard took off across the room, toward the new hole in the back wall. The rest of them fell in behind, passing through the hole where the doorway used to be.

The back room reeked of smoke. The four of them pulled up short at the sight of Seth standing by himself, brushing dark soot off his clothes.

"Where's Qualtan?" Elladan asked breathlessly.

A wicked grin spread across Seth's lips. "He and his two toadies high-tailed it downstairs with the Boulder hot on their trail."

Lloyd was grim as he raced down the basement stairs. Qualtan had nearly cost him everything—his life, his future with Andrella. Maybe Gryswold had also noticed the change in his old friend. Perhaps he had even called him on it. If so, maybe Qualtan had a hand in the Baron's demise. Either way, Lloyd was determined to put an end to this.

A metallic banging echoed up the stairwell from below. The stairs took a sharp-angled turn at the bottom, opening to a large cellar with a high ceiling. A few torches lined the grey-stone walls, lighting most of the wide area. Yet dark shadows still clung to the corners of the expansive room.

Embedded in the opposite wall was a ceiling-high metallic door. The Boulder stood directly in front of it, methodically beating the door with its great stone fists.

Two armed men stood cowering to one side, their outfits smoldering as if they'd been set on fire. They turned as Lloyd and the others appeared, swords pointed in their direction.

Lloyd and Fafnar swept forward in unison, making short work of the already beleaguered cutthroats. When it was over, Lloyd peered carefully around the partially lit room.

"Let's shed some light on the subject," Elladan said with a wave of his hands. Four globular-shaped lights winked into existence, twisting and turning as if dancing in place. With a second motion, the elven bard sent the globes spiraling toward the center of the room. The cellar was now bathed in a bright glow that radiated into every corner.

The room was empty. There was no sign of Qualtan or the black knight. Across the basement, the Boulder continued its rhythmic beating. The only other exit in sight was a double cellar door at the top of a short set of stone stairs, yet those appeared to be sealed shut.

Elladan let out a short chuckle. "Looks like the Boulder's got Qualtan cornered."

The five of them strode across the room and peered past the stone golem. The metal door had some deep dents in it, but otherwise looked intact. It didn't look like it was going to buckle anytime soon.

Seth turned to Elladan as he cracked his knuckles. "This calls for finesse."

Elladan tilted his chin and nodded. "I think you're right." He held up the hand with the golem's ring. "That's enough, Boulder."

The stone golem halted mid-swing. The large creature slowly turned, and lumbered back to the center of the room. It stopped there and turned once more, its glowing eyes fixed on the stubborn metal door.

Fafnar wheezed a nervous half-laugh. "I don't think it likes being beaten."

Seth snorted. "Not my problem."

The metal door had a large handle with a circular dial above it. Seth examined the mechanism closely, then placed his ear against the door and slowly turned the dial.

"I don't like this," Glo whispered softly. "That black knight could be in there with Qualtan, or even a host of vampires."

"That could be a problem," Elladan agreed. "I'll stay with the Boulder in case we need him. Maybe you should see if Aksel wants to join us?"

"Good idea," Glo said with a tilt of his head. The tall elf's brow knit in concentration, then a slim smile touched his lips. "He's waiting right outside."

Glo went over and unlatched the cellar door. Soft morning light flooded the area as he threw open the double doors. The night had almost passed, and dawn had nearly broken.

As the tall elf retreated down the stairs, the white-robed form of Aksel appeared above him. The little cleric waved his hands in small circles as he joined them in the center of the room.

"Sense anything?" Lloyd asked. The young man's patience was wearing thin. They needed to finish with Qualtan and his undead friends, then get back to finding the Baron's heart.

Aksel glanced at him sympathetically. "Yes, in fact. There is a definite undead presence down here. Very recent and quite strong."

Everyone tensed at Aksel's declaration. Yet the discovery hardened Lloyd's resolve. Now maybe they could finally finish this.

"Quiet!" Seth hissed from the metal doorway. "I nearly have it."

Lloyd watched with growing irritation as the halfling slowly spun the dial. Seth finally stopped, then turned it the other way. After what seemed like forever, a loud *click* echoed across the basement.

"Child's play," the halfling murmured as he stood up and pressed on the handle. There was another loud click and then the door swung open with a metallic *groan*.

Light filtered into the small dark room beyond the doorway. A familiar figure in white robes cowered in the back against a second metal door. He appeared to be alone.

Seth stepped back and ushered Lloyd forward. "After you."

Lloyd strode straight at the cringing Qualtan, determined to finally get some answers.

"Careful," Aksel called from behind him, but Lloyd paid him little heed.

The exasperated young man grasped the abbot by the collar and pressed him up against the door. "I've had enough of these games. Now where did your friends go?"

Qualtan trembled with fear. "F-friends? Wh-what friends?"

Lloyd slammed the abbot's head against the metal door behind him and shouted. "I said stop playing games. Who killed the Baron—and why?"

Qualtan grabbed the back of his head, his eyes dazed as he continued to stammer. "I-I-already told you. Al-Almax did it!"

Lloyd's patience completely evaporated. He hoisted Qualtan up into the air and held him there, while speaking through gritted teeth.

"Stop lying. You are the one who's turned to the dark. Now tell us—where is the Baron's heart?"

Qualtan grabbed onto Lloyd's hands, his feet flailing wildly. Coughing and sputtering, he managed to finally choke out an answer. "The-the-Assassin's Guild—th-they did it—the-the heart-is in-Vermoorden."

The admission made Lloyd see red. His grip on Qualtan grew so tight that the abbot could no longer speak. His face turned bright red as he was slowly deprived of air.

Lloyd lost track of everything else around him until he felt a firm hand on his shoulder. He spun his head to see Fafnar standing there, the noble's eyes filled with sympathy.

"If this were Dunwynn, I'd run him through and be done with it—but this is Ravenford."

Lloyd shuddered with anger, not wanting to loosen his grip on the abysmal abbot. *After all he's done, he deserves to die.* Somewhere in the core of Lloyd's being, his resolve began to waver. *Doesn't he?*

"Gracelynn will want to question him," Elladan's voice called over his shoulder. He could hear the concern in the bard's tone.

Lloyd shuddered once more, then his anger finally abated. The young man let out a deep sigh. "You're right, of course."

He let go his hold on Qualtan, letting the abbot unceremoniously drop to the floor. Lloyd then spun around, an ironic smile on his lips. "Guess this means we're headed back to Vermoorden."

Seth's mouth twisted sideways. "Only if you believe that lying son of a—" The halfling's eyes suddenly went wide. "Lloyd, watch out!"

Lloyd spun around to see Qualtan lunging at him with a knife. His hands went immediately to his blades, but then someone pushed him out of the way. As Lloyd struggled to maintain his balance, he saw Fafnar draw his blade, and in one swift motion he ran Qualtan through. The knife fell from the abbot's hand and with one final gasp, he dropped to the floor.

Fafnar withdrew his sword and gave Lloyd a wry smile as he wiped off his blade. "Looks like I got to run him through anyway."

Lloyd tilted his head in response. "Trust me, I'm not complaining."

"Well, I am," Seth interrupted. "How am I supposed to open that second door with this body in the way?"

Fafnar responded with another half-wheeze half-laugh. He gazed down at Seth with a smirk of his own. "Far be it from us to impede your progress."

Lloyd chuckled and nodded to Fafnar. "Agreed. Help me move him out of the way so Seth can do his job."

"Thank you," Seth said with mock gratitude as the duo dragged the body out of the vault to the center of the main room.

As Aksel bent down to examine it, a loud "whoops" echoed from inside the vault. Seth came rushing out a second later, followed by a loud hissing noise. The halfling motioned to everyone frantically. "Poison gas! Everyone outside!"

16
BRING OUT YOUR UNDEAD

With frightening speed, the monster closed the distance between them

Martan sat behind Haltan's warehouse in the cover of a large, leafy hedge. He was uncomfortably close to Kalyn. A few years ago, he would have enjoyed being this close to her. He might enjoy it now, except that he knew she hated his guts. He didn't exactly blame her.

Kalyn poked him in the elbow, then pointed toward the warehouse, using her hands to sign to him.

How many do you see?

Martan turned his attention back to the warehouse. The large double doors were slightly ajar, lantern light creeping from them and illuminating the night. Martan took his time, watching the figures inside moving back and forth, listening to the soft voices drifting toward them in the darkness. Finally, he turned back to Kalyn and signed his answer.

I count six.

I count the same, Kalyn replied. Martan watched with interest as she pulled an arrow from her quiver. She checked the fletching, then laid her bow across her lap, testing the string before nocking the arrow.

Martan's heart thumped in his chest. If he knew Kalyn at all, he guessed she was planning to bust down Haltan's back door and start shooting arrows into everything that moved. It would be just like her to throw caution and safety to the wind, just for a little excitement.

"Shouldn't we get some backup…"

Before he finished whispering the sentence, Kalyn clamped her hand over his mouth, shushing him. She gave him a warning look that quickly melted away as she pulled her hand back and wiped it on her pants. Cheeks brightening, she motioned for him to follow her further back into the brush. Once there, she fixed him with an acid stare.

"Of course we'll get backup! I ain't that stupid."

Martan opened his mouth to apologize, but abruptly froze, the hair on the back of his neck standing on end. A movement caught the corner of his eye. He grasped his sword hilt as he slowly turned, coming face-to-face with a large red wolf.

Martan thought he was a goner until the wolf whined and wagged its tail. It sat down and raised a paw, then its entire body twisted and changed shape until it shifted into Raina.

The small druid girl smiled at him, then scooted closer to Kalyn. "What do we have?"

Kalyn softly snorted. "A Martan who's afraid of his own shadow."

Martan released the tension from his shoulders as Raina crossed her arms and narrowed her eyes at Kalyn.

"Oh! You mean what do we have in the warehouse?" The corner of Kalyn's mouth rose somewhat. "There are six goons in there, by our count."

Martan responded with a slow nod.

"Shouldn't be too hard for us to handle." Raina winked. "Waiting on Glo's go-ahead, I presume?"

Kalyn tapped her forehead. "Yup. Waitin' to hear him talkin' in my noggin'."

Raina rubbed her hands together eagerly. "Okay. Let's get ready to blow this ant hill wide open."

Kalyn pretended to gasp in shock. "Such vulgar language coming from a druid!"

Raina slapped her friend on the arm. She gave Martan a playful wink, then shifted back into her wolf form. She quietly trotted toward the warehouse doors, pausing inches away from them and peering in. After a moment, she wagged her tail.

Martan watched Kalyn creep from the bushes, her boots barely making a sound. He stood and followed her. He veered off to the left and she to the right, taking positions on either side of the large double doors. Raina continued to watch what was taking place beyond the doors, her black nose and furry ears twitching, occasionally rotating toward Kalyn.

After a few breathless moments, Kalyn shifted on her feet. Martan locked eyes with her. She dipped her chin in a subtle nod, which he returned before drawing his bow and readying an arrow. He watched as she lowered herself to one knee, readied her bow, then made the soft squeaking sound of a mouse.

Raina shifted forms, her shape swelling in size and bursting with muscle until a large red bear stood between Kalyn and Martan. The druid reared up on her hind legs and slammed into the doors, smashing them inward with a *Crash*! She unleashed a terrifying roar and charged in.

Martan leaned around the corner, drawing back his arrow and firing at the first man he saw. His arrow sank into the man's ribs just as one of Kalyn's arrows skewered him through the neck. Before the man could fall, Raina swatted him with a giant paw. The man went flying across the room, where he slammed into a shelf of supplies.

One of Kalyn's arrows jammed into another man's knee. He fell to the floor, his screaming silenced as Raina clamped him with her toothy maw and tossed him across the room.

Martan drew another arrow and fired at a man fumbling with a crossbow. The arrow hit home in the man's shoulder, allowing Raina to drop-kick him into oblivion like the others.

"Don't just stand there, you idiots!" Beyond Raina, a pale man shoved two others toward the bear, a snarl on his face, "Do something!"

The two men shakily drew their swords, eyes riveted on Raina.

Raina scraped her claws across the floor and roared before running forward and slapping one of the men across the room. The second one fell with Kalyn's arrow in his chest.

Unable to get a clear shot past Raina, Martan circled into the open doorway and released his arrow. It hit home in the chest of the last man, knocking him flat on his back.

Raina snorted and shook her furry head, turning toward Martan and Kalyn.

"Easier than bakin' a pie." Kalyn said as she broke cover and strutted inside.

Martan hesitated just outside the doors. "Too easy." He scanned the building from where he stood, an uneasy feeling creeping up his spine.

Raina lowered her head and started sniffing the floor. She shook her head again and scratched at the ground in a perplexed manner.

"What is it?" Kalyn moved forward to join the bear.

A movement beyond Raina captured Martan's attention. Before he could cry out a warning, the man he had just shot sailed through the air and landed on Raina's back. He raised a club over his head and smashed it down on Raina's head with a resounding *Crack!*

The druid grunted and slumped to the floor, her form shrinking until she was just a small body lying at the pale man's feet.

Martan rushed toward Kalyn. He was just able to draw another arrow before the man suddenly appeared directly in front of her. He snarled, baring a pair of long, white fangs.

"Dragon dung! Vampire!" Arrow at the ready, Kalyn pulled it back and released it into the man's gut at point-blank range.

The vampire buckled over with a loud groan, but then pulled the arrow from his body and threw it to the floor. The creature looked up at a stunned Kalyn and smiled, licking his fangs.

Martan drew back his bow and fired an arrow into the vampire's neck. The monster gagged, groping at the arrow. Kalyn drew a wooden spike from her belt and lunged forward, but the vampire was too quick. It swiped its arm through the air, backhanding Kalyn across the face with a loud *Pop!* It hit her so hard, she was tossed back outside, beyond the doors.

"Kalyn!" Martan wanted to rush to her side, but his feet would not cooperate. They firmly rooted themselves in place as the vampire broke his arrow in half and pulled it from his body. The monster dropped it to the floor and twisted its head from side to side, cracking its neck. Heart racing, Martan watched the deadly wound seal itself up, leaving nothing behind.

The vampire glared at him with a snarl. "An eye for an eye, and a neck for a neck!" In a flash, the monster appeared in front of Martan and grabbed him. Before Martan could react, the vampire bared its fangs and sank them into the exposed skin of the archer's neck.

Martan instantly grew lightheaded as blood surged to his neck and was sucked out of his body. He sank to his knees, one hand pushing against the vampire's face, and the other groping for his knife.

Only a few seconds had passed before he felt completely sapped of strength.

So this is how it ends? Martan let his arms fall to his sides as the world around him grew dark.

Kalyn sat up slowly. The world spun around her, the right side of her face throbbing with pain. She patted the ground, trying to find a weapon. As her vision cleared, her eyes fixed on the blurry image of Martan slowly sinking to the ground. The pale man stood over him, his mouth affixed to Martan's neck. It only took her a moment to understand what was happening.

"No, Martan! Get away from him, you…" Kalyn stopped short when a bright beam of red light zipped past her and directly over the vampire's head.

The vampire looked up in Kalyn's direction and snarled.

"Burn, you creep!" Andrella appeared next to Kalyn, mumbling something as she thrust her hand forward. A fire red ray leapt from her fingers and sped toward the vampire.

The monster dropped Martan to the ground and twisted, just barely avoiding the scorching hot ray of light.

"You think this is a game?" Andrella took another step forward.

This time, Kalyn heard two soft words fall from her lips in a strange language. Another fiery beam shot from Andrella's fingers.

The vampire screamed as the spell hit him square in the chest, setting his clothes on fire.

"Grilled vamp is on the menu tonight!" Kalyn shouted.

"I hope you like them well done, because I think I feel a fireball building in my fingers!" Andrella took another step forward, her hands twisting in a strange pattern.

The creature hissed and spun in a tight circle, his entire body evaporating and turning into a cloud of mist. It shot past Andrella and Kalyn and disappeared beyond the bushes outside.

Andrella reach a hand down to Kalyn. "Are you okay?"

Kalyn struggled to her feet, ignoring the question. "Please, check on Raina." She nudged her head in the druid's general direction while staggering over to Martan. Kalyn dropped to her knees next to the downed archer. She turned his face and looked at the bleeding wound in his neck. Even though her right eye was swollen shut, she could tell he was very pale. His lips were almost blue and he was barely breathing.

"No, you idiot. You made a promise, remember?" She pulled a handkerchief from her pocket and pressed it up to the wound, staunching the bleeding.

"Wake up, Martan!" She gently slapped both sides of his face with her other hand.

"Hold on, Kalyn. I can help."

Kalyn looked up and watched Raina stumble toward them with Andrella's help, blood caking a few of her dreadlocks. She squinted and grimaced as she knelt down next to Martan, reaching a hand up and resting it against her forehead. She tugged a bag from her belt and opened it.

"Fran said I might need these." She pulled a rolled parchment from the bag, along with two diamonds. She rested the diamonds on Martan's moving chest and unrolled the parchment. Speaking in the same strange language as Andrella, Raina slowly read through the scroll. When she finished, the scroll and the diamonds vanished in a flash of light.

Instantly, Kalyn's pain disappeared and her swollen eye opened. Raina sighed in relief.

Martan sat bolt upright with a gasp and looked around, his brown eyes finally coming to rest on Kalyn. "Are you all right?"

Kalyn hit him in the arm. "Of course I am! It'd take more than a sucker punch from a vampire to do me in."

Unable to help herself, she wrapped her arm around his neck and pulled him into a tight hug. She bit her lower lip as forbidden tears stung her eyes.

Martan hesitantly patted her on the back. "I'm… okay."

"Only thanks to Raina and Andrella… and Fran!" Kalyn shoved away from him, "Your toes were almost six feet under the daisies!"

Raina stood to her feet. "You're both lucky. That was just a vampire spawn."

Kalyn cocked her head to one side. "Vampire spawn?"

"One that's been recently turned, and hasn't quite come into its full power. If that had been a true vampire, we'd all be dead."

Kalyn touched the side of her face. "For a wimpy little spawn, that thing hit pretty darn hard."

Raina's gaze remained grim. "If a real vampire'd hit you, you wouldn't have a head left."

Kalyn's eyes went wide. She exchanged a horrified glance with Martan.

Raina shifted her attention to Andrella. "It was a good thing you came when you did."

Andrella smiled, hands resting on her hips. "It was a good thing that vamp spawn left when it did. That was my last spell!"

Andrella's admission abruptly lightened the mood. Kalyn let out a sigh, her lips bending sideways. "A good thing, too! A fireball in a warehouse is almost as bad as one in a lighthouse."

Martan snorted, actually cracking a smile for the first time since he and Kalyn had been reunited.

Raina, however, did not appear to get the reference. Her countenance remained stern. "Which way did the vamp go?"

She nodded as Andrella and Kalyn both pointed in the same direction, "It's probably too late, but I'll try to track him down."

With that, she shifted into a wolf and darted off.

"Be careful!" Everyone shouted after her.

Aksel and the others fled outside just ahead of the ever-growing cloud of poisonous green fumes. A group of town guards awaited them there, led by the Lady Gracelynn, Captain Gelpas, and Shalla.

The Baroness hurried over to them, her tone frantic. "Andrella wasn't down there with you, was she?"

Aksel glanced around at his companions. "Not as far as I know."

Lloyd pushed his way forward, his face suddenly pale. "Has something happened to her?"

Gracelynn and Gelpas exchanged a frantic glance. "We don't know. She told each of us she was with the other."

Aksel's hand went to his chin. He couldn't say he was surprised. Andrella had made it clear she wanted to be involved in the assault, but Gracelynn had forbidden it. While Aksel did not agree with Andrella's methods, he had to admit it was rather clever.

"Let me check with the others," Glo offered. The tall elf's brow knit with concentration as he mentally reached out to Kalyn. Due to the nature of the contact, Aksel heard every word.

Kalyn, is Andrella there with you?

The young Deepwooder responded immediately. *Yup! She's right here.*

Is she okay?

Yup! Fine n' dandy. Funny, I was just about ta reach out ta ya…

Just a minute, Glo interrupted her. "She's okay. She's with the others down at the warehouse."

Gracelynn threw up her hands in exasperation. "Whatever am I going to do with her? Tell her to get back here at once!"

Aksel had to sympathize with the monarch. He knew loss only too well, having been orphaned at a very young age. For a long time, he hadn't let anyone get close, but Seth and Glo had changed all that.

Aksel compensated by promising himself that he would never lose anyone again. That's why he took up leadership of the group. Someone with common sense had to watch over them. The burden rested heavy on Aksel's small shoulders, yet he couldn't imagine how much more difficult it must be for a parent.

While these thoughts raced through Aksel's mind, Glo relayed Gracelynn's message to Kalyn. *The Baroness is having a fit. Andrella might want to get back here.*

Kalyn paused a moment before responding. *That might not be the best idea. We sorta ran into a vampire… spawn. Andrella scared it away with some bing, bang, boom fiery magic-ray stuff, but now we found a vamp coffin. Raina wants ta burn it first, then we'll all head up back yer way.*

Aksel did his best not to react. Kalyn and the others were extremely lucky it had only been a vampire spawn. If it had been a true vampire, they would all be dead. He exchanged a glance with Seth, who was also part of the mental link. The halfling rolled his eyes, but otherwise remained silent.

Thankfully Glo was on the same page as the two of them. The elf purposely left out the more perilous details of the encounter. "She says she'll be back soon. It appears they found a vampire coffin, and Raina wants to burn it first."

Unfortunately, Glo's omissions were not quite enough. Horror spread across the Baroness' face at the mention of the word vampire. She barked at the Captain of the Guard, "Gelpas, take some men and get down there right now!"

"Right away!" Gelpas responded, motioning for three guards to follow him across the field.

"I'm going, too!" Lloyd cried, starting after them.

"Wait, Lloyd!" Glo yelled. "The vampire's gone. In fact, it was Andrella who scared it away with fire rays."

Aksel's brow raised in astonishment. He'd heard Andrella had studied with Maltar, but didn't realize she had advanced as far as wizard spells of the second order.

Shalla's lyrical laugh echoed around them. "That definitely sounds like Andrella. The other night, she was throwing around spells at the Golden Golem—broke up a fight with those Dunwynn knights."

Fafnar's jaw dropped in disbelief. "My sky knights?"

Shalla cast a withering glance at the noble. "Yes. Albeit, they'd been in their cups, but they were still rather rude nonetheless."

Fafnar's face reddened with embarrassment, but then hardened with annoyance. "My apologies, good woman. You have my word, they will receive a stern reprimand for their abysmal behavior."

Shalla's expression softened at the noble's unexpected response.

Aksel found himself amazed as well. Fafnar had changed markedly since their first meeting. While still a bit stiff, his haughtiness had all but disappeared. According to Glo and Elladan, Lloyd was directly responsible for the transformation. His good heart and genuine nature seemed to win over even the most arrogant of folks.

Yet the unassuming Lloyd appeared unaware of his effect on people. At the moment, he was beaming with pride at Andrella's accomplishments. "So she stopped the fight?"

Shalla grinned at the ardent young man. "She sure did."

The news seemed to mollify Gracelynn somewhat. She appeared calmer, though lines of worry were still etched across her brow. "Well, Maltar always said she had talent. I just wish she was a bit more practiced."

The monarch's eyebrows raised slightly as an idea came to her. She cast a sly glance at Glo. "Perhaps you could work with her, Glolindir?"

The color abruptly drained from Glo's cheeks. He hesitated before answering. "I've never had a student before, but I can try."

A delicate smile formed across Gracelynn's lips as she reached out and grabbed the elf's arm. "Anything you can do would be greatly appreciated. She's always been headstrong, but since her father's death she's gotten even more so. If she continues down this path without proper guidance, I'm afraid of what might happen to her."

Glo gulped, his face strained with uncertainty. The wizard had certainly gained confidence since Aksel first met him. He was far more seasoned now, but Aksel imagined teaching to be a daunting task. Furthermore, Glo's father had been his first instructor. Aksel could only imagine the issues that might raise for his elven friend.

A forced smile touched Glo's lips as he nodded to Gracelynn. "I'll do my best."

Gracelynn responded with a genuine smile and a squeeze of the wizard's arm. "Thank you, Glolindir. Your involvement eases my mind."

That makes one of us, came the blithe thought from Seth.

Aksel bit his tongue as not to laugh, while Glo cast daggers at the halfling with his eyes.

"I'll talk to her as well, Lady Gracelynn," Lloyd said. The young man resumed his stride after Gelpas.

"Hang on there, Lloyd," Elladan called after him. "We still might need you here. We haven't found the guy in black armor, and you have that holy sword now."

Lloyd halted in his tracks, then spun around with a sheepish grin. "Oops. I nearly forgot about that."

Aksel frowned as he gazed from Lloyd to Elladan. "And when were you planning on telling me about this?"

In the rush to head off Qualtan's escape, they hadn't had time to adequately prepare themselves. They should have had wooden stakes and holy water, at the very least, but a holy weapon was a veritable gift from the gods. A vampire wouldn't spontaneously heal from the wounds inflicted by such a weapon.

Elladan stared back at Aksel with a partial smile. "It was just a little something I picked up for him in Tarsmoor."

Aksel responded with a grim nod. Elladan's foresight might just end up saving them from this impromptu situation.

"What about Qualtan?" Gracelynn interjected. Her mind now eased, it had returned to the wayward abbot.

Fafnar hung his head. "I'm sorry, Lady Gracelynn, but I'm afraid he's dead."

Gracelynn's face went white, a sudden gasp escaping her lips. "What happened?"

Lloyd strode over and placed a hand on Fafnar's shoulder. "Qualtan tried to stab me in the back, your ladyship. Fafnar was only trying to protect me."

The Dunwynn noble gazed up at Lloyd, his eyes filled with gratitude.

Mixed emotions played across Gracelynn's face, ranging from horror to sadness. The hint of a tear welled in her eye as she let out a long sigh. "Ah well, you did what you had to. It appears he was farther gone than we thought."

Aksel watched the monarch with sympathy. In the last few days, she had lost her husband and one of her oldest friends. "Lady Gracelynn, we will bring up his remains so that you may decide what to do with him."

Gracelynn gave Aksel a slight smile. "That would be most appreciated."

Aksel nodded, then swept his eyes around the group. "The poison gas has probably dissipated by now. If the black knight is still inside, he's probably in that second vault—either dead from poison, or undead."

"My money's on undead," Seth noted dryly.

Aksel tilted his head to one side. "Most likely. If that is the case, then it's probably best if just Lloyd and I go down there."

No one looked happy with Aksel's declaration. Fafnar in particular began to object, but Seth cut the Dunwynner off.

"Fine by me. I like my blood right where it is."

Fafnar stared at the halfling for a moment, then firmly shut his mouth.

Elladan narrowed an eye at Aksel, then pulled off the Boulder's ring and held it out to him. "Suit yourself, but you're probably going to want this."

Aksel climbed cautiously down the steep basement steps, waiting for his eyes to adjust to the dim light. Elladan's 'dancing lights' had long since run out, leaving just the glow from a few scattered torches. Still, his gnomish vision was better adapted to the dark than a human's.

The cellar was empty. There was no trace of the poisonous green cloud that had erupted from the vault and driven them from the basement. The little gnome gingerly sniffed the air. Even the noxious odor that accompanied the cloud was gone.

"Is it safe?" Lloyd whispered from behind him.

"As far as I can tell," Aksel murmured over his shoulder.

An eerie silence surrounded the duo as they trod carefully across the floor. They passed the Boulder, the stone golem as motionless as a statue, its glowing eyes fixed on the open vault doorway. Qualtan's body still lay at its feet in the same exact position they had left it.

Aksel nudged his head at the body and whispered, "Why don't you drag that over to the door while I take a peek in the vault."

"Be careful," Lloyd whispered as he sheathed his weapons. He grabbed the dead abbot's arms and slowly dragged him across the stone floor toward the exit to the outside.

Meanwhile, Aksel continued his slow advance. He halted in front the entrance to the vault. Aksel warily peaked inside, his keen eyes sweeping across the small room beyond. At first he saw nothing, then his eyes fixed on a small cloud of dark vapor hovering near the second vault door.

"Lloyd—we're not alone!" Aksel cried as he slowly backed away from the vault.

The vaporous cloud followed him, changing as it went. It swiftly expanded into human form—a man dressed in black with long dark hair, eerie red glowing eyes, and a pale complexion. The creature snarled at him, revealing two large fangs protruding from its upper jaw.

"Aksel, get back!" Lloyd cried from across the room.

Yet before Aksel could move, the creature lunged forward and grasped his arm in a vice-like grip. A strange sensation came over the little gnome. He felt as if a part of him was being pulled out of his body. A sudden weariness came over him, his head feeling light and his knees buckling.

Abruptly, the creature let go. It vaulted backwards, hissing loudly as a flaming black blade swiped at the place where it had just been standing. Lloyd's tall form suddenly appeared in front of Aksel, the blade in his right hand crackling with fire, the blade in his left glowing a brilliant white.

Aksel staggered backwards, his body weak and achy, as if he were sick. Even speaking felt like a chore, but he had to warn his friend. "Be careful... Lloyd! That's a... true vampire."

The tall man responded with the briefest of nods. The vampire and Lloyd slowly circled each other, the creature's red eyes fixed on the glowing white sword in its opponent's left hand.

Abruptly Lloyd feinted with his black blade, then lunged at the creature with his holy sword. The vampire underestimated Lloyd's speed, the warrior catching the creature in the shoulder before it could move out of the way.

The blade left a gaping hole in the creature's shoulder, though no blood seeped out from the wound. The vampire hissed in a deathly voice as it pulled away. "You'll regret that, mortal. I'll drain your life essence, too."

Aksel knew that was no idle threat. The creature moved in again, swiping at Lloyd from various angles while avoiding his holy blade. The young warrior scored numerous cuts with his flaming blade, but the vampire just shrugged them off. Each wound healed almost as quickly as it was made.

Aksel had to do something before the creature overcame Lloyd. With a great effort, he forced himself to stand straight. The little cleric then slowly backed away until he hit something solid. Aksel gazed upward, the massive form of the Boulder towering above him.

At that same moment, the vampire finally broke through Lloyd's guard. It grabbed his wrist, twisting the black blade right out of his hand.

Lloyd flailed at the creature with his gleaming white sword, forcing it to let go and draw back. Yet the damage had already been done. The young warrior staggered away, reeling as if the wind had been knocked out of him.

The vampire bared its fangs in a wicked grin. "I told you I would drain you."

With frightening speed, the monster closed the distance between them. It knocked Lloyd's other blade from his hand and grasped him by the throat.

Aksel watched with horror as the young man slumped in the vampire's grasp, his skin visibly paling and dark circles forming beneath his eyes. Realizing it might already be too late, Aksel gave in to gravity while grasping the golem's ring in his hand. He hit the floor with a *thud*, but forced himself to speak nonetheless. "Go… help… Lloyd…"

The glow in the Boulder's eyes flashed, then the creature stepped over him and lumbered forward.

The vampire leaned in to finish its prey, but looked up as the Boulder closed on it. The creature paused a moment, then negligently tossed Lloyd off to the side. The young man slammed into the wall with a loud *crunch*, and slid to the floor in a heap.

The vampire then turned to face its new opponent, throwing up its arms and covering its face. Moments later, two great fists slammed into it from either side.

Bam! Bam!

Aksel had seen those same strikes stun a giant serpent, yet the vampire appeared unfazed. It dropped its arms with a hiss, then lightning-quick struck, back at the huge golem.

A pale fist landed in the Boulder's midsection with a loud *crack*. The force of the blow sent the golem staggering back a few steps. Small pieces of the stone creature chipped off from the point of impact, falling to the ground at its feet.

Aksel's eyes went wide with disbelief. *This is bad. Really bad.*

The Boulder had barely righted itself as the vampire moved in for a second strike. Suddenly a red-hot beam arced across the basement. It caught the vampire in the chest, causing it to recoil. A sharp cry escaped the creature's lips.

It felt that!

Aksel glanced over his shoulder. Glo stood on the outside steps bathed in an aura of sunlight, looking like an angel descended from the heavens.

Though the wound Glo inflicted was only temporary, its effect sent a shock of renewed vigor coursing through Aksel's veins. Ignoring the pain in every limb, he forced himself up as he pushed his palm outward.

"*Lux... acribus.*" The two words rolled off his tongue as a ray of white light shot from his outstretched palm. The blinding beam raced across the cellar, catching the vampire in the torso. The creature screamed louder this time.

Before it could recover, the Boulder swung at it again.

Bam! Bam!

Unprepared this time, the vampire reeled from each blow. Still staggering, the nearly indestructible creature was caught off-guard when a figure in red suddenly appeared behind it. A white blade flashed in the dark, slicing straight through the vampire's abdomen.

The undead creature stared in disbelief at the blinding blade sticking out of its chest. It screeched in agony, the horrific sound sending continual chills up Aksel's spine as it reverberated off the cold basement walls.

Lloyd held the blade there until the creature burst into flames, then pulled it out and fell back to the ground. The vampire continued to burn until its body collapsed to the basement floor. Moments later, there was nothing left but a pile of ash.

17
A MATTER OF TRUST

It's a thankless job

Andrella could feel the butterflies in her stomach as Gelpas escorted them back to her mother. The Captain had been curt with her, his stern gaze more than enough to express his disapproval.

Andrella respected Gelpas almost as much as her father. He had always been there for her family. He practically was family. Seeing that she had disappointed him upset her a lot. Still, his silent ire was nothing compared to what awaited her at Haltan's.

As soon as she laid eyes on her mother, she could tell she was in big trouble. Gracelynn's expression was calm and collected, though her raised eyebrows hinted at her unspoken displeasure. Her mother's gaze swept over her, making sure she was alright.

Once Gracelynn was satisfied, she fixed Andrella with a sharp, cold stare. "There will be consequences."

Andrella couldn't help but cringe at how even and collected her mother sounded. She would have preferred that Gracelynn yell at her. The young lady's lips formed into a pout. *She doesn't understand! If I hadn't been there, Kalyn, Martan, and Raina might have died.*

Andrella opened her mouth to say as much, but Shalla appeared at her side, gently taking her by the elbow. "Andrella, do you have a moment?"

Shalla smiled at Gracelynn as she pulled Andrella closer to the house with Kalyn and Raina. Martan stepped forward in Andrella's place, and launched into a report of everything that had happened at the warehouse.

Kalyn took a deep breath and blew it all out as the girls formed a loose circle. "Wow. Yer mom looks ready to chop wood with ya."

Shalla shushed her. "Someday, you'll be a mom too, then you'll understand." She turned to Andrella. "Learn to pick your battles. Your mother is under a lot of stress, and there is no point in arguing with her."

Andrella crossed her arms and let out a defiant *humph*. "Martan might have died if I hadn't gone!"

Shalla's cheeks lifted as her lips pressed together. "Everyone will understand that in due time, but you gave your mother quite the scare. Give her time to cool off." Shalla's mouth softened into a warm smile. "Like I said, you'll be a mom someday too, and then you'll understand."

"It's a thankless job."

Everyone looked at Seth. The halfling leaned against the nearby house, his arms folded.

Kalyn gasped mockingly. "Short stack! I didn't know you were a mother!"

Seth's eyes dropped to her feet. "Is that a snake?"

"Where?" Kalyn shrieked as she leapt away from where she stood. The young woman frantically scanned the ground, her face darkening as she realized she'd been had.

Kalyn cast an acid glare at the halfling and grumbled, "I should've let that orc squeeze you to death."

A wicked grin spread across Seth's mouth, but before Kalyn could say anything further, a sudden scream split the air.

The sound sent a shiver up Andrella's spine. She whirled around, counting heads. "Where's Lloyd?"

Shalla placed a hand on Andrella's shoulder. "He and Aksel went back into the basement."

"And Glo just went down after them!" Elladan's attempt to mollify her was obvious, though she could detect a note of apprehension in his voice.

A second scream made Andrella spin toward the basement door, but Shalla's grip on her shoulder tightened before she could move. The bardess leaned in close. "Easy, Andrella. You're in enough trouble already."

Despite Shalla's discretion, Gracelynn already guessed her daughter's intentions. She spoke to her in a commanding tone. "Andrella, you must stay with the rest of us!"

Yet Andrella had already made up her mind. She swatted Shalla's hand away as she marched forward. "What we need to do is get down there and help."

Before she'd gone two steps, Kalyn blocked her path. "Hold yer bonfires, blondie! Aksel is a bonafide undead expert. If anyone can handle things that go bump in the night, it's him and Lloyd. Besides… you told me you was fresh outta spells."

Andrella paused, biting her lower lip.

"Not to mention, Seth ain't goin' down there, and that should say something." Kalyn jerked her thumb back at the halfling standing next to the basement door.

Andrella glanced around at the many eyes staring her way. Self-doubt momentarily gnawed at her, but then she swiftly brushed it aside. *Don't they get it? I finally found a keeper. Lloyd is one in a million. I'm not about to lose him now!*

She opened her mouth with a snappy retort, but stopped as a blood-curdling scream erupted from Haltan's basement. "That does it! I'm going down there."

Andrella shoved Kalyn aside, and rushed for the basement door, but before she got two steps, Raina snagged her by the dress sleeve.

"Wait! That wasn't a human scream."

Andrella jerked her arm away from the druid, charging ahead

once more. Just as she drew up next to Seth, Glolindir's head popped out of the entryway.

There were thick creases across the elf's brow as he gazed at Seth, and then past the girls toward Martan. "Would you give me a hand down here?"

Kalyn drew up to Andrella's side. "What happened?"

Andrella's heart pounded against her chest. "Is Lloyd okay?"

Glo shot them a quick look, his eyebrows knit with concern, eyes shifting with calculated thought. "I'll let Lloyd and Aksel explain that when they get up here."

Seth and Martan followed Glo back down into the cellar, while everyone waited breathlessly outside. After what seemed like hours, Seth stumbled out with Aksel. The small gnome was barely able to stand on his own.

Andrella peered at him closely. He looked older somehow. Moments later, Glo and Martan stumbled through the entryway with Lloyd hanging on their shoulders. The hair around his temples had grayed, his skin paled.

"Lloyd!" Andrella cried as she rushed forward. The young man jerked his head up at the sound of her voice.

"Lloyd, what happened to you?" Andrella swooped in and took Lloyd's arm from Martan, looping it over her own shoulders.

"V-vampire," Aksel groaned as Seth helped him sit down. "Lloyd killed it… but it drained our… life essence."

Raina knelt down next to Aksel, looking him over carefully. "Not all of it, thank goodness, but enough that you need to be fixed up as soon as possible. If not, the effects could be permanent." She glanced up at Andrella and cringed, her expression mournful. "Unfortunately, Fran only gave me one scroll."

Andrella's stomach churned, her mind racing as she tried to think of something. Yet nothing would come, her emotions raging so loud it was impossible to think. With nowhere else to turn, she looked at her mother. "Can you help them?"

Gracelynn's eyes were wide with horror. She took a deep breath and slowly shook her head. "I'm sorry, I cannot. However, Huorgan at the temple can. I suggest they be taken there immediately."

"Can't it wait?" Lloyd struggled to stand up straighter, taking some pressure off Andrella's shoulders. "We still haven't found… the black knight."

Andrella's mouth fell open, but Kalyn laughed. "Lloyd, yer tougher than rocks, but not that tough!"

Andrella gave the young woman a grateful nod as she pulled Lloyd closer. "Exactly! The state you're in, what good would you be if you found him? You can barely stand."

Fafnar strode up, taking Lloyd's other arm from Glo and looping it around his shoulders. "She is correct, my friend. It's in your best interest to be healed first and foremost."

"So, it's clear down there?" All eyes turned to Seth. The halfling knelt next to Aksel on the opposite side from Raina.

Aksel nodded with some effort. "Should be… though we… never got to… the second vault."

"Don't worry about it!" Elladan gave them a nonchalant wave accompanied by that familiar half-smile. "You two run—well, walk— along and get healed. The rest of us can handle things here."

Aksel sighed and tugged the golem ring off his finger, shakily holding it out to Elladan. The bard took it, patting the little cleric's hand.

Lloyd slowly pulled his arm away from Andrella. "I can walk."

Andrella gazed at him with disbelief. *Gods, he's stubborn!*

Still, she couldn't help admiring his determination. It was one of the things she loved about him. Andrella put her hands on her hips, doing her best to suppress a smile. "Well, I'm coming with you anyway."

Fafnar nodded toward Aksel. "If I may suggest such, my lady, perhaps you could help our friend cleric while I assist Lloyd?"

Dropping her arms, Andrella looked to Aksel as Raina and Seth helped the gnome stand. He looked so frail and shaken right now, a far cry from his normal, steadfast self. Andrella smiled at him reassuringly. "Oh, of course. It would be my pleasure."

Andrella stooped and took Aksel by the arm, placing another hand around his shoulders. She then gazed back at Lloyd. Thankfully, he had accepted Fafnar's assistance without any further complaints.

Andrella cast a furtive glance over at her mother. She could see the deep concern in her eyes as the four of them set off at a slow pace toward the temple. Andrella suddenly felt terrible for making her worry so. She was starting to understand what Shalla meant about being a mom.

Fafnar steadied Lloyd as they took the lead. "So, first a dragon, now a vampire? The tally marks are adding up. Not bad, my friend."

Lloyd managed a smile, a small thing that made Andrella feel better.

Those two are surprisingly chummy. Andrella couldn't believe the change in Fafnar. She knew it was all thanks to Lloyd. It made her beam with pride.

While the duo continued to banter, her thoughts strayed to the future. *Lloyd is going to make a great diplomat someday. He's still a little rough around the edges, but I'll smooth those out.*

Aksel stumbled, but Andrella caught him. As she steadied the little cleric, Andrella wondered how much life the vampire had drained from the both of them. She didn't know vampires could do such a thing at all, until now.

She glanced back at Lloyd, her eyes drifting to the silvery locks at his temples. A delicate smile crept across her lips. *He looks pretty distinguished like that. We are going to get this fixed today, but… it's nice to know he is going to age like fine wine.*

Soft morning light swept through the square opening that led down into the basement. The warm rays illuminated the cold stone stairs and a small portion of the cellar below. Beyond that, all grew quickly dim.

Seth led the way down the steep steps. Kalyn and Martan, with swords drawn, followed the halfling down. Neither looked comfortable—Kalyn in particular held a long wooden spike in her off hand.

"Can ne'er be too careful," she whispered before descending the stairs.

Raina went immediately after her, then it was Glo's turn.

Glo took a step down, but paused as the vision of a pale creature with long white fangs and evil red eyes flickered through his mind. The creature abruptly morphed, in his mind's eye, into a knight in black armor with the symbol of a green tree on its chest. The image sent a shiver running down Glo's spine.

A gentle touch on his shoulder nearly sent him leaping out of his skin. "Are you alright?"

Glo turned to see Shalla and Elladan gazing at him with concern. He arched an eyebrow at the comely duo. "I'm fine."

The elven wizard resumed his descent into the darkness, but truth be told, he wasn't fine. Glo hadn't been quite himself since Elistra had disappeared nearly a week ago. He had grown quite close to the blonde seeress, and her abrupt departure had shattered his self-confidence. With her at his side, he could face almost anything, but now he felt strangely hollow.

Glo stopped at the base of the stairs, waiting for his eyes to adjust to the dull light. Between the Serpent Cult and the Baron's assassination, he hadn't had time to think about Elistra. Yet for some reason, his feelings chose now to bubble to the surface. Glo grimaced at his emotional weakness. *There is too much at stake right now. I must remain focused.*

The elf's eyes had grown accustomed to the flickering torch light. Seth, Kalyn, Martan, and Raina fanned out before him. Just beyond stood the hulking form of the Boulder, at the spot where the vampire had fallen. Dim shadows filled the rest of the basement, but he could clearly see the door to the second vault still lay closed.

"Cras Placerat." A pair of voices behind him spoke the spell tongue in perfect unison. A flood of light expanded outward to all corners of the room as two sets of quadrupled glowing spheres spiraled past the tall elf.

"Phew." Martan let out a sigh of relief.

Kalyn nudged the grim archer in the arm and admonished him quietly. "Stop being such a baby."

A faint smile crossed Glo's lips. He had momentarily forgotten that humans couldn't see through the shadows like elves.

Glo glanced over his shoulder as Elladan and Shalla exchanged a grin. It was most likely at Martan's expense, but they looked so happy together.

Glo's eyes went wide, the answer to his emotional dilemma suddenly obvious. Elladan and Shalla—Kalyn and Martan—they were the reason his feelings had resurfaced. The two bards had been close from the moment they met. As for the archers, Glo had seen them watch each other when they thought no one was looking. Though they were loathe to admit it, there was definitely something between them.

A movement in the corner of his eye caught Glo's attention. Elladan and Shalla drew up on either side of him, the elven bard holding up his hand and giving Glo a conspiratorial wink. "Don't worry. If anything moves, I'll sick the Boulder on it."

A genuine smile spread across Glo's lips as he noted the golem's ring on Elladan's finger. Though the bard had misread the source of his anxiousness, Elladan was ever the faithful companion.

Shalla, on the other hand, was frighteningly discerning. She slipped her arm through the crook of Glo's elbow and whispered in his ear, "It's okay to miss her."

Glo arched an eyebrow at the bardess. *Is it that obvious?*

He was saved from responding by Seth. The halfling's semi-hushed voice echoed across the stone walls of the cellar. "Gonna open that second door."

"Everyone be ready," Elladan added.

Glo gave Shalla a slight smile and patted her hand before extracting his arm. Everyone then fanned out, weapons ready as Seth fiddled with the vault door.

The elven wizard found a spot that gave him a clear angle to the second vault. Yet as he tried to focus on a spell, his thoughts wandered back to a heart-shaped face with honey-blonde hair and an amazing pair of violet eyes.

Stop that, Glo admonished himself.

"Got it," Seth announced as the wizard wrestled with his wayward thoughts.

Everyone tensed as the halfling heaved the vault door open. The light from the spinning globes revealed another small room identical to the first vault. That room was empty, though, except for a long, fancy wooden box.

"It's another vamp coffin," Kalyn hissed, sword and spike leveled at the ornate container.

No one moved until Elladan strode past everyone and waved them all to stand back. The bard then pointed at the coffin and two simple words fell from his tongue. "Boulder smash."

Glo and the others moved swiftly aside as the large stone golem lumbered past them. They all watched silently as it shambled through the first vault and stopped over the lone coffin. The Boulder then raised its two great fists and brought them down with terrific force on the box at its feet.

Crack!

The coffin splintered into dozens of pieces, debris flying in every direction. Glo had to duck as a huge chunk of wood came careening toward him. When he looked back up, the Boulder stood over the remains of an empty coffin.

Glo let out a heavy sigh, quietly relieved that the black knight wasn't there. He hadn't exactly relished the thought of facing the creature without Lloyd and Aksel. Still, it begged the question, where had the knight gone?

Elladan called off the Boulder as Raina went to inspect what was left of the coffin. The rest of them gathered around the curly-topped druid as she cast a spell over the wooden remnants. White circles of light formed around her hands as she swept them from one end of the coffin to the other. When she was done, she glanced around the gathering. "This belonged to a full-fledged vamp, just like that first coffin we found."

Kalyn's hands went to her hips as she gazed at Raina with a tri-umphant smirk. "So we were right about there being two vamps in town."

"It would appear so," Raina agreed, though she didn't seem as pleased as her friend.

Elladan, on the other hand, seemed to share Kalyn's enthusiasm. "Well that's one down…"

"…and still one too many to go," Seth finished for him.

Elladan chuckled at the halfling. "Can't argue with that, but at least he'll never use this coffin again."

Raina's expression remained unenthusiastic. "That's all well and good, but I wouldn't be surprised if it has a second coffin somewhere nearby. Albeit, probably not as fine as this one, but still it would suffice."

Elladan's smile faded until Shalla strode up and interlocked arms with him. "Still, we did good here. The shop is clear, and we found Qualtan. Guess all that's left is taking his body up to Lady Gracelynn."

Seth swept his eyes around the cellar as he waved the rest of them toward the exit. "You go ahead. I'm gonna take another look around."

Kalyn folded her arms and eyed the halfling curiously. "Looking fer traces of that black knight?"

Seth's mouth twisted sideways. "Even vamps don't just disappear."

"Fine." Kalyn nodded to the rest of them. "Y'all go ahead. I'm gonna stay down here with short stack."

Raina placed an arm around Kalyn's shoulder. "I think I'll stay as well, then."

Elladan shrugged. "Suit yourselves."

The bard led the rest of them out of the basement, Martan stopping to pick up the dead abbot's body. The Lady Gracelynn, Captain Gelpas, and a group of guards awaited them outside. Martan carefully placed the abbot's body down on the grass, but as the morning light hit him, his features changed before their eyes.

Gracelynn gasped. "That's not Qualtan."

Glo bent down with Elladan and Shalla to examine the body. It was indeed not the abbot, but instead someone roughly disguised to look like him. Yet it had appeared just like the abbot earlier.

Glo grew angry at himself as the truth hit him. He peered up at the Lady Gracelynn. "My apologies, your ladyship. It was most likely a spell, one that has since faded."

Shalla placed a gentle hand on the wizard's arm. "I think the dim light of the basement helped to draw out the charade."

Gracelynn's eyes were soft as she gazed down at them. "It's alright, my friends. We caught a glimpse of him during the battle, and it did appear to be Qualtan."

The Baroness let out a weary sigh. Dark circles had formed under her eyes. Gelpas held out his arm to the exhausted monarch. "Your ladyship, we've been up all night now."

Gracelynn stifled a yawn and gratefully took his arm. "You are correct, Captain. I think it best we retire back to the keep for now."

Glo, Elladan, and Shalla all stood up. The bard executed a deep bow to the monarch. "Go ahead, milady. We'll stay here in case Seth finds anything else."

Gracelynn looked at them with a genuine if weary smile. "Thank you all for your help."

Gelpas then led the Baroness and the castle guards back toward the road. In the meantime, Glo continued berating himself. "I should have known that wasn't Qualtan. Outside of Maltar, he might have been our best bet to find the Baron's heart."

Shalla gave him a sympathetic smile. "You really need to stop being so hard on yourself." She glanced at Elladan. "Tell him."

Elladan gazed at him with that familiar semi-smile. "She's right you know. Don't worry, my friend. We'll find him."

Glo wanted to thank the pair for their support, but was interrupted by a shout from the basement. It was Kalyn. "Come on down here, y'all! Seth found something!"

Elladan's half smile turned into a grin. He clasped Glo on the shoulder. "See, what did I tell you?"

Shalla grabbed Glo's arm as Elladan strode back toward the house. She called after the bard, "Give us a minute, would you, love?"

"Don't be too long," Elladan cried back as he disappeared down the basement steps.

Shalla spun Glo around, then stepped back and looked him over. Her penetrating gaze left Glo feeling partially confused and partially embarrassed.

"What is this about?" he asked her tentatively.

The bardess pressed her lips together and placed her hands on her hips. "I heard what happened with Elistra. You do realize she was just trying to protect you, don't you?"

Glo grimaced and hung his head in resignation. "I didn't at first, but I've come to realize that."

Shalla's expression visibly softened. "Do you have any idea how hard it is to love someone like that? Enough to let them go?"

A sheepish smile crept across his lips. "I suppose so. I-I just wish she had trusted me enough to tell me the truth."

A hint of moisture appeared in the corner of Shalla's eyes. "Oh, Glolindir. If she had done that, she might have never left."

Her words struck something deep inside of Glo. All this time, he thought Elistra hadn't cared enough to face him. Yet now he realized it was the exact opposite—she cared too much, in fact. A warm feeling rose up from his abdomen and reached all the way up to his face. The tall elf flushed and grinned stupidly at the lovely bardess. "You think so?"

A warm smile graced her lips. "I know so."

The bardess stood on her toes and kissed him on the cheek. Glo blushed even more, if that were possible. Shalla then grasped his arm and pulled him toward the house. "Now let's go and see what Seth found."

Glo went along with Shalla, but his mind was elsewhere. He silently wondered where Elistra was now and whether she was safe.

18

WHAT ARE LITTLE GIRLS MADE OF?

Click!

"Child's play," Seth murmured, punctuating the sharp sound. A moment later, he pushed against a section of the wall, revealing a secret door in the south wall of the basement.

Kalyn's eyes went wide, thoroughly impressed with the halfling's latest accomplishment. "I wanna learn to pick locks like that…"

Seth cast a dubious glance in her direction.

"Not that I'd ever use it," she quickly amended. Kalyn stepped up to the door and peered into a black, yawning tunnel.

"That tunnel looks… dark," Martan commented over her shoulder.

Kalyn rolled her eyes toward the archer, spiking an eyebrow.

A wan smile pressed across Martan's face as he shrugged sheepishly.

Seth grunted. "Probably used for smuggling."

Elladan chuckled at the halfling's remark. "Guess our old buddy Haltan was running more than one business." The bard clapped Martan on the back. "We need someone to watch our backs. Shalla is staying upstairs, because she doesn't 'do' the damp and dark. Would you mind remaining here and keeping an eye on things?"

A look of relief flooded across Martan's features. "Sure. I can do that."

Kalyn bit her tongue, a cutting remark on the tip of it. *Stop hounding him. He's brave when it counts—you owe him your life twice now.*

Glo stepped next to Kalyn, peering down the dark tunnel. "Should I cast light?"

Seth snorted as he crossed his arms. "Sure. Let's announce that we're coming."

Kalyn held back a giggle as Glo shot the halfling an acid glare.

Raina moved closer to Seth and looked up at Glo. "If you are worried about Kalyn and me, we can manage in the dark just fine."

Kalyn jerked her thumb toward Seth. "Yeah. I'll try not to step on darkness incarnate over here."

Raina smiled. "Just follow me, Kalyn. I'll make sure you won't step on or trip over anything."

With that, she shifted into a wolf, wagging her long tail.

Seth looked at Raina, then up at Kalyn with a twist of his lips. "At least I don't need a seeing eye dog."

Raina bared her teeth with a snarl, her green eyes glaring between Seth and Kalyn.

Kalyn held her hands up defensively. "He said it, Raina! Not me! I take death fluffies like you very seriously."

She leapt back as Raina snapped at her, drawing a snicker from everyone in the room.

Seth shook his head as he disappeared into the tunnel. "If everyone could *try* to be quiet..."

Raina sniffed the tunnel, then looked up at Elladan and Glo with a questioning expression.

Elladan gave her a quasi-smile. "Ladies first."

Kalyn slipped her bow over her shoulder and moved up next to Raina.

"Um… Kalyn?"

She paused and glanced back at Martan with a tilt of her head.

The grim young man took a deep breath, his sad brown eyes searching hers. "Just… be careful in there."

Kalyn nodded with a smile. "I'm with the Heroes! What could go wrong?"

A snort echoed off the walls of the waiting tunnel.

Kalyn shifted her gaze toward the entrance, but it was too dark to see Seth. "What was it you said about being quiet, short stack?"

Her question was met with stark silence.

Kalyn stepped into the tunnel next to Raina, using the occasional brush of the druid's fur to guide her through the darkness. The tunnel ran fairly straight and appeared to be clear of debris, making it easy to travel. She wasn't comfortable near the front of the line, but wanted to stick close to Raina, and keep the elves who could see in the dark behind her.

A few minutes in, Kalyn found herself growing bored. It was pitch black, her eyes all but useless in the darkness. There was no sound except for the shuffling of feet, and the only smells she detected were those of mold and damp dog fur.

Her mind started to wander when she suddenly felt Raina halt and bristle. Kalyn crouched and waited breathlessly next to her friend, resting her hand on a wooden stake in her belt.

Raina shifted her stance, and Kalyn felt the hairs on her arm stand on end.

"Zombies." Seth's voice came from directly in front of her.

Kalyn squeaked, barely holding back a scream. She jumped backward, bumping into Glo.

Seth snickered, his voice laced with sarcasm. "They're locked behind a door."

Kalyn growled. "Well, how was I supposed to know? I'm as blind as a beholder with no eye!"

"Shhh! You'll jinx us!" Elladan hissed from behind.

Kalyn jumped again when Glo rested a hand on her shoulder. "Perhaps I can shed some light on the subject?"

Seth let out a deep sigh. "If you must."

A soft light appeared behind Kalyn. Squinting, she turned and found Glo shielding a bright light at the end of his staff. Her eyes quickly adjusted and scanned everyone in the group. When she was sure everyone was there, she nodded to Glo. "That's a lot better. Thanks."

"Of course." Glo smiled at her, his blue eyes shifting down to Seth. "How many zombies are there?"

Seth held up two fingers.

"Only two?" Kalyn put her hands on her hips. "Why didn't ya stab them or something?"

Seth cocked his head slightly and narrowed his eyes. "You've never fought a zombie, have you?"

Raina suddenly stood up, taking on her normal form. "You can hack, stab, and slice zombies until the sun goes down—it won't make a difference. There's only one way to handle them quickly and effectively." She looked at Glo with a demure smile and a twinkle in her green eyes. "I hear you're good with fire."

Seth snorted and Kalyn covered her mouth, trying to hide the smile crawling onto her lips.

The elven wizard sighed and shook his head. "Never living that down."

"We didn't say a word." Elladan chuckled softly.

"Exactly." Glo moved past Kalyn and walked with Seth, further down the tunnel to a solid wooden door. They both paused and listened at it for a moment before cracking it open an inch.

Glo lifted his hand. "Now, Seth!"

At the wizard's command, Seth shoved the door wide open, revealing two crooked figures in an open room. Glo pointed a finger, two magic words rolling off his tongue. "*Radius Ardens.*"

A split second later, two flaming darts leapt from his fingertips and raced down the tunnel into the room. With a series of pops and loud hisses, the flames engulfed the zombies. In a matter of seconds, the two figures had shriveled into giant lumps of charcoal.

Kalyn waved her hand in front of her nose as the stench of burnt flesh permeated the air. "That was it? Seriously?"

Seth eyed her with obvious irritation. "You could've stayed back with Martan."

Kalyn crossed her arms and mimicked his stare. "I wasn't complaining! I just thought they'd be harder to kill is all."

"Fire and light magic are a zombie's greatest weakness," Raina explained as she moved around everyone and into the room cautiously. She inspected the smoldering bodies, shaking her head.

Kalyn lowered her arms. "That's another thing—I thought we were hunting vamps, not zombies and imps! Where are they coming from?"

Raina turned back to the group, her expression grim. "We saw this in Twin Oaks. Vamps tend to surround themselves with lesser creatures, like zombies and spawn."

Seth crossed his arms and stared around the group. "Wonderful. Why are we doing this again?"

Kalyn's mouth dropped open in shock at the flippant question. "Well, to save Ravenford, of course!"

Seth shook his head as if that answer wasn't good enough. "No. Seriously. Why?"

Glo tilted his head and narrowed an eye at the halfling. "Because the Baron and Baroness have been so good to us?"

Seth shook his head yet again. "One more time."

Elladan chuckled softly as he entered the room. "Because Lloyd is in love with Andrella."

A wicked grin spread across the halfling's lips as he nodded toward Elaldan. "Yeah. That."

Kalyn huffed and crossed her arms in aggravation. "Yer hopeless, short stack."

Seth ignored her and moved into the room, skirting around the charred bodies.

Raina nudged Kalyn in the side and whispered. "Just hopeless? Or a hopeless romantic?"

Kalyn giggled with her friend, watching from the corner of her eye as Seth cast a narrowed glare back at them. They fell silent, however, when he reached a door at the other side of the room and held a finger up to his mouth.

Hand resting on the stake in her belt, Kalyn waited as Seth listened at the door. After a moment, he frowned and cautiously opened it. Everyone moved forward as one when he signaled that it was clear.

As she passed through the door, Kalyn paused briefly until Glo's magical light had filled the room. It was a much larger room than the one before, furnished with a dusty, hexagonal table and six chairs. There was another door on the east side of the room, and the yawning mouth of another tunnel in the south wall.

Spying a few small, round objects on the table, Kalyn approached and picked one up. She was instantly disappointed to find they were only painted wooden coins.

"What is this?" She asked, turning and flipping the wooden coin to Elladan.

Elladan caught it and looked it over, then smiled wryly. "This is a gambling chip. It seems Haltan *was* running several businesses."

Kalyn picked up another chip from the table. "Gambling chips? Are they worth anything?"

Glo moved closer, looking the chips over. "Only if you're gambling."

Seth humphed. "Gambling is for amateurs."

Kalyn dropped the chip and turned toward the south tunnel. She suddenly froze when her eyes fell on a small shadow lingering in the opening, just out of the light's reach.

"Whoa!" She drew the stake from her belt and fell into a defensive crouch. Everyone in the room followed her example. Kalyn blinked when a sad sniffle drifted from the tunnel.

"Please don't hurt me," a small voice whimpered. "I just want my mommy."

Kalyn relaxed, standing straight. "Come where we can see you."

A little girl, not much older than eight years, slowly stepped into the light. She wore a lacy pink dress with puffy sleeves. Her curly blonde hair was tied out of her face by two pink bows on either side of her head. She blinked her blue eyes, her lower lip quivering. "I just want my mommy."

Kalyn moved to comfort the small girl, only stopping when Seth put his hand out. She gave the halfling a dark look, which he returned with a barely noticeable shake of his head.

With a sigh, Kalyn looked back at the little girl, but held her ground. "It's okay. Don't be scared. What are you doing down here all alone?"

The little girl reached up and rubbed her eyes as tears began to fall. "I'm lost!"

"Oh, it's okay. Don't cry." Kalyn took a step forward, only stopping when a firm hand grabbed her by the shoulder. She gazed back to see Elladan staring at the little girl, his brows knit with suspicion.

"Where are your parents?" he asked.

"I lost my mommy!" The little girl sobbed and lowered her hands, her eyes locking onto Kalyn's. A strange glow appeared in them that made Kalyn's head fuzzy. All the tension abruptly left her shoulders.

The little girl tilted her head, the side of her mouth twitching with a queer smile. "Are you my mommy?"

Eight pale bodies suddenly appeared out of nowhere, four on either side of the tunnel opening. A horrible stench filled the room. Kalyn blinked as Elladan jerked her back sharply.

The little girl hissed, baring a sharp pair of fangs. "I want you to be my mommy!"

Raina's voice cried out in alarm, though it seemed so distant. "Ghouls! Don't get bitten!"

Kalyn tried to understand what was happening, but it was difficult to think. She looked up as one of the pale bodies lumbered toward her. Her eyes grew wide and her mind suddenly cleared when she saw a sickly long tongue hanging past a row of long, sharp teeth.

The monster hissed, its pale arms reaching for Kalyn as it shambled closer. A shrill song from Elladan made it pause just long enough for Kalyn to draw her wooden stake and slam it into the monster's collar bone. The creature shrieked in agony and shoved Kalyn away, knocking her into Elladan.

From the corner of her eye, Kalyn saw Seth dodge another one of the monsters, cutting it with a knife. Behind him, Raina's form abruptly doubled in size, shifting into the form of a bear. The druid lumbered over the top of Seth and slammed into the monster, punching it into a wall.

The monster screamed, then sank its teeth into Raina's shoulder. The druid bear roared in agony, raking her claws across the monster's face, prying it away from her.

The little girl suddenly appeared in front of Kalyn, reaching out to her. "I said I want you to be my mommy!"

Panic set in, and Kalyn grabbed a small canteen at her side, popping the lid as quickly as she could. "Drink holy water, vamp brat!"

The little girl's eyes went wide and she disappeared in a puff of smoke just before some of the liquid sloshed from Kalyn's canteen onto the floor.

Glo rushed back to the door where they had entered the room. "Quick! Back this way!"

Raina plowed over a couple of ghouls, grabbing one chasing Glo and flinging it to the back of the room. She snapped at some others, barely avoiding their long claws as she kept herself between them and the group's only way out.

Elladan and Kalyn grasped each other's hands and rushed through the door after Glo and Seth. Seth grabbed the door and Glo began weaving a spell, glowing orange sparks flying wildly around his fingers.

Kalyn gasped as Elladan pulled her further down the tunnel. "Raina! Hurry!"

She watched, heart racing, as her friend took a wide swipe at the advancing monsters before turning and charging for the door.

A brilliant ball of fire formed between Glo's hands as Raina's galloping form twisted and shrunk back to her small body. She slipped through the open doorway just as Glo shoved his hands forward and sent the fireball blazing into the room beyond. Seth slammed the door closed behind it, then everyone high-tailed away down the tunnel.

They hadn't gotten far when a massive explosion rippled through the walls of the passage. Screams echoed from the room beyond, and heat filled the tunnel as angry flames erupted through the cracks of the closed door.

All at once, everything went silent. Kalyn grabbed Raina, the duo holding each other breathlessly as everyone listened for any sort of sound.

After a short while, Seth stole back to the door. After pausing to listen, he cautiously opened it and peeked inside. A few moments passed till he looked back at the others and nodded, closing the door again.

Elladan sighed and clapped Glo on the shoulder. "I'll never joke about your fire spells again!"

Glo arched an eyebrow at the bard. "Yeah, right."

Kalyn pulled back from Raina and looked her over. Her eyes instantly came to rest on a large wound in the druid's shoulder. Her stomach churned. She had seen wounds from hunting accidents before, but this looked different. It oozed green, as if infected.

Kalyn's mouth fell open in a stammer, the words rattling out of her mouth faster than she could think. "That looks bad. What do I do? How can I help? I don't know what to do."

Raina put her hand over Kalyn's mouth. "It's bad, but don't worry. I know what to do. With a little time and rest, I can fix myself up." She lowered her hand and took a deep breath, her brows knitting with a mixture of pain and curiosity. "Did I hear you yell something about holy water?"

Kalyn nodded and held up her canteen, wafting it under Raina's nose.

Raina frowned as she smelled it. "That's not holy water! That's Fran's 'moonwater' from her still…" The young druid paused, then started chuckling despite her obvious pain. "Oh. I see. Can I have a drink?"

Kalyn laughed. "Go ahead. Fran swears it's a cure all!"

Martan stood alone in the basement of what until recently had been Haltan's shop. Those spinning lights of Elladan's and Shalla's had long since winked out. That left the sunlight streaming down the outside steps as the only reliable source of light.

A few feet beyond the stairs, the basement grew dim, lit only by a couple of torches that lined the high stone walls. Dark shadows hung like lurking beasts in the corners of the wide room. That, and the eerie silence that pervaded the cellar caused Martan to subconsciously shy toward the sunlit steps.

The others had disappeared a while ago, down a secret passage that Seth had discovered in one of the basement walls. Martan had heard nothing from them since, and was starting to worry.

The gloomy archer pulled an arrow from his quiver and nervously straightened the fletchings as his imagination played havoc with his mind. *Aksel is the only sensible one of the bunch. Sometimes Elladan, but not always.*

The creases on Martan's brow deepened. *But Kalyn seems enamored with them nonetheless—like they're some sort of heroes.*

Twice now those 'heroes' had almost gotten him killed. Martan silently hoped their recklessness didn't get Kalyn hurt, or worse. He had just reunited with the young woman. Though he didn't quite believe he deserved it, he still hoped they might reconcile one day.

The archer put the arrow he was fingering back in its quiver. He went to grab another one when a sudden sound made him jump.

"Help me," a small voice called from the shadows.

Martan immediately fell into a crouch. His heart raced as his hand dropped the arrow and strayed to the sword hilt at his waist.

"W-who goes there?" he stammered, his eyes sweeping the surrounding darkness. Abruptly they settled on a shadow near the doorway where the others had disappeared.

Martan held his breath as the shadow moved closer. It halted just outside the ring of sunlight, the afterglow revealing the form of a small girl. The girl wore a cute little dress that was tattered in spots, her hair tied up in pigtails on either side.

Martan's fear abruptly faded, replaced by a mixture of concern and astonishment. *Where in the devil did she come from? She couldn't have slipped by me.*

The little girl gazed at him with a pair of big blue eyes, her expression plaintive. "Please help me. I've lost my parents."

Martan's mouth fell agape. "Lost your parents? Where are they?"

The girl turned sideways and pointed back at the place Martan dreaded—the entrance to the secret tunnel. "They're somewhere in there."

Martan gulped, his mouth suddenly dry. "I–in there?"

The young girl nodded, the pigtails on either side of her head bobbing up and down.

The girl's response set off all kinds of alarms off in Martan's gut. Years of tracking had taught him to trust his instincts. It was how he had managed to stay alive this long. The grim archer narrowed his eyes and pointed a thumb over his shoulder. "These stairs lead outside. I have a friend waiting up there. Why don't you go and wait with her while I find your parents?"

Martan expected the girl to move or at least say something. However, she merely stood there staring at him with those wide blue eyes.

Martan hunched down and looked the girl in the eye. "There's nothing to be afraid of."

Still she didn't budge. He gave the girl a feeble smile and held up his finger. "Wait here a moment."

The archer stood and backed up to the base of the stairs. He cupped a hand next to his mouth and called up outside. "Shalla? Can you come down here for a moment?"

"Be right there!" the bardess' voice drifted back as if from far away.

Martan turned toward the girl with a forced smile, but she was no longer standing where she had been. The archer swept his eyes all around the cellar, but there was no sign of her. The hairs on the back of his neck stood on end. *This is really getting strange.*

"Where did you go?" he called out.

The young girl's voice immediately echoed back from the secret tunnel. "Come. Follow me. They're in here."

"Dragon dung," Martan swore under his breath. He started toward the tunnel when a familiar voice sounded behind him.

"What's going on? Have you heard anything?" Shalla stood at the top of the stairs, the lovely bardess squinting as her eyes adjusted to the dim light.

As if in answer, the little girl's voice sounded once more from the tunnel. "They're in here. Are you coming?"

Martan gazed at Shalla and shrugged. "Just that."

Shalla's comely brow knit, her lips pressing together with concern. "Is that a little girl?"

A moment later, the girl reappeared at the edge of the ring of sunlight. Her big blue eyes fixed on Shalla, moisture welling in their corners. Her tiny voice quavered as she spoke. "I lost my mommy. Are you my mommy?"

Shalla's eyes teared up as well. "Oh, you poor thing."

The bardess quickly descended the stairs and rushed toward the girl. Martan's gut wrenched inside. Not certain why, he leapt to intercept Shalla.

At that same moment, a blinding ray of red light came flashing out of the secret tunnel. It struck the little girl in the back, prompting an inhuman cry from the small waif.

Shalla and Martan both grabbed their ears, staggering back as the unearthly cry echoed off the stone walls. Abruptly the little girl disappeared in a puff of smoke. The duo grasped each other and stared wild-eyed as Seth, Glo, Raina, Kalyn and Elladan emerged from the dark passage.

Martan, quaking himself, could feel Shalla shaking as she stammered, "W-what was that?"

"Little vamp," Seth answered in a matter of fact tone.

Shalla gulped as she continued to shudder. "Well she sure knows how to tug on your heart strings."

"Tell me about it," Kalyn and Raina answered simultaneously.

Martan noted the curly-topped druid leaning heavily on Kalyn's shoulder. "What happened to her?"

"Long story," Seth answered as he swept by Martan and Shalla, up the basement stairs.

Elladan drew up to them next, Shalla switching into his arms.

Kalyn and Raina followed, Glo behind them, keeping a watchful eye on the tunnel they had just exited. Kalyn nudged Martan in the shoulder. "Well, don't just stand there gawking. Give me a hand with her."

"Oh, right." Martan tore his eyes from the vigilant wizard and wrapped Raina's free arm around his shoulder.

This is crazy, Martan swore to himself as he assisted the two women up the stairs. But he knew Kalyn—once she made up her mind on something, there was no talking her out of it. Even if he decided to leave the 'heroes,' she would stay.

The sullen archer made a decision as they reached the top of the stairs. He would stay with Kalyn no matter what. He owed her that much after all he had put her through, even if it ultimately meant giving his life for hers.

19
PLAYING WITH FIRE

There were intricate carvings along the limbs that appeared to be flames

Lloyd's eyes gradually opened to strangely familiar surroundings. He lay in the midst of a large four-poster bed, swaddled in deep cushions and a soft comforter. Sunlight streamed in through a pair of tall cathedral windows, brightening up the lavishly furnished room. The young man could've sworn he'd been here before, but his head felt foggy and he couldn't quite remember where he was.

A familiar voice gently chastised him. "It's about time you woke up, sleepy-head."

Lloyd sat up, the cobwebs in his brain still lingering as his eyes sought out the source of that voice. They settled on Andrella, the young lady seated in a chair she had dragged over next to the bed.

Lloyd opened his mouth to respond, but a yawn snuck out instead.

Andrella giggled. "Oh my word. If I didn't know any better, I'd say you were hung over."

The young man smiled at her, stifling what was left of the yawn, when it all suddenly came rushing back to him. After the vampire attack, the others had insisted he and Aksel get healed. Andrella and Fafnar had taken them to the temple, where the old cleric had worked on them for nearly an hour.

Afterwards, Lloyd no longer felt weak, but was still extremely tired. Andrella had insisted they both be brought to rooms in the keep. Lloyd had been too tired to argue.

The young man threw off the covers and leapt out of bed, but immediately regretted it. His muscles were stiff, causing violent cramps in his arms and legs.

Andrella swiftly rose to his side, sudden creases lining her brow. "Are you alright?"

Lloyd grinned sheepishly at her as he sat down and vigorously rubbed the circulation back into his extremities. "I'm fine. Just a bit sore is all. Is everyone else okay?"

Andrella's hands went to her hips, her lips spread into a knowing smile. "Oh, my dear, sweet Lloyd. Always worrying about everyone else."

The young man raised an eyebrow. "Am I that predictable?"

Andrella broke out into keen laughter as she sat down and threw her arms around his neck. "Absolutely… but I wouldn't have you any other way."

Lloyd gazed fondly back at the lovely young woman, her sudden proximity doing wonders for his circulation. Still, she hadn't exactly answered his question. "Well?"

Andrella let out a short sigh. "They're all fine. Aksel's resting in the next room. Once you're dressed, we can go and see him…"

Without warning, the young lady threw all her weight against him, toppling them both into the deep cushions of the bed. Andrella lay there on top of him, the warmth of her body pressing against his. When she spoke, her tone was deep and throaty. "Of course… there's no hurry… is there?"

Lloyd gazed up into her electric blue eyes and suddenly forgot all else. He swept an arm around her waist and the other behind her neck, gently drawing her down into a deep, passionate kiss.

Knock, knock.

"Is anyone in there?"

Lloyd bolted upright, nearly knocking Andrella off the bed. He caught her at the last moment, saving her from a less-than-graceful fall.

Knock, knock.

"Lloyd? Andrella? Are ya in there?"

Lloyd got up, gently helping Andrella to her feet. Her face was red as a beet as she called out in a feigned pleasant voice. "Just a moment!"

"Great timing, Kalyn," she muttered irritably as she quickly straightened her hair and dress.

Lloyd swiftly grabbed his clothes as she went to the door. He briefly caught a glimpse of Kalyn and Raina as Andrella closed the door behind them. Once he was dressed, he let them all back in. The two girls seemed quite amused as they entered the room.

Lloyd narrowed an eye at the pair. "Did I miss something?"

Kalyn cast a sidelong glance at Andrella. "Sounds like just the opposite to me."

Andrella gave the young woman a dark look as she jabbed her with an elbow.

"Ouch!" Kalyn wailed as she seized Andrella's arm. "What'd ya do that fer?"

Andrella tried to wrestle her arm away, but gave up as she caught Lloyd's confused stare. Kalyn peered from Andrella to Lloyd, abruptly letting the young lady go as she, too, saw his puzzled expression.

Andrella cleared her throat as the blood rose to her cheeks. "What Kalyn meant to say is… you're more than fine the way you are."

"Ahem, I'll be the judge of that," Raina interrupted them. The curly-topped redhead motioned Lloyd back toward the bed. "Take a seat while I check you out."

"I feel fine…" he began to protest.

"…except you could hardly get out of bed a couple of minutes ago," Andrella finished for him.

"Traitor," Lloyd murmured quietly.

Still, she was right. He gave up and lay back on the bed without further comment. Raina stood over him, running her hands a few inches over his body. After about a minute, she stopped and took a couple of steps back. "Your life energy has been restored, but the incident has taken a toll on your body."

Lloyd felt his heart leap in his chest. "Is it… permanent?"

A bright smile crept across Raina's dimpled face. "Oh, no, no, no. You'll be fine with a bit more rest."

Lloyd felt the tension drain from his shoulders as he rose from the bed.

Kalyn nudged Raina in the side. "I heard Aksel's up as well. We can go see him now, if ya want."

Raina's freckled face reddened slightly at Kalyn's suggestion. When she responded, her tone was strangely stiff. "I was headed there next anyway… to check on him, as well."

"We'll all go," Andrella stated, looping her arm through Lloyd's. "After all, we all want to see him, don't we?"

"Yup!" Kalyn grinned at Raina for some reason Lloyd couldn't fathom.

The young druid ignored her friend, rigidly spinning on her heel as she led the way out the door. Kalyn continued to grin as she strode after her.

Aksel Alabaster felt lucky to be alive. Their encounter with the vampire had not gone well at all. It was only by sheer chance that they hadn't been killed, or worse, turned. Still, he and Lloyd had paid a price for their folly.

Aksel lay the blame squarely on his own shoulders. They had been ill-prepared for an encounter with a true vampire. Everyone should have been armed with weapons for fighting the undead. That was a mistake he intended to rectify as swiftly as possible.

Ten hours after their battle, Aksel awoke in a guest room in Ravenford Keep. Seth and Glo had come to visit, the duo seated at the foot of the bed as they detailed all he had missed. Aksel had not been surprised to learn of the secret passage in Haltan's basement. Nor had it shocked him to hear of the various undead gathered in those tunnels.

Glo and Seth were just finishing their account when they heard a knock on the door.

"Come—in!" the little cleric croaked, his throat drier than he had anticipated.

The door opened to reveal Lloyd, Andrella, Kalyn and Raina all standing out in the hallway. The four of them shuffled in one at a time as everyone exchanged greetings.

Raina was the only exception. The curly-topped druid barely acknowledged the others, her eyes focused on Aksel as she strode across the room. She halted by his bedside.

"Lie back down," she said in a firm tone. There was an intensity in her eyes that Aksel found strangely unnerving.

"I'm—I'm fine," he stuttered in response, not sure why the young druid suddenly made him feel uncomfortable.

"Yes, yes, I'm sure all your patients tell you the same thing. Now lie down!" Her eyes widened, her voice rising as she repeated her request.

Seth snickered at the foot of the bed. Lloyd whispered to Glo in a voice so low that Aksel barely caught the end of it.

"…taste of his own medicine."

The duo chuckled softly at his expense.

Aksel sighed. *They're right. I've been equally firm with them in the past.* The little cleric finally gave up and laid down as Raina had asked.

"Now was that so hard?" Raina said, a delightful smile playing across her lips.

"Not really," he admitted.

Aksel's discomfort swiftly disappeared as the young druid ran her hands over his body. Her movements were precise, her focus intent. He grew more impressed as she halted over the exact spots where he still felt sore.

After a few minutes, Raina finished. She looked up and fixed him with another delightful smile. "Your life energy has been completely restored. With a bit more rest, you'll make a full recovery."

"Thank you." Aksel smiled back, his eyes lingering on her briefly. For the first time since they had met, he noted something vaguely familiar about her. There was a faint coppery tone to her complexion that was almost gnomish in nature. Considering her bright red hair and green eyes, if her skin were just a shade darker, she could probably pass for a tall gnome.

While Raina examined Aksel, Glo explained to Lloyd and Andrella what they had found in the tunnels. As expected, Kalyn would occasionally interject her two cents, and Seth continued to poke fun at the odd Deepwooder.

Glo reached the point where he had left off with Aksel as Raina finished her exam. "…so we retreated back out of the tunnels and went to report to the Lady Gracelynn. Elladan figured we were somewhere under the southeast side of town near the bay."

"That's when Lady Gracelynn told us 'bout the old burnt-out guardhouse," Kalyn interjected in her Deepwood accent.

A slim smile formed on Glo's lips as he gave the archer a sidelong glance. "Yes… so, anyway, after we all got some sleep, Elladan and Shalla went to take a look. They took Martan with them."

Kalyn narrowed an eye at Seth. "I'm surprised you didn't go with them, short stack."

"That's because I was waiting for you," Seth responded without batting an eye.

Kalyn placed her fingers on her chest, her eyes wide. "Me? What'd I do now?"

The corner of Seth's mouth quirked up slightly as he pulled a blanket from behind his chair. There was something long and thin wrapped inside the thick cloth.

Kalyn's expression grew suspicious. "There ain't any snakes hidden in there?"

Seth let out a sinister chuckle. "I could put some in if you'd like."

Kalyn blanched and waved her hands in front of her. "No, no. That's just fine."

The young archer tentatively took the blanket from Seth. She slowly unwrapped it to reveal a finely crafted long bow. There were intricate carvings along the limbs that appeared to be flames.

Kalyn's jaw dropped. "Is this…"

"…a flaming bow," Seth finished for her, the halfling's eyes dancing in amusement.

Kalyn gaped at the weapon a few moments longer, then glanced back at Seth. "Where'd ya get this?"

The smirk on Seth's lips widened. "After we finished with Gracelynn, I went back to Haltan's. Everything was destroyed except for this."

Glo moved in for a closer look. "It is a handsome weapon—one that would be handy against the undead."

Kalyn nodded, not taking her eye off the bow in her hands. After a long pause, she shook her head and held it back out to Seth. "I really, really appreciate this, but I can't part with my family bow. I think Martan should have it."

Seth eyed her a moment, then shrugged. "Suit yourself—you give it to him."

Kalyn grimaced at the halfling, then set her jaw. "Fine. I will."

Kalyn was obviously torn at giving up the flaming bow, but Aksel understood her desire to keep a prized family heirloom. Still, it wasn't the only way she could be useful against the undead. The little cleric cleared his throat. "Kalyn, I've got nothing else to do the rest of today. If you want, I can enchant your family bow, and make it a bane to all undead."

Kalyn shifted her gaze to him, her entire face brightening. "Holy troll snot! Yes, yes, yes, yes, yes!"

"I think that was a yes," Seth noted dryly.

Kalyn went to hand Aksel her family bow, then paused for a moment, her face clouding over. "Will it change the bow in any other way?"

Aksel gave her a small smile. Family obviously meant a lot to her. "It is purely an enchantment. All it will do is make it work well against the undead."

Kalyn let out a deep breath, then handed him the bow. "Okay, just be careful with it."

Aksel gave her a solemn nod. "I'll treat it as if it belonged to my family."

Kalyn gave him a nervous smile, then spun on her heel. "No use in waitin'. Might as well give this to Martan now."

The side of Seth's mouth curved upward as he cast a glance Aksel's way. "I'll go, too. Someone needs to check up on Elladan."

Aksel nearly laughed aloud as Seth took off after Kalyn. *Seth checking up on Elladan?* Talk about your pot-and-kettle situations. There was no telling what trouble those two could get into if left to themselves.

Raina drew up beside Aksel and ran a gentle hand across Kalyn's bow. "This is finely wrought." She gazed up at Aksel while biting her lower lip. "You know, I'm pretty handy at crafting. I can stay and help you, if you want."

Aksel hesitated a moment, then shrugged. Crafting was usually a tedious process. It would be nice to have someone to talk to, and there were things about this Raina that intrigued him. "Sure, why not?"

A bright smile spread across the young druid's face.

As the two of them began to discuss what they'd need, Andrella cleared her throat. "Ahem…"

Aksel and Raina looked up at the young lady. Andrella had a hand on both Lloyd's and Glo's arms and was dragging the two of them back toward the door. "We'll just be going now. You two kids have fun!"

Aksel thought the young lady was acting rather oddly. He exchanged a perplexed glance with Raina, then promptly dismissed Andrella's strange behavior. He hardly noticed as the trio left the room, his concentration fixed on the enchanting of Kalyn's bow.

Lloyd was surprised, but not unhappy, when Andrella dragged them out of Aksel's room. The young warrior was not used to inaction. He wanted to follow Seth and Kalyn, and said as much to Glo and Andrella. The moment the words left his mouth, he regretted it.

Andrella crossed her arms and fixed him with a hard stare. "Must I remind you, Raina said you need a bit more rest before you've completely recovered."

Lloyd cast an imploring look at Glo, but the wizard shook his head. "I think it can wait till first thing tomorrow. We already killed one full-fledged vampire, and the other is in hiding. In the interim, Gracelynn has the town guards and the Dunwynn sky knights patrolling Ravenford. Not to mention, everyone is being told to stay indoors at night."

Glo's explanation did little to ease Lloyd's frustration. Still, there was no use arguing with his friends—especially not with Andrella. Once the young lady made up her mind about something, there was no reasoning with her.

Lloyd let out a deep sigh, his shoulders sagging. "I guess you're right."

Andrella moved in closer and placed a hand on his cheek while smiling up at him. "Of course I'm right. I'm always right."

Lloyd was not the smartest man in the world, but he knew better than to challenge that statement.

Glo arched an eyebrow at Lloyd, then thankfully redirected the young lady's attention. "Andrella, since we appear to have some time on our hands, would you like me to work with you on your spell casting?"

"Do you mean it?" Andrella spun toward Glo, her entire face lighting up with glee. Her exuberance was so infectious that it lifted Lloyd out of his glum state.

Glo's lips creased into a faint smile. "Yes, dear. I think it would be in all our best interests."

"Well then, yes! Sure. Absolutely!" Andrella threw her arms around the wizard and squeezed him tight.

Lloyd noted the tactful way that Glo had broached the subject. Andrella might not have reacted so well if she knew it was her mother's idea. Still, Gracelynn had a right to be concerned. Lloyd was also worried for Andrella's safety. Smart and talented as the young lady was, he knew firsthand just how dangerous the world could be.

With little else to do, Lloyd escorted a beaming Andrella down to the courtyard. He listened with thinly veiled amusement as she pelted poor Glo with all sorts of questions about spellcasting.

To his credit, Glo took it all in stride. He answered each one of

Andrella's questions with profound patience. Lloyd knew the wizard's greatest fear was ending up like his father. Yet from what Lloyd could see, he had little to worry about. Glo was the exact opposite of the critical mage.

The trio had just exited the keep when a familiar voice called out his name. "Lloyd!"

The young man swept his eyes around the courtyard till they settled upon Sir Fafnar. The Dunwynn noble held up a hand as he strode across the yard in their direction. Lloyd turned to Glo and Andrella as they descended the steps. "You two go ahead. I'll catch up with you shortly."

The pair waved to the Dunwynn knight as they trod off toward the practice yard. Fafnar greeted them in kind, then pulled Lloyd across the courtyard in the opposite direction.

Mixed emotions played across the knight's face as he spoke. "I'm glad to see you doing so much better, my friend."

Lloyd let out a hollow laugh. "Yeah, better enough to be up and about, but not enough to fight."

Fafnar responded with that strange half-snort, half-laugh. "I totally understand. We men of action find it hard to sit idly by whilst others do the work."

Lloyd grinned. A warrior like himself, Fafnar truly got him. Yet there was something off about the knight. "Is something troubling you, my friend?"

Fafnar cast a look over his shoulder, then let out a deep sigh. "I could be in much trouble for telling you this, but you and your friends have proved valiant allies."

Fafnar halted and turned to face Lloyd, his expression pensive. "There's no easy way to say this. My brother, Ignar, is on his way here and will arrive sometime tomorrow. He intends to occupy the town."

Lloyd's mouth fell open at the shocking pronouncement. "But that's absurd—especially now that we've finally got things under control."

Fafnar's mouth stretched into a grimace. "That's indeed what I reported back home. However, the Duke does not see it that way. He wants a 'stable' Dunwynn presence in charge of the town."

Lloyd felt anger well up inside him. That statement was a slap in the face to all parties involved—his comrades, Fafnar, and the Lady Gracelynn. Only someone as arrogant as the Duke of Dunwynn would make such a pompous proclamation.

Lloyd took a deep breath to calm himself, then grasped Fafnar by the shoulders. "Surely you can reason with your brother?"

Fafnar lifted an eyebrow at Lloyd. "Do you have any brothers?"

Lloyd nodded. "One. My older brother, Pallas."

"And would he listen to anything you have to say?" Fafnar asked in a soft voice.

Lloyd opened his mouth to reply, then stopped himself. The truth was that Pallas never listened to Lloyd. As far as he was concerned, Lloyd was his younger idiot brother.

"No, not really," Lloyd finally admitted. "I take it Ignar is your older brother?"

Fafnar's expression grew even more pained. "Yes, though he is not the oldest. My brother Klinkar is the eldest and by far more reasonable. Ignar, I'm afraid is an ambitious brute."

Lloyd did not like the sound of that at all. Still, as he had learned these last few months, everyone had their weak point. "Any suggestions on how to deal with him?"

Fafnar half-snorted again as he clasped Lloyd on the shoulder. "At the end of a blade, perhaps?"

Lloyd eyed the knight with uncertainty. "Do you really want us to challenge your brother?"

The side of Fafnar's mouth rose slightly. "I dare say you could take him one-on-one, my friend, but he'll have at least a platoon of soldiers with him."

Lloyd's brow creased at hearing that. He and his friends were quite skilled, but might be hard pressed to stand against fifty or more men. Further, innocent townsfolks might get hurt in such a confrontation.

Fafnar patted him on the shoulder, then dropped his hand. "I understand your dilemma, my friend. In truth, were I to stay, I would stand at your side against my brutish brother. However, I've received new orders and must leave Ravenford immediately."

Lloyd gave the noble knight a wan smile. "Thank you, Fafnar.

You've done more than you should by just warning us. I would not ask you to do more."

He extended a hand to the Dunwynn noble. "Godspeed on whatever your new mission is."

Fafnar clasped hands with him. "May the gods watch over you as well, my friend, whatever you decide to do."

With that, the Dunwynn knight turned and strode away.

Across the yard, Lloyd spied Andrella hard at work with Glo. They seemed quite engrossed in firing spells off at standing targets.

Lloyd decided not to bother them just yet with this alarming news—nor would he disturb Aksel. First and foremost, he would inform the Lady Gracelynn. Once the others returned, they could put their heads together and decide what to do about the impending invasion.

Andrella led Glo to the end of the courtyard, opposite the gardens and Maltar's tower. There was a wide dirt area there, with standing wood dummies for the castle guards to practice on.

Glo's stomach felt somewhat queasy at the thought of training the young lady. Visions of his father kept popping into his head. *You're barely an adequate wizard yourself. How do you expect to train someone else?*

Glo railed at the image in his mind. *I may not be as experienced as you, old man, but at least I won't scar her for life.*

Andrella lined up at the edge of the dirt square and took aim at one of the mannequins at the other end. She gazed uncertainly at Glo. "Does this look right?"

Glo stared blankly at the young lady, suddenly feeling quite inadequate. *What in the world am I doing? I have no idea how to train someone?*

The tall wizard cleared his throat. "Ahem… sure. Go ahead. Um… I'll watch you."

Nice, Glo. Real smooth and confident, the wizard derided himself. Yet as he observed the young lady, he started to notice little things. First, she held her breath. Second, her brow scrunched and her eyes narrowed to slits. Finally, her shoulders rose nearly to her ears.

"*Radius Ardens*." The familiar words fell from her lips as a red hot ray streaked from her outstretched finger. It raced across the yard and missed its motionless target by nearly two feet.

"Dragon dung!" Andrella swore, balling her hands into fists. She cast a glance at Glo, her cheeks reddening and her hand going to her mouth. "Oops. Sorry."

Glo's lips curved into a thin smile. "It's quite alright. I can't tell you how many times I've said the same thing when a spell's gone awry."

Andrella let out a bell-like laugh. "Fair enough. Just promise not to tell my mom."

Glo chuckled softly. Andrella's mom was a pussy cat compared to his father. "I promise. Would you care to try again?"

The young lady nodded. "Alright—though I'm not sure it will be any better."

Andrella's ability to laugh at herself eased Glo's tension tremendously. He believed he could help her, but vowed to do it in a non-critical way. *I refuse to criticize her like my father did me.*

A subtle approach suddenly came to mind. Glo inched closer to the young lady as she prepared another spell.

Andrella shifted her gaze to him uncertainly. "What is it?"

"If I may?" The wizard slowly reached out and placed his hands on her shoulders. He gently pushed on them until they relaxed under his grip.

Andrella's mouth twisted sideways. "I had no idea I was doing that. Is there anything else?"

Glo gave her a weak smile. "It might help if you actually breathe through your casting."

The young lady's brows knit together. "I'm holding my breath, aren't I?"

Glo merely nodded in response.

Andrella let out a closemouthed laugh. "Maltar always chastised me for doing that."

Glo grimaced at the mention of the irritable mage. Maltar had been nearly as critical as his father. "Yes, well, Maltar chastised everyone for everything."

"He was an ornery old coot," Andrella agreed.

Glo arched an eyebrow at her. That did not seem like something she would normally say.

Andrella saw his puzzled expression and chuckled. "I guess I've been spending too much time with Kalyn."

"Probably." Glo laughed as he spoke, his own tension now all but gone.

Andrella narrowed an eye at him. "Do you think you could show me how it's done?"

"Certainly." Glo lined up the target in one fluid motion, and with practiced ease brought his will to bear. "*Radius Ardens.*"

The red ray leapt from his fingertips, arching across the yard and striking the dummy square in the chest.

"That was perfect!" Andrella said with clear admiration.

The wizard slowly dropped his arm and faced his pupil. "Actually, it was hours and hours of practice."

Andrella's face clouded over as she bit her lower lip. "Do you think it will take me that long?"

A deep compassion welled up inside him for the apprehensive young lady. He understood only too well what it felt like to doubt yourself. Glo placed a reassuring hand on her shoulder. "I think you're farther along than you realize."

He gently spun her back around to face the dummies across the yard. "Now it's your turn. Take a deep breath and let it out slowly as you aim."

Andrella gave him a weak smile, then did as he suggested. She took a deep breath and let it out gradually as she raised her arm.

Glo continued to direct her, his tone smooth and even. "Keep your body relaxed. Empty your mind of all else but the spell."

Andrella's shoulders remained loose this time, but her forehead creased once more.

"Don't overthink it," Glo cautioned softly. "It's a simple spell. No need to force it."

Andrella gave him a small smile, the lines in her brow disappearing.

"Very good," Glo praised as he circled around behind her. From what he could see, she was lined up perfectly. "When you're ready, just say the words."

Andrella hesitated a couple of moments, then spoke the words in the spellcasting tongue. The red hot ray jumped from her fingers, speeding toward the dummy and striking it dead center.

Andrella leapt up into the air with glee. "I hit it! I hit it!"

She spun around and threw her arms around Glo's neck, while still jumping up and down. "Did you see that? I hit it!"

Glo was nearly as enthused as she, but could have done without the leaping about. He put his hands on her waist and stopped her from shaking him. "I did in fact. That was very well done."

Andrella let go and gave him a quirky smile. "Well, I had an excellent teacher."

Glo felt the warmth rise to his cheeks. "I don't know about that. After all, I just gave you a few pointers."

Andrella's hands went to her hips, her mouth pressing into a thin line. "You're too modest, you know. Now I see why you and Lloyd get along so well."

Glo cocked his head to one side and nodded. "We do have some things in common."

Andrella's hands dropped from her sides. She shook her head, then turned to face the target again. "One more for good luck?"

Glo ushered her forward. "Be my guest."

Andrella lined up the target perfectly. She let out a slow breath and raised her arm in one smooth motion. *"Radius Ardens."*

The ray sped from her fingers, colliding with the dummy's head. Flames erupted from the appendage, and a moment later it fell off the top of the dummy to the ground below. In mere seconds it had burnt to ash.

Glo raised both eyebrows. He had never seen such a raw display of power before.

Andrella peered back at him, her mouth hanging wide open. "Is that supposed to happen?"

Glo forced himself to smile at the young lady. "Not exactly."

Andrella's face abruptly fell.

Nice going, Glo, the wizard silently chastised himself. He immediately stepped forward and placed an arm around her shoulder. "Look at it this way—I'd hate to be on the receiving end of that."

Andrella gazed up at him, a smile returning to her lips. "It was pretty awesome, wasn't it?"

"It was indeed," Glo agreed, though he silently wondered just how much power lay hidden within the young lady.

Kalyn strode next to Martan on their way back from the burnt-out guardhouse. A sweep of the structure resulted in the discovery of a trap door below the building. Any further search was cut short, though, as the day was nearly done.

Martan and Kalyn now headed up the hill toward Ravenford keep. It had been decided it best for everyone to stay the night there, to be near Gracelynn and Andrella.

Martan softly cleared his throat as they passed under the portcullis. "So… what happened to your bow?"

Kalyn looked at him with a puzzled expression, then down at the bow resting on her shoulder. Her eyes widened as she realized it was the flaming bow that Seth had given her.

"Oh! Aksel has mine. He was gonna magic it into a weapon that'll make the undead deader 'n a doornail." She slipped the flaming bow off her shoulder and ran her hands along the length of it. "Seth gave me this one. That was awful sweet of him, but I just can't part with mine, it being a family heirloom and all."

She held it out to Martan, her lips twisting as his eyes widened. "Go on. You take it."

Martan held his hands up and took a step back. "Kalyn, I couldn't. It was a gift to y…"

Kalyn shoved the bow into his hands. "Nope. I'm giving it to ya. Now, let's go see what it can do!" She grabbed him by the arm and pulled him toward the training grounds, giggling.

After shooting a few flaming arrows into an already scorched and decapitated target, Martan paused and ran his hands along the bow.

"It's impressive. Well built." He looked at Kalyn. "Are you sure you want to part with it?"

Kalyn grimaced. "No—but hold on to it anyway." She kicked some of the turf with a sigh. "I just wish we could do more against those undead."

Martan nodded, his expression thoughtful. "Too bad we can't fire wooden stakes from our bows."

Kalyn's mouth slowly fell open as an idea occurred to her. "That's brilliant, Martan!"

Martan's eyes shifted from side to side. "Wha… what is?"

"We can take the metal tips off our arrows and sharpen them into wooden stakes. Granted, they'll lose their balance in the air, but we can tweak the fletching to accommodate for it. Come on! Let's get busy!"

The two of them made their way to Maltar's tower. No one else was there. Kalyn dumped their quivers on the floor and separated the arrows into groups. She paused when she came to one arrow wrapped in green linen.

"Is that what I think it is?" Martan's voice was low, almost a whisper.

Kalyn's eyes darted up to him as she grabbed the wrapped arrow and held it out. "Yeah. An original mystic arrow, made by my grandpa."

Martan took the arrow, unwrapping it to reveal a dark green shaft, with owlbear feathers for fletching, and a silvered tip. "Didn't he give this to you on your swee… sixteenth birthday?"

Kalyn nodded as she took the arrow back and ran her hands across the smooth shaft. "He taught me how to make them before he disappeared."

Martan's eyes widened. "Do they work?"

"Darned if I know! Ain't nobody had use for one since who knows when. Most folk think it's just superstitious hullabaloo, and ain't no shifters or powerful mages messed with Deepwood to test the theory out—though I thought about using it on old skull head." Kalyn's mind briefly flashed back to the evil mage who had kidnapped her sister. She had finally gotten her revenge on him when the Heroes took down the Serpent Cult.

The young Deepwood archer twisted the study arrow between her fingers. "I wonder if it would work on vamps?"

"Only one way to find out, I guess." Martan knelt next to her. "It's the only one you have?"

Kalyn nodded, wrapping the arrow back up in the green linen. "I'll make ya one of yer own when I have a chance. Ya never know when a mage-slaying arrow might come in handy." She looked at him as she slipped the arrow back into her quiver. "Now, remember, ya can't tell anyone. It's silly, but grandpa always said these arrows are as much a curse as a blessin', and they need to be protected."

Martan gave her a grim nod. "If they work like the stories and songs say, I would hate for someone like the Duke of Dunwynn to get a hold of them. It might be the end of every elf caster in Thac." His paused a moment, his head tilting to one side. "Then again…"

Kalyn punched him in the shoulder. "Martan, Glo's an elf caster!"

Martan slowly bowed his head. "Yeah… guess you're right…"

"Anyway… the stories are true." Kalyn's lips twisted sideways. "Still, I don't think it would make a difference. I ain't so sure that block-headed duke can tell the difference 'tween an arrow and a ham skewer."

20
LETTERS FROM A DEAD CLERIC

Two small figures knelt over the prone form,
with their heads buried in its neck

Andrella sat on the porch of the Golden Golem beside Lloyd, Elladan, and Shalla. The group of them watched with idle curiosity as Kalyn, Martan, and Raina ambled in boredom around the Boulder. The large golem stood stalwartly to the side of the porch as a fixture to attract local business.

Everyone waited for Seth, Aksel, and Glo to return from the temple with holy water. Those present were quiet for the most part, but Andrella could sense the tension in the air. No one was looking forward to the task that lay before them. Thankfully, the three Deep-wooders provided more than adequate entertainment.

Andrella giggled softly as she watched their antics. Martan looked skeptical as Kalyn fearlessly poked and prodded around the Boulder. Raina followed the duo, calmly answering Kalyn's questions.

"I wanna climb it." Kalyn latched onto the Boulder's arm and began to shimmy upward.

Martan narrowed an eye at the young woman. "Sure you want to do that?"

Kalyn grunted as she climbed. "I'm just… trying to… kill… time."

Elladan chuckled, raising a hand, the sun glinting off the finger with the golem's golden ring. "I wonder what would happen if the Boulder started to dance?"

"Kalyn would fall on her rear, that's what." Lloyd said with a snort.

Andrella giggled, grabbing his hand and interlacing her fingers with his. "The rest of us would have fun, though."

"You're gonna fall, Kalyn." Martan's said in a deep monotone.

"I climb… trees… for a livin'… worry wort!" Kalyn sighed as she finally made it to the Boulder's rocky shoulders. Once she had found a comfortable perch there, she looked toward the keep sitting on the hill a short distance away. "Oh! Andrella, I can see your house from here!"

Raina shielded her eyes from the light and looked towards the keep. "What a coincidence, so can I!" She crossed her arms and looked straight up at Kalyn, a lopsided smile on her lips.

Andrella shifted in her chair, wiping away a tear that her giggling had squeezed from her eye.

Shalla chuckled. "Just be aware that the Golden Golem Inn is not responsible for any injuries you may incur as you climb down, Kalyn."

"However, if you do fall and get hurt, I'm sure Seth would get a hoot out of it." Elladan added.

"He'd probably pay her to reenact it." Lloyd chuckled as Andrella giggled again.

Martan let out a deep sigh as he watched Kalyn atop the Boulder. The young woman kicked her legs back and forth from her rocky perch. "Martan, why don't you show everybody what your new bow can do?"

"If I have to." Martan responded glumly. The archer slipped the bow off his shoulder, nocked an arrow into place, and drew it back. Everyone watched as flames appeared, wrapping themselves around the arrow without burning it.

Kalyn gave a drawn-out sigh. "Mine doesn't do that. How am I s'pposed to know if Aksel's 'chantment works?"

Raina huffed. "I was helping Aksel the entire time; he did a good job. It'll work." The little druid crossed her arms, peering up at Kalyn through narrowed eyes. "Unless you don't trust us?"

Andrella got to her feet, leaning her hands on the porch railing. "Oh, you were helping Aksel the entire time, huh?"

"Such generous souls, helping one another out like that." Elladan turned to Shalla, "Remember when we used to help each other out like that?"

Shalla smiled. "Seems like it was just yesterday—we were so young then."

Raina's freckled cheeks turned several shades of red. "Okay, okay, stop changing the subject."

Kalyn pulled her braid over her shoulder, fidgeting with it. "I trust ya, Raina. I don't question Aksel's skill—he's a hero, after all—but I'd like to know my bow works before we go into a vamp lair, if ya know what I mean."

Andrella held back a heavy sigh. She knew how Kalyn felt. Glo had pulled her aside earlier in the morning and taught her a new spell, but she wasn't sure if she had what it took to actually cast it in the heat of combat.

Lloyd wrapped his arms around her shoulders, planting a kiss on her head. Andrella smiled. He always seemed to know just what to do to make her feel better.

Raina huffed again, drawing Andrella back to the conversation. "Well, Kalyn, you'll see soon enough, and I promise that it'll be just fine. Aksel put hours of work into it."

Elladan chuckled. "He put in hours of work, huh?"

Raina shot the bard a withering glare while Shalla laughed unabashedly, but Kalyn interrupted her before she could retort.

"Wish there were some Dunnies 'round here to test it on. Pretty sure it would prove they were creatures of undeath."

Andrella looked up at Kalyn just in time to see the archer wink. "Ya know, Andrella, I'll pay money to watch you tear a new one into Sir Fafnar's brother when he shows up."

A dangerous smile crossed Andrella's lips as she pushed her shoulders back. "Oh, don't worry. You'll get a front row seat to that."

Kalyn lips warped sideways. "Hope yer mom don't kick us outta town before then."

Andrella shifted her gaze to the Keep, her mind drifting to her mother. Gracelynn had shocked everyone this morning when she allowed Andrella to accompany the heroes. Andrella wasn't quite sure whether it was due to Glo having taken her under his wing, or the news of the upcoming Dunwynn occupation. Either way, she was grateful for her mother's change of heart.

"Here comes Glo and the short ones!" Kalyn's announcement directed everyone's attention to the elf, gnome, and halfling as they approached the inn.

Everyone was given a bottle of holy water and a wooden spike before they split into groups. Lloyd, Glo, Seth, Martan, and Aksel headed eastward back to Haltan's. Andrella, Kalyn, Raina, Elladan, and Shalla, with the Boulder in tow, made their way to the burnt-out guardhouse.

They headed south across the eastern bridge, and then took the road east where they passed several rows of fisherman's homes and small docks. The abandoned guardhouse stood at the very end of the dusty street, a short distance from the bay.

Andrella lifted her gaze as they approached the tower. There were signs of fire damage around the windows and door. Otherwise, the building looked solid and sturdy, though eerily quiet and dark inside.

Andrella gazed back at Kalyn, still sitting on the Boulder's shoulders. "You and Seth checked this out yesterday, right?"

The Boulder came to a halt and Kalyn quickly climbed down its arm, dropping to the ground. "Yup! Martan was with us, too. We found fresh tracks, and Seth found a trap door under a bed, but other than that, it was clear. I'll check it again, just to be safe."

The archer warily walked up to the door of the guardhouse, Raina right behind her, and the twosome began scanning the ground. They gave everyone pause as Kalyn crouched and lingered near the door, her and Raina staring closely at the ground.

"Fresh tracks." Kalyn looked up at Andrella. "Something passed through here before dawn, I reckon."

Andrella felt Shalla shudder next to her. "I bet we know what that was."

Kalyn stood and readied her bow, while Raina silently shoved the door open. The Boulder stomped up to the door and halted, while the archer and druid disappeared into the darkness.

Andrella hurried closer to the door, spying Kalyn's shadow checking the corners of the room beyond. She called out to her in a semi-hushed voice. "Anything to test your bow on, Kalyn?"

Kalyn responded with a silent nod. Another minute or so passed till the archer sauntered outside, followed by Raina. "Looks clear in there."

Elladan nodded to the Boulder. "Normally, I would say 'ladies first,' but under the circumstances, I think it best if our large friend here takes the lead."

Andrella waited as the large construct stooped and squeezed past the door, then she filed into the building with the others. The scent of old smoke lingered in the air of a large room. Remnants of tables and chairs were scattered about, and a blackened glass mirror sat behind the charred remains of what had probably been a bar.

"Guards are allowed to drink on the job? Where do I sign up?" Shalla chuckled.

Andrella rolled her eyes at the bardess, a smile on her lips. "Ha! Guards drinking on the job. What do you think this is? Lukescros?" She laughed. "The hardest thing they were allowed to serve here was apple cider."

Elladan chuckled softly. "Lukescros does have its perks!" He swept his eyes around the room. "So, where is the trap door?"

Kalyn jerked her thumb to an open door on the east side of the guardhouse. "Captain's quarters, under the bed."

Elladan looked up at the Boulder and pointed in that direction. "Go into the room and move the bed."

The Boulder lumbered across the large room and through the open door. Once inside, it picked up the charred bed with ease to reveal a stone panel in the wooden floor beneath.

"Why would the guards have a trap door here?" Andrella wondered aloud.

"Let's find out. Boulder smash!" At Elladan's command, the large golem dropped the bed, drew back a massive fist, and slammed it straight through the stone trap door.

The thundering of stone colliding with stone shattered the morning silence, making Andrella flinch. The trap door crumbled into a black tunnel, the stones clattering to the ground somewhere far below.

"You aren't exactly the quiet type, are ya, Elladan?" Kalyn asked, pretending to clean out her ears.

A half-smile turned up the corner of Elladan's mouth. "I do prefer a big entrance."

"Let's light up this stage, shall we?" Shalla stepped up closer to the mouth of the tunnel. With two words and a sweep of her hands, she conjured four torch-sized lights and sent them spiraling down the hole.

Andrella leaned in as close as she dared, watching as the lights followed a ladder to an empty chamber about fifty feet below.

Raina shimmied next to Andrella, peering into the long shaft. "Before anyone moves, I want to do something." Her hand went to her belt and pulled a scroll from it. She unrolled the parchment and read aloud the arcane language written on it. When she finished, the scroll disappeared in a twinkle of light that spun around the group of them, before bursting and showering them with sparkles.

Kalyn gasped in awe. "What was that?"

"A magic aura to protect against evil. It'll keep the vamps off our throats." Raina looked at Andrella and winked, then carefully stepped into the hole. "I'll go first, just in case."

"Be careful, hon. We don't know what's waiting for us down there," Shalla cautioned.

Kalyn jumped down after Raina, followed by Elladan, then Shalla. Andrella decided to go last. She had promised her mother that she would be careful and not take any more risks than necessary. She was about half-way down the ladder when she heard a hiss that made her freeze and lock her eyes onto Raina.

The young druid dropped to the floor, landing in a crouch, her eyes trained to the ceiling. "We've got company."

Andrella narrowed her eyes as Shalla lifted her orbs of light to the ceiling, just above where Andrella clung to the ladder. Two little boys stood side-by-side on the ceiling, not fifteen feet from her, as if they were standing on a floor.

One of them looked directly at Andrella, his eyes taking on an eerie glow. "Is that you, mommy?"

For a split second, Andrella felt her head get fuzzy, but then a sparkling aura flashed around her, and her head instantly cleared. The other boy hissed, baring a sharp pair of fangs. One ran across the ceiling and began crawling down the wall toward the group below. The other came directly for her.

Andrella nearly panicked, but then she heard Glo's voice as if he was speaking in her mind. *Take a deep breath and breathe through the spell.*

With a sharp intake of air, she pointed a finger at the boy and two words fell from her lips. "*Radius Ardens.*"

Fire sped from her fingertip and punched the little vampire square in the chest.

"Owie!" he shrieked and turned to mist, floating away from her.

Two glowing arrows appeared in the other little boy, one piercing him straight through the heart. With an unearthly howl, he exploded, filling the air with ash.

Andrella wrinkled her nose just before she sneezed.

Kalyn giggled and shrieked excitedly. "My bow has magic powers! I can't believe it!"

"That's nice, dear," Raina called from the darkness below. "Shalla, can you send your lights down here?"

"I'll do it," Elladan answered. Four new orbs appeared at floor level and floated across the room about thirty feet, revealing a door on the other side. A little gray cloud hovered there. It shifted back and forth uncertainly, then slipped through the cracks of the door.

Shalla's voice squeaked as they all finally reached the floor.

"That is so creepy!" Her eyes nearly bugged out of her head, and her lips were pulled back in an uncomfortable grimace. "I wish we could bring the Boulder down here with us. It would make me feel better."

"Did you see how my bow smoked that little vamp? Did you?"

Kalyn skipped to Andrella's side and shook her bow in the air. "I have a magic bow!"

Andrella grabbed Kalyn around the shoulders, giggling. "Who needs the Boulder when you've got us, Shalla?"

Shalla's eyes shifted between Andrella and Kalyn, one delicate eyebrow slowly lifting. "I'm beginning to think Seth is right about you two."

"It's too quiet."

"Isn't that a good thing?" Aksel responded in a hushed voice.

Seth regarded his friend skeptically in the soft light from Glolindir's staff. Aksel's expression was deadpan, but Seth knew the gnome well enough to appreciate his dry sense of humor. "Only if you like ambushes."

Aksel's eyes lit up at the comment. "The thought had crossed my mind."

The duo stood in the underground room where they had previously encountered the group of ghouls. Glo, Lloyd, and Martan huddled nearby, all keeping a watchful eye on the encroaching darkness. The passage here from Haltan's basement had been clear. So had the little room between this one and the tunnel. Seth had even checked the east door, and found a bare kitchen with a cold hearth.

"S-so you think the vampires know we're coming?" Martan stammered nervously. The archer's grip tightened on the bow with the decorative flames in his off hand.

Glo gave him a grim nod. "It's a logical assumption. The little girl was a vampire, and she saw us down here yesterday."

Martan blanched at the mention of the little vamp.

Lloyd clasped the archer on the shoulder as he moved past him toward the south tunnel. "Even if she did warn them, we're ready for them this time."

Seth exchanged a curious glance with Aksel. Lloyd was acting just a bit too overconfident, even for him. Seth assumed he was overcompensating. That last encounter with a vampire had left Lloyd in a drastically weakened state. It must have been infuriating for someone like him, who relied so heavily on his physical strength.

Glo must have been thinking the same thing. "You're not wrong, my friend. We are indeed better prepared. Just don't get carried away. Vampires are devious creatures."

Lloyd grinned sheepishly, his hand going to the back of his neck. "Am I that transparent?"

Seth let out a derisive snort. "Heh. Like a gelatinous cube."

Lloyd narrowed an eye at him, but any response he might have had was abruptly cut short.

Boom!

The loud sound echoed down the corridor to the south.

Martan nearly jumped out of skin. "What was that?"

Boom!

The second thump followed shortly after the first. All eyes turned in the direction of the south tunnel.

Aksel nudged Seth in the arm. "You did complain it was too quiet."

"Do you think it's the vampires?" Martan asked, his voice laced with more than a hint of fear.

Seth felt a touch of sympathy for the disheveled archer. After all, he had nearly been killed by a spawn just the day before. "Nah. My money's on Elladan. Things get smashed when he and the Boulder are together."

His comment elicited a round of chuckles from the group.

"I agree with Seth," Glo added. "Vampires tend to be just a bit more subtle."

"If you say so," Martan responded, though from his tone, he didn't sound quite convinced.

Seth led the way down the south corridor. It ended after a few dozen yards at another door. He pressed his ear to it and listened for any sounds from the other side. It was all quiet.

Unlike the other doors, this one was locked. Seth swiftly opened it, revealing a wide room similar to the one they had just left. A hexagonal table lay in the center of that room, adorned with more wooden chips.

The room had three other entrances, one on either side, and another door on the wall opposite from where they had entered. They all filtered into the room, when shouts erupted from behind the southernmost door. The companions all froze in place.

"That sounds like Raina," Martan whispered.

Aksel motioned the group forward. "They might be in trouble. Everyone get ready."

The others lined up while Seth went to check the door. Lloyd had both blades unsheathed, Martan held his bow ready, a flaming arrow nocked on its string, and Glo and Aksel wove their hands through the air with prepared spells.

This door was also locked, but Seth picked it in seconds. He was just about to pull it open when a puff of gray smoke slipped through a side crack in the door. Seth instinctively leapt back out of the way. "Watch out!"

Everyone's eyes were glued to the grey cloud. They all watched as it floated slowly across the room, then disappeared through a crack in the door to the west.

The group let out a collective sigh, before Aksel barked out a few more orders. "Martan, go watch that door. Seth, open this one. Everyone else be ready."

Seth waited till they were all prepared, then swiftly swung the door open. On the other side, they found another wide chamber, this one brilliantly lit by multiple sets of dancing lights. Andrella and Kalyn stood near a metal ladder that led up the side of the chamber, the former with her arm around the latter. Elladan, Shalla, and Raina stood nearby, all five of them laughing gaily.

It was the last thing Seth expected to see after that puff of vampire smoke had drifted from this room. The halfling exchanged a curious glance with Aksel, Lloyd, and Glo, then returned his attention to the revelers. "Sorry to disturb your party."

The others turned to face them, Andrella's face lighting up when she saw Lloyd. She ran over to him and threw her arms around his neck. "You should have seen it. I totally scared off that little vamp!"

Kalyn strode over as well, followed by the rest. "She totally did! That girlfriend of yours is meaner than a Deepwooder at a Dunwynn tea party."

Andrella swung her eyes toward Kalyn. "Says the girl who totally dusted a vamp."

Kalyn's face turned a bright shade of scarlet. "Aw, shucks. Twasn't nothin'. Aksel deserves all the credit for enchantin' my bow."

All the praise flying back and forth made Seth want to wretch. "Yeah, yeah. Save it for later—after we kill all the vamps."

Thankfully, his words squelched the others unwarranted zeal—all except for Kalyn. The archer stuck her tongue out at him. "Party pooper."

The retort Seth had on the tip of his tongue was cut off by Aksel. "Seth's right. We still have to route the vampires, as well as find the real Qualtan."

The little cleric's declaration quelled even the effervescent Kalyn.

Seth folded his arms across his chest and watched with keen satisfaction as they all quietly shuffled back into the other room. Once they were all gathered there, Seth pushed his way past them and checked the door where Martan stood guard. It wasn't locked.

Seth listened carefully at the door, but heard nothing on the other side. He pushed it inward and Elladan sent his swirling lights through the open doorway.

A long hallway lay before them, lined on either side with a number of closed doors. The hall ended at a single door a few dozen yards down.

The companions carefully searched the side rooms. They were all set up like the others, each with a hexagonal table surrounded by a few chairs. Wooden chips lay spread across most of them, and there were a couple of decks of playing cards as well.

"Looks like Haltan was running a full-fledged gambling den," Elladan noted with a wry smile.

"He wouldn't be the first merchant to do so," Shalla responded drolly. "I know one or two in Lukescros and Lymerdia."

Elladan chuckled. "I think I know the same ones."

Lloyd turned to Andrella, his expression curious. "When did the guardhouse burn down?"

Andrella cocked her head to one side and tapped her chin with a single finger. "A couple of weeks ago… just after you all left for Vermoorden."

"That's about the same time that shipment arrived in from Twin Oaks—the one with the first vamp hidden in it," Raina noted softly.

Seth exchanged a glance with Aksel. "Well that doesn't sound suspicious at all."

Glo steepled his hands in front of his mouth. "It's all starting to make sense. This underground establishment would be the perfect place to hide a den of vampires."

Aksel peered from Glo to Seth. "It's a definite possibility. Either way, we still have that end door to check."

Everyone filed back out into the hall. Seth inched up to the last door at the end of the hallway. Like all the others, it was not locked. The halfling leaned against the door and listened carefully. A soft noise emanated from the other side of the door—a low sucking sound.

Seth motioned for the others to be ready, then carefully swung the door open. The room beyond was the same size as the others, except that the table had been moved to the side. In its place stood a small bed with a dresser, a wardrobe, and a desk lining the other walls. A small hearth was inset into the back wall.

In front of the hearth, on a small carpet, lay a prone figure garbed in white robes. Two small figures knelt over the prone form, with their heads buried in its neck. As the door opened, they sat up and spun around, their mouths open with fangs bared, and smothered with deep red blood.

Seth immediately crouched down, grasping the knives he had hidden up his sleeves. The one "child" was the little girl vamp they had run into in these tunnels earlier. The other appeared to be a young boy, not much older than the little girl.

The girl's blue eyes fixed on Kalyn, her face contorting into a pout. "You're not my mommy. You're mean."

Before anyone could move, the little girl puffed into a cloud of smoke.

"Where ya goin?" the little boy cried. "We've got fresh meat here!"

He started to rise when a flaming arrow whizzed by Seth's ear and planted itself left center of his chest. The little vamp's mouth fell open, a silent scream on his lips. A moment later, his body crumbled into pile of dust on the floor below.

"Nice shot," Kalyn murmured, attesting to the fact that Martan had made the kill.

Seth did not turn, however, his eyes remaining fixed on the cloud of smoke that had been the girl vampire. He watched as it floated toward the hearth, then disappeared up the chimney. It was the third time the little girl vamp had gotten away from them. Seth made up his mind it would be the last.

"Take care of the body. I'm going after her," he called over his shoulder as he vaulted up the hearth shaft.

"Just be careful!" Aksel's voice drifted up after him.

Aksel stood over the dead body of what once was the Abbot Qualtan. The little cleric had cast a spell to ensure this time it was indeed the abbot and not just another disguise. The abbot must have been terrified at the end, his face contorted into a mask of fear. Aksel almost felt sorry for him.

"Poor Uncle Qualtan," Andrella murmured, a stray tear streaming down the side of her face. She gazed at Lloyd. "He wasn't always like this, you know. He was actually kind to me as a child."

Lloyd wrapped his arms around the distraught young lady and pulled her head to his chest. "I believe you. I've seen it happen to the best of men."

"And elves as well!" Elladan added from over by the wardrobe. He and Shalla had taken to searching Qualtan's things in hopes of finding some answers.

"I can attest to that," Martan murmured from the nearby doorway. The archer was not a fan of the elves. He had been held captive in the elven halls of Kai Arborous before the companions had met him.

Martan kept in line of sight with Kalyn and Raina, both of whom had stationed themselves at the other end of the hall. It was a prudent move, one of which Aksel highly approved. Who knew how many vampires were roaming around down here? The last thing they needed was to be cornered in this dead-end room.

Andrella cast a strained smile at Lloyd and Elladan. "Thank you for that, but I'd still feel better if I knew what had changed him so."

"I might be able to answer that."

All eyes turned toward Shalla, who stood in front of Qualtan's desk. Every drawer had been opened, one in particular looking as if its lock had been broken off. Shalla held up her hands as she strode over to rejoin them. One held a small box covered in blue velvet, and the other two pieces of parchment.

Aksel noted that one of the parchments had yellowed with age.

Shalla handed the newer one to Andrella. "Read this."

Lloyd let go as the young lady wiped her eyes and scanned the thick paper. "This is dated a little over a week ago." She read the contents aloud for all to hear.

> *Q,*
>
> *Be patient. As promised, the heart has been delivered to our friend DW. Come the full moon, your adversary will be gone forever. A second emissary will arrive soon. In the meanwhile, continue our work in the catacombs.*
>
> *D*

Aksel's eyes went round at the mention of the full moon. It confirmed his suspicions on why they had taken the Baron's heart.

Andrella nearly dropped the parchment, moisture welling in her eyes once more. Her voice was hollow as she spoke. "I can't believe it. Uncle Qualtan had Daddy murdered."

Lloyd grasped her from behind and held her tight while trying to console her. "There must be a reason. Good men don't just turn evil."

"If one is to believe this letter, he seemed to view Gryswold as his adversary," Glo pointed out softly.

Elladan placed a hand on the tall elf's shoulder and nodded. "That checks with what we saw at dinner the other night. Qualtan seemed to harbor quite a bit of resentment for his former comrades."

Lloyd gazed at the two of them while still holding Andrella tight. "That false Qualtan said the heart was taken to Vermoorden."

Elladan snapped his fingers at the mention of the town. "Vermoorden. How much you want to bet that 'DW' is the Mayor DeWyness?"

Glo steepled his fingers and nodded to the bard. "That makes sense. So if this letter is true, then we now know where the heart was taken. What I don't like is the sound of that 'gone forever' come the next full moon. That's only a few days from now."

Aksel had heard enough. It was time to share his suspicions with the others. "Ahem. I didn't say anything before because I wasn't certain, but this letter confirms it. Gryswold's soul is trapped in his heart, probably to be used in some sort of dark ritual."

Andrella's demeanor abruptly shifted. Her tears halted, and her eyes blazed with anger. There was a strained edge to her voice as she spoke. "That does it. We are going to Vermoorden. I'll find my father's heart if I have to tear the whole town apart brick by brick!"

"We both will!" Lloyd declared ardently as he grasped her by the hand. The pair exchanged a heated gaze, their countenances equally grim.

Aksel knew Lloyd to be overzealous at times, but Andrella's sudden shift in attitude worried him. The strain of these last few days may have been too much for the young lady. He gazed at her with keen sympathy. "I completely understand, Lady Andrella. Once we have finished here…"

A sudden gasp interrupted his speech. All eyes turned once more to Shalla. The bardess stood with her mouth agape, the blue velvet box in her one hand now opened. Inside lay a beautifully crafted silver ring inset with a deep blue sapphire.

Shalla's eyes were filled with sadness as she held out the older parchment toward Andrella. "You need to see this."

Andrella warily took the parchment from Shalla and looked it over. Her eyes narrowed as the scanned the yellowed paper. "This has a date from nearly twenty years ago." She paused a moment, her voice catching. "Why, this is in mother's handwriting!"

Lloyd moved closer once more and grasped her by the shoulders.

Andrella gave him a weak smile, then proceeded to read the letter out loud. Her voice caught a few more times, but she managed to plow through to the end.

My Dearest Qualtan,

It is with the deepest regret that I must return your lovely ring. It is a generous gesture, one that is truly appreciated. However, I must confess that my heart belongs to Gryswold. I do not know if he will have me, but if he will, I intend to be his bride. Please know that no matter what happens, you will always have a fond place in my heart.

With the greatest affection,
Gracelynn

Elladan let out a low whistle. "That explains why Qualtan had it out for Gryswold."

Andrella, her expression aghast, let the paper fall from her hands. "Why wouldn't she tell me…"

Lloyd wrapped his arms around her once again, yet Andrella merely stood there as if in shock.

Aksel picked up the fallen parchment as Shalla crossed over to Andrella. She gave Lloyd a subtle nod and the young man let Andrella go. Shalla placed an arm over Andrella's shoulder. "You have to see your mother's side of things. It's not exactly something you want to tell your kids."

Andrella peered into the bardess eyes and slowly nodded, the color returning to her cheeks. "I guess not."

Aksel tucked the aged letter away for safekeeping. He assumed at some point Andrella would want it back, but for now it would probably only serve to distract her. He cleared his throat, with every intention of focusing them back to their mission. "Ahem. I understand how disturbing this must be, but…"

A sudden noise made everyone spin toward the hearth. Seth had reappeared at the base of the firebox, vigorously brushing dark soot off his cloak. The halfling gazed up at them, his eyes hard. "We've got trouble."

21
FIENDS IN THE DARK

About twenty yards away from him stood more than three dozen pale creatures

While Aksel and the others searched Qualtan's room, Seth had been busy chasing after the little girl vamp. The agile halfling scurried up the hearth shaft till he reached a squared-off opening in the back stone wall.

Far above, Seth spied daylight, but there was no sign of the puff of smoke he had been chasing. The hole in front of him appeared to be a long, square stone duct just wide enough for a halfling to fit. Seth squinted, but couldn't see farther than a few feet into this side shaft.

With a silent shrug, the halfling launched himself into the dark hole. He slowly crawled forward on his belly, carefully listening for any sounds in the shaft ahead. Yet all he could hear was the sound of his own heart pounding in his chest.

This was a stupid idea, Seth chided himself. *Been hanging around with Lloyd too long.*

A short distance ahead, he reached a 'T' intersection. *Just great. What now?*

Seth listened down all three shafts, but heard nothing to indicate which one the little vamp had taken. With another shrug, he chose the duct to the left. The halfling continued his slow crawl until he finally reached another opening. It was still dark, but from what he could see it appeared to be another hearth.

Seth lowered himself into the vertical shaft, and cautiously climbed down till he reached the bottom. He swept his gaze around what appeared to be a small room until recognition dawned on him.

Dragon dung! It's that kitchen we passed.

Seth highly doubted the little vamp came this way. He was willing to bet a few gold pieces that she had scurried back to warn her fellow vamps. With a great sigh, the halfling vaulted up into the hearth chute and made his way back into the ductwork.

Figuring the little vamp was long gone, Seth hurried back through the ducts. He swiftly reached the 'T' intersection, and this time chose the shaft going straight. He had only gone a few feet, when the sound of voices reached his ears.

Got you! Seth thought with grim satisfaction.

Dim light shone ahead as he neared the end of the shaft. A metal grating barred the exit, but Seth scuttled up to the grille and peeked through. A large cavern lay before him, dim light streaming in from somewhere off to his right. In the distance he thought he could hear the lapping of waves, and the air was filled with the faint smell of salt.

The floor of the cavern was lined with a few rows of long boxes—coffins, no doubt. A group of shadowy figures stood gathered in their midst.

Seth could hear the murmur of voices wafting up from the cavern floor. He strained his ears, picking up the high-pitched voice of the little girl vamp.

"…and they killed Henry! With an arrow, no less! They're so mean. All we were doing was feeding off what was left of that dumb old abbot."

A tall shadow towered over the form of the little girl vamp. It shifted its stance and Seth caught a faint glint of light off dark armor.

The Black Knight! Found you.

The knight's deep voice rumbled up from the cavern floor. "It's fine, little one. Let them come. Soon they will all be one with us."

The knight's declaration was met with a round of hissing and low laughter.

Seth had heard enough. He slowly backed away from the grate, then spun around and began the long crawl back to warn the others.

Lloyd Stealle barged headlong into the dark cavern, brilliant red and yellow flames crackling around the blades he held in either hand. He halted about ten steps in from the entrance, then fell into a fighting stance and shouted, "Alright vamps—if you're in here, show yourselves!"

The young warrior's rash challenge was answered with dozens of hisses and growls from the darkness around him. Lloyd nervously adjusted his stance, rattled at the sheer volume of the vampires' response.

Thankfully he wasn't alone. As if on cue, two voices sang out behind him, overshadowing the guttural noises emanating from the darkness. *"Cras Placerat."*

Bright light flooded the cavern as two sets of glowing spheres spiraled past him, out and up into the chamber. The brilliant glow revealed a vast, natural rocky cavern stretching back as far as the eye could see. About twenty yards away from him stood more than three dozen pale creatures. They were lined up in front of an equal number of wooden coffins.

"Whoa, that's a lot of vamps!" Kalyn blurted behind him.

"You can say that again," Elladan concurred emphatically.

Lloyd agreed as well, but remained silent as his eyes were drawn to a tall figure at the very center of the undead horde. Clad in black armor, the creature positively reeked of power—a force so evil that despite Aksel's protection spell, it made Lloyd's skin crawl.

A deep voice echoed ominously from beneath the dark knight's helmet. "We've been waiting for you."

Lloyd nearly blanched from the malevolence in that voice. It took all his will to shake off the feeling of dread. He responded through gritted teeth. "Good, because I'm here to kill you."

A wicked laugh burst forth from the armor, reverberating off the walls of the chamber. "But I'm already dead—and you will be, too, soon enough." The black knight motioned its brethren forward. "Go, my children. Feast on their blood and souls."

"Get ready," Aksel's voice sounded from a few feet behind Lloyd.

The vampires swelled forward as one, slowly at first, but quickly picking up speed. Lloyd felt his muscles twitch as the horde closed half the distance to them in just a few seconds.

The young warrior tensed himself for the inevitable clash when two balls of brilliant red light streaked down from the back of the cavern. In a flash they slammed into the midst of the horde, exploding outward in a fierce onslaught of fire and light.

Lloyd shielded his eyes, the impact so close that he could feel his face and hands burning from the intense heat. It only lasted for a few seconds, then the flames receded and the fire went out.

Lloyd swiftly peered around the cavern. Where there had previously been nearly forty vampires, less than a dozen now stood. Burnt piles of ash were all that was left of the rest of the undead army.

Cheers went up behind Lloyd, but he knew this was far from over. The black knight still stood virtually unscathed in the midst of the remaining vampires.

Without another thought, Lloyd rushed forward, a battle cry on his lips as he charged the knight.

"Wahoo!" Kalyn cried with glee at the sight of all the charbroiled vamps. Their plan had worked.

When Seth told them about the cavern, he mentioned it might have another entrance out by the bay. Andrella backed up the notion, saying that she knew of a cave along that part of the shore. That gave Elladan a brilliant, if crazy idea.

Glo and Andrella flew out to the cave while Lloyd and the others acted as distractions. It all hinged on the wizard and his apprentice catching the vampires off guard with dual balls of fire. Elladan estimated that the damage from the twin explosions would incinerate most of the spawn before they had a chance to heal.

Thankfully he was right. Most of the vamps were now nothing but ash. Only a few remained standing, most of whom were singed and partially burnt.

The black knight, however, looked untouched. As Lloyd charged the imposing creature, some other vamps moved to bar his way.

Kalyn hissed to Martan, "Let's clear the path for Lloyd!"

The two archers loosed a flurry of wood-tipped arrows from their bows. The three vamps directly in Lloyd's way took direct hits to the heart, exploding into dust before they could deter him.

Other spawn moved to intercept the warrior, but the dark knight waved them off. "Get the archers, my children. I'll handle this one myself."

A brutal game of dodge and strike ensued with the approaching vamps. Inspiring music flooded the cavern as Kalyn and Martan fired round after round. A translucent battle axe floated into the fray, taking deadly swings at the rushing creatures. Yet the vamps were faster than Kalyn imagined.

The creatures bobbed and weaved their way forward, forcing axe and arrow to miss their marks. They continued their onward plummet, yanking stray shafts out of their torsos as they went.

Suddenly, a large furry blur shot past the duo, cutting off one of the remaining creatures. Raina in bear form plowed into the spawn, grappling the creature paw to hand.

"Be careful, Raina!" Kalyn shouted, remembering how the last spawn had knocked her friend out cold. Yet she had no more time to watch the battle as the rest of the vamps continued their forward rush.

Andrella didn't quite know how to feel. She had been exhilarated to join the companions in the first place, and flying turned out to be an incredible experience. Glo even praised her on how easily she took to the air.

"When I learned to fly, I flailed around like a beached whale," he confided.

Yet her nerves screamed as she led Glo through the cave entrance.

Everyone was depending on her—especially Lloyd, who was to be the main bait.

Glo had only taught her this morning how to cast a ball of fire. He assured her that she was ready. She had even managed to coalesce a flaming ball between her palms, but it fizzled out before she could cast it.

Glo had taken the lead, holding Andrella by the hand as they flew toward the back of the dark cave. She whispered to her mentor, "Are you sure I can do this?"

Her voice squeaked a lot more than she had intended.

Glo squeezed her hand gently. "I know you can. Just breathe through the spell, like I taught you."

It was nice that he had so much faith in her, but Andrella's nerves would not relent. Her stomach continued to twist into knots. "But… I failed this morning…"

Glo was silent for a few moments, then squeezed her hand again, his tone kind but firm. "Andrella, I've been doing this for nearly one hundred years. Trust me when I say you're ready."

Andrella raised an eyebrow. *One hundred years?* She'd almost forgotten how long-lived elves were. Glo didn't look much older than her. *He's quite handsome, in fact…*

Her thoughts were interrupted as a bright light appeared just ahead of them. She could see now.

The rocky cave expanded into a large cavern a short distance further on. Lloyd and the others stood at the opposite end, maybe one hundred yards from where she and Glo hovered in the air. Between them stood a great number of vampires.

Andrella nearly gasped, covering her mouth barely in time. *There's no way they can survive that.* The young lady's resolve abruptly hardened. *I have to do this. Lloyd's as good as dead if I don't.*

Glo squeezed her hand once more and whispered, "Are you ready?"

Andrella set her jaw and nodded. "Let's do this."

The duo flew forward side by side, picking up speed as they went. Andrella forced all other thoughts from her mind, weaving her arms as Glo had taught her. They were almost above their targets when the vampires suddenly rushed the others.

Andrella nearly lost it at that point, but something inside her took over—some instinct that demanded she protect the ones she loved. Driven by those strong emotions, the young mage cupped her hands together, feeling rather than seeing the flaming ball appear between them. She pushed her palms outward together and spat a single word, "*Augue.*"

The bright red ball streaked from her hands, crossing the cavern at incredible speed. A second sphere joined it, the two rushing toward their targets. In less than a second, they covered the distance to their quarry.

The twin orbs slammed into the cavern floor, exploding into dual hemispheres of brilliant red and yellow flames. The half spheres expanded in size till they nearly overlapped each other, completely engulfing the unsuspecting vampires.

Harsh screams and guttural howls erupted from the conflagration, yet they were quickly cut short. A few seconds later, the flaming spheres winked out. Only a few vampires still remained standing— the ones on the outskirts of the attack, and the black knight, of course. The rest were no more than piles of ash.

Andrella let out a deep breath, not realizing she had been holding it the entire time. "We… we did it!"

Yet Glo didn't quite seem to share her enthusiasm. "Yes, that mostly worked, but there are still quite a few vampires left standing."

Andrella rolled up her sleeves and fixed the wizard with a grim smile. "Then let's fix that, shall we?"

Martan did his best to hold back his terror as he fired arrow after arrow at the approaching vampires. *Why in Thac are we doing this again?*

The morose archer had thought the idea of baiting the creatures insane in the first place. He had even tried to convince Kalyn it was a bad idea, but she wouldn't hear a word of it.

"I'm sure the Heroes know what they're doin'."

Sure, Martan thought to himself. *They know how to get those around them killed.*

Yet by some miracle, Elladan's plan had worked. Glolindir and the Lady Andrella had taken out almost all of the vampires—almost.

Dragon dung! These things are too fast. Martan had a bead on a vampire's heart, but the creature somehow managed to bend out of the way of his arrow at the very last moment. The arrow embedded itself in the vamp's arm, only to be immediately yanked out.

"They're getting closer," he warned Kalyn.

"Shut up and keep firin'," the young woman yelled back at him.

Martan took a deep breath and nocked another arrow to his bowstring. The arrow came alight with flame as he drew a bead on the nearest vamp. *Synopei, please let this one hit.*

With that silent prayer, he let the arrow fly. It sailed across the intervening distance straight for the creature's heart. Yet once again at the last moment, the vamp began to change direction.

All of a sudden, a flaming beam lanced down from above. It caught the creature in the back, causing it to howl in pain. Momentarily stunned, Martan's arrow caught the vamp right in the heart. Its eyes went wide, then the creature exploded outward in a cloud of dust.

"Booya!" Kalyn cried exultantly. She had just experienced similar success with an assist from the Lady Andrella. Kalyn gave the flying duo a quick salute. "Slicker n' snot, guys! Keep it up!"

Martan gave them a feeble smile as well. *At least they're trying to keep us alive this time.*

All of a sudden, a vampire leaped up into the air. It caught Glolindir by the edge of his robe and slammed the elf down to the ground with a bone-cracking *crunch.*

"Glolindir!" Kalyn screamed. The young woman took off toward the fallen elf, arrows flying at the vamp who had taken him down. Yet none hit their mark.

"Dust already!" Kalyn yelled at the stubborn creature. Unfortunately, she neglected to keep an eye on her surroundings.

Martan watched in horror as a second vampire slammed into Kalyn, knocking her flat on her back. His heart was in his throat as the creature leaped on top of her and bared its fangs.

The grim archer's fingers moved without thinking. An arrow leapt from his bow without him realizing it and sped across the short distance, straight into the vampire's heart.

Yelling and kicking at the creature straddling her, Kalyn got a mouthful of dust as it exploded. Choking and spitting, the young woman shot up and took aim at the vamp on top of Glolindir, but it turned out to be unnecessary.

A fiery ray shot down from above and caught the vampire in the head. The creature howled as it burst into flames and crumbled to ash over the fallen elf.

Martan's eyes went wide as Andrella strafed by overhead. *Holy Thac! Remind me never to tick that lady off.*

Aksel had had his doubts when Elladan suggested the dual fire ball scheme. Andrella was still a novice wizard. She had barely mastered spells of the second order the previous day. Yet Glo assured him that she would be able to handle this third order spell.

Against his better judgement, Aksel agreed to the plan. In the end it had worked rather well, leaving only a few of the vampires to deal with.

As the vampires rushed them, Aksel conjured a spiritual battle axe and sent it into the creatures' midst. He swung repeatedly at them, but the vampires were too agile to land a strike.

"I'm going out there," Raina declared suddenly.

Aksel shifted his gaze toward the red-haired druid just in time to see her shift. The small woman abruptly expanded, fur sprouting from her skin, her face elongating into a snout. Moments later, a red-furred bear loped forward and crashed head-on into one of the approaching vampires.

Aksel watched with clear admiration as she locked paws with the creature and held it at bay. It was obviously only a spawn she faced, but such creatures were quite strong. Yet now the pair were deadlocked in a dangerous dance.

A sinking feeling hit him in the pit of his stomach. He had taking a liking to this strange young woman. She was smart, funny, and rather daring. The last thing he wanted was to see her get hurt.

With a flick of his fingers, Aksel sent his spiritual battle axe to help the young druid. He brought it up behind the vampire and swiped the creature across its back.

The vampire howled in pain, obviously injured by the holy-powered weapon. Raina took the opportunity to shift her hold on the creature. She spun it around and lifted it from behind, immobilizing it in an unbreakable bear hug.

"Turn it this way!" Aksel cried out to her.

Raina heard his voice and shifted toward Aksel, the creature still pinned in her massive arms. The vampire beat its fists against its captor, but it struggled to no avail.

Aksel pressed his lips into a thin line as he pushed his palm outward. "*Lux acribus.*"

A blinding beam of white light shot from his outstretched hand, hitting the pinned vampire in the torso. The creature screamed, then exploded into a cloud of dust.

Aksel's lips curved into small smile as the red bear did a short dance of triumph. *Well, that could have gone far worse.*

Elladan held his breath when the twin fire balls went off. He had faith in his plan, and trusted Glo's estimation of Andrella. His sole concern was how many vampires would be caught in the crossfire. When the flames finally winked out, only a handful of vampires were left.

Shalla nudged him in the arm. "Look at that. It actually worked."

Elladan flashed her a pearly smile. "Did you ever have any doubts?"

The bards conjured their instruments and played like mad as the battle ensued. Fingers danced up and down the strings, sending waves of inspirational magic coursing through the air.

Lloyd took on the black knight as Kalyn and Martan dusted a few vamps. Raina held off another while Aksel lent her his support. It all seemed to be going well, when a vamp suddenly dropped from the ceiling right in front of Shalla. It hissed at the startled bardess, its eyes filled with a feral red glow.

Elladan moved without thinking. He grabbed a stake from his belt and leapt in front of the hissing vampire. He stabbed at the creature with his stake, but it was far too strong and fast. It caught his arm and threw him to the ground, immediately leaping on top of him.

Elladan could smell the creature's foul breath as it bore down on him. Stake still in hand, he struggled to wedge it between himself and the pale creature. The vamp was now only inches from his neck. In a last-ditch effort, Elladan twisted his body and slammed the stake into the creature's chest, fervently praying that he had hit it in the heart.

The vampire abruptly halted its descent. Its red eyes went glassy just before it erupted into a cloud of dust.

"Got 'im!" Elladan cried in triumph as he sat up and wiped the dust from his eyes. That was when his gaze fell on Shalla. The bardess stood with a crossbow in hand, a tantalizing smile upon her lips.

Elladan shrugged and gave her a bent smile. "Okay, maybe you got 'im."

Shrouded in his invisible cloak, Seth watched intently as Lloyd faced off against the black knight. The knight was brutal, pressing forward with huge overhead swings of its great blade. If just one of those hit, Lloyd would have been cloven in two.

Yet the young warrior proved as fast as the knight. Time and again, he caught the big blade, pushing it aside with one sword, then spinning and striking a savage blow with the other.

Still, it was not enough to hurt the knight. There was something strange about the creature's armor. Lloyd's holy sword should have been deadly to it, but instead, the blade merely bounced off the knight's black mail.

Lloyd's star metal sword proved far more effective. The ebon blade cut through the armor, leaving thin gaps in the dark steel mail. Unfortunately, any damage to the vampire itself healed too fast to make any difference.

Things were looking dire for the young warrior. He couldn't truly hurt his opponent, and one wrong move on his part would prove fatal.

Just when Seth thought it was hopeless, Lloyd did something that truly impressed him. The young warrior completely avoided a huge swing, then caught the knight twice in its midriff. The first strike with the black blade left a clean cut in the vampire's armor. The second strike hit in the same exact spot, going straight through the armor and slicing into the undead creature's flesh.

The resultant howl attested to the effectiveness of the maneuver. Unfortunately, it did not leave Lloyd enough to time to retreat. With surprising speed, the knight leapt forward and grasped his wrist, wrenching the holy sword from Lloyd's hand. The knight then pushed Lloyd to the ground and raised its blade for a killing blow.

Not sure what good it would do, Seth grasped the hidden daggers up his sleeves. He prepared to toss them, but stayed his hand as Lloyd performed an ingenious maneuver.

Howling with rage, the black knight stepped over Lloyd's body, and threw its entire weight into one deadly blow. At the same moment, Lloyd brought up his black blade and used the creature's own momentum to skewer it straight through the chest.

Seth watched with fascination as the knight froze in place, the other end of the black blade sticking straight out of its back. It hung there for a few moments, then an evil laugh echoed from underneath the dark helmet. "Were I alive, that would have been fatal. Too bad for you."

Slowly and inexorably, the black knight pulled itself off Lloyd's blade. Lloyd did not move. The young warrior lay on the ground, his face pale and his breathing heavy.

It's drained him, Seth realized. *Lloyd's a goner for sure, unless…*

The halfling's eyes narrowed as he stared at the black knight's armor. There was a hole in the back of its chest, just big enough for a knife or… a stake!

Seth swiftly sheathed his daggers and pulled out a stake as the black knight straddled Lloyd once more. It hissed at the fallen warrior as it lifted its huge blade into the air. "I was going to turn you, but you damaged my nice black armor."

As the creature admonished Lloyd, Seth took off at a dead run. The blade had just begun its downward arc as the halfling leapt into the air. Seth slammed the stake with all his might through the hole in the armor.

"Ahhh!"

The knight tensed, a terrifying shriek emanating from its black helmet. The sword clattered out of its hands as it tried to reach behind its back and pull Seth off.

Seth wriggled from side to side, staying out of the reach as he ground the stake further into the armor.

Abruptly the knight froze in place. A horrid wail sprang from the armor, and then a cloud of dust exploded out of the hole and the knight's visor.

The stake went slack in Seth's hand as he fell to the ground and tumbled out of the way. The black armor collapsed into a heap at Lloyd's feet.

Seth stood up and brushed himself off. "Seth one, black knight zero."

The young man peered up at the halfling, a weak grin on his face. "Guess you've graduated… from killing mages…"

The side of Seth's mouth twisted upward as he helped Lloyd off the ground. "Just don't tell Glo. It makes him nervous."

Seth surveyed the cavern floor as he helped Lloyd back to the others. There were no more vampires in sight, but Glo had been badly hurt.

Raina looked Lloyd over as Aksel healed Glo. "He's going to need another visit to the temple."

Lloyd grimaced at her pronouncement. "Not again."

Andrella threw her arms around him and hugged him tight. "I'm just glad you're in one piece."

Glo moaned from where he laid on the cavern floor. "Yes, be thankful you don't have any broken bones."

"Hush," Aksel admonished the wizard. "Unless you don't want them to mend right."

Glo arched an eyebrow at the cleric, then pressed his lips together firmly.

"So did we get them all?" Lloyd asked wearily.

Raina shook her head. "Not quite. I saw a couple of spawn puff into smoke and disappear back into the tunnels. They'll have to be hunted down, but for now I think it best to take care of our wounded."

"I quite agree," Andrella nodded. She pulled Lloyd's arm over her shoulder and called over to Martan. "Give me a hand taking him over to the temple."

This time, Lloyd didn't argue.

Once they left, Raina motioned to Seth and the others. "Give me a hand with what's left of these coffins. Don't want those spawn sneaking back in here and using them."

Seth helped to go around and destroy the coffins that were still in one piece, and poured holy water on the dirt within. At the far end, he came across one that was rather ornate. There was a symbol emblazoned on it—a green tree over a yellow background. It was the same design as on the black knight's armor. There was an elvish symbol carved beneath it.

Seth waved Elladan over. "Come check this out."

Aksel was still working on Glo's shattered bones, but everyone else gathered around the ornate coffin.

Elladan took one glance and pronounced, "That's a 'D.'"

Shalla raised a delicate eyebrow. "Hmm. As in the 'D' in that letter to Qualtan?"

Elladan gave her a sly wink. "I'd bet money on it."

Kalyn folded her arms across her chest, her lips rising ever so slightly. "So this proves that Qualtan was workin' with the vamps…"

Shalla nodded at the young woman, then shifted her gaze back to Elladan. "…and if 'DW' really is the Mayor DeWyness like you guessed, then so is she."

Elladan wrinkled his nose as if smelling something foul. "Which has to make you wonder, what's really going on in Vermoorden?"

Seth had been thinking the same exact thing. He pulled out a dagger and fingered the blade meaningfully. "Let's go 'ask' Mayor Darkness…

22
INVASION OF RAVENFORD

It appears we are wanted criminals in Dunwynn

Andrella's footsteps echoed up and down the throne room as she marched toward the side meeting room. As she approached the closed door, she could hear voices beyond. She took a deep breath, straightened her shoulders, then turned the latch and stepped inside.

Everyone gazed her way, the room falling silent. Gracelynn sat at the head of the table, looking as composed as ever. Still, Andrella couldn't help but notice the dark circles under her eyes.

Gelpas stood at her mother's side, his shoulders tense. Elladan, Shalla, and Raina were also in the room, their faces grim.

"How's Lloyd?" Shalla asked.

Andrella took a deep breath. "He's okay. The vamp barely touched him. He's sleeping it off now in the guest room upstairs. He should be fine in a couple of hours." She angled her eyes down toward Raina. "How's Glo doing?"

"He's also in a guest room upstairs, being harassed by Kalyn and Seth. He's gonna be sore for a day or two, but he'll make a full recovery."

Gracelynn sat back in her seat. "I'm glad everyone's alright. It was no small battle, as I understand, and thus no small service that all of you provided to keep us safe." With that, she lifted a parchment from the table.

Andrella raised her eyebrows when she spotted an older parchment lying there next to the blue velvet box they found in Qualtan's quarters.

Gracelynn sighed, making eye contact with her. "Based on this, we believe your father's heart was taken to Vermoorden. Further, the Mayor DeWyness may be involved."

Andrella clamped her teeth together. "I never liked DeWyness. She always seemed too wrapped up in her own affairs to care for her town and people."

"I noticed the same thing." Gracelynn stared hard at her daughter before speaking again. "Andrella, as soon as the others are rested and ready to travel, I want you to go with our friends here to Vermoorden and recover your father's heart."

Andrella started, her mouth falling open. "Mother! What about you? Ignar is due to arrive sometime soon."

"Actually, his ships were spotted rounding the coast of Cape Marlin a short while ago." Shalla crossed her arms, looking between Andrella and Gracelynn. "Three ships in total, filled to the rafters with Dunwynn troops."

Andrella blinked, impressed by how the bardess seemed to know everything that was going on in and around town.

Gelpas shifted on his feet, peering down at the Lady Gracelynn. "That only gives us a couple of hours before they pull into the harbor."

Andrella turned back to her mother.

Gracelynn sat up straighter in her seat and pushed her shoulders back. "Don't worry about me, daughter. I can handle Ignar." The duchess' eyes twitched toward Elladan. "The others, however, really need to leave before he arrives."

Andrella's brows slowly drew together. "Why?"

Elladan chuckled softly. "It appears we are wanted criminals in Dunwynn."

"What?" Andrella could feel the heat of anger crawling up her neck. "On what grounds? I thought we settled everything at the tournament."

Elladan fixed her with one of his patented half-smiles. "Our good 'friend' Princess Anya of Lanfor claims we stole her property."

Andrella was silent for a moment in frustrated thought. "What could you have stolen? You blew it all up!"

Elladan let out a deep rolling laugh. "I wouldn't phrase it that way in front of Glolindir."

Shalla spoke up as Elladan continued to chuckle. "We think she is referring to Vestiralana."

Andrella's mouth fell open as shock and rage swirled in her chest. "Who does she think she is? Lady Ves is a person, not property!"

Gracelynn sighed, drawing Andrella's attention back to her mother. "Unfortunately, the current Dunwynn law does not recognize any non-humans as having rights."

Andrella looked twice at her. "Lady Ves is human, isn't she?"

Elladan cleared his throat. "Actually, Ves and her sisters are all dragons."

Andrella stared at him, her mouth half open. "They're… dragons? Ves, Ruka, and little Maya?" She narrowed her eyes. "Why am I just being told this now?"

Elladan held up his hands. "We were sworn to secrecy."

"As were your father and I, dear. It was for their own protection at the time." Gracelynn let out a heavy sigh. "But back to the point— I've been instructed to throw all the Heroes in the dungeon. That is why all of you must leave before Ignar arrives."

Andrella felt overwhelming emotions bubbling up inside her. She didn't know whether she wanted to break something in a rage, cry out in frustration, or both. All of this was so unfair.

Shalla walked around the table to Andrella, wrapping an arm around her shoulders. "It's going to be alright. While you are with the others, saving your father, Gelpas and I will keep an eye on things here."

Gelpas dipped his chin. "Indeed we shall."

"And I'll be staying here as well," Raina interjected. "Someone needs to hunt down those last few vamps."

Andrella took a deep breath to calm her nerves, then peered intently at her mother. "Are you sure about this? Are you sure you want me to go?"

Gracelynn stood and walked around the table to Andrella, grasping both her hands. "Elladan and Shalla related the entire vampire battle to me. I think you handled yourself quite well. We"—her voice caught for a moment—"I believe you are ready for this."

Andrella felt her cheeks warm as a smile turned up her lips. She drew her mother into a tight embrace. "Thank you for believing in me." She pulled back, resting her hands on her mother's shoulders. "Just promise me that you'll be careful. We don't know anything about this Ignar, and I don't trust him."

Gracelynn laughed for the first time in weeks. It was good to hear it once again. "Neither do I, but I've dealt with far worse. I can handle myself." She turned and walked back to her chair, gently sitting down.

Andrella also pulled out a chair and sat down, drumming her fingers on the table lightly. "So, only a couple of hours before Ignar arrives? That doesn't give us much time."

Elladan sat forward in his seat. "It does if we use Maltar's teleportation circle."

"Can it be set for Vermoorden?" Andrella's lips twisted to the side as Elladan shook his head.

"No, however it can take us to Lukescros. That would put us just a few hours' ride south of Vermoorden."

Andrella nodded. "Good. That will allow Lloyd and Glo to rest until the last minute."

"Then we are all agreed?" All eyes turned to Gracelynn.

Andrella nodded and stood, peering at Elladan. "We'll inform the others of the plan, then I'll help you prepare the teleportation circle."

Shalla strode toward the door, pausing next to it. "I'll get you set up with supplies." She gazed at Gelpas. "Captain, would you mind giving me a hand?"

Andrella lifted an eyebrow as Gelpas' face brightened. "Of course, Mistress Shalla."

The pair left the room talking through a list of items to acquire.

Elladan chuckled as he stood and pulled out Raina's chair for her. "Sounds like Shalla is going to make sure our packs are heavy."

"Better than being too light." Raina smiled.

"Very true!" Elladan made his way toward the door, pausing only to look back at Gracelynn. "I will tell Martan to keep a look-out from the tower and let us know the minute he spots Dunwynn sails."

Gracelynn dipped her chin. "Excellent idea."

"And I will go tell the others our plan." Raina chimed in.

"I'll meet you in Maltar's tower when I've finished." Elladan smiled at Andrella, then he and Raina left, shutting the door behind them.

Andrella hesitated, her eyes drifting toward the blue velvet box sitting on the table. With everyone gone, now was as good a time as any to address why it and that old letter were in Qualtan's room.

Andrella crossed the space between them, leaning over and picking up the box. She opened it, keenly aware that her mother had tensed, and pulled out the ring. Andrella spun it around on her finger, locking eyes with Gracelynn.

"So, Mother, is there anything you'd like to tell me?"

Gracelynn took a deep breath, a heavy sigh escaping her lips.

Elladan had loved maps ever since he was a little kid. As a youth, he would spend hours at the great library in Kai Arborous, poring over the pages of every atlas he could get his hands on. Each page would take him to a different place, as if he were traveling the entire world of Arinthar. It was a dream he vowed to fulfill in person before his long life was over.

All those hours of studying maps came in handy now. With his sharp mind, Elladan had memorized the longitudes and latitudes of most of the important places in the world. Thus, pinpointing Lukescros' location in the pipes and rods that hung from the ceiling above the teleportation circle was child's play for him.

"A few more feet to the left." Elladan motioned with his hand from his vantage point outside the crisscrossed glowing blue rings of the circle.

Andrella hovered a few feet above the ground, holding the rod attached to the sphere of Arinthar in both hands. Elladan watched with admiration as she pushed the orb along the track in the direction he had specified. She had seen Glo cast the spell earlier that day and already had it memorized.

Elladan chuckled softly to himself. *She's a sharp one, alright. Glo better watch out, or at this rate she'll surpass him.*

"How's that?" Andrella peered down at him from where she had stopped the sphere.

Elladan narrowed an eye as he gauged the position of the orb. He waved his hand again. "A half a foot further."

Andrella nodded, her face scrunching up as she inched the model of Arinthar forward. She cast another glance over her shoulder at him.

Elladan responded with a thumbs-up. He was just about to praise her accuracy when the pounding of footsteps resounded down the stairwell.

Martan appeared at the bottom of the stairs, the grim archer huffing from exertion. He halted and crouched down, his hands on his knees, as he glanced at Elladan. "They're… here…"

Elladan cocked his head and narrowed an eye at the breathless archer. "You mean Dunwynn?"

Martan bobbed his head up and down. "Three ships… pulling up… to the docks…"

Elladan let out a short breath and shifted his gaze toward Andrella. The budding wizard gracefully descended to the ground, her eyes fixed on his. Mixed emotions played across her face.

Elladan sympathized with the inner turmoil she was feeling. Part of her was obviously bursting with excitement to leave. Yet another part of her was clearly concerned with leaving her mother behind just now. The bard placed a comforting arm around her shoulder as she drew up next to him. "Guess that's our cue to leave."

Andrella peered up at him, a strained smile on her lips. She gently patted his hand, then headed toward the stairs. "I'll go get my things."

Martan graciously moved aside for her, his eyes filled with compassion for the troubled young lady. As soon as Andrella passed, he cast a glance at Elladan. "I'll go get the others."

Elladan gave him a swift nod.

Martan then bounded up the stairs after the Lady Andrella.

A short while later, Andrella returned with Aksel, Glo, Kalyn, and Lloyd in tow. Lloyd looked sleepy, but otherwise seemed fine. Glo, on the other hand, appeared rather stiff.

Aksel glanced around the basement. "Where's Seth?"

Elladan responded with a mild shrug. "He'll be back shortly. He had a 'small' errand to attend to."

Aksel lifted an eyebrow, but turned as a shout drifted down from the stairwell.

"We've got your supplies!"

Shalla appeared a moment later, followed by Gelpas, Martan, and Raina. Each held at least one backpack in hand, the packs literally bulging at the seams.

"Sure you packed us enough there?" Lloyd noted drolly as the bardess and the others handed the packs out to the companions.

Kalyn nudged her head toward Andrella with a snort. "Count yer blessins' this one's got a portal bag, or you'd be carryin' three times what ya got already."

Andrella cast a sour glance at Kalyn. "Have you learned nothing from me? It's not lady-like to traipse around in the same clothes day in and day out."

Kalyn's hands went to her hips, her cheeks puffing into a pout. "I wash the clothes I wear"—her voice dropped to a whisper as she turned her head and stared at the ground—"every few days or so."

Andrella slowly shook her head, a deep sigh escaping her lips.

"Well then," Shalla gracefully changed the subject, "the ships have docked. We got a rough headcount and there's easily a hundred troops on board."

Elladan raised both eyebrows. "That's a serious occupation force."

The corner of Shalla's mouth lifted slightly. "That's not all. Just after each ship docked, an iron golem detached from the bow and are wading their way ashore."

Aksel nervously rubbed his chin. "Not even the Boulder could stand against that."

Andrella huffed, her face reddening. "What in Thac is my uncle thinking, sending a force like that? Is he planning on waging a war?"

Lloyd placed a comforting arm around the young lady's shoulder. "On the bright side, I doubt they'll have any problems with those remaining vampire spawn."

Andrella peered up at the young man, her angry expression giving way to a smile. "I guess that's true."

"A force like that will have little trouble keeping the town safe," Gelpas agreed, "though my men will most likely be displaced."

Andrella shifted her gaze to Gelpas, her expression growing troubled once more. "What about you?"

A wry smile edged across the Captain's face. "Oh, don't worry about me. They'll have to keep me on—at least for appearances."

Shalla placed a slim hand on Gelpas' arm. "And I'll be the go-between for the Captain and his men."

Elladan noted how her hand lingered on the tall Captain's muscular arm. He experienced the slightest twinge of jealousy, but immediately pushed it aside. Elladan was leaving, to return only the gods knew when, and Shalla was a grown woman.

A quasi-smile crossed the elf's face as he pulled the lovely bardess aside. "Just promise me to be careful."

Shalla placed her hands on his arms and gazed up at him with a playful smile. "I always am."

"All done!" a voice interrupted them. Seth had appeared at the base of the stairwell.

"What's done?" Aksel asked.

The halfling wore a satisfied smile as he strode over and dropped a golden ring in Elladan's hand. "I hid the Boulder in Haltan's vault."

Shalla shifted her gaze between Seth and Elladan, then gave an approving nod. "That was clever."

Elladan exchanged a grin with Seth. "We do our best." He then held out the ring to Shalla. "Hang on to this for safekeeping."

Shalla eyed the ring for a moment, then took it, a playful smile crossing her lips. "Why Elladan, you shouldn't have."

The bardess slipped the golden circle on her finger, then stood on her toes. Elladan went to kiss her on the lips, but at the last moment, she moved her head to the side and kissed him on the cheek instead.

A half-smile formed on the bard's lips as Shalla gently disengaged herself, her eyes filled with mixed emotions. Elladan could guess what was going on in her mind. He decided to keep things light with a quick grin and a wink.

Meanwhile Raina and Kalyn said their goodbyes.

"When this is all over, come visit me in Bendenwood," the curly-topped druid told the young archer.

"I will for sure this time," Kalyn responded somberly. She stepped forward and caught the smaller woman in a firm embrace.

"Sure you will," Raina said dryly as the two women let go of each other.

Elladan noted the way the young druid and Aksel gravitated around each other these last couple of days. Yet they both appeared quite shy. Ever a fan of love, he decided to give them a little push. "Is that an open invitation?"

Raina's brow crinkled as her eyes turned toward him. "Sure…" She cast a quick glance in Aksel's direction, then dropped her gaze to the floor, her cheeks reddening slightly. "As druid friends, you're all welcome… anytime…"

Elladan had studied the fairer sex long enough to read the signs. She was definitely interested in the little gnome cleric. He nudged Aksel in the arm. "What do you think? Want to visit Bendenwood when this is all over?"

Aksel eyed Elladan as if trying to determine his ulterior motive. After a moment or two, he merely shrugged and shifted his gaze toward Raina. "I don't see why not. It's an interesting place, and I wouldn't mind learning more about the druids."

Raina's expression turned bubbly, her voice practically squeaking with excitement. "I'll be happy to show you around when you come visit."

Aksel simply nodded. "That would be most appreciated."

As everyone gathered their things, Andrella grew more emotional.

Without warning, she threw her arms around Gelpas and hugged him tight around the waist, burying her head in the Captain's broad chest.

For the first time since Elladan had met him, Gelpas' stern expression disappeared. He held the young woman in his arms and gently patted her on the back.

A number of seconds passed before Andrella finally let him go. She stepped back and wiped a stray tear from her eye. "Please keep an eye on Mother."

Gelpas stared at the young woman with an almost fatherly expression. "I give you my word."

Lloyd gently grasped her arm. "Andrella… it's time…"

Andrella took a deep breath, then threw back her shoulders and spun on her heel. "Then let's be going."

She grasped Lloyd by the hand and purposely strode with him into the teleportation circle. With everyone now lined up, Shalla went over and threw the switch.

Elladan silently wondered if it would be the last time he would see the lovely bardess. He gave her one last grin as Ravenford faded away.

23
THE CAGE

Donatello found himself in a lush meadow of wildflowers, vibrant yellow and orange blossoms stretching off as far as the eye could see. Tall green trees dotted the meadow here and there, reaching up to a cloudless blue sky overhead.

For the life of him, Donnie couldn't remember how he had gotten here. The last thing he remembered was standing in the blue rings of the teleportation circle in Gaither's tower in Tarsmoor with his friends and the sour-faced Sir Fafnar.

Glo had set the circle to send them back to Ravenford. Yet now neither his companions nor the town were anywhere to be seen.

Donnie cupped his hands together and called out their names. "Elladan! Glo! Lloyd!"

Yet no answer came. The confused elf gazed up to the sky, shading his eyes as he tried to get his bearings. A sudden voice behind him nearly made him jump out of his skin.

"You call for them, but not for me?"

A chill went up Donnie's spine as he heard that familiar voice. He spun around, his heart nearly leaping out his chest. There before him stood his first love.

"Miranda?" Donnie barely managed to choke out the name.

A breeze kicked up across the meadow, adding to the chill he already felt. The sandy-haired blonde smoothed out her long-sleeved white and blue dress, then stared at him intently with her deep emerald green eyes. "So, you do still remember my name…"

Donnie's voice caught in his throat as he took her pale, slim hands in his. "Of… of course I do. I think about you… every day…"

The side of her mouth upturned ever so slightly. "I bet you do, especially with that little dragon girl constantly making eyes at you."

"It's not like that…" Donnie began, then stopped. His eyes narrowed. "How did you know about Ruka?"

A stronger wind suddenly kicked up across the meadow, uprooting flowers and blowing them in Donnie's face. The slender elf shielded his eyes, but the gust abruptly halted once more.

Donnie returned his gaze to his love, but something was different. Her blue and white gown had been replaced with a dark leather tunic and long black boots. The only other thing that had changed was the smirk on her lips had grown more pronounced.

"Perhaps you prefer me more like this?"

Donnie's eyes nearly bugged out of his head. "Ruka? Was it you the whole time?"

The dragon girl folded her arms across her chest and stared back at him, her eyes ablaze. "Didn't you know? It's always been me."

Donnie's jaw dropped open. He tried to speak, but all that would come out is gibberish. "But… how… it's not… is it?"

The wind kicked up again, a fierce gale this time. Dark clouds swept swiftly through the skies, obliterating the sun in mere seconds. The winds grew so strong Donnie found it hard to stand his ground.

Ruka stood there calmly watching him as they were blown farther apart.

"Ruka! Miranda!" The distraught elf cried in vain, but his voice was lost in the gale force winds.

As everything went dark around him, Donnie heard her voice once last time. "Save my father…"

Donnie's eyes snapped open. The wind was gone, and so was the meadow. Instead, he lay in some sort of chamber on a cold, hard surface. Strange sounds reached his ears, groans and cries off in the distance.

The lean elf attempted to sit up, but his body felt stiff, and the fast movement caused his head to spin. Thankfully, it lasted only a few moments.

With the dizziness past, Donnie took in the rest of his surroundings. He sat in a barred enclosure, covered on all four sides with some sort of opaque grey material. Light filtered in through the bars of a single metal-framed door, providing the only clear view of the world beyond.

A cage, then, Donnie thought to himself.

Learning from his previous mistake, the wiry elf slowly rose to his feet. He stretched a bit to loosen his stiff joints, then looked himself over. His body was drenched in sweat, but otherwise he appeared wholly intact. Furthermore, whoever his captors were, they had left him with all his gear, including his rapier. *Either they're not very bright, or they're so powerful they just don't care.*

The fact that he had been caught so easily made him think it to be the latter. Erring on the side of caution, Donnie stole quietly over to the door. A peek through the bars proved not very useful.

From his limited vantage point, he spied two small enclosures covered with the same opaque material as the one that held him captive. The material was thin enough that he could see the shadows of the occupants of those other cells.

One was short and squat—a dwarf, perhaps. The other was larger than a man or elf, with a huge head. The grunts emanating from that cage made him guess it to be an ogre or a troll.

Donnie let out a deep sigh. He had been hoping to find Ruka or Miranda, but in truth, it had probably just been a dream. *Either way, I need to get out of here.*

Luckily, Donnie had spent enough time with Seth that no ordinary lock could hold him. He pulled a hidden pick out of his boot and inserted it into the cage door.

Bam!

The slight elf was thrown nearly across the cage. The world around him spun out of control, but eventually slowed and finally stopped.

Donnie carefully rose to his feet and crossed to the door again. A close examination of the lock revealed no physical traps. *Magic, then. I have just the thing.*

The cunning elf reached into his pack and pulled out a pair of red leather gloves laced with black striations. He slipped one onto his right hand, then gingerly poked the cell door with his index finger.

A purple flash erupted from the door, then expanded outward across the walls of the cage. Donnie watched as the twin lines of light raced around to the opposite wall, where they collided and abruptly disappeared.

A faint smile crept across Donnie's lips. *That seems to have worked. Only one way to be sure, though.*

The cautious elf braced himself as he inserted his pick into the lock once more. This time, there was no magical backlash. A classic pin and tumbler mechanism, he had it picked in no time.

Donnie carefully opened the cage door and stepped outside, only to be met with a frightening sight. He stood in the middle of a vast chamber, the ceiling dozens of feet above his head. The walls were even farther away, probably four to five times the size of the first floor of the Darkwoods Monolith.

Even more alarming was the number of cells in this room. There were dozens and dozens of cages, stretching away as far as the eye could see. Now outside his cage, the volume of grunts and groans echoing across the chamber nearly deafened him.

Donnie's jaw hung open as he gaped around the enormous chamber. *Who in Thac built this place? And who are they holding in all of these cages? Better yet, why?*

A cage larger than the rest caught his eye. It lay behind the two cells in front of him. Donnie silently skirted between the two, doing his best to avoid the cell with the ogre. His eyes went wide when they fell on the shadow in the large cage. It had the shape of a sleeping dragon.

Save my father…

The words from his 'dream' echoed through Donnie's head.

Could it be? Is that Ruka's father?

Perhaps the dream had been some sort of premonition.

Donnie swept his eyes across the huge cage, but there was no door in sight. *It must be around the other side.*

The furtive elf tiptoed along the length of the enclosure, but halted abruptly as he rounded the corner. Down the aisle stood two small scaly creatures with twin horns, long tails, and clawed hands and feet.

Demons.

The word sent chills up Donnie's spine. Demons were creatures of pure destruction, hell bent on killing and devouring anything living, both body and soul. Even two small demons such as these were no laughing matter. Given the size of this place and the number of prison cages, there had to be an army of demons in these walls.

Donnie edged back around the corner and cautiously peeked down the aisle. The two small demons had parked themselves in front of a cage and gibbered at the closed door in their guttural tongue. Donnie did not speak demonic, but it appeared as if they were taunting the prisoner inside.

A voice cursed back at the demonic pair—a harsh but decidedly female voice. "Open the door, you spineless cowards! I'll show you how 'soft' I can be."

Donnie was torn. The smart thing would be to back away and go around the other side of the huge cage. Yet his conscience wouldn't let him. *I failed Miranda all those years ago. I'll be damned if I fail another woman in distress.*

His mind made up, Donnie silently drew his blade and crept back around the corner toward the unsuspecting creatures. The first demon went down with a single thrust through its horny skull. Unfortunately, the second one let out a hair-raising shriek and bolted before he could stab it.

Nice going, Donatello.

The little demon was too fast—there was no way he could catch it now. He knew it was only a matter of time till it returned with more of its kind. With no other recourse, the slim elf turned back toward the cage.

His eyes widened as they fell on its occupant. Inside stood an imposing woman. Nearly as tall as Lloyd, she was garbed from head to toe in dark scalemail overlaid with a polished steel breastplate, armguards, and kneeguards. Both sets of guards were adorned with shining steel wings. Atop her head lay a polished steel helm, also adorned with wings on either side. Flaxen hair draped down her oval face to the long black cloak that hung across her broad shoulders.

Just as he, she retained her weapons. A longbow was slung over the warrior's back, an arrow-filled quiver strapped across the other side. She planted the end of a steel spear into the ground, then gazed at him with an amused expression.

Donnie responded with one of his sparkling smiles as he went to unlock the cage. "Fear not, milady, I'll have you out in a moment."

Two deep brown eyes fixed on him intently from underneath that winged helm. "Aren't you a little short to be a hero?"

"Good things come in small packages," Donnie quipped as he dispelled the magic field around the cage with his gloves. A few seconds later, he picked the lock and swung the door open.

Donnie stepped back and ushered her forward. "After you."

The tall warrior's brow furrowed as she strode out of her prison. "Maybe you're useful after all."

Donnie flashed her another smile and executed a quick bow. "Donatello at your service. Donnie for short."

A slight smile touched the warrior's lips. "Well met, Donatello. I'm Karathralla, but you can call me Kara."

Off in the distance, the demon's shrieks could still be heard above the din of grunts and groans that surrounded them. Yet now those shrieks were being answered in kind.

Donnie gazed in the direction of those cries, then fixed Kara with a wan smile. "Looks like we've worn out our welcome."

"I think you're right," Kara responded, her keen eyes sweeping about the vast chamber. A few seconds later, her gaze fixed on a point in the distance. Her eyes narrowed as recognition dawned on her face.

"This way." She motioned for Donnie to follow. Kara led him back the way he had come, past his former prison.

At the next aisle, Donnie spied the door to the large cage containing the dragon. A thin gasp escaped his lips when he caught a glimpse of the creature's tail. *It's bronze!*

The startled elf stopped in his tracks, unsure as to what to do next. He felt a firm hand grasp his arm.

"What is it?" Kara whispered in his ear.

Donnie pointed to the large cage. "I think I just saw my friend's father." He started toward the cage door when the hand roughly yanked him back.

"Look out," Kara whispered harshly in his ear.

Down at the other end of the aisle, a large form lumbered into view. A massive creature, it looked like some monstrous toad, but stood upright with thick arms in place of its forelegs. The creature's huge maw hung open, displaying a deadly row of sharp teeth. Its reddish skin was mottled with spikes, and long spines ran down the length of its back.

Donnie ducked back behind the corner, his heart thumping in his chest. "That was close. What is that thing?"

"Hezrou," Kara hissed between her teeth. "Seven-hundred and fifty pounds of pure demon. They're brutally strong, and hard to kill."

Donnie gulped. "That's a lot of demon."

Kara inched her way around him, their bodies so close he could feel the heat of her breath on his brow. Despite her tough demeanor, she was actually quite lovely. *If circumstances were different...*

The warrior swiftly pulled back, dragging Donnie with her. She hunched down and drew him so close that their noses practically touched. "It hasn't seen us yet. Sorry, but there's no way we can take that thing on by ourselves. We'll have to come back for your friend."

Donnie hesitated, the proximity of Kara's comely features having an intoxicating effect on him. It took a few moments for what she said to register. "We?"

Kara's mouth curved into a slight smile. "Yes, we. It's my job to stop these demons. Plus, I owe you."

Donnie responded with a pearly grin. "Can't argue with that."

A soft laugh escaped the warrior's mouth. Donnie was slowly breaking through the chinks in her emotional armor.

The duo took off again, Kara once more in the lead. They wound their way through so many cages that Donnie eventually lost count. Though they continued at a good pace, the shrieks and roars definitely drew closer.

After what seemed like an eternity, the duo finally reached the edge of the prison camp. Before them lay a set of impossibly large double doors reaching nearly to the ceiling far above.

Donnie marveled at the sight. He doubted he could budge even one of those doors. Thankfully they were partially open, revealing the night sky beyond.

Unfortunately, the doors were guarded by a pair of tall creatures that could only be demons. Roughly humanoid, they resembled scarlet skeletons with a thin layer of leathery skin stretched across their bony frames. Pointed ears jutted from their skulls, their jaws filled with long razor-sharp teeth. Both creatures held a long spear in its hands.

Kara grabbed Donnie and pulled him back behind the last cage. At the same time, the screaming and shrieking grew louder.

"We need to leave now," Kara hissed softly.

Donnie peered around her toward the doorway. One of the demons had left its post and was headed toward the prison cages. Thankfully, it hadn't spotted them yet.

He shifted his gaze back to Kara. "Do you think you can take those things?"

The warrior woman slowly shook her head. "One, maybe, but not two at once."

An idea began to form in Donnie's head. He narrowed an eye at her. "You any good with that bow?"

Kara pressed her lips together and nodded. "Some."

A sly smile crossed Donnie's lips as a plan crystalized in his mind. "Follow my lead."

The slender elf stepped out into the open just far enough for the nearest demon to see him. It took a few seconds, but its baleful blank eyes eventually turned his way.

Donnie held up his hands to his ears and waved them while sticking out his tongue at the creature. "Nah, nah, nah, nah, nah. You can't catch me!"

The creature stared at him for a long moment, then raised up its spear with a hideous shriek. It started toward him at a loping run.

Donnie held his ground as the demon approached, doing his best to gauge its speed. *Gods, that thing is fast.*

He would never outrun it, but if his plan worked, he wouldn't have to. When the demon got close enough, Donnie took off in the opposite direction from Kara. He glanced back over his shoulder just as the creature rounded the corner. His plan had worked. The demon was so intent on him that it hadn't seen her.

Donnie's eyes widened in wonder as Kara drew out her ornate bow. Carved wings matching her armor decorated the limbs. As she nocked an arrow and drew it back, it began to glow white like Alana's sword.

The sight enamored Donnie so much that he nearly lost his footing. The demon, sensing its chance, leapt at him with a wild shriek. It was in mid-air when the first arrow pierced its neck. A second one immediately followed, skewering it through the skull.

The tall demon crashed to the ground at Donnie's feet, with two glowing arrows protruding from its body. The thin elf cautiously nudged it with a boot, but it remained still.

Donnie flashed a grin at Kara, but stopped when he saw the grim expression on her face.

"The second one's coming!" she called out to him.

Donnie knew the same tactic wouldn't work twice. Plus, they didn't have the time for it—those other shrieks were drawing even closer. With no other choice, the wiry elf drew his rapier and called out to Kara, "Get ready to shoot."

He was off, dodging between the cages and out in the open before she could respond.

The second demon immediately spotted him. A terrifying scream escaped its jaws as it veered his way. Answering screams responded from somewhere close within the camp.

Yet Donnie couldn't worry about that now. *I've got only one shot at this, and have to time it just right.*

The crazed elf plunged headlong toward the approaching demon, all the while gauging the gap between them. A second before they clashed, Donnie threw himself to the ground, tucking and rolling as he did so. He felt, rather than saw, the demon's spear pass over him as his forward motion propelled him right into the demon.

Though not very heavy, his momentum took the creature's legs out from under it. The nimble elf shot upright at the end of his roll, immediately spinning around to face his horrific foe. Yet the demon was nearly as agile as he. It was already back on its feet and turning to face him.

The creature opened its maw and shrieked, exposing those deadly razor-sharp teeth. Yet before its cry had ended, the tip of a glowing arrow appeared between its jaws.

The demon's cry abruptly halted. It went to turn, but its body shuddered twice more, then slowly collapsed to the ground. Three glowing arrows stuck out of its torso, attesting to Kara's skill with the bow.

Donnie went to nudge the fallen demon as Kara came rushing by. She grasped his hand and pulled him along with her as more shrieks and screams erupted from the nearby camp.

She grinned at him for the first time since they had met. "Nice going. Are you always this reckless?"

Donnie shrugged as they continued to run. "It's a talent."

The two of them reached the huge double doors just as more demons tumbled out of the camp. Kara and Donnie exchanged a quick glance, then slipped through the doorway and out into the night.

The sound of shrieks echoed behind them as the harried duo raced down the stone steps. Donnie and Kara swiftly reached the bottom and darted across the rocky hillside. A silvery moon lit their path, but at the same time made them far too visible. The forest was only a short distance away now, but the cries of pursuit grew louder and more frequent.

Donnie glanced back over his shoulder. A tall tower rose high into the night sky, its vast shadow blocking out most of the mountain behind it. Once again, it reminded him of the Darkwoods Monolith, but this structure was far larger. High above, a strange glow emanated from the very peak of the tower. Yet Donnie did not have time to contemplate on it, for demon after demon now poured out of the front doors.

"Quickly, into the woods," Kara hissed at him.

Donnie turned his gaze forward and plunged into the forest after the warrior. The next hour was a blur of trees and rocky terrain as they weaved their way through the woods. Kara led them in a serpentine pattern in an attempt to throw off their pursuers. It must have worked, for the sounds of the chase eventually died down behind them.

Donnie thought they were home free until a chilling howl echoed through the night. Kara came to a sudden halt, Donnie stopping right behind her.

"What in the seven hells was that?"

"Not hell, the abyss," Kara corrected him.

Another howl sounded through the trees, this one closer than the first. It was answered by a third howl off in the opposite direction.

Donnie cast a worried glance at Kara. "Are those…"

"…hell hounds." Kara nodded, her expression grim. "They've got us surrounded on three sides. They'll catch us for sure, unless…" She paused a moment to sniff the air, turning her head from side to side. She finally stopped, her eyes going wide. "Quick, this way!"

Kara took off through the trees, Donnie rushing through the night after her. She followed a straight line this time, no longer concerned with misdirecting their pursuers.

Donnie wondered where they were going, but kept his mouth closed. There was no sense in tipping off their enemies to their exact location.

The howls continued behind them, growing closer with each passing minute. Yet they were soon joined by another sound, a steady noise that grew louder the farther they raced onward.

I know that sound—it's rushing water.

Donnie was impressed. Kara was leading them to the one thing that could cause the hounds to lose their scent.

A few minutes later, they broke through the trees and came to a screeching halt. The duo stood at the top of a cliff, another bluff visible far off in the distance.

Donnie inched his way to the edge and peered downward. Moonlight glinted off the racing waters of a wide river far below. It was a sheer drop from where they stood, with no obvious path down the cliff face.

Behind them, the howls had grown quite loud. Donnie could hear something crashing through the trees in their direction.

A firm hand latched onto his. Donnie glanced at Kara and saw the intense look in her eyes.

"It's a fine night for a swim!" He exclaimed with a forced smile.

Without thinking, he stood on his toes and kissed her. The kiss was over as quickly as it had begun, but her lips were surprisingly soft.

Kara narrowed an eye at him.

"For luck," he explained with a charming smile, then leapt off the cliff with her, hand-in-hand.

24
ALLIANCES

Glolindir thought he was used to teleporting. Thus, he expected the disoriented feeling that came with being displaced a great many miles. Yet this time was different. It felt as if his body was being wrenched sideways as Ravenford disappeared around them.

Moments later, everyone reappeared dangling in mid-air about three feet above a river. With cries of alarm, the group tumbled en masse into the sparkling waters.

Glo took a deep breath just before submerging, yet moments later his feet connected with something solid. He instinctively pushed off, almost immediately popping up above the surface. The tall elf wiped stray strands of wet hair from his brow and looked around.

The river they had landed in was rather wide, but thankfully they had been deposited near the bank of a small isle. The rest of the party surfaced around Glo, all sputtering as they broke the water line.

"What in the seven hells… was that?" Elladan cried in between coughing out water. "I thought we'd reappear… in another circle…"

Glo arched an eyebrow at his elven friend. "Apparently some force is interfering with teleportation."

Aksel pushed back a mass of coppery hair that had been pasted over his eyes. "Possibly the same thing that led to Donnie's disappearance."

Glo nodded as he treaded water. "Probably best we avoid teleporting for the time being."

"Ya think?" Seth snorted as he side-stroked his way toward the nearby shore.

The companions all fell in behind the halfling as they swam to the bank. They slowly waded onto the isle and wrung out their clothes as they took in their surroundings.

The small island was empty, except for a stone structure surrounded by wide steps and dozens of red and pink potted flowers. In the very center stood an open alcove containing an exquisite, clear crystalline statue in the form of an angel.

Two bridges exited the isle, leading to larger islands on either side. The island to the left consisted mostly of open ground, except for a few dozen large tents and a couple of large half-built structures. The isle to the right supported a town consisting of countless brown and white buildings of all shapes and sizes.

Kalyn's jaw hung open at the sight. This town was more akin to a city, easily five times the size of Ravenford.

"Where are we?" the Deepwooder drawled.

"Oh, this is Lukescros," Lloyd immediately answered. He drew up next to the gawking young woman, pointing around as he spoke. "In front of us is the famous Crystal Angel Shrine. The north island is where the faire is held. You can see they've already started to set up the amphitheater and the arena. The southern island houses the main town…"

"…which has dozens of shops…" Andrella interjected with clear enthusiasm.

Lloyd grinned at the excited, if wet, young lady. "…a half-dozen inns, craft halls of all kinds, and a few hundred homes." He then directed their attention to one last island down river from the rest. "And that's the eastern isle. That's where the town hall is, the Bardic college, and embassies for ambassadors from other cities."

Kalyn shivered. She briskly rubbed her arms as she cast a pleading glance at Andrella. "Please tell me Ravenford has one of those. I need ta change out'a these wet clothes."

A weak smile crossed Andrella's lips as she slowly shook her head. "I'm afraid not. Ravenford is only a small barony"—her eyes suddenly lit up—"but Penwick should have one."

All eyes turned to Lloyd.

The young man gazed at them sheepishly, his hand going to the back of his neck. "Yeah, well… that may or may not be a problem."

Elladan shifted uncomfortably on his feet, the puddles growing around his soggy boots. "That was as clear as mud. If there's a problem, spit it out already."

"Yeah, before we all turn into icicles," Seth added, still wringing the water out of his cloak.

Lloyd grimaced as he searched for the appropriate words. "It sort of depends on who's currently in charge at the embassy—let's just say not everyone in Penwick is a fan of the Stealles."

Glo was taken aback by the admission. The way Gryswold had painted Lloyd's father, one would have thought all Penwick favored the great hero and his family.

Andrella summed it up nicely as she laced a soggy arm through Lloyd's. "Sounds like pure politics to me—someone, or a few someones perhaps, are jealous of your father's fame?"

Lloyd's pained expression faded, his eyes filled with gratitude and more as he peered down at the astute young lady. "Not just Dad, but Mom too. She's sunk a small fortune into the city's reconstruction. Some folks claim she's trying to outshine the barony."

Kalyn coughed into her hand. "Dragon dung! Anyone can see by the way you're raised that your momma ain't no boot-lickin' politic'er."

Lloyd's brows drew together as he stared at Kalyn. "Thanks… I think…"

Andrella wiped a hand over her mouth to hide a smile. "Anyway, there's an inn that we normally stay at when we come for the faire." She glanced over at the southern island. "In fact, I believe it's just over the bridge."

Elladan drew up next to her and followed her gaze. "I probably know it. What's the name?"

"The Bright Angel."

The Bright Angel turned out to be a very elegant establishment, with marble columns in front and a large entryway adorned with a shining angel. The main inn was not overly large. It stood only two stories high, but sizable towers rose at the four cardinal corners.

By the time the companions walked into the foyer, it was already late afternoon. With an eight-hour ride to Vermoorden in front of them, Aksel determined it was probably best to get rooms for the night. Thus, Elladan worked his magic and acquired them one of the tower rooms—a suite with a living area and four bedrooms attached. The companions had soon changed into dry clothes and decided how to spend the evening.

Aksel went to pray at the Temple of Angels. Glo headed over to the library to do further research on teleportation. Elladan went to the Faire grounds to sign up for the bardic competition. Kalyn, hearing there was an archery contest, dragged Martan along with her. Seth went to check out what rumors were circulating in the local taverns.

Despite any initial reservations, Andrella convinced Lloyd to take her to the Penwick embassy. The duo now walked arm-in-arm through the bustling town, until they crossed another bridge at the east end of the island.

Andrella gazed around in wonder when they reached the other side. "Wow, this is like an entirely different world."

Lloyd chuckled. "I think the inhabitants prefer it this way."

The path ahead became a dirt road. Lush vegetation stretched in all directions topped with hundred-year-old oaks and pines. Invisible birds fluttered far overhead, their end-of-day songs wafting down from the tall tree tops.

Lloyd pointed down the path. "The college campus and the town hall are nestled together on the west side of the island, in a park-like setting. The embassy estates are spaced evenly along the eastern shore."

Andrella enjoyed the guided tour. Lloyd seemed so much more in his element here. She liked this side of him—he was far more self-assured. "So, how far is it to the Penwick embassy?"

Lloyd pressed his lips together. "About halfway up the island."

"And what about Dunwynn?"

The young man narrowed an eye at her. "All the way at the north end. Why do you ask?"

Andrella could feel the tension in his arm. She was touched by his response—it showed that he cared about her. As long as he didn't become too overprotective and try to lock her away somewhere, they'd get along just fine. She wrapped both her arms around his and snuggled in close as they strode side-by-side. "Don't worry, silly. I have no intention of going there."

"Okay." Lloyd's frown melted, the color rising to his cheeks.

As they walked along the dirt path, spaces appeared in the brush. Six-foot-high brick walls stretched along there, paralleling the road. A few times they passed a thick wrought iron gate, though nothing could be seen beyond but dirt paths with more brush and trees.

"Not all the estates are occupied all year round," Lloyd confided in her. "Only ours and Dunwynn's have permanent residents."

The first sign of humanoid life finally appeared ahead of them. Two guards stood post at the next gate. Both men wore scarlet tabards with the symbol of a lion undercut by two crossed swords. Andrella immediately recognized it as the coat-of-arms of Penwick.

Lloyd strode up to the guards and gave them a crisp salute. Both men saluted in turn, exchanging a surprised glance.

"Why, if it isn't the young Lord Stealle!" The first guard cried.

The second guard wore a confused expression. "Begging your pardon, Sir, but last we heard, you had set out from Penwick to fight injustice." He stepped forward and held a hand to the side of his mouth. "If you don't mind us asking, what brings you back so soon?"

Lloyd cast a quick glance at Andrella, a single eyebrow raised. He leaned in as well and dropped his voice to a near whisper. "Let's just say that injustice has found its way closer to home than we'd like to think."

A brief smile flashed across Andrella's face. He had handled the question rather skillfully. With a bit more polish, he definitely had the makings of a diplomat.

The two guards' eyes went wide. "Indeed, Sir, it may be as you say. We've heard tidings of undead sightings in the town of Three Forks. Lord Hightower sent a contingent of troops out to investigate a few days ago. We've heard nary a word since."

It was Andrella's turn to raise an eyebrow. If memory served her right, Three Forks was about a day's ride west of here. *First Twin Oaks, then Ravenford, and now Three Forks? This undead problem is growing into an epidemic.*

Lloyd exchanged a knowing glance with Andrella, then changed the subject. "Did you say Lord Hightower?"

The guard nodded. "Indeed, Sir. He's the current Lord of the manor."

Lloyd's face brightened visibly. He leaned next to Andrella and whispered, "Lord Hightower is an old friend of the family."

The first guard went to open the gate, while the second one beckoned to them. "Please, Sir, you and your guest may follow me inside. I'll inform Lord Hightower of your arrival."

The guard led Lloyd and Andrella up a winding road through the wood. A few dozen yards in, the trees separated, revealing a sprawling building set on a small hilltop.

Andrella's eyebrows rose simultaneously. *Mansion is the appropriate word.* The brick structure stood three stories tall and was lined with numerous windows, multiple chimneys, and thick ivy crawling up its sides. If Andrella had to guess, she'd estimate it a third the size of Ravenford Keep.

Behind the main building stood multiple secondary structures, including stables and barracks for military personnel. Andrella was quite impressed. *This is more of an encampment than an estate.*

The guard led them through the double-doored entry into a wide foyer. The floor here was a white and black marble, with white columns on either side, stretching up to the ceiling three stories above. It reminded Andrella of Ravenford Keep.

"Wait here, please."

Andrella held onto Lloyd's arm as the guard ascended one side of a double set of stairs that wound up to all three floors. In the center of the staircase hung a large banner displaying the Penwick coat of arms.

They didn't have to wait long until a booming voice called down from the second-floor landing. "By my word, if it isn't the young Master Stealle!"

A tall man with greying hair and a thick grey mustache stared down at them. Despite his age, the man looked quite robust. He confirmed Andrella's first impression by practically running down the stairs to greet them.

"That's Lord Hightower," Lloyd whispered in her ear.

The Lord Hightower drew up and grasped Lloyd by the hand, pumping it vigorously. "It's good to see you, Lloyd!" His steel-grey eyes took on a shrewd cast as he looked the young man over. "You look the same, and yet… there's something different about you…"

The older man's sharp gaze fell on Andrella, the corners of his mouth rising. "Perhaps it has something to do with this lovely young lady?"

Lloyd's cheeks reddened slightly. "Oh, excuse me, your Lordship. This is the… *Lady Avernos.*"

Andrella dipped her chin as she curtsied, hiding the smile that graced her lips at Lloyd's attempt to conceal her identity. It was actually a rather astute precaution, one that made her even more proud of him.

Lord Hightower's eyebrow lifted as he executed a short bow. "Welcome to Penwick Manor, *Lady Avernos.* Our Baron is an Avernos as well. Perhaps you are somehow related?"

Lloyd cleared his throat before she could answer. "If you don't mind, your Lordship, can we talk about that later? Right now we have some urgent business to discuss with you." He leaned in closer and eyed the older man meaningfully. "Perhaps in a more private setting?"

Lord Hightower stepped back and appraised the young man anew. After a few moments, he nodded approvingly. "Well, I was right. You have done some growing up in these last few months."

He winked at Andrella. "I can barely remember getting two words out of this one not more than six months ago."

Andrella gave the old gentleman a warm smile. *I think I'm going to like this one.*

Lord Hightower held out an arm to her. "Well then, let us adjourn to, as you say, a more private setting."

Andrella took the old gentleman's arm, with Lloyd following close behind.

Lord Hightower's tone was exceedingly amused as they ascended the stairs. "So tell me, Lady Avernos, is it you who's had such a marked effect on young Lloyd here?"

Andrella couldn't help giggling at the old gentleman's cheerful query. "Among others, your Lordship. Let's merely say he's been surrounded by more than one 'good' influence."

Hightower arched a gray eyebrow at her phrasing, a wide smile lifting his thick mustache. "A very diplomatic answer, young lady." He glanced over his shoulder at Lloyd. "I dare say, I can't wait to meet your other 'tutors.'"

Andrella giggled again, imagining how Lord Hightower's first meeting with Seth would go. Lloyd must have been thinking the same thing, his cheeks paling.

Lloyd didn't realize just how much he missed home. He'd been so busy protecting the people of Ravenford that he hadn't had time to even think about it. Yet now surrounded by Penwick tabards and reunited with a man who was practically his uncle, it hit Lloyd full in the face.

Lord Laegaire Hightower escorted Lloyd and Andrella to his private chambers. The main room was rather spacious, with a long table at one end and a cozy hearth surrounded by plush seating at the other. An ornate desk stood in front of a wide window, its entire top covered with papers.

Hightower led them over to the fire and bade them sit on the lavish couch. A butler came in with refreshments and snacks, set them on a nearby table, then swiftly left.

Hightower, glass of brandy in hand, stood next to the hearth and took a brief sip. The firelight played across his face, accentuating the circles under his eyes. "Have you heard about Three Forks?"

Lloyd responded with a solemn nod. "The guards brought us up to date." He then relayed the news from Twin Oaks and what they had encountered in Ravenford.

Hightower's brow furrowed at Lloyd's recounting. "It's just as we feared—the undead are on the rise again."

Lloyd stood and placed a hand on Hightower's broad shoulder. "Our friends in Bendenwood specialize in this sort of thing. We could send word to them."

Hightower looked him in the eye, then smiled, the tension in his shoulders releasing. "Their help would be most appreciated. We could send for a group of the Priestesses of Arenor, but I'd hate to take them away from Penwick without knowing where these devils will appear next."

The old gentleman set his brandy down, then place both hands on Lloyd's shoulders. His keen eyes were filled with warmth. "Look at you, young Lloyd—making alliances all over the map. I'll have you know, Gryswold sent word of your deeds in Ravenford"—his tone turned somber—"before his untimely demise."

Lloyd stole a glance at Andrella, but the young lady showed no reaction. He supposed that came from her diplomatic training. It was a talent Lloyd was sure he'd never master.

Hightower followed his gaze, a shrewd look dawning in his eyes. "Our main concern is the whereabouts of the royal family of Ravenford. Rumor has it they've been all summoned to Dunwynn. That would indeed be a shame."

Lloyd exchanged a glance with Andrella. The young lady nodded and rose to her feet.

"Not all, your lordship," Lloyd assured him. "May I present the Lady Andrella Avernos, daughter of Baron Gryswold and the Lady Gracelynn."

Andrella executed a lavish curtsey. "Your lordship."

A grin lifted Hightower's thick mustache. He took Andrella's hand and bowed. "Lady Andrella—it is an honor to have you here among us. Please consider this mansion your home away from home."

Andrella dipped her chin in thanks, but before she could respond, Hightower wrapped both his hands around hers. His steel grey eyes were filled with compassion. "Your father and I were old friends, my dear. Please think of me as an uncle."

Andrella's breath caught at the heartwarming gesture. She swiftly recovered, a warm smile gracing her lips. "Why thank you—Uncle Hightower."

Hightower's cheeks turned rosy from her charming response.

Lloyd practically beamed with pride. *Andrella definitely has a way about her.*

A sudden nudge in the arm brought Lloyd's attention back to Lord Hightower. "And you, young Lloyd Stealle, having the Lady Andrella right here under my nose all this time.

The old gentleman chuckled softly, then ushered them back to the couch. "Please, both of you sit down and tell me how this all came about."

Lloyd and Andrella seated themselves, taking turns relaying the lesser-known details of Gryswold's demise. They shared all they had learned about Qualtan, the vampires, and the Assassin's guild in Vermoorden. Andrella finished with her mother's request to join the companions in the recovery of her father's heart.

Hightower nodded thoughtfully when they were done. "Well, you can count on Penwick's support in all this. Just say the word and you shall have whatever you need."

Lloyd grinned at the old gentleman. "I was hoping you would say that."

Hightower's gaze shifted to their laps, a knowing smile suddenly spreading under his mustache. Lloyd glanced down and saw that he and Andrella had unwittingly clasped hands.

Hightower cleared his throat. "I dare say Gryswold approved of this union."

Lloyd felt the blood rise to his cheeks. He glanced at Andrella, then back at Hightower. "He did tell me he was happy that a Penwick man loved his daughter."

Andrella let out a short gasp, her hand going to her mouth. Little drops of moisture welled in the corners of her eyes. "L-Lloyd—you love me?"

It abruptly dawned on him that he had never actually said those words to Andrella. Yet before he could say anything else, she threw her arms around his neck and kissed him soundly on the lips.

Lloyd lost himself in that tender embrace—the smell of her hair, the warmth of her lips. When Andrella finally pulled away, she was practically breathless. "Oh, Lloyd… I love you… too…"

Lord Hightower cleared his throat, his broad grin testifying to his amusement at the duo. "Lloyd, you do realize you are courting the heir apparent to the Duchy of Dunwynn?"

That fact was not new to Lloyd. It had been brought to his attention more times than he cared to count by his 'supposed' friends. Seth, in particular, reveled in referring to him as the 'Lord Avernos Dunwynn.'

Lloyd merely shook his head. "I'm quite aware of it, Lord Hightower, but frankly I really don't care. I love Andrella for the intelligent, charming, and sometimes headstrong"—he flinched as Andrella smacked him on the arm—"woman she is. Not for some title she has now, or in the future."

"Oh, Lloyd…" Andrella threw her arms around him once more.

Lord Hightower seemed more than impressed with his response. He lifted up his glass of brandy. "I say this calls for a toast."

Andrella stood and hoisted Lloyd up by the arm with her. "I quite agree."

Hightower poured drinks all around. Lloyd and Andrella lifted their brandies as the old gentleman proposed a toast. "To the both of you—may your love light the way to new friendships between the people of eastern Thac."

Lloyd and Andrella clinked glasses with Hightower. "To new friendships between the people of eastern Thac."

25
STOP DRAGON MY HEART AROUND

Even the demons are gonna sympathize for ya when I'm finished sending you to them!

The Black Pig was your typical waterfront tavern. Located in the poorer section of town, it sat just off the Penderbun River where the bridge crossed over from the Faire grounds on the north isle. It was a perfect location for working-class folks looking to end their day.

Seth sat quietly at one end of the bar, inconspicuously nursing an ale. From his vantage point, he had picked up all sorts of information. Much of it he already knew, but some he did not.

Gryswold's assassination had been a main topic. The general consensus was that *the Duke o' Dunwynn finally had him killed for stealin' his sister away all them years ago.* Though totally inaccurate, Seth found the allegation quite amusing.

There was also a bit of speculation about the continued disappearance of magic users. Many thought it a dark sign that the Magic Council had all mysteriously left Lymerdia.

If they'd turned tail and run,' then somethin' evil must be a brewin'.

That led to the topic of the undead rising in Three Forks. Seth arched an eyebrow at that one. It sounded too much like what had had happened in Twin Oaks, and almost in Ravenford. The only other thing that piqued Seth's interest was talk of the irritable new wizard teaching up at the Bardic College. It turned out to be none other than Maltar.

I'd hate to be in his class, Seth thought wryly.

The topics recycled as a new batch of townsfolk wandered in for an end-of-day drink. Seth downed what was left of his ale, dropped a few copper pieces on the bar, and then made his way outside.

The sun hung low on the western horizon as Seth exited the rustic tavern. He scanned his surroundings, intent on heading back to the Bright Angel, when he spied another tavern a few buildings in the opposite direction. The sign above the door read the Grey Swan.

Seth nearly turned away when a solitary figure exited the tavern. It was a young, fair-skinned human female with long, golden-blonde hair. Her body was hidden behind a dark grey cloak, but Seth had the strangest feeling he'd seen her before.

The woman gazed briefly in his direction, providing Seth a glimpse at her eyes. They were blue-green.

The halfling wrinkled his nose as recognition dawned on him. *Ves?*

The young blonde spun on her heel and strode away. Completely bemused, Seth took off after her. He kept his distance until she abruptly turned down a back alley. Seth hurried to the alley entrance, but when he peered down the long corridor, the woman had disappeared.

Seth investigated the alley thoroughly, but there was no trace of the woman who looked like Ves. With a shrug, the halfling gave up and headed back to the Bright Angel.

On entering the lobby, Seth found Aksel, Glo, Martan, and Kalyn waiting there. Elladan stood at the front desk speaking with the clerk.

"What'd I miss?" Seth asked blithely.

Aksel turned toward him and smiled. "There you are. We were just thinking about dinner."

Seth rubbed his stomach gingerly. "I'd rather be eating it."

Elladan wore a half-smile as he strode up to rejoin them. "Looks like we can go ahead and eat. Lloyd and Andrella ditched us."

Glo gave the bard a puzzled look. "And why's that?"

"Unlike us poor folk, they were invited to dine up at the Penwick embassy." Elladan winked.

"Just as well," Martan drawled. "I don't think most of us'd fit in up there anyway."

Elladan lifted an eyebrow. "Speak for yourself, friend."

Kalyn nudged Martan in the arm. "Yeah, I've had proper lady training.'"

"Yeah, yeah. Less talk and more food," Seth complained. He hadn't eaten since before their encounter with the vampires earlier that morning. As if to punctuate his point, his stomach made a loud rumbling noise.

Glo looked at him with mock horror. "Oh gods, he's turning into Lloyd!"

Kalyn placed a hand on her chin and eyed him sharply. "Now that ya mention it, I think he's a bit taller."

"Maybe you've shrunk," Seth shot back as he moved past her toward the common room.

Dinner turned out to be excellent. The food here was possibly the best Seth had ever had. There was everything from roast chicken to plump dumplings and apple pie with thick cream. While he stuffed his face, Glo told them what he found at the library.

"There wasn't much on recent teleportation incidents. Still, I found references to similar disappearances around the time of the fall of the Naradon Empire. Of course, that was seven hundred years ago."

Aksel, finished with his food, sat back and absently stroked his chin. "I wonder what the correlation could be between then and now?"

"That's an awful long time for there ta be a corra-lashun." Kalyn struggled with that last word.

"About the lifetime of an elf," Glo murmured softly.

Finally full, Seth threw down his fork and knife. "Okay. Now for some rumor mongering."

Everyone sat forward as Seth told them all he had heard. They seemed as amused as he at the Duke being the prime suspect in the Baron's death. The news from Three Forks, on the other hand, had them all troubled.

Kalyn nudged Martan in the elbow. "Maybe we should message Raina 'bout that one."

The thought of Maltar teaching classes left Glo wide-eyed. "I hope he doesn't force his students to duel to the death. I can just see him kicking the loser and shouting at him to get up already."

Seth ended with his strange encounter with the woman that looked like Ves. When he mentioned her name, Martan nearly choked on a forkful of pie.

Kalyn slapped Martan hard on the back, forcing him to swallow. Martan teared profusely after that.

Kalyn's eyes narrowed as she looked from Martan to Seth. "Who's this Ves?"

Martan abruptly blanched and got up from the table. "Excuse me. I just remembered something I forgot."

Seth broke out into fits of laughter as the archer strode briskly away.

Kalyn watched him go, then turned back to Seth with a dangerous undertone to her voice. "Okay, spill it. Who's Ves?"

Seth nearly rolled off his seat and onto the floor. *This is going to be good.*

Martan cursed his luck as he ascended the stairs to the tower suite. Things with Kalyn had just begun to smooth out. She had forced him to sign up for the archery contest, but just the fact that she wanted him there was a good sign. Afterward, they'd fired a few rounds at the practice range, kidding and teasing like old times.

Fine time for Ves' name to pop up.

He hadn't thought about the Greymantle girl in at least a few days now—definitely not since Kalyn reappeared. A vision of Ves suddenly popped into his mind. She was standing over him, concern in her eyes as he woke up from his fall off the cliffs at Cape Marlin. She was absolutely the most beautiful woman he had ever laid eyes upon.

The vision abruptly shifted, the dulcet face replaced with the snout of a large bronze-colored dragon. Ves' voice reverberated through his mind. *Martan… please don't be mad at me.*

Martan halted on the steps and shuddered. It was a frightening sight, yet, at the same time sort of sad. *Maybe I was too harsh on her?*

A faint sound ripped Martan from his thoughts. Someone was on the steps below. They were trying very hard to be quiet.

Martan's survival instincts kicked in. He hurried up the rest of the stairs, turned the corner, and flattened himself against the wall. He listened intently, but heard nothing more.

Less than a minute passed before a cloaked figure rounded the corner. Martan sprang on them, grabbing them by the shoulders. As he did so, the figure's hood fell off.

A familiar face stared back at him, one he had just envisioned moments ago. Martan's jaw went slack. "Ves? Is that really you?"

The young woman stared back at him, a sly smile crossing her lips. "Who else do you think it'd be?"

She sounded just like Ves, but her tone was softer and a bit breathier than he remembered.

Martan abruptly realized he was still holding her by the shoulders. He let her go and stepped back, the blood rising to his cheeks. "But what are you doing here? The last I saw, you were flying off toward the coast."

The corner of Ves' mouth curved upward. She lifted a finger and poked him gently in the chest. "That was over a week ago, silly. Do you have any idea how far a dragon can fly in a week?"

Martan's eyebrows knit together as he thought it over. Actually, he had no idea.

Ves took a step closer and flattened her hand on his chest. The contact felt very warm and made Martan quite uncomfortable. "Do you have a room up here? It's been a long flight, and I'm really quite tired."

"Of-of course," Martan stammered. "Where are my manners? Right this way."

Martan led Ves down the hall to the tower suite. He unlocked the door and ushered her inside.

Ves strode in and glanced around the large main room. "This is very nice. Where are the others?"

Martan, still quite unsettled, walked in behind her, words nervously spilling from his mouth. "They're all still finishing dinner. Care to sit down? Can I get you anything? I could run down and get you something to drink—or eat."

Ves spun around and placed a slim hand on his face. The warm touch made him blush all the more. "That's okay. I'll just wait here."

Ves stepped back and undid her cloak. It fell to the ground at her feet, revealing a very low-cut black dress.

Martan's eyes nearly bugged out of his head. His cheeks burned as he forced his eyes to meet hers. "A-are you sure there's n-nothing I can get you?"

Ves yawned and stretched, revealing far more than Martan thought it proper for him to see. "Actually… I'm kind of tired. Is there anywhere I can lay down?"

Martan gulped hard. "There—there are four bedrooms in this suite."

Ves took a step forward and ran a finger up his chest. "Where's yours?"

Martan gulped again, his voice failing him. He pointed toward the door to his room.

"Oh, good," Ves said. She grabbed Martan firmly by the shirt and dragged him toward the bedroom with her.

Kalyn slapped her hand on the table, irritated that Seth was still laughing. "Come on guys! Who is this Ves person? What did I miss?"

"Alright, Seth," Aksel sighed and turned to Kalyn as Seth caught his breath. "Ves and her sisters, Ruka and Maya, helped us with the sunken ships off Cape Marlin."

Kalyn cocked her head to one side. "Was that before or after the lighthouse burnt down?"

Again, Seth fell into fits of laughter, nearly falling out of his chair.

Aksel huffed and leaned forward. "Seth. That will do."

Seth sat up and frowned at Aksel. "Kill-joy."

Aksel turned back to Kalyn. "As I was saying, Seth and Martan were scouting the area around the lighthouse when, for various reasons, Martan fell down a cliffside."

Kalyn crossed her arms and leaned back in her chair with a snort. "That sounds like Martan."

"He nearly died," Aksel continued, his face grave. "Ves saved his life."

Kalyn felt her shoulders slump, her eyes drifting down. She could feel the others staring at her.

"One look at Ves and Martan was a goner," Seth snorted.

Kalyn felt a wrenching in her chest. Her eyes shot up and bore into the halfling. Seth merely ignored her, casually stuffing a piece of pie in his mouth.

Glo sat forward before Seth could say anything more. "You should really ask Martan about the rest of it."

Kalyn looked up at the elf, her eyes widening. "What? That's a terrible idea."

"Glo is full of those." Seth's lips twisted upward as the elf glowered at him.

Elladan chuckled. "Glo is right. It would be better if you asked Martan about it, instead of getting the whole spiel from us."

Kalyn shook her head. "I'm not good at talking about stuff like that, and Martan ain't good at talking at all. How's this a good idea again, fellers?"

Elladan chortled louder this time, then waved a serving maid over, handing her some copper. "Please bring us a whole apple pie and two glasses of milk on a tray."

Seth's mouth curved sideways. "He's gonna need something a lot stronger than milk."

Kalyn looked between Elladan and Seth. "Who's the pie fer?"

A few minutes later, Kalyn found herself walking up the stairs toward their suite, carrying a tray with a warm pie and two cups of milk. She sighed as she approached the door, repeating what Elladan had told her.

"Just stay calm, ask, and then listen." She repeated it a couple of more times. "That ain't hard, Kalyn. It's so simple, Seth could do it." She thought about that for a moment, then shook her head, reaching out for the door handle.

She paused, her brows knitting into a frown when she heard soft voices on the other side. She cautiously stepped into the room, her eyes scanning the suite, only to stop on Martan's door. It was cracked open an inch, and muffled voices and feminine giggles drifted from the other side.

Kalyn's frown deepened as her heart started to race. *Who'd Martan be talking to up here? And who on Synopei's green earth is doin' all that ear-bleedin' giggling?*

Feeling the heat of anger creeping up her spine, she marched up to the door and kicked it open. The giggling came to an abrupt halt. Kalyn's jaw dropped, the tray nearly slipping from her hands. Half a strangled scream caught in her throat at the scene before her.

Martan was lying on the bed, his shirt and vest on the floor, along with his belt. His brown eyes were wide as they locked onto Kalyn and the color drained from his face.

A beautiful blonde woman was straddling him, her slinky black dress barely staying put on her pale shoulders. She stared at Kalyn, a smile on her lips as her blue-green eyes looked her over. "We didn't call for room service, *girl.*"

Everything turned blood red for Kalyn. The burning candles turned red. The walls turned red. The blonde turned red. Even Martan's ghost-white face turned red.

"K-Kalyn, I can explain…" Martan began as he tried to push the blonde off.

Kalyn gripped the edges of the tray and thrust it forward. The contents sailed through the air, covering the bed and its occupants in a sea of white. The cups bounced off the bed and crashed to the floor with a shattering of glass, and the pie landed directly on top of the blonde's head with a *splat.*

The blonde shrieked as Martan launched off the bed, dumping her to the floor.

He raised his hands defensively as Kalyn came toward him with the tray raised. "K-Kalyn, wait just a moment!"

"I'm gonna skin you alive and feed you to a den of snakes, you worthless son of a sea hag!" Kalyn jumped onto the bed and slammed the tray over Martan's head twice, breaking it.

Martan dashed out of the room, Kalyn throwing the pieces of the tray at him.

"Hold still, you spineless tree fungus! I'm tryin' to kill ya!" Kalyn rushed by Martan as he bolted for the door, blocking his escape. Gritting her teeth in a snarl and never taking her eyes off his quivering form, she stooped and grabbed the nearest solid object available—a brass spittoon next to the door.

Martan held his hands out in front of him, backing away slowly. "Kalyn, if y-you would just c-calm down…"

Kalyn took a swing at him with the spittoon, just brushing his hair as he ducked beneath the blow. "Don't you tell *me* to calm down, you sorry zombie kisser!" She charged after him as he spun on his heel and jumped over a couch, picking up a vase and holding it up as a defense. "Even the demons are gonna sympathize for ya when I'm finished sending you to them!"

Elladan didn't know what to expect as Seth pushed open the door to their suite. They had heard the screams all the way down the hall and rushed to their friends' aid. Yet what waited there on the other side of that door left them all speechless.

Kalyn raced after Martan around the long couch in the center of the room. The former held a large spittoon over her head and the latter was shirtless. Kalyn's face was a mask of rage as she shouted at the top of her lungs. "Stand still, ya lily-livered goblin licker, so I can brain ya!"

Martan's expression was one of terror as he tried to reason with the enraged young woman. "Kalyn! Kalyn! Would you just let me say one word?"

Kalyn paused for a moment, a mad look in her eyes, the spittoon waving dangerously over her head. *"One... word..."*

"Kalyn..." Martan pleaded frantically.

Before he could say anything more, the young woman darted after him again. "I'm gonna tie yer arms n' legs into knots so that blonde hussy can't ever get your shirt off!"

Elladan heard Aksel whisper to Seth, "Should we do something?"

"Nope. This is way too funny." Seth snickered.

Elladan couldn't deny that, but amusing as it was, Martan was bound to get hurt in the end. The bard took a deep breath and stepped into the room. "What's going on here?"

Kalyn halted, and spun toward him, a maniacal look in her storm grey eyes. She threw the spittoon at Martan and shrieked, "Ask him! Tell them, Martan! Tell them all about your little blonde friend."

Martan barely dodged the flying metal object, then stood back up, his face drooping as he stared at Kalyn with rueful eyes. He opened his mouth to speak, then closed it again and grimaced.

"That's what I thought," Kalyn snarled. She spun on her heel and stormed off to her room, slamming the door behind her.

The room around them looked as if an air elemental had hit it. Chairs were strewn on the floor, drapes were torn down, tables were overturned. Poor Martan stood in the center of it all, white as a sheet.

Elladan walked over to the beaten archer and placed a hand on his shoulder. "Martan, what happened?"

The haggard young man took a deep breath and looked Elladan in the eye. "Ves is here."

Elladan swept his eyes around the room again, but saw no one else. "Ves? Where is she?"

Martan's expression was strained as he pointed toward the bedroom that he shared with Elladan.

Elladan's brows drew together. Martan seemed ridden with guilt and Kalyn had acted like a jealous fish wife. Yet the Ves they knew was a proper young lady. *Something here just doesn't add up.*

The bard exchanged glances with the others. Aksel and Glo wore expressions that mirrored his own confusion. Seth, in contrast, wore a lopsided grin.

"Oh, this I have to see."

The halfling strode over to their bedroom, the rest of them falling in behind. The door hung open ever so slightly. Seth rapped on it gently. "Ves? Are you in there?"

"Are you decent?" Martan called from behind the others.

Elladan cocked an eyebrow at the archer, but refrained from saying anything.

Glo, on the other hand, grew quite incensed. He glared at Martan with his hands on his hips. "Martan? Just what were you doing in there with Ves?"

Martan threw his hands up in front of him, his face gone ashen. "We weren't doing anything… at least… I wasn't trying to…"

Meanwhile, there had been no response from the other side of the door. Seth pushed it open and they peered inside, but the room lay empty.

All eyes turned to Martan. The archer wore a puzzled frown as he pushed past them. He swept his gaze all around the room and even poked his head under both beds. The archer finally stood back up, his eyes wild as he shook his head. "Well, she was here ten minutes ago."

Seth narrowed an eye at the gaunt man. "You sure Kalyn *didn't* hit you over the head with that spittoon?"

Martan let out an exasperated sigh. "No. Ves was here—Kalyn can attest to that—but she was acting awfully strange."

Aksel began to pace back and forth, quietly rubbing his chin. "Seth, any chance that Ves could have followed you back here?"

Seth tilted his head sideways and eyed Aksel with clear annoyance. "She'd have had to be a ghost."

Martan still seemed extremely frazzled. Elladan put an arm around his shoulder. "Why don't you sit down and tell us the whole story from the beginning."

Martan's bed was soaked in milk and covered in pie, so they sat on Elladan's instead. The glum archer then recounted his tale from when he first encountered Ves in the hallway, 'til they had walked in on him and Kalyn. The room grew quiet when Martan finished.

Glo was the first to break the silence. "There is no way that *was* Ves."

Aksel, however, did not seem quite convinced. "I don't know. Mind control can mess with someone's psyche."

Glo paused a moment as he mulled that over, then shifted his gaze to Elladan. "You saw her after we rescued her. Did she seem like herself?"

Elladan briefly flashed back in his mind to their escape from the airship. After a few moments of reviewing those events, he nodded. "I believe so. She was a bit shaken, but her first instinct was to draw the other dragons away from us."

A thin smile crossed Glo's lips as he folded his arms and stared at Aksel triumphantly. "I told you so."

Aksel let out a deep breath. "Well, if it wasn't Ves, then it had to be someone who knows her to pull off that good of a disguise. Further, they'd have to know of our association with Ves."

Elladan let out a soft whistle. He could think of only one person who fit that bill and she was crazier than hellbat dung. "Anya? But what would she be after?"

Glo cocked his head to one side and squinted at him. "Didn't you say she accused us of stealing her property?"

Elladan shrugged. "Well, yeah, but we all thought that was Ves. What would be the point of sending us someone who looked like her?"

Seth let out a derisive snort. "To get us to reveal where the real Ves is."

A single brow lifted on Glo's forehead. "But we don't know where she is."

Aksel's eyes suddenly came alight. "True, but Anya doesn't know that."

Aksel's epiphany gave Elladan an idea of his own. "Glo, can I borrow that *friendship pearl* of yours?"

Glo wore a curious expression as he handed the pearl over to Elladan. The pearl was a gift from Ves to the wizard, a means of communicating with the sisters from afar. All three girls had their own, but Glo hadn't used his since Ves was kidnapped by Anya.

Elladan held the pearl up to his mouth and spoke into it aloud. "Is anyone there?"

A few moments of silence went by until a young girl's voice answered. "Who's that?"

Another voice immediately followed. "Shut up, Maya."

Elladan recognized the second voice as Ruka's. It sounded like she had the same idea as him—that someone else might be listening in. Elladan waited a few seconds more, then tried again. "Anya, I know you're there."

A high-pitched laugh emanated from the pearl, the sound like tiny bells ringing in a meadow. "What is it, my love?"

Elladan's mouth bent into a half-smile. His hunch had been right. He spoke again into the pearl. "We know you're looking for us. What is it you want?"

Anya laughed again. "Oh, Elladan, always straight to the point. That's what I like about you." There was a momentary pause. "It's very simple—you took something that belongs to me and I… want… it… back…"

Elladan felt anger rising deep within his gut. He forced himself to take a long breath before he responded. "But Anya dear, Ves is a person. She doesn't belong to you."

There was another short pause. "Oh, my poor, sweet, Elladan. I don't want Ves. I have plenty of other dragons. I just want the item you stole from my ship."

Elladan's eyes widened. "Hold on a minute, my dear." He peered at Seth. "You didn't happen to take anything from Anya's ship, did you?"

Seth looked him straight in the eye. "Nope."

Elladan glanced around at the others. "Anyone? No?" He took another deep breath and spoke into the pearl in a calm, even tone. "Look hon, we don't have whatever it is you think we stole."

"And I'm supposed to take your word for it—after you just up and left me?"

Elladan was surprised to hear the hurt in her voice. It almost sounded like she actually had feelings for him. Yet he knew her type. The world revolved around Anya, and only Anya. Still, it was better to have her talking instead of threatening them. "Look, we have something we must take care of first. As soon as we're done, we'll meet with you and sort this all out."

"And when will that be?" Anya responded in a petulant tone.

Elladan kept his voice smooth. "A couple of days at most. We'll meet you back here in Lukescros."

There was another pause as Anya thought it over. "Very well, but don't keep me waiting too long."

26
UNEXPECTED FRIENDS

"Trust me. My friends specialize in trouble."

It was later the next day as Elladan and Martan road through Vermoorden. They had left Lukescros earlier that morning after a fitful start.

Aksel had contacted Shalla and found the Lady Gracelynn was put onboard a ship to Dunwynn. Ignar had left as well, but instead headed south down the coast. That left Ravenford in the hands of a small Dunwynn occupation force.

The news upset everyone, but Lloyd was especially concerned about Ignar. There was some sort of treaty between Penwick and Dunwynn where neither city's ships would cross an imaginary line along the coast.

Upon reaching the Penwick embassy, Lloyd warned the Lord Hightower. The old gentleman in turn said he would notify Lloyd's father, the Admiral of the Penwick Navy. Hightower then provided them with mounts and supplies.

The ride to Vermoorden proved uneventful, but the companions split up just before reaching the town. Seth stole past the guard station, while the others donned disguises. Glo, Kalyn and Aksel dressed as traveling monks, Lloyd and Andrella as a noble couple, and Elladan and Martan as performers.

Elladan, now dressed all in black, guided his horse down the road toward the *Theater of the Festive Spirits*.

Martan drew his mount up beside him. "I thought we were meeting the others at the burnt-out farmhouse?"

Elladan gave the archer a quasi-smile. "Just making a quick stop is all. While I was signing up for the bard competition, I heard a disturbing rumor. Someone said that Balmaroh had been assassinated."

Martan pointed at the large building just ahead of them. "The rumors might be true. The place looks closed up."

Martan was right. The doors and windows of the theater were boarded up. A sign on the front door read, *Closed Indefinitely*.

Elladan exchanged a worried glance with Martan, then swept his eyes down the street. There was a small stone cottage next to the theater. On a hunch, he flicked his reins and rode toward it.

"Where are we going now?" Martan asked.

"The last time we were here, I swore Balmaroh said he lived next to the theater."

Martan shrugged. "I guess it's worth a shot."

The cottage was well groomed, surrounded by a short white picket fence and a row of hedges along the sides. Elladan and Martan tied their horses to the post out front, strode up to the door, and knocked.

The front door opened a crack, a thin hawk-nosed woman peering at them from inside. Elladan immediately recognized her as Balmaroh's assistant, the wizard Newin.

Newin stared at them a moment, then did a double take. "Elladan? Is that you?"

The elven bard gave her his familiar half-smile. "It's me."

Newin's cheeks turned slightly red as she opened up the door. "Please come in, the both of you."

Newin ushered them into a comfy little home. Before them a

narrow hallway paralleled a set of stairs leading upward. An archway opened to their left into a good-sized living area with a couch, a few chairs, a harpsicord, and an open hearth at the opposite end.

Newin bade them sit down and then announced their arrival. "We have visitors! It's Elladan!"

A large black dog padded in from down the hall and stared curiously at them. Martan immediately fell on his knees and petted the furry fellow. The dog was followed by a short, mousy-looking man with spectacles—Balmaroh's other assistant, Rhith.

Rhith seemed rather nervous to see them. "Elladan… wh-what are you doing here?"

Elladan eyed the small man curiously. "I heard some disturbing news in Lukescros, so I came to check on Balmaroh. Is he around?"

Rhith exchanged an anxious glance with Newin. "You-you didn't hear?"

Newin cleared her throat and brushed back a lock of her long hair. "Balmaroh is no longer here. He's…"

"…been replaced," a high-pitched voice squeaked from behind the two.

Rhith and Newin stood aside as a small figure pushed its way between them. A brown, scaly-skinned bipedal creature, shorter than Aksel or Seth, strode over to a chair and plopped itself down. It had a reptilian head, a long tail, three-fingered hands, and three-toed clawed feet.

Elladan's forehead creased as he exchanged a glance with Martan. The dour archer's eyes were narrowed as he mouthed the word *kobold*.

Kobolds were distant kin of dragons, yet the contrast to their magnificent cousins marked the entire race with feelings of inadequacy. Thus, kobolds tended to be mean-spirited toward anyone who made them feel inferior.

Elladan leveled an eye at the small creature. "And who's replaced him?"

"Me, of course," the creature squeaked. The kobold waved a short arm in the air and a lute appeared within its grasp. Elladan watched with amazement as it ran its three-fingered hands across the strings.

A masterful tune echoed forth, the bard losing himself in the melody. When it was done, Elladan clapped in earnest. "Where did you learn to play so well?"

The kobold turned its snout toward him. "You could say… Balmaroh taught me everything I know."

Elladan's suspicions were aroused even further, but before he could say another word, Rhith interrupted him.

"So-so what are you gentlemen doing here?"

Elladan shifted his gaze to the timid illusionist, his voice lowering to just above a whisper. "We're taking down the assassin's guild."

The kobold shot up in its seat. It slammed a three-fingered fist on the small table beside it, nearly knocking the thing over. "It's about time!"

Elladan peered at the creature again, his eyes narrowing. *I wonder…*

This time Newin interrupted him before he could finish his thought. "What do you want us to do?"

Elladan swept his gaze back to the timid illusionist and the tall, thin wizard. "Meet us by the burnt farmhouse north of town after sunset. Invite anyone you think is trustworthy."

"We'll be there!" The kobold squeaked.

Aksel had been a bit shaken on seeing the remains of the burnt farmhouse. He could still envision the huge red dragon standing in the midst of the wreckage, holding a tiny Seth in its immense claws. Charred wood and melted roof tiles lay strewn in all directions, yet by some miracle, two partial walls of the main cottage had been left standing.

Kalyn carefully scouted the rubble, her jaw dropping upon finding a set of dragon tracks. "Holy troll snot, these here claw prints is easily three feet long." She spun her head toward Aksel. "How big did ya say that dragon was?"

Aksel threw his hands up in the air and shrugged. "I don't know. Maybe fifty feet from head to tail?"

Kalyn gulped hard. "I knew dragons was big, but that's bigger than most huts back home."

Glo gazed at her with a weak smile. "That's merely an adult red. Ancient dragons can grow anywhere between 80 to 120 feet."

Kalyn squinted at the tall elf. "Now yer just funnin' me."

One of Glo's eyebrows shot upward. "I kid you not."

Kalyn gazed from Glo to Aksel, whistling as she rose. "Then I've got no idea how you and Seth survived that meetin'."

Aksel let out a hollow laugh. "Quite frankly, neither do I."

The three of them were soon joined by Lloyd and Andrella, both of whom still wore elegant attire. Kalyn pretended to gush as they dismounted and tied up their horses. "Well if it ain't the fancy nobles. Come to slum with us poor folk?"

Andrella put a hand to her forehead, her expression one of feigned distress. "Oh my. Whatever shall I do? I've lost my retinue. How will I survive in this desolate wilderness?"

Lloyd glanced from one lady to the other and shook his head. "Have you two been taking acting lessons from Shalla?"

Andrella grabbed Kalyn by the arm and grinned. "Guilty as charged, good Sir." Yet the smile on her face swiftly faded as her eyes fell on what was left of the farm. "This place looks like a tornado hit it."

Kalyn nodded solemnly. "A fifty-foot red dragon. according to Aksel."

Andrella's face darkened further. "I remember seeing wreckage like this in Ravenford when I was still young."

Lloyd's voice was soft as he placed an arm around her. "From the black dragon attack?"

"Yes." Andrella nodded, laying her head on his shoulder.

Kalyn climbed into the trees and kept lookout while the rest of them set up a makeshift camp between the two partial walls.

Shortly thereafter. Elladan and Martan arrived. The bard briefly described their encounter with Rhith, Newin, and the strange little kobold. Though Elladan seemed pleased at their pledged support, he voiced some suspicions as to the kobold's true nature.

Aksel thought it best not to comment. He still felt it too risky to expose the plan Seth had set in motion.

It was right about that time that the halfling appeared in the middle of the camp. Aksel nearly jumped out of his skin. "Seth! You nearly gave me a heart attack. Do you enjoy doing that?"

"Immensely." A wicked grin spread across the halfling's face.

Aksel took a deep a breath and let it out slowly before speaking again. "Very well. Where have you been?"

"I'll tell you in bit." With that, Seth picked up a stone and sat on the ground. A knife magically appeared in his hand and he began to sharpen it.

Aksel exchanged an exasperated glance with Elladan, but the bard merely laughed. The little gnome closed his eyes and took a deep breath. *Seth is Seth. No amount of cajoling will get him to talk before he's ready.*

Elladan left to help Lloyd and Andrella prepare a quick dinner. Martan, in the meantime, took up a post on the opposite end of the camp from Kalyn.

Aksel's gaze swept from the grim archer to the young tracker up in the trees. Anya's trickery had created a huge rift between the two. Aksel felt bad for them both. Though Martan was partly to blame for what happen, he didn't quite deserve the icy treatment Kalyn was giving him. Yet Kalyn had been too deeply hurt to just let it go.

Aksel sighed again and peered out over the lake. The sun now hung low over the mountains to the west. Brilliant reds and yellows streaked across the horizon as the reddish orb slowly disappeared. The sky to the east darkened and the blanket of night fell across the earth. Tiny stars poked their way through the firmament, their twinkling lights sparkling like diamonds in the black velvet of the night sky.

Nearly an hour after sunset, the hoot of an owl sounded from the tree where Kalyn sat. It was the signal that they would soon have company. At the same moment, a black dog suddenly appeared next to Seth. Aksel almost jumped again 'til he realized it was Balmaroh's dog, Wraith. The creature seemed to take great pleasure in teasing Seth.

"The one up in the tree there is far more observant than you."

Seth didn't even look up from his knife. "I heard you coming a mile away."

"I doubt it." The dog scoffed. "Anyway, my masters are nearly here, and they brought some friends."

A few minutes later Rhith and Newin entered the camp. The pair were accompanied by the strangest little kobold. All three were followed by the inn owner, Barmann, along with most of his staff.

Aksel had to admit it was more than he expected. Still, he wasn't planning on getting any of them involved in actual battle.

Elladan greeted their guests. "Thank you all for coming on such short notice." He ushered them to sit around the campfire. Once everyone was seated, the bard spoke again. "Alright, let's get down to it. We're here to take down the assassin's guild."

His statement was met with some soft muttering.

"Yeah."

"About time."

A half-smile spread across Elladan's face. "There are a few things we'll need to do first, though. One, we need to figure out where their lair is. Two is to find out who in town is involved, and three is to neutralize them before they can warn their guildmates."

Some more murmurs went around the crowd, 'til Barmann finally spoke up. "Philmar, the potion vendor, and Captain Morled both stay at the inn. They've been seen talking with that shady guy with the eye patch that comes in every once in a while."

Seth stood outside the circle, casually leaning against one of the half-walls. "He's a member of the assassin's guild."

Barmann squinted at the halfling a moment, then nodded. "That's what we thought."

Aksel shared what they had previously discovered about Philmar and Morled's connection to the Mayor. That news didn't seem to surprise anyone.

Once again, Barmann spoke for the group. "We all figured DeWyness was dirty. Either she's part of the guild, or they pay her off."

Murmurs of agreement went around the campfire. Aksel frowned as the kobold tugged on Newin's robe, then whispered in her ear. The thin wizard nodded at the creature, then addressed the gathering.

"The same could be said for the Magistrate and her apprentices. If anyone even mentions assassins, they shut them down really quick."

Aksel had suspected as much from the Magistrate. Fraith had made it painfully obvious he was the Mayor's toady on their first visit to Vermoorden. Aksel also knew that DeWyness was a wizard, but what caught him by surprise was that she had apprentices.

Glo must have been thinking the same thing. The tall elf raised an eyebrow as he gazed at Newin. "And just how many apprentices does the Mayor have?"

The firelight danced across Newin's face, adding to her grave expression. "Four altogether, and they're nothing to sneeze at—though they don't compare to DeWyness herself." Her eyes narrowed as they bore into Glo. "Watch out for her—she's very powerful."

Glo exchanged a knowing glance with Aksel. The little cleric gave him a curt nod. *Five deadly casters—this is going to be far riskier than we anticipated.*

A thick silence had fallen over the campfire.

Lloyd was the one who finally broke it, his eyes burning with a fierce intensity. "That's a good start. At least we know what we're up against." His fiery attitude seemed to lift everyone's spirits. "So, does anyone have ideas on how to find their lair?"

"I do."

All eyes turned to Seth. The halfling hadn't moved from his spot against the nearby wall. "When we first got here, I set up a meeting with old one eye. Supposed to meet him at the inn in about an hour."

Aksel was impressed. "You thinking he'll lead us back to his guild?"

The halfling shrugged. "Something like that."

Barmann gave Seth an approving nod. "Not bad—so what do you want the rest of us to do?"

There was a momentary pause, then a bent smile formed on Elladan's lips. He leaned in closer to the fire and motioned for everyone to gather around. "Here's the plan…"

"So how far is it to this… Ravenford?"

Donatello glanced up at Kara as they strode through the darkened streets. It was a couple of hours after sunset. He couldn't really see her face—the houses had thinned on this side of town and there were no street lights here.

The slim elf shrugged. "A couple of days' ride at most."

The duo continued in silence until they rounded the next corner. A short distance ahead stood a multi-storied structure, its levels dotted with shining windows.

"And you're sure your friends will be able to help us?"

Despite the surrounding darkness, Donnie gave Kara a pearly smile. "Trust me. My friends specialize in trouble."

"Making it… or handling it?"

Donnie chuckled. "A little bit of both, actually."

The large building was set back a bit from the road. The area surrounding it was fenced in, but the front gate lay open. Donnie turned down the walkway, with Kara following close behind.

The sound of voices drifted out of an open door on the first floor. Figures milled about inside. Above the doorway hung a single light that illuminated a worn wooden sign. Scrawled on the plaque were the words *House of Barmann*.

Donnie let out a sigh. It had taken them a few days to get here. The high plunge to escape the demons had knocked him out cold. By some miracle, both he and Kara survived, washing ashore downstream beyond the mountains. The woods they woke up in turned out to be none other than the Darkwoods.

The duo built a raft and followed the river downstream, eventually reaching Lake Strikken. There, a boat picked them up and brought them to Vermoorden.

Like the gentleman that he was, Donnie ushered Kara before him. The slight elf followed close behind, his eyes swiftly adjusting to the lights inside the inn.

Silence fell over the room, all eyes turning toward the tall blonde warrior in front of him. Donnie chuckled softly to himself. *She is a rather impressive sight.*

While Kara drew all the attention, Donnie swept his eyes around the room. It was emptier than he thought it would be. There were a few patrons at the bar. A well-dressed couple sat at one table. Their backs were to him, but his gaze was drawn to their copper-haired child. Donnie thought it strange that neither parent had red hair.

The sharp-eyed elf continued his sweep across the room, his eyes suddenly catching on another table. Three people sat there: a man with flaxen hair, a woman with chestnut hair and storm-grey eyes, and a second man with jet-black hair garbed in black.

Donnie's nose wrinkled. The woman definitely looked familiar, yet his gaze stuck on the man in black. Other than the human ears, he was the spitting image of Elladan.

Elladan's look-alike had been staring at Kara, but locked eyes with Donatello a moment later. The man's jaw went slack. "Donnie?"

The man with flaxen hair spun around in his seat. Despite the magically altered ears, Donnie immediately recognized Glolindir.

The three of them strode up to greet him, Elladan firmly embracing Donatello. Donnie was initially surprised by the warm greeting—he was not used to having real friends. Something melted inside him as he embraced Elladan back.

The bard finally pushed away, the slightest trace of moisture in his eyes. "I thought we lost you for good this time!"

The corner of Donnie's mouth upturned slightly. "*I* thought I was lost for good. Would have been, too, if not for Kara here." He pointed a thumb at the tall warrior next to him.

Kara's arms were folded, yet she wore an amused expression. "You had a hand in our escape."

"Escape from where?" A familiar voice sounded from behind the others.

Donnie glanced past Glo and saw the noble couple approaching. He arched an eyebrow when he realized who they were. *Lloyd and Andrella.*

Donnie looked them over with clear appreciation. *They make a cute couple.* His eyes then fell on their 'child.' Up close, it was obviously Aksel, but Donnie couldn't help ribbing them about it. "Have I been gone that long? When did you two start having kids?"

Andrella put a hand over her mouth and giggled, but Lloyd nearly choked.

"Yeah, yeah, real funny, Donnie."

Donatello would have known that sarcastic voice anywhere. Seth's head poked out from behind one of the other patrons at the bar. "How about we stow it for later."

Aksel cleared his throat. "Seth's right. We're kind of in the middle of something here."

Elladan placed a hand next to his mouth and whispered, "We're taking down the assassin's guild."

Donnie cast a quick glance at Kara. The tall warrior responded with a grim nod. He peered back at Aksel. "Count us in."

Elladan grasped Donnie by the arm. "Good. Now grab a table and try to look inconspicuous."

Donnie swept his eyes around the room. All the male patrons were still staring at Kara. The lean elf shrugged. "Okay, we'll do our best."

Elladan led them over to a table off to one side. Glo then cast a spell on Donnie to make his ears look human. Donnie made a mental note to see if he could learn it. *Might come in handy one day.*

The others went back to their original seats. The bartender brought Donnie and Kara some ales and they ordered dinner. Meals had been scarce these last few days.

Kara chugged down her ale in one long swig, then wiped her mouth and eyed him curiously. "Interesting group of friends you have there. Is the gnome the leader?"

Donnie cocked his head to one side. "More or less. They're not exactly a regimented unit."

Kara pursed her lips together. "And this is the group we were going to find in Ravenford?"

Donnie gave her a subtle nod. "They're far more capable than they appear."

Kara sat back and stretched her long arms, then fixed him with an intense stare. "Very good. I shall observe their prowess in battle with this 'assassin's guild.' We shall see if they are up for a siege on the Demon Tower."

Donnie stared back at her and gulped. *I'm not sure I'm up to a siege on the Demon Tower.*

The thin elf swept his gaze around the room once more, his eyes falling on Lloyd and Andrella. He had nearly forgotten how large the young man was—taller than Kara, in fact. Yet he was more surprised by the Lady Andrella's presence here.

Donnie observed the couple, noting a difference in them both. Lloyd seemed to carry himself with far more confidence. Andrella did as well, but her attitude had changed markedly. She had been clearly affected by the death of her father, yet this was something more. *Maybe I've been gone longer than I thought.*

Over at the other table, Elladan and Glo were deep in conversation, while Kalyn sat quietly and listened. The lively Deepwooder seemed far more subdued than usual. She had said nary a word to either Donnie or Kara. Elladan hadn't changed at all, still poised as always, but Glo appeared even more focused. Last Donnie had seen the flaxen-haired elf, he was still dealing with being "dumped" by Elistra.

Donnie returned his attention to Kara, his apprehension slowly fading. He gave her a pearly white smile. *Together we might be up to the challenge after all.*

Seth was as surprised as anyone to see Donatello. *Figures—we just get Philmar and Morled settled down, and now Donnie has to show up.*

The seedy duo were at the tavern when Seth and the others arrived. The half-drunken Philmar had nearly recognized Aksel. He started to raise a fuss, but Andrella managed to sidetrack him with her feminine charms. Needless to say, Lloyd was none too happy about it.

Surprisingly, Kalyn chose to charm the also-inebriated Morled. It was quite out of character. It also completely devastated Martan, which was quite likely why Kalyn had done it.

The girls lured the drunken duo to Philmar's room, where an angry Lloyd and Martan pummeled them senseless. Martan elected to stay back there and keep an eye on the pair.

A few minutes later, Donnie waltzed in with the tall blonde warrior. It was impeccable timing—old one-eye was scheduled to arrive any minute now. Thankfully Seth was able to steer them all back on track. Everyone spread out once again with Donnie and his new 'friend' Kara at an out-of-the-way table.

It was none too soon. Not five minutes had gone by when old

one-eye walked into the tavern. He and Seth exchanged a nod, then the short, dark-cloaked man strode to a corner booth at the back of the room.

Seth waited for another minute, then went back to join him. He slid into the seat opposite the one-eyed man and silently finished his ale.

The man pursed his lips. "Nice job you did there. Why'd you skip town?"

Seth shrugged. "Things got a bit too hot—so I left. Now I'm back."

A wicked grin spread across old one-eye's face. "It did cause a bit of a stir. We weren't sure you'd be back... but a deal's a deal." He cast a quick glance around the room. Seemingly satisfied, he pulled a bag from under his cloak and covertly pushed it across the table. "Here's your money."

Seth took the pouch and opened it, carefully inspecting the contents.

The one-eyed man chuckled. "Still don't trust no one?"

"Nope." Seth pulled the drawstrings closed, pocketed the bag, then slid to the end of the booth. "Nice doing business with you."

Old one-eye nodded. "Heh. Likewise. If you ever want more work, let us know."

Not looking back, Seth gave him a curt wave as he strode away to the bar. The halfling ordered another ale and waited 'til old one-eye left. The second he exited, Seth jumped from his seat. He grabbed his cloak to turn invisible, when Aksel came running up to him.

"Hang on. I've got something which will help."

Seth eyed his friend anxiously, but waited as the cleric weaved a spell. He finished with the words, "*Ambulate in Aerem.*"

Seth suddenly felt a lot lighter on his feet. He cocked his head to one side. "What was that?"

"An air walk spell. Now go!" Aksel waved him toward the door.

Seth gave Aksel an irritated look, then grabbed his cloak and turned invisible.

By the time Seth got outside, old one-eye was nowhere in sight. *Thanks a lot, Aksel.*

Quickly running out of options, the halfling chose to take to the air. It was a bit strange at first, walking with nothing underneath him, but Seth quickly acclimated to it.

He just reached the tree tops when he spied a diminutive dark-cloaked figure up the road to the north. Seth tried to race after him, but swiftly found he could not run in mid-air. *Son of a…*

Seth thought about landing, but the dark-cloaked figure abruptly veered off the road to the east. Chancing that one-eye couldn't see the invisible, Seth took off at an angle across the grass. Thankfully he caught up with the dark figure as it swept around the hillside that led up to the keep.

All of a sudden, the figure halted.

Caught out in the open, Seth froze in mid-air. He pulled his cloak tight around him, thankful that the moon hadn't risen yet. *Even if he sees me at this distance, I'm a tiny patch in the night sky.*

After what felt like an eternity, the figure moved again. Seth waited a few moments, then followed.

The figure continued to skirt around the keep. They drew so close that Seth could see the men on the parapets. Erring on the side of caution, he floated down below the trees. Unfortunately, in doing so, he lost sight of his quarry.

Seth carefully scanned the area until a subtle movement caught his eye. A dark shadow crept along the castle wall, but Seth's keen eyes could make out the shape. It was the dark-cloaked figure he had been following.

Seth floated over to the castle wall, keeping below the parapets, but above and behind his quarry. He continued to follow it 'til the figure stopped. A half minute went by when the dark-cloaked figure suddenly disappeared.

Seth descended to the ground at the spot where he had last seen his quarry. He ran his fingers over the wall, carefully studying each individual stone. Abruptly he felt one move under his hand.

Seth pushed against the stone. There was a soft *click* and then the section of wall next to it swung inward. Beyond the opening, a set of stairs led down into the keep. Far below, Seth could see a dim light at the bottom of the stairwell.

The halfling's lips twisted into a smug smile. *Got ya.*

27
ASSASSIN'S LAIR

*Their friend disappeared from sight as the cloud expanded
down the corridor*

Nearly forty-five minutes had passed since Seth returned to the inn. It had taken that long to sneak everyone through the woods, and across to the secret entrance. The last part had been facilitated by a clever bit of fog, conjured by the crafty Newin.

Donnie now led the way down the dark stairwell, inwardly surprised that Seth had let him go first. The halfling wasn't exactly the supportive mentor, but Donnie was determined to prove his skill. The nimble elf examined each step with extreme care, only moving downward when he was sure it was safe.

Lloyd and Kara stood a few steps up from him, swords and spear held at the ready. The rest of the companions lined up beyond the two warriors, along with Rhith, Newin, the little kobold, and their dog.

Donnie didn't think the theater folk battle-ready. Yet for some unknown reason, Aksel agreed to let them join the others. Either way, Donnie couldn't worry about that now.

They proceeded downward nearly a hundred steps before the stairway ended. Donnie hadn't found a single trap on the stairs, a fact that made him all the more nervous.

A stone corridor opened before them. There were a few torches along the walls, spaced to provide a minimal amount of light. There was an opening at the other end, perhaps a few dozen yards away.

Donnie crept down the passage with extreme caution. Again, he found no traps of any kind—not a pressure plate, a trip wire, or anything that would set something off. His inner senses screamed at the unbelievability of it all.

More anxious than ever, Donnie reached the end of the corridor. A circular chamber opened before him, this one far better lit than the passage they had just traversed. On either side of the room stood a stone statue of a female warrior, each holding a pair of swords crossed against their breasts. The chamber ended a dozen yards down in another corridor.

Donnie eyed the statues cautiously, then took a step into the room. The moment his foot touched the floor, the statues began to move.

A sardonic chuckle echoed from back down the corridor. Yet Donnie didn't have time to respond to Seth's nonverbal chastisement. He reached behind him with an empty hand and simply said, "Spear."

A metallic shaft was thrust in his hand as the two statues advanced on him. Donnie didn't wait for them to strike. He rushed forward, spear raised as if to meet their charge. At the last second, he tumbled between them.

The stone women spun haphazardly, trying to catch him with their blades. Instead, Donnie caught one of the statue's legs with the end of the spear.

Between the odd angle and his forward momentum, the statue was upended. It fell to the floor with the resounded echo of stone on stone.

"See, even stone women fall for me!" Donnie quipped as he leapt to his feet.

Groans echoed down the corridor as Lloyd and Kara charged

into the fray. With two swings, Lloyd parried a blow from the upright statue and lopped off its arm with his black blade.

Kara held out a hand as she rushed the prone statue. Donnie hurled the spear out in front of her. In one fluid motion, she caught it and jabbed downward with all her might. The hard metal pierced the statue's chest, the stone cracking and splitting apart.

Meanwhile, Lloyd parried another blow, then spun around and swiped the statue's head clean off its torso. It crumbled to the ground in a heap.

Donnie grinned at the two warriors, then peered past them at the others. "See, no problem at…"

The rest of his words were brusquely cut off as a loud gong sounded from somewhere above. The metallic clash reverberated up and down the chamber, slowly and inexorably dying out.

Seth eyed Donnie darkly from the edge of the corridor. "So much for the stealthy approach."

A strained smile spread across Donnie's lips. "Maybe no one heard the giant gong?"

"No one heard it? *No one heard it?*" Seth's eyes widened, his voice rising with anger. "Well I'm sure if they missed the gong, they heard the stone statues hitting the ground, or Kara over there clanking"— he waved a hand at the tall warrior—"or maybe, *just maybe*, they heard one of your sassy quips. They're probably lining the corridors right now, honing their knives and setting traps for us."

Seth huffed, his cheeks bright red.

Donnie's mouth hung open, stunned by the sudden outburst. He'd been on the receiving end of Seth's sarcastic wit, but he'd never actually seen him get angry.

Aksel strode up and gazed at the halfling, his eyes filled with concern. "Are you alright?"

Seth pressed his lips together and glared at the gnome. "No, I'm not alright. Why is it always something with you people? Do you know the meaning of the word stealth? I swear, one of these days you're going to get us all killed."

Seth folded his arms and glared at everyone indignantly. The others stared back, their faces filled with shock and dismay. Even Elladan was left speechless.

Donnie squinted at Seth with a sheepish grin. "So… does this mean you want to go first?"

Seth fixed Donnie with a look that could have bored holes into his skull. "What do you think?"

The truth was Donnie didn't know what to think at this point. He gave him a tentative shrug. "Yes?"

Seth's lips bent into a contemptuous smirk. "Sorry, but that's incorrect. The answers you were looking for included, no, nope, not on your life, not on my life, not on your horse's life, no way in the abyss, and I'm sorry Seth, I'll go first instead."

Donnie eyed the halfling carefully. He had no idea what was going on with him, but this was neither the time nor the place. "Very well, Seth. I'm sorry… I'll go first instead."

"Thank you," Seth responded, overemphasizing each word. The halfling then spun on his heel and stormed his way to the back of the line.

Kalyn shook her head as Seth blew by her. She gave Donnie a wincing smile. "Wow—that may be the most speakin' Seth has done in his entire life."

Donnie smiled weakly back at her. He appreciated her attempt to lighten the mood. The embarrassed elf gave Kara an awkward glance. He couldn't imagine what she thought of this group after that outburst. Yet the tall warrior did not seem the least bit phased. Instead, she stared back at him expectantly. "Whenever you're ready."

"Same here," Lloyd agreed, blades still in hand.

Donnie gave them both a grateful smile, then started for the next corridor.

✶

Elladan was as surprised as anyone by Seth's 'meltdown.' The halfling's sarcastic wit was usually enough to get his point across. Still, they had been through a lot these last few weeks and even Seth had a breaking point.

Thankfully, Donnie did not escalate things. The furtive elf now led Lloyd and Kara deeper into the assassin's lair. Elladan and the others followed close behind.

A few yards from the circular chamber, the passage reached a dead end. Donnie ran his hands carefully over the wall. After a minute or so, he whispered something over his shoulder.

Lloyd and Kara retraced their steps, the former quietly passing on Donnie's message. "There's a secret door with a trap on it. Donnie says we should all stand back."

Elladan exchanged a quick glance with Aksel and Glo, then the entire party backed out all the way to the circular chamber. They all waited anxiously until they heard Donnie's frustrated cry.

"Crap."

"Run!" The slim elf shouted a moment later.

A loud hissing noise echoed down the passageway as Donnie turned and dashed toward them. He hadn't gone more than three steps when a green cloud overtook him. Their friend disappeared from sight as the cloud expanded down the corridor.

"Donnie!" Elladan cried.

Kara started forward, but Lloyd grabbed her by the arm. "Wait. That could be poison gas."

Kara turned on Lloyd, her expression a mixture of fear and anger. "We can't just leave him in there!"

Lloyd stepped in front of Kara. "Don't worry, I'll get him."

"No, you won't!" Seth raced to the front of the line. "Everyone get out. I've got this."

"But Seth…" Aksel began.

A wry grin spread across the halfling's face. He pointed to his belt. "Poison immunity."

Without another word, Seth launched himself into the rapidly expanding cloud. Everyone else retreated to the opposite end of the circular chamber.

The gas had just started pouring into the room when Seth reappeared, dragging Donnie with him. Lloyd and Kara rushed forward to give him a hand. They brought the slight elf back with them and laid him down on the hard stone floor.

Donatello's skin looked positively green. Everyone gathered around as Aksel knelt and ran his hands over the unconscious elf. A few moments passed 'til he sat back, his expression haggard. "I'm afraid the poison's spread too far for even my magic."

They all stared aghast at the little cleric.

Elladan could hardly believe he was going to lose his old friend. Abruptly, something clicked in his mind. "Wait a second, I might have something!"

Elladan pulled the portal bag from his belt and reached an arm inside, all the way down to his elbow. He rummaged around for a few seconds 'til his hand touched the thing he was looking for. A moment later, he pulled a large box out of the bag.

Aksel came over as he laid it down on the floor. "Is that…"

"…Philmar's stash." Elladan nodded. The bard had 'liberated' the potion vendor's merchandise after they had dealt with him and Morled.

Elladan popped the lid open. Inside the box stood nearly fifty vials filled with liquids of all different colors. Aksel ran his hands over them and grabbed one containing a black liquid.

"This is it!" the gnome cried. He spun around and ran back to Donnie while waving to Lloyd and Kara. "Quickly, lift up his head!"

They both raised the light elf while Aksel popped the cork off the vial. "Open his mouth."

Kara propped his mouth open and Aksel poured the contents of the vial down his throat. Nothing happened at first, then Donnie's color started to change. The green pallor faded and he sputtered.

"Um, guys… I think we may need to back out o' here altogether."

Elladan looked at Kalyn, then back across the chamber. The gas cloud had now filled three-quarters of the room and was still expanding. "Just how much of this stuff is there?"

"We can fix that," a high-pitched voice squeaked.

Elladan's eyes fixed on the little kobold as he whispered to Newin. The wizardess nodded, then rolled up her sleeves and strode out in front of the others.

Elladan could feel the magic build as she waved her hands in a calculated pattern. She released the spell with the words, *"Impetus de Ventus."*

A rush of air emanated from her outstretched hands, slamming into the expanding green wall. The cloud continued to billow against it, but Newin held her ground firm. Sweat beaded on her brow until finally the gas started to give way. It slowly receded across the chamber, then back into the corridor from where it had come.

Meanwhile, Donnie sat up, his color nearly normal. He gazed around and rubbed his head. "What'd I miss?"

A full smile crept across Elladan's face as he stared at his hapless friend. "Oh, nothing much. Seth just saved your life."

Donnie's nose wrinkled as his eyes searched out the halfling. "Seth?"

Seth poked his head out from behind Glo and Andrella. "What?"

"Um, thanks." Donnie gave the halfling a grateful smile.

Seth shrugged, his expression indifferent. Elladan, however, detected the slightest bit of compassion in the halfling's eyes.

In the meantime, Newin had completely dissipated the poison cloud. Glo nodded to her appreciatively. "That was nicely done."

Newin dipped her chin in gratitude, but the kobold let out a high-pitch laugh. "Oh, she's had lots of practice dispelling fog."

Elladan eyed the kobold closely. He'd had a sneaking suspicion for a while now, but the kobold's statement just confirmed it. He strode in front of the little creature, his hands on his hips. "Alright, it's time we clear this thing up. You're Balmaroh."

The kobold gazed up at him with a toothy grin, then turned to Rhith and nodded. The illusionist made a pattern in the air with his hands, magic releasing from his fingertips. A moment later, the kobold disappeared. Standing in its place was a thin, light-haired man garbed in a puffy white silk shirt with a fancy vest, light brown pants, and knee-high brown leather boots.

Balmaroh gazed at Elladan with a sly grin. "Master Seth covertly approached me and detailed the assassin's plan to have me murdered. He figured if we staged an assassination, they'd leave me alone. So, we enlisted the aid of Rhith here, and voila, Balmaroh was no more..."

Elladan turned an eye toward Seth and fixed him with a half-smile. "Wow, you are just full of surprises today."

The side of Seth's mouth curved upward. "Yeah, yeah. I'm a regular prince. Now, can we get back to business?"

Lloyd breathed a sigh of relief when Donnie sat up again. They'd nearly lost him. If it weren't for Elladan's quick thinking, they certainly would have.

It came as a shock that the little kobold was actually Balmaroh. Yet it didn't surprise him that Seth had set the whole thing up. He acted like he didn't care, but Lloyd knew that underneath it all, the sardonic little halfling really did.

With the green gas dissipated, they could once again head deeper into the assassin's lair. They were just gathering up when Lloyd felt a slim arm entwine with his.

Andrella peered up at him, her eyes large and glistening. "You weren't really going to run into that poison cloud, were you?"

Lloyd gazed down at her with a rueful smile. "I couldn't just leave him in there."

Andrella squeezed his arm tighter, moisture welling in the corners of her eyes. "Oh, Lloyd. I love that you care so much, but please promise me you'll be more care..."

Before she could finish her sentence, a bright flash lit up the chamber, followed by the crack of thunder. Lloyd instinctively leapt backward, dragging Andrella with him. He slammed into the wall, but somehow still managed to catch her.

Donnie and Seth had tumbled to either side of the chamber. The duo sprang up simultaneously, each flinging a dagger down the passageway.

Their efforts were met with a strangled cry. A blue-robed figure stood at the end of the corridor, a knife sticking out of her shoulder. There was an opening in the wall behind her. She stepped back through it and slammed the door shut.

Andrella's body felt limp in Lloyd's arms. He turned her around and gasped. The arm of her dress was shredded, the skin beneath blackened in spots.

Another cry echoed across the chamber. Balmaroh and Newin knelt over the fallen body of their friend Rhith. The illusionist's robes were in tatters, his skin burnt almost beyond recognition. Tears streamed down Newin's face, Balmaroh's head hung low.

Aksel knelt next to the pair, all three looking a bit singed. He ran his hands over Rhith's body, though it was obvious it was beyond healing.

Meanwhile, Seth came over and examined Andrella. He gave Lloyd a grim nod. "Lay her down. I'll take care of her."

Lloyd gently laid the unconscious young lady on the stone floor. The young warrior then grit his teeth and drew his blades. "I've had enough of this."

Kara drew up next to him, spear in hand. "I'm with you."

"As am I," Donnie chimed in.

"Wait one second." Glo and Elladan hurried over to them, both also somewhat singed. They cast a couple of swift spells to make the warriors stronger and faster.

Kalyn and Martan joined them, neither appearing hurt. The young woman gazed down at Andrella, her face darkening. "I want a piece of the toad licker that did this."

"Count me in," Martan said, his expression grave.

Elladan glanced between the pair and shook his head. "I feel the same way, but someone needs to watch our rear."

Kalyn nodded grimly. "Will do. Come on, Martan." She smacked the gloomy archer on the back and headed back the way they came. Martan stumbled forward a bit, but followed without a word.

Still angry, Lloyd swept his gaze between Kara, Donnie, Glo and Elladan. "Are we all ready?"

Everyone nodded.

"Then let's do this."

A pair of knives flew at Lloyd as the door swung open. Thankfully, they bounced off the steel rings of his elven chain shirt. At the same time, a red-hot beam lanced out and caught Donnie in the chest. Kara responded with a pair of arrows in quick succession, then Lloyd and Donnie were through the doorway.

Lloyd caught a brief glimpse of a blue-robed arm as a door in the back of the room slammed shut. After that, he had no time to think.

A fierce battle ensued with a small group of assassins and casters; it was over as quickly as it started. Black-robed bodies lay strewn on the floor, their souls off to meet their dark god.

With the battle won, Kara bent down and looked Donnie over. "Are you alright?"

Donnie winked at the others. "I'm fine. We elves are made of tougher stuff than we look."

Under other circumstances, Lloyd would have laughed. Yet things had taken a dire turn, and the scorch mark on Donnie's chain shirt looked rather ominous.

"Looks like we missed all the fun." Seth stood in the entrance with Andrella at his side.

"Don't worry, there's bound to be more," Donnie quipped.

Andrella appeared a bit pale, but the burn marks on her arm were gone. Lloyd rushed over and swept her into a tight embrace. She hugged him back, then pulled away. He narrowed an eye at her. "Shouldn't you be resting or something?"

Andrella stared back at him, her expression as hard as stone. "My father's heart is in here somewhere. I won't stop until we find it."

Lloyd's lips flattened into a grim smile. "That makes two of us."

Donnie nudged his head toward the other end of the room. "Can't wait to see what's behind door number two."

Seth shrugged. "Only one way to find out." He went to check the door. "It's locked…"

A tiny pick appeared in his hand. He thrust it into the keyhole and jiggled it around expertly 'til there was a soft click. "And now it's not."

Lloyd, Kara, and Donnie lined up in front of the others as Seth opened the door a crack. He peeked through, then pulled back, holding his nose. "Phew, that stinks."

"What stinks?" Glo called from behind them.

"A cloud."

"Poison?" Donnie asked immediately.

Seth shook his head. "Don't think so."

A moment later, Lloyd smelled it, too. It was a noxious odor, like rotten eggs.

"I'll go check it out." Seth weaved his arms in a quick motion, two soft words falling from his lips, too quiet for anyone else to hear.

Without warning, the door flew open. The corridor beyond was filled with a thick yellow cloud. Lloyd's eyes went wide, as a fiery red ball about the size of a fist, burst through the fog and raced straight for them.

Lloyd reacted without thinking. He leapt in front of the others, instinctively connecting with his inner spirit. Time slowed in a deadly race to cross his blades as the ball rushed forward. With a herculean effort, he forced them into place. Energy coursed through his arms and into his swords as the fiery ball struck.

It exploded into an arc of fire, flaring out all around him. His blades grew hotter and hotter as the flames grew longer and longer. Sweat formed on his brow, his arms shaking as he held back the storm of fire.

As suddenly as it had appeared, the raging fire winked out.

Lloyd could hardly move, his muscles burning from exertion. Tendrils of smoke rose from his blades as the heat they absorbed slowly dissipated.

With a deep breath, he willed his body to relax.

Cheers went up all around him and a familiar pair of arms wrapped themselves around his waist. "Lloyd, that was amazing!" Andrella gazed up at him, her eyes filled with a mixture of awe and concern. "Are you alright?"

Lloyd winced as a firm hand clasped him on the shoulder.

"Well done! I have never seen anything like that." Kara stared at him with clear admiration.

Lloyd forced himself to smile as he shifted in order to gently dislodge her hand. "Thanks. Just give me a minute to recover."

Kara gave him a crisp nod. "Don't worry. We'll take it from here."

An invisible Seth clung to the ceiling in the corridor beyond the door. He had seen the ball of fire as the door flew open, and instinctively leapt out of the way. Now the halfling crept forward over the top of the putrid cloud.

Seth held his nose, his eyes tearing as the noxious smell wafted up to greet him. Thankfully, the cloud ended a couple of dozen feet down the corridor. The passage went another few feet and ended at a closed door.

Seth leapt down and listened at the doorway. He heard a voice on the other side saying, "Don't let them through."

It was followed by heavy footsteps approaching the door.

Seth ran back to the edge of the cloud and jumped to the ceiling as the door opened behind him. He caught a glimpse of two heavily armed figures as he crawled over the fog.

Seth hurried over the cloud, leaping to the ground as soon as he was past it. He ran through the door, keeping his voice low. "We've got company."

Kara and Donnie lined up in front of the door, with Glo and Elladan just behind them. Lloyd tried to join them, but Andrella held him back. "Oh, no you don't. You need to rest."

Before he could protest, two heavily armed figures charged out of the cloud. The moment they appeared, Elladan released a spell. A pool of black liquid appeared on the ground in front of them.

As soon as the figures hit the pool, their feet went out from under them. They clattered to the ground, landing in a heap a few feet from the door.

Donnie cast a quick grin at Elladan. "Nicely done."

"My pleasure," Elladan responded with a bent smile.

Donnie then gazed at Seth. "Shall we?"

Between Donnie's boots and Seth's spell, they waded into the grease with no problem. The hapless warriors were quickly dispatched.

Elladan dismissed the pool, and they prepared to move forward when Aksel, Martan, and Kalyn entered the room.

"How's Rhith?" Glo asked somberly.

Aksel merely shook his head, his face ashen.

Seth winced inwardly. He had gone to great lengths to keep Balmaroh alive, and now the bard's friend was dead. Still, this was no time to weep.

"Who's watching our backs?" Elladan asked softly.

"Balmaroh's dog, Wraith," Aksel said flatly.

Seth gave an approving nod. *Even I couldn't sneak past that dog.*

Donnie cast a hesitant glance at Seth. "Did you want to go first?"

The side of Seth's mouth twisted upwards. "Nah. We'll go together."

Andrella was starting to get the hang of this caster thing. She joined in with zeal as the companions faced more assassins and casters in the next corridor and the side rooms off of it. After a fireball by Glo, along with some fancy archery and swordplay, they dispatched all of them except for one caster. That same woman in the blue robes got away through the door at the end of the corridor.

Andrella watched as Donatello leaned in close to the door. He listened intently for a moment, then grimaced.

"They dropped a beam into place on the other side."

Andrella looked up at Lloyd as he growled under his breath and stomped up to the door. His face was flushed, hands clenched. "She's not getting away that easily." He turned to Kara and nodded. The tall warrior stepped up next to him, bracing herself. They counted to three, then slammed into the door. It creaked and snapped inward, shrieking on its hinges.

Andrella stood straight and looked past the duo, her eyes widening.

Staring back at the group, faces pale with shock, were four men wearing blue and gold tabards carrying the insignia of Vermoorden—a black hawk on a golden field.

Those aren't assassins…

She gasped as Lloyd and Kara moved forward, weapons drawn. "Don't hurt them!" Her words brought the two warriors to a quick halt.

"Boys, I think it's time for a nap." Elladan strode forward, fingers picking a haunting melody from his lute. The four guards slowly slumped to the floor with yawns, their eyes drifting closed.

Seth stepped up, pulling a rope from his pack to tie the men up.

Everyone froze, and Andrella's gaze snapped toward a partially open doorway as a muffled whimper drifted from it.

Lloyd strode purposefully over to the doorway and cautiously pushed it open further. Three people quickly scampered away from the door. The one in front was a man wearing a stained apron with a white cap on his head. Two maids cowered behind him. The man raised a butcher knife, hand shaking.

Lloyd sheathed a single blade and waved a dismissive hand at him. "Put that down, I'm not going to hurt you."

Andrella quickly moved to his side, raising her hands in a non-threatening gesture. "We mean you no harm."

The cook's eyes darted between Lloyd and Andrella. "Who… who are you?"

Andrella and Lloyd exchanged glances before she responded. "We have traced some very evil people here to Vermoorden, and we mean to root them out." She turned to the side and pointed at a set of stairs back in the corridor. "Where do those go?"

"Why… in-into the keep, of c-course." The cook stammered.

Andrella reached into the pocket of her dress and pulled out a few silver coins, holding them out to the cook. "Thank you for your help. Stay here until things quiet down."

The cook hesitated, then opened his hand and let Andrella drop the money into it.

"You… you aren't going to kill us?" One of the maids squeaked behind him.

Andrella shook her head with a warm smile. "No, dear. We're not the bad guys here. Now, stay out of sight until someone tells you it's clear."

She and Lloyd backed out into the other room, closing the kitchen door behind them.

"Those servants are not a part of the cult. I doubt these soldiers are, either." She drummed her fingers on her chin thoughtfully. "What did we miss?"

Donnie cleared his throat. "There was an empty side passage back a ways. Maybe we should check it out?"

28

AN EVIL DISCOVERY

What stood behind the altar made Glo's blood run cold

Donnie and Seth led the way back to the empty side passage. The hall remained as unremarkably bare as before. The only thing in sight were a few torches affixed at regular intervals along the walls. A plain door stood at the other end of the corridor, perhaps a dozen yards away.

Seth gave Donnie a curt nod, then climbed up to the ceiling. Donnie crept carefully down the hall, the halfling mirroring his movements above.

The duo reached the other end without incident. Donnie stopped in front of the door. He scoured it and the surrounding floor and walls for any signs of traps, but found nothing.

Donnie glanced up at Seth. The halfling silently shook his head.

Certain the door was clean, Donnie carefully checked the handle. It wasn't locked. He then pressed his ear up against the door. He heard nothing at first, but after a few moments, a faint shuffling sound reached his ear. It gradually grew louder 'til the door began to vibrate.

Donnie's eyes widened, his lips curling downward. *Whatever's behind this door sure is big.* He continued to listen until the shuffling faded away once more.

Donnie gazed up at Seth and signaled for him to retreat. They met up with the others halfway down the hall. Donnie kept his voice low. "There's something large on the other side of that door."

Glo arched an eyebrow. "What's it sound like?"

"Large feet pacing up and down a wide area."

Lloyd exchanged a confident glance with Kara. "We're ready for it."

"So are we," Kalyn exclaimed, swatting Martan hard on the back.

The glum archer nearly choked as he nodded his assent.

Aksel peered at Glo, Elladan, and Andrella. All three nodded, the young lady's expression extremely determined.

Aksel gazed at Donnie and Seth. "Okay, let's do this."

Seth climbed back up to the ceiling, then he and Donnie proceeded as before. Once at the door, Donnie looked back over his shoulder.

Lloyd and Kara stood ready, weapons in hand. Glo and Andrella were right behind them, fingers raised and spells on their lips. Aksel and Elladan stood in the back. The bard had his lute out, prepared for a soft but inspiring tune. Martan and Kalyn lined up against either wall, arrows nocked to their bowstrings.

A brief shiver went up the elf's spine. *Note to self—as soon as the door is open, go low.*

Ruka's dagger in hand, Donnie listened at the door, waiting 'til the footsteps were at their loudest. When they reached their peak, Donnie cranked the handle. In one swift motion he pushed the door open, then dove through the archway off to one side.

Donnie had entered a tall, wide chamber, bathed in a deep reddish glow. He caught a brief glimpse of what looked like pews trailing off on either side. Any further view was blocked by a huge yellow-skinned figure holding a large club at its side.

The size of the Boulder, the creature stood not five feet from him. Its exaggeratedly muscular body was barely covered by a fur loin-cloth and hide wrappings around its lower legs and wrists. A squat head sat on its obscenely thick neck, sharp yellow teeth protruding from its oversized jaw.

Donnie's heart leapt into his throat. *Ogre.*

Ogres were exceedingly strong and would kill and eat just about anything. Thankfully, their vast strength was offset by their weak minds.

A pair of large beady eyes fixed on Donnie for a moment, then the huge mouth opened, a deafening roar echoing across the chamber. Yet its bellow was cut short as a barrage of fiery rays and arrows lanced into its torso. The ogre took a step backward and grabbed its burnt chest in clear confusion.

Here's my chance.

Donnie launched himself forward and stabbed the creature in the leg as he tumbled by. Seth had mirrored Donnie's actions, catching the behemoth in the other leg.

The ogre appeared momentarily stunned, then it raised its club with a terrifying roar.

At that same moment, Lloyd and Kara came rushing into the room. Blades ablaze, Lloyd swept into the creature, cutting and slicing with deadly accuracy. The tip of Kara's spear glowed as she rammed it into the creature's thick hide. It sunk deep into the ogre's leg, causing the creature to rear back in pain.

A huge roar escaped its lips as the ogre swung wildly at the lady warrior. Despite her heavy armor, she easily dodged the first blow, yet the backswing caught her unprepared, sending her flying across the room in Donnie's direction.

"Kara!" he cried, scrambled after her.

Donnie intercepted the airborne warrior, wrapping himself around her armor-clad torso just as she hit the ground. The elf took the brunt of the impact, his slight form flattened between Kara and the hard floor. His head reeled from the blow.

Kara's face hung over him when his vision finally cleared. "Are you alright?"

Donnie ached all over, but forced himself to grin through the pain. "I'm… fine. We elves are tougher than we look. How about you? That was one heck of a blow you took."

Kara laughed as she helped him to his feet. "It'll take more than some stupid ogre to lay me out."

Back across the room, Lloyd dodged and slashed expertly around the creature. Intermittent arrows, fiery beams, and blinding rays continued to pelt the huge target.

Kara hefted her spear, then gazed back at Donnie. Without warning, she leaned in and gave him a quick kiss on the cheek.

Donnie blinked. "What was that for?"

"For luck!" she said with the hint of a smile. Before he could respond, she darted away, back into the fray.

Donnie chuckled softly to himself, then ran after her. The nimble elf circled around the battle, looking for a chance to strike.

The ogre appeared haggard, burnt, and bleeding from multiple wounds. Yet it hadn't quite given up the fight. It caught Lloyd with a glancing blow as he danced away after a particularly deadly strike. The young warrior was flung into the pews back behind the huge creature.

Yet the ogre was left staggering as well. Lloyd had practically shredded its leg. No longer able to stand, the creature dropped down on one knee.

Donnie saw his chance. He ran forward and leapt onto the ogre's back. Using its belt as a foothold, he scrambled upward. A huge hand tried to grab him, but he dodged under it.

The agile elf continued his mad climb until he reached the creature's thick neck. Taking Ruka's dagger in both hands, he plunged down with all his might. The dragon-scale blade sunk all the way to the hilt, into the ogre's thick neck.

The ogre roared in pain. It grasped Donnie in its huge hand and flung him away, across the room. Donnie ended up in a heap, right next to a rising Lloyd.

"You all right?" Lloyd asked with clear concern.

"Been better… been worse…" Donnie grumbled as he slowly extricated himself from the toppled pews.

Across the room, the ogre flailed around wildly. The casters and archers appeared to be running out of ammo. Kara couldn't seem to get close.

"I'm… going to… end this…" Lloyd huffed with exhaustion.

The young warrior took his black blade in both hands, then closed his eyes. His face took on a serene expression, then his body abruptly disappeared.

Across the room, Lloyd reappeared, right on the ogre's back. The warrior lifted the black sword high, then sunk it into the ogre's neck right next to Ruka's blade.

The ogre's body jerked in response. Blood spurted from its mouth, then the creature went rigid. A moment later, it fell on its face, causing the entire room to shake.

Glo breathed a sigh of relief when the ogre finally fell. He had held Andrella back when Lloyd went flying, counseling her instead to *"keep the thing busy."*

Andrella had pelted the creature with fiery rays, all the while screeching, *"Die you son of a warg!"*

It would have been comical had the situation not been so dire. Elladan certainly seemed to think so. In the midst of battle, he had switched tunes to his classic, *Hell Hound.*

Now, with the ogre felled, Andrella rushed to Lloyd's side. A second later, Seth appeared in the doorway.

"You have to see this."

Glo's jaw dropped as they followed him into the chamber. They had found an underground temple, replete with nearly two dozen pews and a long altar. A pair of giant urns decorated either side of the altar with tall red flames dancing atop them. Their light bathed the temple in crimson, yet what stood behind the altar made Glo's blood run cold.

A statue as large as an ogre stared down at them. From the waist up, it depicted a beautiful woman with long flowing hair, adorned with only fine jewelry. Yet from the waist down it melded into the thick coils of a giant snake. Six arms sprang from the statue's torso, each holding a large sword.

Donnie eyed the statue warily. "Is that…"

"…a demon," Kara finished for him, her eyes burning with clear hatred.

"A maralith, to be precise," Aksel added, with only slightly less abhorrence than the lady warrior.

Seth let out a derisive snort. "Well, that's no coincidence."

Kalyn joined them along with Lloyd, Andrella, and Martan. "Ya think they're in league with the Serpent Cult?"

Glo steepled his hands in front of him. "If they worship a maralith, there's a pretty good chance it's Salisma Tanj, the Serpent Cult's supposed 'goddess.'"

"She's no goddess," Kara declared vehemently. "She's a lieutenant of the Lord of All Demons."

Glo gave her a curt nod. "We already knew as much. Lysandra—the High Druid of Bendenwood—informed us."

"Which—if we're to believe Elistra—also ties them in with the Thrall Masters," Elladan pointed out.

Glo cast a quick glance at the bard. Things had been so crazy, that he hadn't thought about Elistra since they left Ravenford. She had originally warned them a Thrall Master might be behind the Serpent Cult. The fact that one of the Thrall Masters controlled demons added weight to her warning.

"Well, isn't this just one sick, twisted web." Andrella trembled slightly.

Lloyd wrapped his arms around the young lady and pulled her close.

Glo abruptly shivered as well. The air in the chamber had suddenly grown cold.

"Look!" Donnie cried.

The air above the altar had started to swirl around. It turned a reddish-purplish color and took on the consistency of water. As they watched, the circle widened, and a hole formed in its center.

Glo immediately recognized what it was. "It's a portal!"

Portals were gateways to other planes of existence. They worked much like *portal bags*, but instead of being used for storage, they enabled passage between planes.

A familiar visage appeared in the opening, one that sent chills up Glo's spine. It was a beautiful woman with porcelain skin, framed by long, raven-black hair. Her thin nose was bordered by extremely high cheekbones and blood-red lips. The woman positively radiated power, her dark eyes freezing the companions in place as they swept across the room. Her lips parted, revealing two large fangs that protruded from her upper jaw.

"Puny mortals. I told you there was more than one way into your world..."

Glo involuntarily flinched at the malevolent voice. He had heard it twice now—once while examining an evil black gem, and again in the altar room at Serpent's Hollow. It belonged to the powerful demoness, Salisma. They had stopped her from entering Arinthar back then, but she had warned them she would soon find another way.

Amazingly, Kara stepped forward. She waved her hand at the large demoness in a dismissive gesture. "You don't belong in this world. Be gone, foul demon."

Salisma laughed, a low wicked sound. "*I don't belong here? You're one to talk, little *thul dunin.*"

There was a momentary silence, then four words echoed around the chamber. "*Magicae Circuli Contra Malum.*"

Glo felt the release of magic as a white circle engulfed them all. The circle swiftly faded, but he could still feel the mana radiating from Aksel.

Glo no longer felt frozen in place, but the portal continued to widen.

"The flames!" Seth cried.

Glo glanced at the urns on either end of the altar. The crimson flames burned higher and grew by the second. He watched, dumfounded, as Seth drew a flask from his pack and threw it at one of the urns. The fire shrank in response.

Glo's eyes narrowed. *Of course. That's holy water.*

Seth whirled around and yelled to the others. "Quick, everyone! Throw your flasks."

During the vampire hunt back in Ravenford, Seth and Aksel had given all the companions holy water. Now everyone pulled out those flasks and threw the contents on the two urns. The flames slowly died down and the portal shrank in response.

Salisma's visage watched the process with clear annoyance. "You got lucky once again, mortals, but you can't keep me out forever. Eventually I will enter your world, and then I will hunt down each and every one of you."

The flames abruptly went out and the portal collapsed in on itself with a whooshing sound.

As soon as it completely disappeared, Andrella turned to Kalyn. "Is she always that pleasant?"

Kalyn dropped her voice down low and mimicked the demoness. "Yada, yada... gonna enter your world. Yada, yada... gonna kill you all. Sheesh, ya think she'd learn a different tune."

Seth was not a believer in the grace of the gods. He always felt they helped those who helped themselves. So even though he wouldn't pray, he'd use whatever tools the gods provided. Thankfully, in this case it had done the trick.

Elladan gave him one of those half-smiles. "That was some quick thinking there."

"Good thing, too, or we'd be neck-high in snake coils right about now," Donnie added glibly.

Kalyn, standing next to the thin elf, yelped and turned white as a sheet.

Normally Seth wouldn't miss an opportunity to taunt her, but something nagged at the back of his mind. "Is it just me, or was this room better protected than any we've seen so far?"

Aksel rubbed his chin gingerly. "Other than the fact that it's the assassin's temple, I'd tend to agree."

Glo raised an eyebrow. "So, what you're saying is they hid their treasures in here?"

Seth shrugged. "I would."

Donnie narrowed an eye at Seth. "You take one side, I'll take the other?"

"Sure."

They split up and executed a brief search, eventually ending at the altar. Shortly thereafter, Donnie called out, "I found something."

The elf had discovered a camouflaged door behind the statue of the maralith. There was a corridor behind it that went back about a two dozen feet, then turned a corner. Interestingly, the side walls and ceiling here were lined with spikes.

Donnie eyed the floor dubiously. "Trapped?"

"Definitely."

The duo glanced at each other, then carefully crept into the corridor side by side. A few feet down the hall, they discovered a trip wire that set off a slashing blade trap. They easily cut it.

A little farther down the hall, they found a second trip wire. Seth noted some rather square indentations across the floor beyond. He pointed them out to Donnie. "Those are spinning blades that pop up from the floor."

"Lovely," Donnie intoned. "Let me guess, if you trip the wire, or step on those squares, it goes off?"

Seth grunted. "Something like that."

The cynical elf proffered a hand to Seth. "Well then, be my guest."

"Heh," Seth snorted as he examined the wire. He followed it to a hidden lever at the base of the wall, then pulled out his knife and carefully cut it. Everything appeared fine, when all of a sudden, the lever flipped on its own.

"Crap baskets!" Seth leapt back as spinning blades popped out of the floor.

Donnie drew up next to him. "You alright?"

Seth grimaced. "Stupid lever was weighted. As soon as I cut the wire, it sprang the trap."

Donnie nudged his head down the corridor. "Well, that looks pleasant."

Three tall spokes now stuck out of the floor, reaching almost to the ceiling. Each was fitted with multiple sharp blades at various heights along their length. As they spun, the blades extended almost all the way to the side walls.

Seth let out a deep sigh. "Oh well, guess it's time for a blade dance."

"Your funeral," Donnie chuckled.

Seth's lips twisted sideways. "What? You're not coming?"

Donnie raised his hands in front of him. "I'll wait for you to get through first."

Seth shrugged. "Suit yourself."

The halfling watched the blades intently until he discerned a pattern, then launched himself into their midst. It was a crazy dance down that hallway, and he got nicked a few times, but ultimately Seth made it to the end without losing too much blood.

Around the corner sat a large chest rather conspicuously against a blank wall. Seth squinted at the floor in front of it. There was a faint indentation all the way across that he immediately recognized as a pressure plate. There was no way around it—you'd have to step on the plate to reach the chest. The halfling bent down for a closer look. There was a familiar rune symbol over the locking mechanism.

"How you doing down there?" Donnie called to him.

"Just peachy!" Seth responded in an acid tone. "Found a chest and more traps."

"What kind?" Donnie yelled.

"Pressure plate and a fireball rune."

"Sounds wonderful. One false move and bye-bye treasure."

Seth got on the floor and looked under the plate. There were four springs there. He had to disconnect each one to remove the plate, then disarm the trigger.

Seth easily managed to unhook the first two, but as he disconnected the third spring, the last spring snapped. Before he could catch it, the plate fell on the trigger. Small openings appeared in the wall behind the chest and green gas started to pour out.

Poison gas. How original.

Seth yelled at Donnie. "Get everyone away from here!"

"What about you?"

"I'll be fine."

"Okay."

Seth shook his head as he waited for the gas to dissipate. Once it was gone he re-examined the rune. Unlike other magical traps, this one had no moving parts. There was nothing for him to disable.

"How's it going down there, Seth?"

Seth looked up to see Aksel standing on the other side of the spinning blades. Donnie, Glo, Lloyd, and Andrella all crowded around him.

"Marvelous. Care to join me?"

Aksel eyed the spinning blades dubiously. "No thanks, I'll pass."

Seth heard Donnie explain the rune trap to the others.

The color drained from Andrella's cheeks. "But my father's heart might be in there…"

Lloyd placed a comforting arm around her shoulders. "Don't worry. I'm sure we'll think of something."

Glo exchanged a glance with Aksel. "If you could see the chest from here, you could probably dispel the rune."

"It's too big for me to move," Seth answered before they asked.

"Guess it's up to me then," Donnie sighed. The slender elf reached into his pack and pulled out his red leather gloves with the black striations. "Be right there," he called to Seth.

Donnie squinted at the spinning blades for a few moments, then launched himself forward. The wiry elf twisted and dodged rather nimbly through them. He reached Seth a minute later with nary a scratch. "That wasn't so bad."

Seth glared at him without a word.

Donnie knelt and touched the rune with his glove. There was a momentary flash of red, then it disappeared. Of course the chest was locked, but Seth picked it in ten seconds flat.

Donnie gingerly lifted the lid. Inside lay three boxes, one bronze, one silver, and one gold. Donnie took the first two while Seth took the third.

The duo then wound their way back through the blades with the boxes in hand. It was far harder and neither escaped without some nasty cuts.

Donnie grinned at Seth when they reached the other side. "That was a close shave."

Seth grimaced. "Must you?"

Donnie chuckled. "Sorry, force of habit."

Andrella could hardly contain herself as the three ornate boxes were laid out on the altar. *One of these must hold daddy's heart.* The young lady held firmly onto Lloyd as Seth examined the bronze box.

The halfling carefully lifted the lid. Inside sat a black crystal skull. The surface of the skull shimmered with a dark glow as it was exposed to the light. A blast of cold air suddenly rushed over them, and the magic circle Aksel had cast earlier winked out.

"Close it! Close it!" Aksel cried in dismay.

Seth pushed on the lid, but it wouldn't budge.

Lloyd extracted himself from Andrella's grasp and strode forward to grab the lid. He pushed on it and it started to close, but he was obviously struggling.

Kara drew up next to him and added her weight to his. Between the two warriors, they were finally able to shut the lid.

Kalyn stood bug-eyed next to Andrella. "What in the unholy name of Dunwynn was that?"

"I don't know, and I'm not sure I want to." Glo exchanged a puzzled glance with Elladan and Aksel. Both shook their heads.

"Moving on," Andrella urged them as she wrung her hands together. *We've come this far—it has to be in one of these.*

Seth opened the silver box next. Thankfully there was no dark artifact in there, but neither was the Baron's heart. Instead they found a silver scroll case with an ornate design on it.

"I recognize that symbol," Elladan exclaimed. "Anya's got a plaque with the same design in her state room."

"So you're saying this belongs to Lanfor?" Glo asked him.

Meanwhile, Kalyn whispered in Andrella's ear. "I wonder what Elladan was doing in Anya's 'state' room?"

Andrella looked at Kalyn with a raised eyebrow. "Playing his instrument, perhaps?"

Both ladies giggled under their breath.

In the end, Elladan took the scroll for safekeeping.

Seth stood in front of the last box, the gold one. "Third time's a charm."

Andrella felt Lloyd's arms wrap around her again as she held her breath. *Please be daddy's heart. Please. Please.*

Seth opened it a crack and peered inside. A strange expression spread across his face. He cast a glance over his shoulder at Aksel. "Is that normal?"

The little cleric stepped forward and peeked through the crack. He seemed momentarily puzzled, but then gave Seth a nod. "It's a bit strange, but probably nothing more than an animation spell."

"Just open the lid already!" Elladan cried, mirroring Andrella's own internal angst.

"Fine," Seth spat. The halfling stepped to one side and threw open the lid. Inside lay a perfectly healthy, still-beating heart.

There was a moment of hesitation, then cheers went up around the chamber.

Tears came unbidden to Andrella's eyes as Lloyd hoisted her up into the air. He brought her down into his arms and she hugged him tight.

"We found it! We found my father's heart!" Andrella sobbed with joy. After everything they'd been through, it felt surreal to finally see her father's heart. She had hoped they would find it, but there was always some part of her that feared they wouldn't.

Everyone had grabbed someone else and danced around with them—Kara and Donnie, Glo and Elladan, Seth and Aksel, even Kalyn and Martan.

Andrella saw the two trackers out of the corner of her eye in a close embrace. She snickered as Kalyn abruptly stopped and shoved Martan away, her face bright scarlet.

Their revelry was abruptly cut short as Wraith appeared in their midst. "Sorry to interrupt, but there's something large waiting for us outside the keep."

29
WELCOMING PARTY

Glolindir rose above the mists, the world around him painted in a silvery landscape. Directly below, thick fog billowed from the rear of the keep—a prelude to the ensuing battle.

News of an impending ambush had caught the companions at the worst possible time. They were all exhausted, both physically and mentally. Things might have been dire, were it not for Aksel's pragmatism and Elladan's quick thinking.

The pair broke out Philmar's stash and ransacked it to bolster the party's diminished capabilities. The duo then gathered all the companions around for a quick strategy session.

Twenty minutes later, an invisible Glo hung suspended in air over Newin's rolling cloud of fog. The elf swept his keen eyes over the clearing, immediately spying two huge figures outlined in the pale moonlight.

Glo gulped, then notified the others via telepathic mind link. *It's as we thought—a troll and an ogre.*

DeWyness isn't fooling around, Aksel noted grimly.

Speaking of which, have you spotted her yet? Elladan interjected.

A few smaller figures hid in the shadows of the surrounding trees, but from this height, none of them appeared to be the Mayor. *If she's here, she's not out in the open.*

Oh, she's here, Seth responded emphatically.

Glo silently agreed with him. They had only met the Mayor once, but she seemed far too controlling to leave something this important to her minions.

As Glo hovered above the mists, he sensed the tinge of magic. A strong wind kicked up, and the thick clouds began to dissipate. *It appears someone doesn't like Newin's fog.*

They're gonna like what comes next even less, Elladan thought wryly.

Before the cloud had completely disappeared, a large figure burst out of its midst and barreled headlong into the unsuspecting ogre. Huge twin blades crackling with red flames sliced at the creature as a double-sized Lloyd weighed into battle.

That's my cue. Glo already held a small piece of glowing material in his hand. He brought his will to bear as he wove a well-practiced pattern with it through the air. Two words rolled from his tongue as he released the spell. *"Murum Ignis."*

A curtain of shimmering scarlet fire suddenly sprang into existence across the center of the clearing. It swiftly rose into the air, reaching nearly twenty feet in height. No troll would cross that barrier. Now Lloyd stood a fair chance against his huge opponent.

The sound of jaunty music abruptly filled the night as the last shreds of mist evaporated. At the same time, more figures came pouring out of the keep.

Glo watched intently from above as his friends engaged the Mayor's followers in mortal combat.

Elladan and Balmaroh stood at the entrance to the assassins' lair, playing a lively duet to bolster their companions. The battle had only just started, but it was already fierce out there. Thankfully, their plan had worked, and Glo had separated the ogre and the troll.

Lloyd now faced the ogre, but the troll was left unchecked on the other side of a raging wall of fire. The dull-witted creature lumbered up to the blazing inferno and took a step into it, only to backpedal a moment later.

The troll briskly brushed off its smoking chest, then lifted its long arms to the heavens and let out a savage roar. An enraged troll would be trouble for any of their friends on that side of the wall. Luckily, Elladan had a plan for that as well.

The bard let Balmaroh continue playing as he reached into his pouch and pulled out a handful of nuts. Elladan brought his will to bear as he moved his arms in a practiced motion. The mana gathered as he beckoned, coalescing in his hands until he released it with the word, *"Turbare."*

A violet circle appeared around the troll, stopping the creature's raging and freezing it in place. A few moments later, it dropped its gaze and swung its head in all directions. Without warning, it flung its club at two nearby figures, one in dark-robes and another in black mail. Both went flying, hitting the ground a short distance away. Neither got up again.

Balmaroh grinned at Elladan. "Nicely done, my friend."

Elladan responded with a partial smile and a shrug. "I have my moments."

As the fog rolled out, Donnie went with it. When the mists began to part, he had already made it into the shadows of the trees. A dark-cloaked figure stood about a dozen feet away, its focus on the keep entrance.

Rapier in one hand, Ruka's dagger in the other, Donnie crept closer. As soon as he reached striking distance, he lunged at the shadowy figure. Somehow it managed to avoid his thrust.

Quickly backpedaling, Donnie caught a sudden movement out of the corner of his eye. The agile elf tumbled out of the way as a knife swept past where his head had just been.

Rolling to his feet, Donnie immediately spun about. Two dark-cloaked figures now stood on either side of him. *Well, this just keeps getting better and better.*

Adjusting his stance for multiple opponents, Donnie flashed a pearly smile at the deadly pair of assassins. "Well, boys, care to dance?"

Andrella had only been in combat once before, against vampires in the catacombs under Ravenford. That time, she had the element of surprise, but now she and Newin were in a pitched battle against two other casters.

In other circumstances it might have unnerved her, but Andrella didn't have time for nerves. A short distance away, the love of her life fought a tremendous battle against a powerful ogre. Less than an hour ago, a similar creature had sent Lloyd flying with one swipe. Even though he was now ogre-sized, Andrella worried nonetheless.

"Andrella, focus!" Newin hissed at her.

The young lady flinched as three purple projectiles exploded against an invisible barrier a mere foot away from her torso. She silently thanked Glo for teaching her the shield spell. Her ire raised, Andrella fired back with her own purple barrage. Surprisingly, they connected with their target.

Bam! Bam! Bam!

Each missile struck with concussive force. Her opponent reeled with each blow, falling backward with the last.

Andrella snickered. "Well, that's going to leave a mark."

"Behind you!"

Newin's sudden shout made Andrella spin around. A dark-robed figure stood not a dozen feet away, its arm pointed directly at her. Andrella could feel the surge of power that was about to be unleashed. She would not survive it.

The young lady's eyes misted over, her fists clenching as rage and regret coursed through her veins. *No. It can't end like this. Not when I've finally found Lloyd and I'm so close to saving Daddy.*

Kaboom! The night suddenly lit up around them, the sound of thunder deafening in her ears.

Andrella wiped the tears from her eyes. The dark-robed figure lay on the ground, arcs of electricity still dancing across its torso and smoke rising from its seared robes. She glanced all around, but Newin was still in the midst of her own battle.

"Watch your back!" A voice called from above.

Andrella glanced up and saw a familiar figure hovering far above her. It was Glo—he was visible once again. He had saved her life at the risk of making himself a target.

Across the clearing, her first opponent had gotten up. Determined to prove she was worth the trouble, Andrella rolled up her sleeves and waged into battle once more.

Martan watched with growing trepidation from the entrance of the assassins' lair. Most of the others were already embroiled in deadly combat; only the archers and the bards had stayed behind. While the bards played encouraging music, Kalyn, Martan, and the new warrior, Kara, did their best to protect their companions.

"Aksel's got a stalker at his nine o'clock!" Kalyn called. Yet before she could get off the shot, a glowing arrow cut across the clearing. It was immediately followed by a second. The first arrow barely missed, but the next one nailed its target.

"Heh," Kara snorted as the assassin fell.

Martan winced. Kalyn did not take lightly to others stealing her kills. Thus, he was amazed when she merely said, "Nice shot."

Maybe she's changed after all, Martan thought hopefully. A moment later, she proved him wrong once again.

"Still… ya think they'd see those glowing arrows from a mile away."

Kara looked down at her, the corner of her mouth uplifting ever so slightly. "And yet somehow they never do."

Meanwhile, Martan continued to sweep the battlefield. Most folks seemed smart enough to avoid Lloyd and the ogre, but Martan spotted a dark-cloaked figure circling the duo.

"Lloyd's got a tailgater!" He called the shot.

Martan had it lined up perfectly. The tip of his arrow lit up in flames as it sped from his bow across the clearing. A moment later, a glowing arrow took off after it. Martan watched wide-eyed as his arrow closed on its mark. At the very last second, the assassin seemed to bend out of the way, only to be skewered by the second arrow.

The sullen archer cocked his head to one side and peered at Kara questioningly. "How'd you know he'd move that way?"

Kara snorted again. "I've been watching these assassins as we've fought them. They all tend to move the same way. Once you see the pattern, they're easy to pick off."

Martan exchanged an astonished glance with Kalyn. The young woman gazed at Kara with newfound respect. "That's slicker than troll snot. Gonna have to try that little trick myself."

Kara gave her a warm smile, then returned her gaze to the battlefield. "Anyone see the short fellow—Seth, was it?"

"You won't," Martan said simply.

Kara glanced at him with an arched eyebrow.

"Seth will stay hidden till he finds his target," Martan explained.

Kara's entire brow raised as she gave him a curt nod. "That's very smart."

"Donnie's got company! Nine o'clock and three o'clock," Kalyn called.

The Deepwood sniper let two arrows fly in succession, much as Kara had explained. The first one missed the target, but the second one caught the dark figure in the chest.

Kalyn turned to Martan and smacked him hard on the back. "Oh yeah! Nailed him."

Martan sputtered as he nearly dropped his bow. "It was… a nice shot…"

Kaboom!

A sudden flash cut the night sky in two. Martan spun his gaze to where it had struck. The seared remains of a dark-robed figure lay on the ground a short distance from Andrella and Newin. Martan was mortified. If not for Glolindir, Andrella and Newin might be dead.

The morose archer cast a grim glance at Kara and Kalyn. The three of them exchanged a curt nod, then nocked arrows and went silently back to protecting their friends.

Aksel had spread out with the others, but instead chose the troll side of the wall. There were two figures in black plate mail there, both with the symbol of the dark god, Amon, emblazoned on their chest. Though two against one, Aksel would not let their threat go unchallenged.

As luck would have it, one of the dark clerics stood too close to the troll. Per plan, Elladan cast a spell of confusion on the dim-witted creature. Easily overcome, the confused troll lashed out at everything near it, including the priest.

The odds now even, Aksel set his sights on the other dark cleric. Yet the priest ignored him, instead concentrating on the enlarged Lloyd. Aksel watched with great concern as the dark cleric cast a spell at his friend.

Lloyd abruptly went rigid. The ogre, seeing its chance, reared its club back for a huge swing at the stationary warrior.

Aksel had to do something fast, or Lloyd was a goner. With no time for a spell, Aksel scooped up a rock.

"Hey!" He shouted as he flung the stone at the dark priest's face.

The cleric turned just as the stone reached him. It connected with a crunching sound, shattering the priest's nose as well as his concentration.

Over on the other side of the wall, Lloyd suddenly unfroze. The big warrior ducked out of the way just as the huge club sailed over his face. Had it connected, his head would have been pulped.

Satisfied that his friend was safe, Aksel cast a quick spell. A translucent battle axe appeared next to him and floated toward the priest of Amon.

The black cleric raised its own axe and charged Aksel. The night lit up with a brilliant flash and thunder rolled as they met head-on. The battle between dark and light had begun.

An invisible Seth silently followed Aksel out into the clearing. He had seen the first assassin, but two arrows expertly took it out before it had gotten close. The two dark priests might also have been a threat, but the troll had been 'nice' enough to take one out of play.

Seth continued to hover a short distance from Aksel when a sudden glint caught his eye. Reacting on pure instinct, Seth flung a black dagger at the object. There was a sharp *klink* as it collided with another dagger in mid-air. The two knives bounced harmlessly off each other and fell to the ground nearby.

Suddenly visible, Seth crouched low. *That was meant for Aksel.*

The knife had come from somewhere in the trees. Seth squinted till his eyes fell on a shadow lurking in the darkness of the treeline. A moment later, a familiar figure stepped forth. Seth moved to intercept it, stopping a few yards away from the shadow.

"I had a feeling I'd be seeing you again tonight," One-Eye intoned.

Seth's lips curled to the side. "Aw, did you miss me?"

Knives in hand, the two figures crouched as they slowly circled each other. All at once, they launched themselves across the intervening distance. Lightning flashed with the crack of thunder as the deadly battle ensued.

Lloyd had never felt so powerful in his life. Elladan had given him a potion that made him twice his normal size. Along with that came renewed vigor and an increase in strength. Thankfully the bulkiness had not detracted much from his speed.

A twelve-foot Lloyd now raced through the mists, the ground beneath him shaking as he burst out into the night. The moon sat high in the black velvet sky, its pale beams outlining everything in the wide clearing.

Lloyd's blades were now also twice their size. The flames danced and crackled along their length, radiating a soft red circle of light a few dozen feet in all directions. It easily illuminated the huge frames of both the ogre and the troll. The creatures stood at the edge of the circle, as far from each other as he was from them. Both turned to face this new larger opponent, snarling and grunting in challenge.

Abruptly, a veil of shimmering scarlet sprang up between the pair. The flaming wall rose quickly above their heads and spread across the entire length of the clearing. The troll now stood on the other side of the wall, roaring in anger at the deadly barrier.

The plan worked like a charm.

Lloyd's mouth flattened into a grim smile as he spurred himself forward to face the ogre one-on-one. With his new-found strength, he planted himself and swung his black sword at the massive creature. It sliced across the ogre's midsection, leaving a thin red and black trail in its wake.

The ogre seemed momentarily surprised, then swung back at him with its metal-spiked club. Lloyd made the mistake of blocking it with his off-hand sword. Though he stopped the blow, the force behind it rippled up the length of his arm. The young man immediately backpedaled, his left arm throbbing from the power behind that blow.

The sounds of battle had sprung up around him, but Lloyd couldn't stop to see how his friends were faring. *Even at this size, I'm still no match for this thing's strength.*

Swiftly formulating a new strategy, Lloyd waded back into battle. He swung at the ogre again with his black blade, but this time it back-stepped out of the way and immediately retaliated by lunging at him with its club.

Instead of blocking the blow, Lloyd side-stepped it. Left off-balance, the ogre quickly pulled back, but not before Lloyd took a swipe at its exposed arm. The end of his blade caught it just below the elbow, leaving a deep gash in its flesh.

The ogre leapt backwards, howling in pain. It tried to heft its heavy club, but faltered with its injured arm. A dark expression crossed its brutish face as it grabbed the spiked club with both hands.

Lloyd rushed in again and feinted to his left. The ogre swiped at him, but Lloyd shifted directions at the last minute, easily dodging its shortened swing. He whirled around and cut deep into the ogre's upper arm with his off-hand blade.

The ogre fell back and screamed in pain. The gash in its left arm went nearly to the bone. Had Lloyd's blade not seared the wound, it would be gushing blood.

At that point, the ogre went crazy. It reared its head to the moon and howled with rage. Despite its deep wounds, it managed to heft its club high overhead. With a mad roar, it rushed at Lloyd. Yet in its anger, it had left itself wide open.

Lloyd prepared for the killing blow, but as the monster drew near, something went horribly wrong.

I… I can't move…

His body would not respond, no matter how hard he tried. He watched in horror as the spiked club hurtled through the air, straight for his head.

Time seemed to slow around him. Faces from his past flashed through his mind. His father's stern expression as they trained together in the family barn… His mother's absentminded smile as she waved him out of her private lab… His brother Pallas' smirk as he teased him during a lesson at the academy… His sister Thea's firm but loving expression as she healed a nasty wound he had incurred doing something stupid…

The thought of never seeing them again made him strain with frustration. He willed his body to move out of the way, but it remained unresponsive. Tears formed in his eyes—tears for all the things he would never be.

Andrella…

Perhaps it was that single word, or perhaps some spell had been broken, but Lloyd's body suddenly moved. It flung itself in the direction he had been straining, the spikes of the giant club passing mere inches from his face.

Lloyd backpedaled away, his breath coming in short, ragged bursts. That club would have crushed his head if it had connected.

The ogre nearly fell to the ground as it missed its target. It took a few moments to right itself, then turned toward Lloyd and roared. The enraged creature charged again, its club high overhead.

Lloyd's heart still raced, but years of training kicked in, forcing his breath to slow and his mind to be still. He knew exactly what he had to do.

Lightning flashed and thunder boomed across the clearing as Lloyd launched himself forward for the killing blow.

Andrella was starting to lose concentration. Still locked in a caster's duel, her mind was tired from the strain of the prolonged battle. Luckily, her opponent seemed to be wavering as well.

A second barrage of missiles had proved ineffective against her opponent. She had wizened up and cast her own shielding spell; Andrella shifted to a fiery beam that quite obviously stung. The faltering caster sent one back, but again Glo had prepared her well. A protection spell absorbed all the heat, leaving her completely unharmed.

At the same time, Newin triumphed in her own duel. The opposing caster fell to the ground, choking in a stinking green cloud.

Newin's success spurred Andrella's determination. She prepared another ray of fire when the sky above them lit up. A second bolt of lightning flashed across the heavens, knocking a familiar purple-robed figure out of the air.

Glolindir!

Andrella's mouth fell open as the hapless elf crashed to the ground on the other side of the clearing. Her horror abruptly turned to anger. The young lady followed the trail the bolt had taken up to a hovering figure in the sky.

DeWyness.

At the last moment, Andrella shifted her spell and fired up at the floating Mayor. The beam lanced across the night sky and struck its target dead-on.

"Ahhhh!"

The harsh cry echoed over the clearing, filling Andrella with extreme satisfaction. *That's what you get, you old bag, for harming my friend.*

"Andrella!"

Something crashed into her, knocking her to the ground. Andrella immediately sat back up, her eyes locking on Newin. The thin wizard slowly drooped to the ground, a knife hilt sticking out of her chest.

"Newin!" Andrella screamed, tears forming in her eyes.

Donnie's opponent turned out to be extremely skilled. Seeing his rapier, the assassin had pulled out his own. The duo then engaged in a fierce fencing match.

Donnie carefully tested his opponent, his thrusts easily countered and parried. The assassin did the same. Short thrusts and feints were easily countered.

Abruptly, the assassin executed a complicated maneuver. Donnie thanked his lucky stars he had studied with the best swordswoman on the Pirate Coast. He had seen this move before and deftly countered it.

His opponent drew back and eyed him warily. "Most would have fallen to that attack."

Donnie gave the man a pearly smile. "Most have."

Feeling he now had the measure of his opponent, Donnie began a maneuver of his own. He feinted, then sidestepped, attempting to cross his sword over the other and spin it out of the way. Yet the assassin had been ready for the move.

Donnie found himself barely blocking his opponent's blade with Ruka's knife. *Whew, that was a bit too close.*

Donatello fell back and re-evaluated this assassin. Whoever this was, they were an accomplished swordsman. He could only think of one maneuver that might work against them.

Raising his weapon, Donnie began another assault similar to the previous one. Yet this time, when he crossed swords, he spun his weapon around twice. As the second spiral ended, he flicked his wrist to the side. The motion caught his opponent unprepared, pushing the other blade far out of the way.

Donnie immediately lunged forward, skewering the assassin straight through the gut. The man dropped his weapon and slowly slid to the ground.

"Who… who are you?" The dying man gasped.

"No one of consequence," Donnie answered.

Lightning flashed across the sky, followed by a loud cry. Donnie whirled around in time to see Newin drop to the earth, a knife sticking out of her chest.

"Newin!"

Andrella lay on the ground nearby, so distraught that she missed the peril looming over her. A dark-robed figure held a second knife in hand, poised for throwing at the hysterical young lady.

Donnie reacted by sheer instinct. Dropping his rapier, he flipped Ruka's knife into his main hand and sent it sailing across the clearing, straight into the robed figure's back.

A sharp cry escaped the caster's lips as she arched her back and slid to the ground.

✳

Though a short man, One-Eye had the advantage of reach on Seth. His reflexes were also quite sharp, though Seth thought he had the advantage there. Still, neither seemed capable of landing a blow.

Wielding daggers in either hand, the duo weaved around each other executing lightning quick jabs. Knives flashed almost faster than the eye could see, yet every jab was relentlessly blocked.

Seth tried to take advantage of the assassin's blind side, but it cost him. One-Eye anticipated his move and drew first blood with a swipe across Seth's torso. The halfling flipped backward and stared darkly at his nimble opponent.

"Saw that coming, huh?"

The man snorted. "Heh. Kind of learn to expect that when you've got a bum eye."

Seth's mouth twisted sideways. "I see."

One-Eye's gaze hardened. "Really? Sight jokes?"

Seth shrugged. "Sure. Why not?"

The assassin's shoulders tightened slightly. As he hoped, Seth had gotten under his skin.

One-Eye suddenly leapt forward, coming at Seth with a round of rapid jabs. Seth struggled to hold him off, especially with the man's added reach. One jab was so fast that Seth barely had time to deflect it. It sailed past his chest and ripped through the side of his arm.

Seth tumbled out of the way and came up on his feet, his arm throbbing from where it had been cut.

One-Eye watched him from a short distance away with a wicked grin. "Guess you're not all that good after all."

Seth's mouth bent into an outrageous smirk. "Care to try again?"

The one-eyed man glared at him, then launched at Seth once more. His moves were still lightning quick, but Seth had goaded him into a mistake. One-Eye overextended himself, and Seth took advantage by lashing out with his foot. He caught the man in the midsection and sent him flying backward.

Anger washed across the assassin's face. He leapt at Seth yet again, his stabs filled with even more ferocity. Seth was hard pressed to find another opening. So instead, he slowly gave ground, backing toward the nearest tree.

When his back foot touched the base of the trunk, Seth performed a daring move. He blocked the next jab, and in one fluid motion, let go of his knife and wrapped his fingers around One-Eye's wrist.

Seth used the leverage to run up the side of the tree trunk and vault himself over One-Eye's head. Still holding onto the arm, he wrenched the assassin off-balance and drove his other knife straight into his heart.

Lightning flashed across the sky as Seth pulled the dagger free and watched One-Eye fall against the tree trunk. The assassin slid to the ground and lay there unmoving.

Kalyn's eyes went wide as Glolindir fell from the sky. *But… he's a hero… he can't die…*

The ray of fire that lanced upward, and the subsequent scream, shook Kalyn awake again. *That has ta be DeWyness up there—and Andrella just nailed her.*

Kalyn opened her mouth to shout, *Yeah Andrella, skin her alive!* but the words died on her lips. Newin fell to an assassin's knife, and Andrella nearly did as well. Thankfully, Donnie came to her rescue.

With no more threats on the ground, Kalyn's eyes turned back to the sky. A bright light suddenly spread across the clearing, clearly illuminating the robed-figure as it weaved another spell.

Kalyn didn't hesitate. She pulled one arrow, then another from her quiver and fired them in rapid succession. Both flew up toward their target, nearly reaching it just as the spell went off.

A bolt of lightning hurtled downward as the twin arrows bounced harmlessly off their target. Kalyn's heart leapt into her throat, but thankfully Donatello was there. The wiry elf tackled Andrella, pulling her out of the way as the lightning bolt struck the spot where she had just been.

Up above, the merciless caster began to weave another spell. Kalyn watched helplessly when something suddenly clicked in the back of her mind.

Kalyn's people, the Deepwood Snipers, had been known for their skill in killing mages. It was a well-guarded secret, one not used in a hundred and fifty years, since the end of the Thrall Wars.

The young archer now reached back, pulling a separated shaft from her quiver. It was a *mystic* arrow. She had never used one before, and didn't know exactly how it worked, but that didn't matter now. In one swift motion, Kalyn took aim, drew on the bowstring, and let the arrow fly.

Time seemed to slow as the shaft sailed upward toward its target. DeWyness had nearly reached the end of her spell. Even from this distance, Kalyn could see the sparks igniting in the mage's hands.

A moment later, the arrow reached its target. There was a dull flash as the magical shaft pierced the Mayor's defenses, then it struck her straight in the chest.

DeWyness let out a short cry as the spell died in her hands. She hung there in mid-air for the briefest of moments, then fell from the sky.

"Serves ya right, ya witch," Kalyn muttered in triumph as the leader of the Assassins' Guild slammed into the ground below.

Aksel was engaged in a desperate battle with the dark cleric. The priest of Amon had charged forward, but Aksel had stopped it with his spiritual axe.

As the dark cleric fended off the holy weapon, Aksel drew in his will and pushed his palm outward. *"Lux acribus."*

A ray of blinding white light shot from his outstretched palm. It lanced through the night and caught the black-mailed cleric square in the chest.

The priest of Amon screamed in agony, swatting Aksel's spiritual axe away and turning a dark helmet turned toward him.

Aksel felt a strange tingling sensation, then the world around him wavered and abruptly changed. The clearing disappeared, replaced instead with a hellish landscape. Craggy projections of bare rock spread out in all directions, criss-crossed with pockets and rivulets of golden-red liquid. Fires belched from the ground everywhere, the night sky above replaced with a foreboding canopy of black smoke.

A giant Lloyd still stood nearby, but instead of an ogre, he fought a large demon. Smaller demons battled with Seth, Donnie, Andrella, and Newin.

Aksel shook his head. *This isn't right. It can't be real.* He rubbed his eyes, but the nightmare hadn't disappeared. Uncertain what else to do, Aksel began to pray.

Soldenar, Goddess of all Gnomes, I beseech you. Help me to see the truth.

The lilting voice of his goddess immediately reverberated through his mind. *The truth is it ya seek? And what truth would that be, me lad?*

Aksel grimaced. He had asked for that one. Calming his mind, he rephrased his request. *I ask to see the truth of what lies around me.*

His appeal was met with a short lilting laugh. *Ah, that truth. Normally I'd make ya solve a riddle fer that answer, but I can see ya be short on time. The answer ya seek is to shine a light in the darkness.*

The sky was split by a bolt of lightning, as if to punctuate her reply.

Shine a light? Aksel's nose wrinkled as he thought over her response. All at once, the answer hit him. Once again, the little cleric drew in his will. This time, he reached up to the heavens with both arms as he released the spell. *"Lucem Diem."*

A brilliant white orb appeared in the sky over his head; its light spread out for nearly two dozen yards in all directions. The infernal landscape around him began to waver, then faded altogether.

Aksel was back in the clearing behind Vermoorden Keep. Everything had returned to normal, with the exception of the dark cleric. The figure now stood over him, a black axe raised for a killing blow.

Aksel cringed, but thankfully the gods were on his side. The brilliant orb that hung overhead had temporarily blinded the evil priest.

Aksel frantically drew in his will with a fervent prayer to his goddess. *Soldenar, please give me the power to smite this unholy priest of the dark god.*

So be it! The words reverberated through his mind.

Divine power rippled throughout Aksel's entire being. He channeled the potent holy force through his arms and released it with two words. *"Sanctus Percutiat."*

A ray of white light shot out of him and slammed into the dark cleric. Thunder rolled again as the evil priest was hammered to the ground by the terrific force. A soft moan echoed from the dark helmet, then the black-mailed cleric lay still.

Everything around Aksel had gone quiet. The troll was sprawled on the ground nearby, its entire torso scorched and riddled with arrows. Lloyd stood over the dead body of the ogre, panting with exhaustion.

A soft dirge suddenly rose up from across the clearing. Andrella, Donnie, and Wraith stood nearby as a forlorn Balmaroh knelt over the fallen body of his friend Newin. The bard's voice rose high into the night, its anguish tugging at Aksel's heart.

30
JUST DESSERTS

The still of the night was shattered by a pair of screams

Elladan's heart nearly broke for Balmaroh. He had lost not one, but two close friends this day. Other folks were injured as well. Glo had been hit by lightning and taken a bad fall. Aksel and Seth were working on him now, and neither Donnie nor Lloyd had escaped the battle unscathed.

Furthermore, the skirmish had not gone unnoticed. Even now, there was movement on the castle parapets above.

Lloyd and Donnie drew next to Elladan. The young man had worried lines across his brow. "So now what do we do? We have dead and wounded. We can't just head to Ravenford like this."

Elladan motioned for them to follow him away from Balmaroh and the others. When they were far enough away, he stopped and gazed at the duo with the hint of a smile. "Now we take over the castle."

Donnie narrowed an eye at him. "And just how do you propose to do that?"

"Like this." Elladan peered up toward the top of the keep and cupped his hands together. "Who's in charge up there?"

His query was met with silence at first. Finally, a commanding voice called back down to them. "I am Captain Ascue of the Vermoorden guard! Identify yourself."

"I am Elladan Narmolanya of the Heroes of Ravenford!"

The Captain's response was laced with surprise. "The group that slew the lake monsters two weeks ago?"

"The very same!"

There was another pause before the Captain called down again. "What happened down there?"

Donnie cocked his head to one side. "There's a good question. What are you going to tell him?"

Elladan winked. "Why, the truth, of course."

A sly smile crossed Donnie's lips. "Now this I have to hear."

Elladan cupped his hands together once more. "We were attacked by assassins! We drove them off, but I'm afraid the Mayor didn't make it!"

Donnie began to cough so violently that Lloyd had to pat the lean elf on the back.

"What?" Elladan whispered to his friend. "It's the truth."

"Yeah… but we're the ones… that killed her…" Donnie managed between fits.

Elladan arched an eyebrow at his old friend. "True, but they don't need to know that."

"They will at some point," Lloyd pointed out.

Elladan gave him a firm nod. "Agreed, but hopefully by then we'll be able to prove she was evil."

Any further conversation was interrupted by Ascue's reply. "Where is she now?"

Elladan glanced across the clearing, where the Mayor's body lay crumpled in a heap. Kalyn stood over her, retrieving the arrow she had used for the kill. "Her body is right here! We can bring her to you if you want."

Ascue's response was immediate this time. "No, stay where you are. We'll be down shortly. Oh, and don't think of running. There are a dozen trained archers on this wall and you'll be cut down. If you are who you say, then everything will be fine."

Now who's bluffing? Elladan thought wryly. His elven eyes could see the parapets quite well. There were maybe three men on the wall with bows.

Donnie stared at Elladan with his arms folded. "Well that was 'friendly.' Sure you know what you're doing?"

Elladan's mouth twisted into a semi-smile. "Watch and learn, my friend."

A short while later, a group of perhaps two dozen figures entered the clearing. Aksel's glowing white orb still hung overheard, clearly illuminating their blue and gold tabards—the colors of the castle guard. The guardsmen seemed nervous as they fanned out, their weapons held ready.

"They don't exactly look ready to give us the key to the city," Donnie whispered under his breath.

Elladan leveled his hands in front of him. "Give it time."

With Aksel still healing Glo, and Balmaroh grieving, Elladan strode forward to greet the newcomers. Lloyd, Donnie, and Kara joined him.

The soldiers were led by a tall man with long blonde hair and the hint of a beard and mustache. He and three of his men met the trio in the center of the clearing, while the other guards continued to fan out.

The tall man gave them a curt nod as he looked them over carefully. "Captain Ascue of the Vermoorden guard. Which one of you is Elladan?"

"I am," Elladan responded with a curt bow. "These are my associates, Lloyd, Donatello, and Kara."

Captain Ascue was younger than Elladan had thought. He expected someone more seasoned, like Gelpas. Then again, Mayor DeWyness probably didn't want anyone older in that position. A younger Captain would be far more pliable and easy to keep in the dark.

Ascue exchanged greetings with Lloyd, Donnie, and Kara. "I

recognize most of you from the celebration after the slaying of the lake monsters. You are indeed who you say you are."

He swept his eyes around the clearing, pausing at the bodies of the ogre and the troll. "So, what exactly happened here, and where is the Mayor?"

Donnie pointed over to where DeWyness' body lay. A couple of guards already stood over it. When Ascue looked at them, they responded with a nod.

Ascue closed his eyes and let out a deep breath. "So, it's true, the Mayor is dead."

Elladan could clearly see how shaken the young man was. Ascue was still probably new to his position and way out of his depth here. Elladan decided to take pity on him. He waved for Ascue to step closer and dropped his voice to a whisper. "I'm not sure how to break this to you, but that may not exactly be a bad thing."

"Oh?" Ascue's eyes widened.

"The Mayor was most likely in league with the Assassins' Guild, hidden right here below this very keep." He pointed out the entrance in the back wall that now stood wide open.

Ascue peered at the keep, then back at Elladan, his voice taking on a dangerous edge. "I trust you have proof."

Donnie leaned in and looked the man in the eye. "How about the bodies of nearly four dozen dead assassins, and an evil temple to boot?"

Ascue drew back and straightened his shoulders, his posture going stiff. "Even if that were the case, it still does not point to the Mayor being involved." The young man hesitated, a hand going to his stubbled chin. "I must contact the Magistrate. He will be able to sort this out."

"Wait, Ascue. I can vouch for what they say."

Balmaroh drew up beside them, followed by Kalyn, Martan, and Andrella. The latter had pulled her robe closed and the hood over her head.

Ascue's eyes went wide. "Balmaroh, you're alive?"

The bard's expression grew hard. "Yes, no thanks to DeWyness."

Ascue narrowed an eye at him. "How's that?"

"The Assassins' Guild put out a contract on me. If not for these folks' warning,"—he motioned toward Elladan and the others—"I'd be dead for real."

Ascue's brow wrinkled, his expression uncertain. "Honestly, Balmaroh, I'd like to believe you, but you were never exactly a proponent of the Mayor's…"

Elladan could see Ascue wrestling with his indecision. He was used to someone of higher stature making his choices for him. *Well, if that's what he needs…*

Elladan cleared his throat. "I realize this is a lot to accept, but there is one among us whose word you won't be able to doubt."

Ascue eyed him warily. "And who might that be?"

Elladan motioned to the cloaked figure standing quietly behind Lloyd's tall frame. "Why, none other than the Lady Andrella of Ravenford, sole heir to the Duchy of Dunwynn."

Kalyn coughed violently as Lloyd moved to the side and Andrella stepped forward. The young lady gave Elladan a dark look before removing her hood and putting on a diplomatic smile.

Andrella executed a brief but elegant curtsey. "Captain Ascue."

Ascue's face lit up with surprise. "As I live and breathe, it is the Lady Andrella."

The entire troop of guards gathered around as Andrella outlined their encounter with the Assassins' Guild. She briefly explained how they tracked them down, their valiant efforts in cleansing the lair, and the Mayor's treachery. She ended with a heartfelt thanks to those who died in the fight.

There were loud murmurs among the guards when she finished her speech.

"Can't say I'm surprised."

"I never did completely trust her."

"She had some strange company comin' and goin' out of the castle."

Overall, the young lady's words had the desired effect on them. Even Ascue's face had gone ashen. "I am sorry for your loss, and I do not doubt your word, my lady. Were it me alone, there would be no question, but now it seems I have an entire town to answer to."

There was some dissent among the guards, but Andrella waved them quiet. "I quite understand, Captain. You're only doing your job."

"Perhaps we might find some further evidence in the Mayor's rooms?"

They all spun around to see Glo standing up, the tall elf leaning heavily on Aksel and Seth.

"Glo, you're alright!" Lloyd cried with glee.

The corners of Glo's mouth upturned slightly. "*Up*right, at the very least."

Andrella gave him a warm smile, then turned back to Ascue. "I think that is an excellent idea, Captain. Wouldn't you agree?"

"Why, yes… of course." Ascue nodded.

Elladan found it hard to suppress a smile. The fledgling Captain was like putty in her hands.

Andrella waved around the clearing. "Meanwhile, your men can clean up these bodies and search that wretched assassins' lair to make sure there are none left." She turned to Kalyn and motioned her forward. "Captain Ascue, this is Kalyn Rahn of Deepwood, an expert archer and tracker. She can assist you."

Kalyn actually tried to curtsey like Andrella, but midway through grew self-conscious. She stopped and thrust out her hand toward Ascue. "Capt'n."

A hint of amusement crossed the Captain's face before he took her hand and shook it firmly. "Mistress Kalyn."

Seth nodded to Lloyd. "You take Glo. I want another look around here anyway."

"Guess I'll help too," Martan intoned flatly.

Like Seth, Elladan also wanted another look around. "So will I."

"Very good." Ascue gave them all a curt nod, then went to organize his men as Andrella suggested.

Elladan started after Seth and the others, when he felt a sharp jab in his ribs. Andrella stood there watching him with a single eyebrow raised.

"A little warning next time would be appropriate," she said in a hushed voice.

A wide grin spread across Elladan's face. "But you were so good at it."

"She was, wasn't she?" Lloyd, still holding Glo, practically beamed at the young lady.

Andrella's annoyance swiftly faded, her cheeks reddening from all the praise.

Martan had been leery when the Vermoorden guards flooded the clearing. He thought for certain they would all end up in chains. Lady Andrella's recap of their encounter seemed to sway things in their favor. Still, Martan was not convinced they were out of the woods just yet. He'd had his run-ins with the authorities in the past, and it never turned out well.

For now, Martan stayed behind to help with the clean-up. The Captain kept a couple of guards by his side and sent a pair to help Balmaroh. The rest he divided into two groups—one to gather up the bodies in the clearing, the other to search the guild's lair.

Kalyn had been chosen to lead the latter group. They had just lined up outside the keep when Seth pulled Elladan, Kalyn, and Martan aside.

"The Mayor's body is gone," he told them in a hushed voice.

Kalyn's head drew back, deep lines creasing her brow. "Well, she sure didn't walk off by herself. I got her right in the heart."

Martan found the whole thing highly suspicious. He hurried over to where the body had been, then knelt to examine the ground. "Couldn't have been taken that long ago. The grass here is still flattened."

The woods were less than a dozen yards away. Martan scanned the ground in that direction, almost immediately spying gouges in the earth. The others were not far behind as he followed the trail to the edge of the forest. "There are three sets of tracks here. The middle pair looks as if it were being dragged."

Elladan pointed a thumb back toward the keep. "Kalyn, you go ahead and search the lair. We'll grab a couple of guards and track down the Mayor's body."

"Sure 'nough," Kalyn said. She turned to go, then stopped and pointed a finger at Martan. "Now don't go getting' yerself killed, or nothin'. I ain't done hollerin' at just you yet."

"Yes, ma'am," Martan said simply. He'd learned it best these last few days to say as little as possible to her. He felt a hand on his shoulder as the feisty young woman strode off.

"Son, you've got your hands full with that one," Elladan drawled with the hint of a smile.

Martan let out a deep sigh. "You can say that again."

Elladan grabbed two nearby guards, then all of them entered the woods.

Martan followed the trail as it wound through the trees. It was easy to follow, even in the dark—whoever had grabbed the Mayor was in a rush and did little to hide their tracks. They must have gone about a mile when he called a halt. "There's a clearing just ahead. Stay here while I check it out."

"You mean we," Seth stated firmly.

"We," Martan amended.

The pair crept through the underbrush to the edge of the clearing. The woods around them were unusually quiet. Not a cricket chirped, nor an owl hooted.

Martan cautiously peeked through the thick brush. Silvery light shown down through the treetops illuminating a wide oval area. In the very center lay an oblong lump. Martan stared for a few moments till he realized what it was. *It's the Mayor's body!*

"Now if that doesn't scream trap..." Seth muttered under his breath.

Martan couldn't have agreed more.

Seth went back to warn the others while Martan hunkered down in the nook of a nearby tree. Bow in hand, he waited quietly until a short while later when he heard a soft *klinking* behind him.

Martan peered around the trunk and saw the two Vermoorden guards approaching alongside Elladan and Seth. He signaled for them to halt, but it was too late. A figure darted out of the nearby brush and sped off into the forest. A moment later, Seth took off after it, the halfling moving at an incredible speed.

Martan carefully backtracked to join the others keeping his voice low. "The Mayor's body is still there."

Elladan nodded, then motioned for the guards to fan out on either side of the glade.

"Stick to the trees—and try not to make any noise," Martan whispered.

As the guards spread out, Elladan followed Martan back to his perch. Despite his warning, the men continued to move through the forest like a bull in a magic shop.

Without warning, a mass of glowing purple projectiles shot out of the brush on the other side of the clearing. They wound their way across the glade straight for the *klinking* guards. The still of the night was shattered by a pair of screams, then all went silent.

Martan immediately drew his bow and sent a barrage of arrows toward the bush where the missiles originated. The shafts lanced into the brush one after another, the third one eliciting a short cry.

A robed figure burst out into the clearing, an arrow embedded in its shoulder. It lifted its other arm and sent a red-hot beam hurling directly at Martan and Elladan.

The agile archer pushed the bard out of the way as he tumbled in the opposite direction. He came up in a crouch, and in one fluid motion fired an arrow at the robed-figure.

The arrow found its mark. With a soft groan, the figure fell to the ground, a shaft protruding from its chest.

"I think you got him!" Elladan cried.

Martan certainly hoped so, but experience had taught him otherwise. "I'll go check while you see to the guards."

Martan exited the safety of the woods, bow in hand and arrow nocked. He crossed the clearing with extreme caution, but the robed figure didn't move. On close examination, he confirmed the man was dead. Martan also thought he recognized him.

He saw Elladan crossing the clearing and followed him into the brush. He found the bard kneeling over one of the guards. The man's eyes were closed, his face bruised and his arm twisted in an unnatural direction. "How is he?"

"He's still breathing, which is more than I can say for his friend."

Martan hung his head. He'd seen death more often than he'd have liked, but wasn't sure he'd ever get used to it.

He helped Elladan drag the guard back into the clearing. The bard nodded toward the robed figure Martan had shot as he bandaged the guard's arm. "What about that one?"

"He's dead. I think it was the Magistrate."

A muscle in Elladan's face twitched and his teeth gritted together. "And these were their own men…" His mouth flattened into a grim line. "Martan, go gather up some firewood."

Martan eyed the bard apprehensively. "What are you going to do?"

"You'll see."

The moment the figure darted from the brush, Seth took off after it. The halfling cast a quick spell, muttering two words under his breath. "*Tempore Duplo.*"

Seth suddenly shot forward, his legs moving so fast that he felt as if they would run out from under him. It took him a few strides, but having used the spell before, he swiftly adjusted. His quarry had a good head start, but it didn't last long. With his newfound speed, Seth quickly closed the gap. He could just make out a tall, dark figure weaving through the trees ahead.

Taking a detour around a deep thicket, Seth pulled ahead of his quarry. Planting himself against the trunk of a thick tree, he folded his arms and waited for the figure to reappear. A few seconds later, a tall man in a dark leather tunic came rushing toward him through the trees.

"What's up?" Seth said casually as he went by.

The assassin nearly jumped out of his skin. He whirled around and drew his sword, eyeing Seth as if he'd seen a ghost.

"How did you… what are you…" he stammered. The man glanced around nervously. "It's not my fault. They made me do it."

Seth didn't move a muscle. "Fine, then drop your sword and I'll let you live."

The man hesitated for a moment or so, then slowly stooped down and laid his sword on the ground.

Seth waited till he got back up, then reached for the sword. As he anticipated, the assassin pulled out a knife and took a swipe at him. Seth easily avoided it. "Oh, come on. You're not even trying."

The man in the dark tunic gulped, then spun on his heel and took off through the trees.

Seth shook his head. "Here we go again."

It was a repeat of what had happened before. Seth quickly caught up and passed his quarry, planting himself once again a short distance down his path. As the man ran by this time, Seth said, "We've got to stop meeting like this."

The assassin halted in his tracks, his face going white as a sheet. He fells to his knees and began to pray fervently.

Seth eyed the man skeptically, thinking this was another ploy. "Honestly, you don't have to worship me…"

All of a sudden, the night around them grew darker. The air thickened, filling with an eerie sensation that made Seth's skin crawl. He swept his eyes around the woods, but there was nothing in sight except for himself and the praying man.

Suddenly, the assassin fell to the ground.

Seth cautiously drew closer, but it appeared that the man had stopped breathing. He checked his pulse—the man was dead. It suddenly dawned on him what had happened. The assassin had been praying to his god, the dark god, Amon. His prayers had been answered with death.

Seth gazed on the fallen figure with disgust. "I hate fanatics."

He spun around, and without another word headed back to rejoin the others.

Martan returned a short while later, only to find the bodies of the Mayor and Magistrate atop each other in the middle of the clearing. His arms stacked with tinder, the woodsman gazed questioningly at Elladan. "Where do you want these?"

Elladan waved him toward the pile. "Place that all around the bodies."

Martan's brow wrinkled, but he otherwise refrained from

commenting. The one guard still alive was propped up against a near-by tree, his arm now wrapped in a sling. He seemed to be sleeping peacefully.

"What about him?" Martan asked as he spread the firewood around the bodies.

Elladan glanced at the guard and shrugged. "Oh, I patched him up and played him a lullaby. No use having him interfere with what needs to be done."

Martan narrowed an eye at Elladan. "And what's that?"

"Making sure these two never harm anyone again."

Martan's jaw fell open. "So, you're building a funeral pyre?"

"Of sorts."

The woodsman stared at Elladan as his mind turned over what was about to happen. The Mayor and Magistrate were decidedly evil. They were also both dead at this point. Were either, or both, to be resurrected, they would most likely form another guild of killers.

Martan shrugged. "Fair enough. I'm not a god-fearing man, but shouldn't you say grace or something over them first?"

Elladan cocked his head to one side. "That's a good point. I'll bless them with what they deserve."

The bard strolled over to the makeshift pyre, his back to Martan. As he recited a prayer, Martan heard the distinctive sound of buttons unsnapping, followed by a stream of liquid hitting the ground. The entire scene left Martan speechless. He nearly jumped out of his skin when Seth's voice sounded beside him.

"Are you doing what I think you're doing?"

Elladan didn't turn around. "Just think of it as holy water."

Seth glanced at the bodies. "The Mayor and the Magistrate?"

Elladan nodded.

"And you're burning them so no one can resurrect them?"

"Yup."

Seth folded his arms, the side of his mouth upturning. "I approve."

Martan glanced between the duo, but kept his thoughts to himself. He watched on silently as Elladan lit a fire and Seth added a few flasks of oil. The flames rose high in the center of the clearing, as what was left of the Mayor and her crony went up in smoke.

31
DARK LEGACY

We now have the Thrall Master's gift

Donnie thought Elladan had lost it when he proposed they take over the castle. Yet now, here they were with the Captain of the Guard escorting them into the keep proper. While the matter of proving the Mayor's guilt remained, in her absence, Ascue seemed more than willing to follow the Lady Andrella's 'suggestions.'

Vermoorden Keep was strikingly similar to the one in Ravenford, though perhaps a bit more austere. Composed of dark grey stone, the large structure stood three stories high, but rose to four or five in smaller sections. Two huge wooden doors opened to the first floor. Numerous arched windows filled the stories above.

Ascue led them through the foyer into a two-story great hall. While a large room, it seemed rather uninviting when compared with Ravenford. For one thing, there were no seats in sight. Second, there was little artwork except for a couple of banners emblazoned with the town insignia and a singular portrait of the Mayor hanging on one wall.

Ascue and his men escorted the companions upstairs to the Mayor's chambers. They had barely reached the landing between floors, when a loud *kaboom* resounded from somewhere above.

"What now?" Ascue cried, what little composure he had left unraveling.

They rushed upward, nearly colliding with a young dark-haired boy barreling down the steps. Lloyd, who had taken the lead, caught the frantic lad in his arms. "Whoa, there. What's going on?"

The thin boy huffed heavily, his eyes wide and his face red. "Rota told them not to open the door! They wouldn't listen."

Andrella whispered to Ascue, "Who's Rota?"

"One of the maids," the Captain said softly.

"Don't worry, we'll take care of it," Lloyd promised the boy.

The young man passed the lad off to Andrella, then went running ahead, up the stairs. Donnie exchanged a quick glance with Kara, then they took off after him.

A long hallway stretched in both directions at the top of the stairs. A copper-haired maid knelt on the floor at one end, sobbing hysterically. Lloyd, Donnie, and Kara raced to her side. A trio of figures laid between her and an ornate wooden door. All three were burnt nearly beyond recognition, only identifiable by small tatters of their once-black robes.

Donnie looked closely at the doorframe—there were scorch marks on either side. He nudged Lloyd and Kara, keeping his voice low. "Fire trap."

Lloyd gently grasped the distraught maid by the shoulders. She stood and spun around, her freckled face streaked with tears. She peered up at the tall warrior, then buried her head in his chest. "They... they wouldn't listen to me..."

Lloyd's cheeks reddened as he patted her lightly on the back. "It's not your fault. You tried to warn them."

Andrella, Ascue, and the two guards joined them moments later while Aksel and the young boy helped Glo limp down the hall. The Captain eyed the burnt figures with clear concern. "Rota, who were these men?"

The maid lifted her head off Lloyd's chest, and wiped the tears from her eyes. "I… I don't know, Captain. I… I've never seen any of them… before."

Andrella delicately extracted the young woman from Lloyd's grasp and handed her a handkerchief. Meanwhile, Donnie pointed out the scorch marks to the newcomers. "This was the work of a fire trap. I'm guessing that's the Mayor's room?"

Ascue gave him a grim nod. "Indeed."

"Seems like she didn't want anyone entering her room uninvited."

Donnie glanced over his shoulder to see that Glo had joined them, the wizard still being supported by Aksel and the young boy.

"That—that's right. She warned us never to enter her room when she wasn't there." Rota paused to blow her nose. "I tried to stop them, but they pulled a knife on me. I think they were going to kill me…"

Rota began sobbing all over again. Andrella placed a reassuring arm around her shoulder.

Ascue appeared as if he was about to burst. "Assassins in the keep? This is an outrage!"

"I couldn't agree more, Captain," Andrella said, her arm still wrapped around the anguished Rota. "While we were searching their lair, we found an entrance into the keep. That's probably how they got in."

Ascue's mouth had flattened into a thin line. "An entrance into the keep? Can you show me?"

"We'd be happy to," Lloyd said, his expression nearly as grim as Ascue.

The Captain turned to the young lad. "Torvil, run out back and fetch the guard for me. Tell them to gather in the great hall."

Torvil's face grew very serious. He drew to attention and saluted Ascue. "Right away, Captain!"

The boy turned on his heel and took off down the hall at a dead run.

Once he was gone, Aksel turned to Ascue. "While you take care of that, we'll make sure no one else gets hurt up here."

A brief smile crossed Ascue's lips. "That would be most appreciated."

Andrella nodded toward the bodies on the floor. "Perhaps it might be best for your men to remove these?"

Ascue straightened his shoulders. "Of course, Lady Andrella." He motioned for the guards to move the bodies, then with a crisp salute stalked off with Lloyd at his side. Andrella followed close behind with the hapless Rota.

Donnie stepped around the dead bodies and took a closer look at the door. After a careful examination, he discovered a faint marking at the very top, just below the doorframe. It appeared very similar to the marking on the chest that held the Baron's heart. He pointed it out to Glo. "Is that what I think it is?"

The tall elf followed Donnie's gaze. "Indeed. That's a fire rune."

"Good thing I have these, then." Donnie retrieved his red leather gloves, then stood on his toes as he strained to reach the symbol. Like before, there was a momentary flash of red, which immediately disappeared.

"That should do it." Donnie swiftly picked the lock, then pushed the door open to reveal perhaps the gaudiest room he had ever seen. The entire chamber was colored in red. The walls were red, the ceiling was red, even the furniture was red—cherry wood covered in plush red velvet.

A huge four-poster bed took up most of the room, framed on either side by two tall arch-shaped windows. An ornate desk, a dresser, a wardrobe, a privacy screen, and a large chest lined the rest of the walls. Donnie spied another door off to one side, but decided to search the first room thoroughly before moving on.

All the drawers on the Mayor's desk were locked. Donnie made short work of them and found a couple of interesting books. One volume, bound in black, turned out to be the Mayor's spellbook. The other book was bound in red velour and had yet another fire rune engraved on it.

Donnie handed both over to Glo. "Wow. She loved fire even more than you."

The wizard gave him a sour look. "Really? Isn't it bad enough I get it from Seth?"

Kara peered from Glo to Donnie with curiosity. "Am I missing something?"

Glo leveled a dark stare at the slim elf. Donnie merely grinned at Kara. "I'll tell you some other time."

Donnie dispelled the rune on the journal, and Glo began leafing through it. In the meantime, Donnie examined the chest. Thankfully there were no trip wires or runes here. It was a simple padlock, which Donnie picked in no time.

Inside the chest lay a fine scarlet outfit, adorned with ornate golden lace. It had a high neck with open-shouldered long sleeves, a bustier affixed with a large red jewel, and a long flowing skirt. Below that he found a matching bodice, a pair of scarlet boots, and a single gold metal wrist band.

Donnie shuddered. His mind had unwittingly imagined the middle-aged DeWyness wearing the revealing outfit. The repulsed elf attempted to distract himself by picking up a few pieces of the ensemble and holding them out for all to see. "Anyone interested in this?"

"Not my size," Glo said flatly.

Kara folded her arms across her chest. "Mine either."

"Ooooo, that's pretty."

Andrella and Lloyd stood in the open doorway. The young lady walked over and grabbed the outfit from Donnie's hands. "I've never seen anything like this."

"I have."

Andrella tore her eyes away from the dress and stared at the wizard.

"Or pictures of it, to be more precise. It's magical apparel—a Regalia of the Phoenix," Glo explained.

Andrella's eyes went even wider. "Magical?"

The corners of the wizard's mouth begrudgingly turned upward. "I can show you how to use it, if you'd like."

Andrella practically waltzed over to Glo, her face beaming. "Would you?"

The last traces of Glo's sour disposition faded away as he stared at the enthusiastic young lady. "Certainly."

"So, what happened downstairs?" Aksel asked Lloyd.

The young man let out a deep sigh. "Not much, actually. We led them down to the entrance to the lair, then Ascue told us they'd take it from there."

Andrella looked up from where she had been laying out her new outfit on the bed. "It's just as well, hon. No offense, but you look wiped."

A sheepish grin crossed the young man's face, his hand going to the back of his neck. "Yeah, I guess you're right."

Donnie chuckled softly to himself. They already sounded like an old married couple.

Andrella sighed, looking back at the scarlet dress. "I just have to try this on."

Everyone watched as she picked it up and headed toward the privacy panel. She waved them off with a single hand. "Don't mind me, just keep doing what you were doing."

Donnie raised an eyebrow at Lloyd. The young man appeared completely flustered as pieces of Andrella's clothing were flung over the top of the panel.

Donnie glanced around at the others, his voice rising an octave. "I think we've seen enough. Perhaps we should search the next room."

Kara brushed by him, her lips curled to one side. "I think that's a good idea."

As Donnie expected, the other door was also locked. He checked it carefully, but found no trip wires or runes anywhere. The dexterous elf swiftly unlocked the door and pushed it open.

In sharp contrast to the previous room, this one was painted completely in black. There was a single dark stone altar in the center of the room, adjacent to a large, ebony humanoid statue.

Donnie shivered as he entered the room—the statue practically exuded evil. "I'm afraid to ask who that is."

"That is the dark god, Amon," Kara announced in a matter-of-fact tone.

Donnie was not thrilled with the revelation, but as usual he made a joke out of it. "Oh great, just what we need, the god of darkness and evil."

Aksel drew up next to Donnie and eyed the statue with hatred. "Not surprising, considering the Mayor's priests carried the symbols of Amon."

"Well, if there was ever any doubt that the Mayor was evil..." Donnie quipped.

Aksel cast a disparaging glance at him. "This is an affront to anyone of pure faith and should be destroyed immediately."

Donnie narrowed an eye at the gnome. He seemed rather agitated, not at all his normal self. "Not that I disagree with you, but shouldn't we let Ascue see it first?"

Aksel cast a dark stare at the sandy-haired elf, making him almost flinch.

Thankfully Lloyd came to his rescue.

"As soon as Ascue sees it, I'll help you tear it down, piece by piece."

Aksel peered up at Lloyd and gave him a firm nod. "Deal."

In the meantime, Donnie had started to search the altar. At the very back he found a hollow panel. He pressed on it and it slid back to reveal the altar was not solid. Underneath lay yet another large chest. Donnie asked Lloyd to give him a hand pulling it out.

They dragged the chest to the center of the room, where Donnie swiftly unlocked it and lifted the lid. Pieces of gold coin and jewels spilled over the sides—the chest was literally brimming with treasure.

"Spoils of the guild, no doubt."

All eyes turned toward Andrella. The young lady stood in the doorway garbed in her new scarlet outfit.

Donnie's jaw fell open. She looked positively stunning. Not only was her new wardrobe formfitting, but it was far more revealing than even he had anticipated. Up until now, he had not realized just how well 'endowed' the young lady was. Donnie swiftly caught himself, shifting his gaze back up to Andrella's face.

The young lady wore a satisfied smile. She seemed rather pleased by the reaction her outfit elicited. "And look what it can do!"

She snapped her fingers, and a shimmering red and gold aura enveloped her entire body. It appeared as if she were on fire. Donnie had to admit, it was a pretty impressive sight. Andrella snapped her fingers again and the aura around her disappeared.

Lloyd strode up to the 'fiery' young lady and lifted her into the air. "That was amazing!"

Andrella giggled as he spun her around. "I'm glad you think so."

Lloyd brought her down into his arms and they fell into a rather passionate kiss.

Donnie exchanged a surprised glance with Glo. The shy young man had come a long way since they first met him.

A wistful feeling came over the bemused elf. An image of Miranda passed through his mind's eye, yet it was quickly overlaid with a picture of Ruka. Donnie shook the vision from his brain. *I can't be thinking that way—she's way too young for me.*

Lloyd and Andrella finally pulled apart, the young lady looking past Donnie at the chest full of gold and jewels. She walked over and knelt in front of it, running her hands through the pile of coins. "Well, this will go directly into the Vermoorden treasury."

"All of it?" Donnie gave her one of his most innocent smiles.

Andrella laughed aloud—it was a warm, vibrant sound in the dark room. "Well, I'm sure the good people of Vermoorden would want to compensate you for getting rid of that nasty guild."

They closed the chest and headed back to the Mayor's bedroom. Aksel and Kara stopped in the doorway, each giving one last baleful look at the statue of the dark god. Back in DeWyness' room, Glo sat on the bed leafing through her journal. As they crossed the threshold, the tall elf let out a low whistle. "You have to hear this—it's from the last page."

The retrieval went without a hitch. We now have the Thrall Master's gift. It will be used as planned during the next full moon.

Andrella gasped, grasping tightly onto Lloyd's arm. The young man's face had gone dark, but Aksel's went pale. The little gnome rushed to Glo's side and buried his head into the journal.

Donnie glanced around at the others. "Thrall Master? Did I miss something?"

"Most likely the undead Thrall Master," Aksel said absently as he pored over the journal with Glo.

"We fought a group of vampires in Ravenford," Lloyd explained as he comforted Andrella. "It turns out the Abbot was involved with their leader. He's the one that had the Baron assassinated."

Donnie's eyes lit up with satisfaction. "So I was right! It was the Abbot Qualtan the entire time."

Glo gave him a curt nod. "Indeed. We also found a letter between Qualtan and the master vampire. It stated the heart had been delivered to 'our friend DW.' It even mentioned the full moon."

Aksel looked up from the journal. "The Baron's soul is trapped in his heart. It was to be used in a dark ritual—the creation of a soul gem and the summoning of a demon thereafter."

The mention of demons caused Donnie and Kara to exchange a knowing glance. With all that had gone on this night, they hadn't had the chance to bring up the tower full of demons.

A strained smile spread across the elf's lips. "Funny you should mention that. Once we get this all sorted out, Kara and I have a story to tell you which may be related to all this."

Glolindir and the others had spent the night in Vermoorden Keep. Their discovery of the statue of Amon was more than enough to prove the Mayor's duplicity. Further, their efforts to keep everyone safe had won over both the Captain and the staff.

It was late the next morning when a fully recovered Glo joined everyone in the dining hall. The tall elf was starving after the previous night's ordeal, thus the meal he found waiting for them was a welcome surprise.

A grateful cook had prepared them a combination breakfast and lunch. There were eggs and ham, biscuits, orange juice, pancakes, waffles, sausages, assorted sandwiches, a leafy green salad with a few types of dressing, ale, fresh water, fruits, apple pie, and peach cobbler. Rota and Torvil served them the delightful repast, then left the companions to talk amongst themselves.

Lloyd was the first to speak, in between mouthfuls of pancakes, of course. "So now that we have the Baron's heart, we need to put it back in his body."

Aksel pointed a fork with a sausage on the end at the young warrior. "That may not be all that easy. Remember, we're wanted criminals as far as Dunwynn is concerned."

"Those Dunnies can kiss Seth's fannie," Kalyn drawled as she attacked a grapefruit.

Donnie coughed at the other end of the table. "You do realize that Andrella is sort of a Dunnie herself."

Seth stuffed a forkful of bacon into his mouth, totally ignoring the flippant comments.

Kalyn suddenly looked up at Andrella. "No offense intended, yer Duchess-ta-be."

Andrella threw down her fork and knife. She stared at Kalyn, a muscle twitching in her face. "No, I agree with you. My Uncle can make all the accusations he wants. I'll just take the heart to Ravenford myself."

"And be immediately whisked away to Dunwynn," Lloyd added.

Andrella pushed her chair back and placed her hands on her hips. "They wouldn't dare!"

Kalyn swallowed a thick piece of ham. "Sure ya want to take that chance? If it was me, I'd wanna make sure my daddy was all put back in one piece."

Andrella simmered for a moment as she considered the young Deepwooder's words. "Well then, if we can't go in like normal people, then how about we go by force?" She turned to Lloyd. "You'll back me?"

Lloyd dropped his fork and knife and spun in his seat to face the livid young lady. "I will, but are you sure? I mean, you know I'm no Dunwynn lover, but Fafnar didn't turn out to be so bad." He reached forward and took her hands in his. "And sooner or later, these folks are going to be your people. Do you really want to slaughter a group of them, especially when they're just following orders?"

Glo raised an eyebrow at the young man's appraisal of the situation. *When had Lloyd become so astute?* He exchanged a glance with Elladan and Aksel. The former nodded his head in approval while the latter sat there in wonderment.

Andrella's grim countenance faded into an embarrassed smile. She threw her arms around Lloyd and hugged him. "You're the best." The young lady swept her eyes around the table. "So, does anyone else have any suggestions?"

Elladan cast his gaze at Glo. "Do you still think teleporting is a bad idea?"

"Oh, I know it is," Donnie answered before Glo could speak. All eyes turned to the slender elf.

Elladan leaned forward in his seat. "And why's that?"

Glo was a curious as Elladan. "Does it have to do with your disappearance, by any chance?"

"It does."

Aksel put down his utensils and stared shrewdly at Donnie. "Last night, when I mentioned the soul gem ritual, you said you had a story to tell us. Is this part of it?"

"It is." Donnie had everyone's full attention as he explained what happened after he disappeared.

Glo listened to every detail as the story unfolded. It sounded as if the demons had set up some sort of prison. The question was, to what end?

Donnie went on uninterrupted until he mentioned the bronze dragon.

Lloyd's eyes went wide. "You think it was the girls' father?"

Donnie hesitated, so Glo decided to step in for him. "It would only make sense. It seems as if they're somehow catching folks who can teleport. How many bronze dragons do you know who can do that?"

"Probably as many as you," Seth interjected with a twist of his lips.

Glo cast an acid look at the halfling. Still, he wasn't wrong. They only knew three bronze dragons—the Greymantle sisters.

Donnie continued with his story, finally finishing with their daring escape. When he was done, Seth turned a suspicious eye toward Kara.

"So, who are you again—and how do you know so much about demons?"

"Seth!" Donnie eyed the halfling with clear embarrassment.

Kara held up a palm toward the mortified elf. "It's fine, Donnie. He has a right to ask." She threw back her shoulders as she turned to face Seth. "I am Karathalla Brightwing of the Order of Thul Dunin. I came to this land from the Kingdom of Isandor to investigate the recent disappearances of mages."

"Sounds familiar," Elladan said with a half-smile.

Kara swept her gaze around the table. "The wizards of our order detected disturbances in the astral plane. They determined that there were traps set in that plane to reroute teleporters to another location."

Something clicked in Glo's mind. It finally all made sense. "Of course—that's how teleportation works."

Elladan looked at him with clear amusement. "Care to explain that for us laymen?"

Glo let out a short laugh. "Sorry. Distance has no meaning in the astral plane. So, when you teleport"—he held up one hand—"you're actually traveling through that plane to your destination"—he held up his other hand—"only to reach it moments later."

"Hmm." Aksel absently stroked his chin, then swung his gaze back to Kara. "So, these traps are catching teleporters and routing them to this Demon Tower?"

The tall warrior nodded. "Yes. Our wizards believed they were being shunted to somewhere in the western isles, although they weren't able to pinpoint the exact destination. A few of us were dispatched to each island. I was 'lucky' enough to draw eastern Thac."

Glo murmured to himself as he mulled over what she had just told them. "Traps in the Astral Plane? It's actually quite clever, if you think about it."

"Devilishly clever," Donnie quipped.

The entire table broke out in moans and groans.

"When I arrived here, I tracked them down to the mountains you call the Korlokesels," Kara continued. "I actually drew within sight of the tower when I got caught in one of their traps." She turned a grateful eye toward Donatello. "Thankfully, Donnie freed me before the demons could do anything more."

Elladan's eyes narrowed as he glanced between Donnie and Kara. "So, where exactly is this tower?"

Donnie shrugged. "Somewhere north and west of where the Darkwoods Monolith stood."

Elladan held his hand up with his thumb and forefinger about an inch apart. "Could you be just a bit more specific?"

Donnie threw up his hands. "I didn't exactly have time to draw a map."

Kara stood up and placed her hands on the table with a *thump*. "I could lead you there. All I need is a few true-hearted warriors and I'm sure we can take down this demonic den."

Silence fell across the table as everyone exchanged glances. Seth was the one to finally break it. He sat back in his chair, his arms folded across his chest.

"So, let me get this straight. Here you are, this great warrior of the Thul Dunin. You track these demons to Thac, to the very mountains where they are hiding. You know they're using traps in the astral plane, but even with that information, you still get caught?"

No one spoke as Kara drew herself up to her full height and eyed the halfling darkly. "Yes."

A satisfied smile crossed Seth's lips. "Well then, I'm just pointing out that you're going to need more than just a few 'true-hearted' warriors."

"Gee, Seth, does that mean you're volunteering?" Donnie asked glibly.

Seth fixed the slight elf with a scathing stare.

Aksel cleared his throat before anyone else could speak. "Okay then, this is obviously an important new development." He swung his gaze toward Kara. "I think it's safe to say you can count on us to help against these demons"—his declaration was met with murmurs of agreement around the table—"but first things first."

The de facto leader of the companions swept his gaze around the dining hall. "I traded messages with Shalla this morning. It seems they moved the Baron's body out of the temple and placed it in the family crypt."

Andrella let out an anxious gasp. "Why would they do that?"

Lloyd placed a comforting arm around the young lady's shoulders. "I take back what I said before. Dunwynn has no regard for human decency."

Aksel let out a short sigh. "I think you were right, Lloyd. They are just following orders." He turned his gaze toward Andrella. "The good news is the body is still under a preservation spell."

Andrella visibly steeled herself. "How long do we have?"

Aksel's eyes were filled with sympathy as he gazed at the distraught young lady. "No more than a couple of days at best."

Lloyd slammed his fist on the table. "Then we need to move now!"

"You can count on my help." Kara declared.

Andrella gave the tall woman a strained smile. "Thank you."

Aksel motioned everyone to draw in closer, as he dropped his voice down low. "Okay, there are patrols all over Ravenford, so Shalla offered to meet us on the river northwest of town."

Lloyd was still quite anxious. "I still say we need to leave immediately. It's a two-day ride to Ravenford at best."

"Not necessarily," Glo interjected. All eyes turned to the wizard.

"I learned how to make those spectral horses Sigfus conjured back in the Darkwoods. They are quite fast, and can get us to Ravenford in about eight hours."

Lloyd practically beamed at the news. "Thanks, Glo!" He spun toward Andrella. "Did you hear that?"

The tension visibly faded from Andrella's shoulders. She gave Glo a warm smile. "Yes. Thank you, Glolindir."

"Let's leave after noon," Seth proposed. "That will get us there by dusk. It'll be easier to move around after dark."

Andrella dipped her chin toward the halfling. "That will work perfectly. Captain Ascue confided to me that he knows nothing about running a town. He is holding a town meeting at noontime and asked me to speak."

"Then that settles it," Aksel declared. "We leave later today, right after the town meeting."

32
INTO THE CRYPT

Y—you don't think he turned into a vampire, do you?

A thick canopy of grey clouds hung over the little town of Ravenford. The air felt heavy as the blanket of night slowly encroached on the surrounding countryside. Between the dampness and impending nightfall, the air was colder than it should have been at this time of year.

Andrella huddled next to Lloyd in a thicket northwest of town, not too far from the riverside. The young lady was sorely tempted to light up her dress for warmth, but they were trying to keep a low profile.

As Seth had estimated, they drew in sight of her hometown as the first signs of dusk appeared on the horizon. They had barely dismounted the spectral steeds Glo conjured for them when Martan spotted a patrol of Dunwynn sky knights winging their way inland. The companions immediately ducked into the nearby trees and had been waiting there since.

"How are you doing?" Lloyd whispered in her ear.

Andrella peered at the handsome young man hovering protectively next to her. Even in the dimming light, she could see the concern in his eyes.

"I'm fine," she answered in a soft voice.

The truth is, she was far from fine. Her father was dead, and her mother shipped off to Dunwynn. True, they had finally recovered her father's heart, but she couldn't even set foot in her own hometown without the risk of being whisked away. Worse, they had moved her father's body to the family crypt. It was as if her uncle was trying to drive the last nail into her father's coffin.

"Sure, you are," Lloyd said as he moved closer and wrapped his strong arms around her waist.

Andrella sighed and leaned her head on his chest. He had been her rock in lieu of her father. She appreciated that, but she wasn't about to let him dictate what she could, and couldn't, do. Lloyd hadn't wanted her to come on this trip. He thought it might be too much for her, but Andrella had put her foot down.

"I'll be damned if you're going to rescue my father without me," she had told him in no uncertain terms.

Even after setting him straight, Ascue had nearly wrecked her plans. The townsfolk of Vermoorden had reacted so favorably to her that Ascue asked her then and there to fill in as temporary mayor. It was an honor that Andrella couldn't refuse, but it would have prohibited her from going on this mission. Luckily, she had been able to maneuver her way around that.

Andrella agreed to Ascue's proposal on one condition—that Elladan be made her temporary magistrate. So, when Lloyd asked her who was going to watch over Vermoorden, Andrella answered, *"Why, my magistrate, of course."*

Elladan had laughed at her clever ploy. *"You certainly learn fast."*

Donnie's sudden whisper roused Andrella from her musings. "There's a barge headed this way."

Seth put up a hand. "I'll go check it out." He grabbed his cloak and disappeared into thin air.

They all watched anxiously as the small craft drifted toward this side of the river. Night had just about settled in when the barge anchored itself offshore. A lone figure jumped out and waded onto dry land. Less than a minute passed when a smaller figure appeared next to it. A few moments later, the two figures headed directly toward their hiding spot.

Andrella smelled Shalla's delightful lavender scent before the bardess even spoke. Her eyes misted over as she threw herself into the older woman's arms. "Shalla, I'm so glad to see you."

Shalla seemed taken aback at first, but swiftly recovered, wrapping her arms around the young lady. "I'm glad to see you too, hon." She put her lips up against Andrella's ear. "How are you holding up?"

Andrella brushed back the tears. "I'm… fine"—she forced herself to smile—"and we got daddy's heart!"

"So I heard," Shalla murmured as she pushed back a long strand of hair. Everyone had gathered around to greet the tall bardess. Shalla's eyes flickered around the grove. "Where's Elladan?"

"Oh, I left him to run Vermoorden," Andrella said with a nonchalant wave.

Shalla grew silent. "Are you sure that's wise?"

"Wise is not the word I'd use," Donnie answered wryly.

Andrella giggled. "Trust me, he couldn't make things any worse than they already are." Her gaze fell on the lights that had started to spring up in nearby Ravenford. The smile faded from her lips. "How are things in town?"

"Not good." Shalla shook her head. The bardess painted a grim picture of the state of affairs in Ravenford. Heavy taxes had been levied on the townsfolk. A curfew had been imposed, as well—no one was allowed out after dark. Any stragglers were thrown in the dungeon.

Andrella could feel the heat rising up the back of her neck. "How dare they! Once my father is back, we'll put an end to this travesty."

She felt a pair of strong hands grip her shoulders. Lloyd stood behind her, wearing a grim smile.

"You can count on it."

"So… what about these patrols?" Seth stood a bit back from the others, his arms folded across his chest.

The halfling's question was like a splash of cold water on Andrella's face. He was right. This was no time to lose her temper. They needed to concentrate on the matter at hand. The young lady took a deep breath and let it out as Shalla filled them in on the details.

"There are regular patrols from dusk to dawn—five patrols consisting of five guards each. The rest of the Dunwynn forces stay up at the keep. There are seven heavily-armored ruby knights, five casters, three squads of sky knights, and about a dozen foot soldiers that patrol the walls."

The bardess pulled out a parchment and laid it on the ground. "I brought a map, if you can give us a little light."

"Certainly." Glo bent next to Shalla and spoke a soft word. A small light sprang from a tiny stone in the wizard's hand. Glo held it over the parchment, revealing a fairly detailed map of Ravenford.

"The crypt is up here behind the temple." Shalla pointed. "We'll be pulling in down here by the docks"—she moved her finger to a spot next to the river—"and sneak across the road to this building." Shalla's finger had come to rest on the bait shop.

"Hmm," Andrella murmured. Her forehead crinkled as she knelt next to Shalla. "You'll have to cross the south road. There's not much cover that way—the fish shop, a clump of trees, and maybe the abbey." She traced each out on the map as she listed them off.

Seth snorted. "Heh, won't be a problem for me."

"Me either." Donnie nodded.

"Should be 'nough cover for us—right, Martan?" Kalyn punched the glum archer solidly in the arm.

Martan flinched from the blow. "Um… right."

Kalyn still hadn't forgiven Martan for what had happened with the fake Ves. Andrella couldn't exactly blame her. If Lloyd had embarrassed her like that, she'd have dropped him like a sack of potatoes.

The young Penwick noble knelt quietly next to her, his concentration completely focused on the map. A thin smile crossed her lips as she eyed the creases in his handsome brow. *He's so genuine and caring. I really lucked out with this one.*

Lloyd looked up, his eyes darting between all of them. "What if we use the Boulder for a distraction?"

Seth's lips twisted to one side. "I thought you weren't looking for a fight?"

"It doesn't have to fight back. It could just stand there and scare them like it did with Fafnar's men."

Shalla let out a long sigh, her face taking on a pained expression. "I'm afraid that won't work. The Boulder is gone."

Seth fixed the bardess with a hard stare. "What do you mean, gone?"

Shalla grimaced, her eyelids clamping shut. "I'm not sure how, but they found it in the vault under Haltan's. They sent those iron golems in and pounded it to rubble."

Seth's face screwed up into an angry ball. "Okay, rethinking this strategy about not killing anyone."

"They all just signed their death warrants," Kalyn muttered hotly.

Aksel placed a comforting hand on his friend's shoulder. "Let it go, Seth. There's nothing we can do about it at this point."

Shalla held out a plain gold ring toward the halfling. "I thought you might want this."

Andrella recognized it as the Boulder's ring.

For the first time since she had met him, she noted moisture in Seth's eyes. He reached out and took the ring from Shalla's hand with a quiet, "Thank you."

So, he does have a heart. Andrella felt momentarily sad for Seth, but then drew up her shoulders and steeled herself. She swept her eyes around the gathering and rubbed her hands together. "Okay. So how do we go about this?"

An invisible Seth stole silently across the road and up the hillside that led to the temple. Shalla had transported him, Donnie, Kalyn, Martan, and Aksel back to town on the barge that she had borrowed. The five of them hid under a deep cache of fish in the main cargo hold. It was slimy, and the smell was less than pleasant, but Seth had been in worse situations.

It was just as well—a patrol had stopped them at the docks and questioned Shalla. They threatened to throw her in the dungeon for breaking curfew, but the bardess feigned helplessness.

"I'm sorry, boys, but my fishin' lines got all tangled up. These little ole' arms weren't built for hard work like y'all. My, you do look like quite the strong ones."

Personally, Seth wouldn't have bought it for a minute, but Shalla managed to charm her way past them with a mere warning.

Thankfully the others had stayed behind. Andrella hadn't been happy about waiting outside of town, but she finally gave in. It probably helped that Glo set up a mind link so they could stay in contact.

Seth's eyes darted around as he crept up the hill toward the temple. It was pitch black, the rising moon hidden behind a thick veil of clouds. The temple itself was dark. There were lights on in the abbey, but no movement around the outside. The last patrol had marched by a few minutes ago. There wouldn't be another for at least a few more.

There was no sign of Aksel. Like Seth, the gnome had made himself invisible. He had also cast that spell that allowed him to walk in mid-air. The combination made him pretty much undetectable.

Seth glanced back down the hill. He could faintly make out Donnie, Kalyn, and Martan creeping through the grass toward a thicket of nearby trees. None made a sound as they moved.

Not bad, Seth admitted grudgingly. He had not wanted to bring so many with them into town, but unlike the others, these three at least knew the meaning of the word stealth.

Seth slowly made his way to the hilltop and around the side of the temple. He'd just rounded the corner when he pulled up short. Two guards in powder-blue Dunwynn uniforms stood in front of the stone structure behind the temple. They didn't seem very alert, but they were there nonetheless.

Guys, why are there guards in front of the crypt?

Shalla seemed puzzled. *Guards at the crypt? There are never guards at the crypt.*

It's almost like they're expecting us, Donnie theorized.

Or at least expecting some kind of rescue attempt, Glo clarified.

Seth had heard enough chit-chat for now. *That's nice. Just meet me around back.*

As you wish, came Donnie's dry response.

Seth stole past the guards and around the side of the crypt. He rounded the corner and pulled up short once again as a loud grinding noise emanated from the back of the tomb. Seth watched in awe as a hole appeared in the solid stone and begrudgingly stretched apart.

Aksel, is that you?

No, it's a ghost.

It seemed Seth was not the only one surprised by the sound. The guards around front seemed spooked by the loud noise.

"W—what was that?"

"I—I don't know."

"You don't suppose something is moving around in there?"

"I heard rumors there were zombies and vampires in this town. They say they had to clear them out of the catacombs when we first got here."

"They just put the Baron's body in there yesterday. Y—you don't think he turned into a vampire, do you?"

Seth couldn't help chuckling as he entered the crypt.

While the guards fretted out front, Donnie slipped into the tomb with the others. The inside was not very large. It consisted of a single room with three stone coffins lined up in the center. There were a few unlit torches against the walls. Kalyn and Martan lit them while Donnie went over and examined the coffins.

The outer ones had no markings, but there was a fresh engraving on the one in the middle. It simply read *Gryswold Avernos.*

There was no way to remove the stone lid without making a lot of noise, but the guards' reactions had given Donnie an idea. He motioned Kalyn and Martan over and whispered a quick plan to them. The thin elf then pulled out a pair of knives and stole over to the front door.

When Donnie nodded, Kalyn and Martan pushed the heavy stone lid off Gryswold's coffin. It landed with a resounding crash.

The guards' muffled voices filtered through the thick stone door.

"Th—that sounds like the lid of a coffin!"

"Y—yeah."

The devious elf waited a moment, then raked his knives across the stone door. He added a soft moan, which slowly rose to a wailing pitch. A pair of frightened screams sounded from the other side of the door, followed by complete silence.

Seth and Kalyn rolled with laughter as Donnie joined them at Gryswold's coffin. Inside, the Baron still looked remarkably well-preserved.

"The preservation spell is probably just at its end," Aksel noted in a clinical manner. "Now to get him out of town."

They had already come up with a plan on the barge. While Aksel cast a spell on Gryswold's body, Donnie slipped on the ring that let him breathe underwater. Martan and Kalyn easily lifted Gryswold's body out of the coffin and handed it over to Donnie.

Donnie marveled at how little it weighed. "He's as light as a feather."

Seth eyed him dubiously.

"Okay, maybe not that light."

"Just one more spell," Aksel said as he weaved his hands in a careful pattern. The magic released with a single word and flowed over Donnie. "*Invisibilitate.*"

Donnie glanced down at himself—for all intents and purposes, he had disappeared. He still felt Gryswold's body in his arms, but it had vanished as well. "Alright then—see you all outside of town."

Donnie exited through the back of the tomb and headed down-hill toward the river. A group of soldiers in Dunwynn uniforms were gathered on the road that paralleled the riverside. Two in particular waved frantically to the others and pointed up toward the crypt.

Aksel, I think you're about to have company, Donnie thought blithely. *We're ready for them.*

Glo, Lloyd, Andrella, and Kara waited in a thicket a short distance upriver from Ravenford. It had taken quite a bit of convincing to get the young lady to stay behind. Still, she had been extremely impatient since the others left. Every two minutes, she would ask Glo, "Anything yet?"

Glo breathed a sigh of relief when Aksel relayed the good news. Andrella was immediately on top of him. "What is it?"

"They have your father. Donnie's heading back with him right now."

Andrella's eyes immediately misted over. She threw her arms around Glo and nearly squeezed the life out of him. "Oh, thank you! Thank you."

Glo gently massaged his neck as she let go and threw her arms around Lloyd instead.

"We found him! We found him!" Andrella sobbed with joy.

Lloyd mouthed the word *sorry* to Glo as he held the emotional young lady tight.

Kara's face softened as she watched the touching display. As soon as she realized Glo was watching, though, her expression returned to its normally stoic appearance. "What's happening now?"

Glo fought back the urge to smile. The tall warrior wasn't nearly as hard-hearted as she pretended to be. "Donnie will be here soon. Aksel's going to create a diversion to cover their escape."

"Shouldn't your friend Shalla come with us as well? She'll be in trouble if they find out she helped you."

"That's a fair point." Glo relayed Kara's concerns to Shalla.

Shalla was clearly touched. *Thanks, but I can't leave the others behind. We 'rebels' have to stick together.*

Glo had to admit, he admired her loyalty. He repeated her reply to the others.

Andrella's jaw tightened as she nervously fiddled with her hair. "They might all be thrown in the dungeon after this."

"Not if they can't catch them," Lloyd assured her. "Tell Shalla to have Gelpas, his men, and whoever else, move up to Stone Hill. They can lead any sort of resistance from there."

"That's a brilliant idea!" Andrella hugged Lloyd even tighter.

"Indeed." Glo eyed Lloyd with new found respect. He passed the idea on to Shalla, who agreed it would be a shrewd move.

A few minutes later, there was a loud *kaboom* from the direction of town. From their vantage point, Glo could see flames atop the hill where the temple stood. Shouts drifted through the night, reaching their ears even from this distance.

It wasn't long before the sky knights took to the air. Over a dozen of them lifted off from the keep, sweeping over the burning hill and out into the countryside in all directions.

At just about the same time, Glo spotted a few figures dashing through the trees toward the thicket where they hid. Aksel, Kalyn, and Martan burst into their hiding place, the trio breathing heavy from exertion.

Lloyd glanced all around the grove. "Did Seth come with you?"

"Right here." The halfling appeared out of thin air next to Aksel.

"Where's… Donnie?" Aksel asked in between breaths.

"Over here," Donnie's voice whispered from behind them.

They all whirled around to see a wet Donatello holding the Baron's body in his arms.

Andrella had tried to be patient as she waited for the others to retrieve her father's body. Still, it didn't feel right. It was her father and thus her responsibility to bring him back to life. Yet she couldn't deny the sense of letting the 'stealthy' folk sneak into town. In the end, Andrella capitulated. She reasoned that this was what her mother called delegating.

Yet now that she saw her father, she could no longer hold back the tears. Andrella ran to him as Donatello laid his body gently on the ground. She grabbed her father's cold hand and wept profusely. "Oh, daddy. What have they done to you?"

A pair of strong hands grasped her shoulders. She knew it was Lloyd trying to console her, but still couldn't stop herself from crying.

"There are lights in the forest headed this way," Martan whispered harshly.

"Not to mention those sky knights are getting awful close." Seth added to the general sense of foreboding.

Aksel knelt next to Andrella, his voice filled with compassion. "I can't imagine how you must feel, but I think it's best we hide for now."

Andrella knew the little cleric was right, but something inside her railed at the thought. "No! Resurrect my father. Resurrect him now." That had come out harsher than she intended, but at the moment she didn't care.

She could hear the pain in Aksel's soft response. "I really wish we could, but it's not that simple."

"I don't care. Resurrect him." She knew she was acting like a spoiled child, but right now nothing else seemed to matter.

Everyone around her went silent. Lloyd gently squeezed her shoulders, but said nothing.

A moment later Kalyn knelt next to her. She took Andrella by the hand, her voice choked with pain. "Andrella… I know it's hard… losin' someone… but if we don't hide now… yer just gonna lose him again anyway…"

Kalyn's tearful plea wrenched at Andrella's heart. She silently wondered whose loss had affected the young woman so deeply. Her anger gone, Andrella threw her arms around Kalyn and drew her close.

"Yes, you're right. I'm so sorry." She gazed at Aksel and then up at Lloyd. "Sorry. Sorry."

Behind her she saw Glo casting a spell. The magic coalesced in a blue aura around the coils of a rope upon the ground. The rope shot straight upward as if it were alive, the end hanging a few feet off the ground when it was done. The top of the rope disappeared into the trees above.

Andrella had heard of the spell. It was called *Rope to Nowhere*. It created an extraplanar pocket large enough to fit all of them.

Lloyd gently lifted her father off the ground. "Don't worry, I've got him. You go first."

An overwhelming sense of affection washed over her as she gazed at the tall young man. He really understood her.

Andrella wiped away the remainder of her tears and began to climb. When she was halfway up, she chanced a brief glance over her shoulder. Lloyd was right behind her, with her father's body as promised.

When they reached the top, Lloyd laid her father's body gently down on the fluffy-white floor. He and Andrella sat nearby where she snuggled comfortably into Lloyd's strong arms.

The young lady hadn't realized just how drained she was. She quickly drifted off to sleep with a silent promise to her father. *Soon, Daddy. Very soon.*

33
RESURRECTION

Elladan Narmolanya's mood was somber. With the others gone, he had taken it upon himself to kick off renovation efforts in Vermoorden. Apart from the keep, the entire town showed signs of age, as did the ships that supported its mediocre economy. Further, the town's only tourist attraction, the *Theater of the Festive Spirits*, remained closed.

Thus, the acting magistrate delved into the "town treasury." He doled out funds for both housing and ship repairs. He also made a sizeable "donation" to the town temple, to have both Rhith and Newin revived. Unfortunately, neither resurrection went as hoped.

During the first ritual, Rhith's body had been taken over by a demon. The subsequent exorcism failed, and the clerics were forced to destroy Rhith's vessel. The second ritual also failed—Newin's soul refused to return to the living. Though deeply saddened, Balmaroh took solace in the fact that she had chosen to stay in the afterlife with her life-long companion.

Despite the tragic losses, Elladan's efforts yielded an unexpected bonus. During his search through the former Mayor's chest, he discovered a pretty silver bracelet with four charms along its delicate length. Elladan immediately recognized it for what it was. With all that had befallen the Baron's family since his demise, the trinket might help rectify one rather serious misfortune.

"Do you think their mission was successful?"

Ascue's query roused Elladan from his pensive thoughts. The companions had been spotted on the road north of town only a short while ago. Elladan and Ascue now waited just outside the keep for their return.

The acting magistrate fixed the Captain with a half-smile. "I think we'll know soon enough."

Ascue raised a single brow, but said nothing more. No one had told him exactly why the companions had gone to Ravenford. They figured the less he knew beforehand, the better.

As if on cue, a group of riders emerged from the forest, just north of the keep. All sat on strange translucent steeds that moved without the beat of a hoof. Elladan watched the surreal sight as the riders sped down the road. All continued past the keep, except for three who broke off from the rest.

That small group turned up the hill towards Elladan and Ascue. It was Glo, Donnie, and Kara. All three looked haggard as they drew up on their spectral mounts.

"So?" Elladan said simply.

Donnie gave him a pearly, if tired, smile. "We got him."

Ascue cast a tentative glance at the fatigued elf. "Excuse me, but who is it that you got?"

Donnie's smile spread into a cheeky grin. "Why, the Baron of course. Why else would we ride so hard to Ravenford and back again?"

Ascue narrowed an eye as he swept his gaze around the gathering. "I thought the Baron of Ravenford was dead?"

Glolindir gave him a curt nod. "He still is. The others are bringing his body over to the temple as we speak."

Elladan exchanged a pained look with Ascue. "That might not go quite as you expect."

Glo arched an eyebrow at them as he sat forward in his saddle. "Why's that?"

Instead of immediately answering, Elladan first hoisted himself up behind Glo. "No time to waste. I'll tell you on the way."

Aksel Alabaster felt way out of his element. The Temple of Vermoorden was like no other, its architecture wild and unruly. A wide-open space, there were no seats anywhere in the sanctuary. Pillars sprang up in uneven places, some standing at odd angles. Sunlight filtered down through a large, round window at the apex of the vaulted ceiling.

A wide marble altar was the only familiar sight, but that bore the symbol of the Mad God—a winding, knotted strip with neither beginning nor end.

Like the temple itself, the magics here felt wild in nature, ebbing and flowing with no particular rhythm. Still, the power in this temple was undeniable.

Yet the unruly nature of this place was the least of Aksel's worries. Upon their arrival, the temple curate had shared with them the sad news about Rhith and Newin. Furthermore, the ordeal had drained the head cleric, and he was now indisposed.

The news had caught them all by surprise, but none as badly as the Lady Andrella. She stood with her hands on her hips as she fixed Aksel with an accusing stare. "It was your idea to bring my father here. So, now what do we do?"

Lloyd grabbed her gently by the shoulders and spun her toward him. His expression was filled with sympathy. "Andrella, Aksel had no way of knowing. Plus, what we just learned about Rhith and Newin confirms how risky resurrections can be."

The young lady hung her head as she softened in his arms. "I know, I know. It's best performed in a holy place." She cast a furtive glance at Aksel. "Sorry."

Aksel gave her a silent nod. His heart ached for the young woman. He knew first-hand how hard it was to lose a loved one. Aksel glanced at Gryswold's body, now laid out on the altar. His expert eye noted the first signs of decay—the preservation spell Qualtan had cast two weeks ago was finally wearing off.

Something wrenched deep inside the little cleric. *I have to do something.*

Aksel turned to the curate. "Can you prepare the body for the ritual?"

The curate appraised him for a few moments, then nodded. "I will see to it."

Seth looked at him questioningly. "What are you going to do?"

"Pray for a miracle," Aksel responded as he brushed by his friend.

Vestibules lined the walls of the temple, each dedicated to an individual god of the Ralnain pantheon. On their first visit to Vermoorden, Aksel had set up one with an offering to his god, the Soldenar. The little cleric now went to that vestibule and knelt in front of it.

Aksel knew the mechanics of the resurrection rite. He had watched it performed a number of times, by the clerics at his home temple in Caprizon. He had even practiced it as part of his training, but he had never actually performed it. Few had. Still, at this point there was little choice. If he did not try, Gryswold would be gone forever.

Aksel stilled his mind and concentrated his thoughts in prayer. *Soldenar, Goddess of all Gnomes, I beseech you. Grant me the ability to resurrect the dead.*

The lilting voice of his goddess was tentative as it reverberated through his mind. *Now that 'tis a tall order ya ask, lad. I trust yer aware of the risks involved, as well as the toll on yerself.*

I am. Aksel's response was immediate.

There was a momentary pause. *I see yer firm in yer convictions, laddie. Very well, then answer me this simple query:*

> *What be greater than the gods,*
> *more evil than demons,*
> *the poor have it,*
> *the rich need it,*
> *and if ya eat it,*
> *ya will surely die?*

Aksel winced. It was the same riddle she had asked him once before, when Ruka's life was on the line. Now another life was on the line, and Aksel had no more of a clue to the true answer than back then.

The little cleric wracked his brain, but nothing would come. Yet he had to get it right this time, or everything they had strived for in these last couple of months would come to naught. They would lose another friend, a man who had always treated them with respect. One who had given them a chance when others would not. A man who had been a force for good, a hero in his own right.

No! Aksel's hands clenched together, his body shaking to its very core. *No! I won't give up this time. Nothing should stand in the way of what is right. Nothing!*

Eh, what's that, laddie? The Soldenar's voice echoed through his mind.

Aksel felt as if a bucket of cold ice had been poured on him. He suddenly felt foolish at letting his temper get so far out of control.

Was it nothin' ya said? The Soldenar repeated.

Nothing? Aksel rolled the word around in his mind. Nothing was greater than the gods, nor more evil than demons. The poor had nothing and the rich needed nothing… and if you ate nothing you would die.

That's it! Aksel's brow rose as the realization sunk in.

Nothing. He repeated somberly.

Indeed, nothin' is the answer, the Soldenar confirmed. *Well done, my lad. Ya've earned the right ta the power ya asked for. I just hope yer as prepared as ya think.*

The air around Aksel suddenly grew warm. A tingling sensation started at the base of his spine and spread all over his body. It slowly grew in strength till his entire being vibrated with it. Aksel grabbed onto the walls of the vestibule, feeling the magic course through him as if his veins were on fire.

Sweat formed on his brow and dripped down over his closed eyes. His breath came in short, ragged bursts.

Finally, when it felt like he could take no more, the pulsations ceased. Aksel's arms dropped to his sides. Though the shaking had subsided, he still felt as if the power he now held inside would burst him at the seams.

Aksel took a deep breath to settle his nerves. *Thank you, Soldenar, Goddess of all Gnomes.*

Go now, lad, and do what needs ta be done.

Aksel slowly stood, the warning his goddess had spoken still echoing through his mind. *I just hope yer as prepared as ya think.*

Lloyd Stealle had a strong bond with his family. Despite their many external obligations and your typical sibling rivalry, the Stealles were a close-knit bunch. Thus, the young man was astonished at the depth of his feelings for the Lady Andrella.

Lloyd found it uncanny how close they had grown in such a short time. True, they had similar beliefs, but it was much more than that. There was an undeniable connection between them. When she was happy, he was happy. When she hurt, he hurt.

Now more than ever, Lloyd could feel her pain. Andrella had done her best to keep a lid on her emotions. It had been hard seeing her father's lifeless body. It had been even harder to accept that they couldn't resurrect him then and there. Yet the young lady's anguish had cut him like a knife when they arrived back in Vermoorden.

They had hoped to revive her father at the temple, a place where the magics were strong and positive, yet the high priest was in no condition to help them after what happened with Rhith and Newin. All appeared lost until Aksel implored his goddess for a miracle. Beyond all hope, she had granted him the power to perform the ritual.

"What are they doing?" Andrella whispered.

Lloyd held the young lady gently in his arms as Aksel, the curate, and a few acolytes gathered around the altar. "They have to heal the body first before recalling the spirit."

"Oh."

Andrella's tone was calm, but she fidgeted nervously in his arms. The young man knew how she felt.

When Lloyd was very young, his sister had died. He had sat through her resurrection with the rest of his family—a long, draining process. Thankfully, in the end, his sister had been revived, but as evidenced today, that was not always the case.

The young man gazed around the sanctuary; all their friends were gathered there. Glo, Elladan, Donnie, and Kara sat off to one side, whispering amongst themselves. Martan hung toward the back of the room, wearing his typical glum expression. The usually talkative Kalyn gravitated near him and Andrella, but remained uncharacteristically silent.

Seth sat alone against a pillar behind Aksel, quietly sharpening his knives. Lloyd smiled despite himself. *Leave it to Seth to find the most irreverent thing to do in a temple.*

About an hour passed, but at the end of it, Gryswold's body was completely healed, his heart back where it belonged. With that done, the ritual started in earnest.

Aksel took out seven pea-sized diamonds and placed one at each chakra point along the body. He then stood at Gryswold's head while the curate and acolytes spread out in a circle around the altar.

"What are they doing now?" Andrella asked softly.

Lloyd bent his head down to her ear. "They're forming a spiritual shield around your father."

Her body tensed in his grasp. He pulled her closer and gently rubbed her shoulders. "Try to relax. This could take a while."

She sighed. "Okay."

Lloyd felt the magic build as the clerics wove the shield in place. It took almost an hour, but when they were done, he could see traces of energy coursing through the air between them.

Andrella lifted her head up and peered at him. "Are they done?"

Lloyd gazed at her dubiously until he realized that she couldn't see the spiritual energy. In fact, it was probably only visible to him because of his many years of spiritblade training. He whispered in her ear once more. "He's protected now, so they can begin the real ritual."

Andrella arched an eyebrow, but said nothing more. Still, he could feel the nervous energy flowing off her.

The next couple of hours did little to alleviate her tension. Aksel paced around the altar, humming as he made complex motions in the air and adjusted the diamonds at each chakra point. As time went on, Lloyd could feel the magic building around them. A vast amount of power was being drawn into that singular room.

Andrella leaned back in his arms. "Is it me, or is the air getting thick in here?"

"It's the magic for the spell. It's super concentrated," Lloyd explained in a hushed voice.

Andrella eyed him skeptically, but then nodded and went back to her vigil. The tension continued to mount with each passing moment. Andrella became so wound up that Lloyd thought she would burst at the seams. Just when he thought she couldn't take anymore, Aksel began the final motions.

"This is it," Lloyd whispered in her ear.

She pulled his arms closer around her, her grip so tight that her nails dug into his arms. Lloyd bit his tongue and endured the pain.

Aksel stood once again at Gryswold's head, strands of while light appearing out of thin air and swirling around him. It coalesced into a white aura as he weaved his arms in an intricate pattern. The air had grown so filled with power that the hair on their arms stood on end.

The little cleric thrust his arms up toward the heavens. Three words boomed from his throat and echoed across the chamber.

"*Et vivifica erimus!*"

The magic that had been building for the last few hours released in a rush of mana. It washed over them in a wave so strong that they were all buffeted as it hurtled outward.

Above them, the sun was suddenly obscured. Thick white clouds drew in from all directions. The misty veil began to swirl, coalescing into a circle. A brilliant glow appeared in its center. It grew more and more intense, until a column of blinding light shot down through the window in the ceiling, completely engulfing the altar.

Lloyd spun Andrella behind him, shielding her from the dazzling ray. The entire chamber disappeared in a brilliant flash of white. It lasted for a full half-minute, then finally began to fade.

Lloyd slowly opened his eyes. The room had returned to normal. Everyone faced away from the altar. As one, they turned back around.

The color had returned to Gryswold's cheeks. His chest gently rose and fell, his eyes still closed as if he were sleeping. Everyone held their breath as his eyes fluttered open.

"Daddy!" Andrella flew from Lloyd's arms. Gryswold barely sat up in time to catch her. She threw her arms around his stocky frame and buried her head in his broad chest. Huge sobs wracked her slim form as she held him in a tight embrace. "Oh Daddy! I thought… we'd never… see you again…"

Tears freely flowed from Lloyd's eyes as he tentatively moved to join them.

Gryswold gazed from his sobbing daughter toward the approaching young man. "Andrella? Lloyd?" His eyes widened as they swept around the sanctuary. "Where in blazes are we? And why is everyone standing around?"

Lloyd's lips curved into a sympathetic smile. "I'm afraid you were dead, sir."

Gryswold's brow knit into a deep frown. "Dead? The last thing I remember is… standing in my room." His eyes took on a glazed look. "I was by the bed, looking over some parchments… then I felt this sharp pain in my chest…" He placed his hand over his heart.

"It was an assassin from the guild here in Vermoorden," Glo said quietly.

Gryswold's eyes fixed on the tall elf. "Assassins' Guild?"

Glo gave him a curt nod. "It seems that your good friend Qualtan was jealous of you and Lady Gracelynn. It must have eaten away at him after all these years, and finally turned him down a dark path. In the end, he hired them to kill you."

Gryswold's brow rose as he gently patted Andrella's head. "Qualtan? I always knew he had feelings for Grace, but I would never have expected such treachery." He narrowed an eye at the tall wizard. "I trust you have proof?"

"Yes, Daddy." Andrella pulled herself up and dried her eyes. "We have Uncle Qualtan's letters."

Gryswold peered at his distraught daughter, his voice softening. "May I see them?"

"Ahem." Aksel cleared his throat. "Now may not be the best time, your lordship."

All eyes turned to the little cleric. He appeared absolutely exhausted. His face was pale, dark circles underlining his eyes.

Gryswold squinted at him. "Cleric Aksel? Do I have you to thank for my timely return?"

Aksel shrugged. "It was a combined effort." Everyone backpedaled as the little cleric weaved through them. "I'd like to examine you, if I may?"

Gryswold nodded. "Go right ahead." He switched his gaze to Andrella as Aksel ran his hands over him. "Speaking of your mother, where is she?"

Andrella let out a deep sigh. "It's a long story, father."

Lloyd gently grasped her shoulders. Andrella gave him a wan smile and drooped back into his arms. The last twenty-four hours had taken a toll on her. She was nearly as exhausted as Aksel.

Elladan must have noted her condition as well. "I can explain, your lordship."

Gryswold's face reddened. "Well, somebody better."

The bard went into a brief explanation of how Dunwynn had annexed Ravenford, sent Gracelynn away, and interred his body in the family crypt. By the time Elladan had finished, Gryswold's expression had turned dark.

"Kelvick has gone too far this time."

Aksel had just finished his examination. "Your body and soul have reintegrated nicely,"—he said as he took a step back—"but you might want to…"

Before he could finish, Gryswold swung his legs off the edge of the altar. The stocky man hoisted himself onto to the ground and teetered precariously on wobbly legs. Thankfully, Lloyd managed to catch him before he toppled over.

"…go easy on your body for the next couple of days," Aksel finished with an arched brow.

Gryswold's face reddened once more as he sat back down on the altar. "I can't just sit here. My people… Grace…"

Her father's near-collapse startled Andrella out of her exhaustion. She stepped in front of him, her hands on her hips. "I'll handle Uncle Kelvick, father. They're my people too, after all. And if I'm to be Duchess of Dunwynn one day, then it's high time I give my uncle a piece of my mind."

Lloyd had seen her fired up like this before. He did not envy Kelvick in the slightest.

The anger faded from Gryswold's face, replaced with an expression of pride. "I dare say it's time you did." His face clouded over again. "Still, I don't like Grace being in Dunwynn with him…"

"I think I might have something that will help with that," Elladan interjected. Andrella stepped aside as the bard pulled a pouch from his belt and offered it to the tired monarch.

Gryswold's eyes crinkled as he took the pouch and withdrew a simple charm bracelet. "This is… very nice, Elladan, but… what am I supposed to do with it?"

Glo leaned forward and squinted at the thin silver chain. "Is that what I think it is?"

Elladan nodded, a wide grin on his face.

A smile formed on Glo's lips in response. "Your lordship, picture your wife's image in your mind, then pull one of the charms off the bracelet and throw it on the ground."

Gryswold's features knit into a frown. "Seriously?"

"Seriously."

Gryswold eyed the tall elf for a moment, then held up the bracelet in one hand and grasped a charm between his fingers. He clamped his eyes shut, his brow furrowing even further. The chamber grew silent as the Baron suddenly yanked the charm off the chain and threw it on the floor in front of him.

Lloyd felt magic flow through the air once more. It coalesced over the spot where the charm lay, the air thickening and forming into a grey mist. The mist began to take shape. Colors rose up from the inside—dark grey, chestnut, and off-white. They all swirled around each other as they took form. The mists finally settled into a stately woman with perfectly coiffed chestnut hair, porcelain skin, and a dark grey gown that covered the entirety of her lithe frame.

Gryswold's eyes snapped open once more and immediately misted over. A single word escaped his lips. "Grace."

Gracelynn's entire face lit up. All propriety was throw to the wind as she launched herself into her husband's arms. "Grys!"

Lloyd's heart swelled with joy as the happy couple were reunited. Andrella, equally overjoyed, practically flew into her parents' arms.

"Ahem." Aksel cleared his throat. "Perhaps we should give them a few minutes to themselves?"

Elladan grinned at the gnome. "You took the words right out of my mouth."

Glolindir waited with the rest of his companions just outside the Temple of Vermoorden. All of them were tired, but happy they had been able to reunite the Avernos family.

Elladan, in particular, was back to his effervescent self. "This calls for a celebration!" The handsome bard wrapped an arm around Donnie's shoulder. "Care to help me prepare a feast?"

Donnie narrowed an eye at his friend. "Will there be ale?"

"Of course!" Elladan waved his free arm extravagantly.

"Then count me in," Donnie said with a pearly smile.

Kara grabbed Donnie by the other arm, a thin smile on the tall warrior's lips. "Me as well."

Kalyn punched Martan in the shoulder. "We can help, too. Back home, my folks run a tavern."

"Um…yeah," Martan stammered as he rubbed his arm.

Elladan grinned. "The more, the merrier."

Glo watched the five of them trot off toward the keep, laughing and singing along the way. A smile spread across his face. It had been too long since he had seen them like this.

"You look like something the cat dragged in."

Seth stood over a weary Aksel, who had nodded off on the stone steps. The little cleric's eyes cracked open as he looked up at his friend.

"I'll be fine with a little rest."

"Maybe you should have gone back with the others?" Lloyd suggested quietly.

Aksel shook his head. "Not until Gryswold and Gracelynn are safely tucked away in the keep."

"Did someone mention our names?"

Gryswold stood at the top of the steps with his wife and daughter under either arm. Lloyd immediately rushed up the stairs to help them. Seth assisted a weary Aksel as they escorted the newly reunited Avernos family to the keep.

Captain Ascue was there waiting for them in the courtyard. He executed a low bow to the two nobles. "It is an honor to have you both here in Vermoorden, your lord and ladyship."

Gracelynn dipped her chin to the young captain. "The honor is ours. You are providing us with a sanctuary where our family can safely be together."

A tired Gryswold nodded in affirmation. "It is as my wife said, Captain. We are in your debt. If there is anything we can do for you…"

Ascue cleared his throat. "Actually, now that you mention it… as I already told your daughter, I know nothing of running a town."

Gracelynn extended her hand to the Captain. "No need to ask. We would be more than happy to assist you in any way we can."

This time Andrella cleared her throat. "Actually, mom, they made me temporary mayor."

"Oh?" Gracelyn arched a delicate eyebrow at her daughter.

Andrella steepled her hands together in front of her lips. Glo chuckled softly as he realized she was mimicking him. "Since your adventuring days are over, and mine have just begun… would you mind greatly taking over for me?"

A sparkling laugh escaped Gracelynn's lips. She peered at Gryswold, who responded with a knowing smile. "Seems like she's a chip off the old block, Grace."

Gracelynn mirrored his smile, then shifted her gaze back to Ascue. "I'd be more than happy to, if it's alright with the good Captain."

Ascue nodded enthusiastically. "Why yes, of course. The fairness of the Lady Gracelynn is known far and wide across eastern Thac. I think the people would be more than honored to have you oversee our town until the next elections."

Gracelynn gave the captain a reassuring smile. "Good, then. That's settled."

A loud yawn disrupted any further conversation. Gracelynn

glanced dubiously at Gryswold, then back at Ascue. "My husband seems rather tired after his ordeal. Is there a place he can rest until dinner?"

Ascue drew to full attention. "Why of course. Please follow me."

After a brief round of goodbyes, Ascue helped Gracelynn lead Gryswold toward the keep proper. Andrella started after them, then turned to face Lloyd, her brow lined with concern.

Lloyd grasped her gently by the shoulders. "Go ahead. I'll see you at dinner."

Andrella's frown melted into a winsome smile. "Lloyd Stealle, what ever would I do without you?" She rose up onto her toes and kissed him briefly on the lips. The young lady then bolted across the courtyard after her parents.

"Okay, now that they're safe, are you finally going to rest?"

Aksel peered at Seth through bloodshot eyes. "I think I better."

Glo, Seth, and Lloyd escorted Aksel to his room. Once he was comfortably bedded down, Seth threw himself on a nearby chair. The halfling kicked off his boots and propped his feet up on the table in front of him.

"Comfy, Seth?" Glo asked blithely.

"Absolutely," Seth answered with a smug grin.

Suddenly feeling weary himself, Glo plopped into the chair beside the irreverent halfling. Lloyd slid into the seat opposite him.

The elven wizard stifled a yawn as he swept his gaze around the room. It was just the four of them now, the same ones who had that first encounter back in the Bendenwoods. It felt like ages ago, but in reality it had only been a couple of months.

Glo's mind marveled over all they had accomplished in that short time. Still, there was a lot left undone. The tall elf let out a heavy sigh.

"What's the matter?" Lloyd's brow was creased with concern.

Glo steepled his hands together. "Well… we've revived Gryswold and rescued Gracelynn…"

"But…" Seth's lips were twisted sideways.

Glo slowly shook his head. "You know me far too well. But… Ravenford is still under Dunwynn control, the Princess of Lanfor has a price on our heads, and there is at least one Thrall Master out there somewhere in the world."

"Not to mention… we don't know… where Ves, Ruka, and Maya are…" Aksel's voice wafted over from somewhere underneath his covers.

"Go to sleep!" Seth chided the gnome.

Glo couldn't help chuckling at the halfling's attempt to 'mother hen' their exhausted friend.

Lloyd continued Aksel's train of thought. "We should warn the sisters that their father might be a prisoner in a tower full of demons."

Glo felt a shiver run up his spine at the mention of demons. An image came unbidden to his mind of a cold but beautiful woman with porcelain skin, long, raven-black hair, high cheekbones, and blood-red lips.

The tall elf shook off the feeling of dread and sat forward in his chair. "Speaking of demons, we've somehow managed to keep Salmisa Tanj from entering Arinthar twice now. Yet, if there is a whole tower full of demons, how long before a major one like her crosses into this world? It would be the end of life as we know it."

"Are you done?" Seth idly fingered a sharp knife in his hands.

Glo exchanged a knowing grin with Lloyd. "Yes, I think that about sums it up."

Seth sheathed the knife, then dropped his feet to the floor and leaned forward. "Well there's one more thing we know for sure."

Glo eyed the halfling curiously. "And what's that?"

"We aren't the Heroes of Ravenford anymore."

Lloyd's brow knit into a deep frown at Seth's last statement. "So, what does that make us?"

Glo idly tapped his fingers together. "I think that remains to be seen. Though, there is one more thing we know for certain."

Lloyd cocked his head to one side. "And what's that?"

"Things are obviously far from over."

Here ends Book Five of
the Heroes of Ravenford
Look for further stories of the
young heroes in
Rise of the Thrall Lord

About the Author

F.P. Spirit writes high fantasy fiction inspired by the likes of Tolkien, Eddings, Brooks, and Piers Anthony. An avid science fiction fan, he became hooked on fantasy the moment he cracked open the Lord of the Rings in high school. When he is not writing, F.P. is either spending time with his wife and sons, gaming, doing yoga, Tai Chi, or walking their dog.

A long-time lover of fantasy and the surreal, he hopes you enjoy his fun contributions to the world of fantasy and magic.

You can learn more about F.P. Spirit by visiting his website at:
Fpspirit.com